Also

WHERE THE WILD HEARTS ARE
Wild on My Mind

Sweet Wild of Mine

Laurel Kerr

sourcebooks
casablanca

Published by Sourcebooks Casablanca, an imprint of Sourcebooks
P.O. Box 4410, Naperville, Illinois 60567-4410
(630) 961-3900
sourcebooks.com

Printed and bound in the United States of America.
OPM 10 9 8 7 6 5 4 3 2 1

*For my mother: my first fan
and on-call babysitter*

*For my husband: for all the loads of
laundry he did so this book could be written*

*For my daughter: who has graciously
allowed Mommy writing time*

Chapter 1

"YOU MUST BE NEW TO SAGEBRUSH FLATS."

Magnus Gray reluctantly turned in the direction of the friendly southern drawl. The speaker matched the rich, sexy voice. Blond. Willowy. Tall. Bonny green eyes. Pink lips curved into a welcoming smile.

Magnus didn't trust the woman's grin, so he chose to respond with a neutral expression…not surly enough to be rude, but not pleasant enough to invite further conversation. Unfortunately, the American lass didn't register the subtlety.

Instead, she slid into the booth across from him. This time, Magnus couldn't stop a frown. In fact, he even might have growled a bit under his breath. He didn't want to chat. Couldn't the hen see his open laptop?

"I'm June Winters." The woman beamed like the desert sun.

He grunted. Under good circumstances, he hated introducing himself. Even after years of practice, he always stuttered on the letter *M* in his name.

And this? This was *not* a good circumstance.

"You don't need to be a stranger, you hear? You're welcome to join the celebration. The more, the merrier!" The woman still smiled. Even for a Yank, she was a damn Cheshire cat. Without breaking eye contact, she waved her hand in the direction

❖

of a group of rowdy locals congregated around a rustic bar decorated with antlers. Some people might have found the decor quaint, but not Magnus. He'd given up quaint when he'd finally escaped his boyhood home on a remote Scottish isle in the North Sea that was part of the chain of islands that made up Orkney.

Despite his silence, the woman kept blethering. "My friend and her husband just found out they're going to have twins. The whole town is just as happy as ants at a picnic. Drinks are on the house, well, all except for the new mama-to-be. She's having sparkling grape juice!"

Magnus could only stare at the woman in disbelief. This was why he avoided small towns. All the endless gossip. Why would he want to know about her friend's drinking habits or the fact that she had a trout in the well? Next, the lass would be telling him just when and where her friends had shagged to conceive the bairns.

He'd chafed under the scrutiny that came with growing up on an isle with a population of less than five hundred. No privacy. No boundaries. No peace. Even though he'd lived with his da on a speck of an island offshore from the larger one, he'd still found himself entangled in the sticky threads of town gossip. They'd trapped him as surely as a spider's silk did a struggling beetle. Against the odds, he'd broken free…only for his editor to send him straight into another web. A dusty, arid one, at that.

At nineteen, Magnus had penned his first book between his shifts as a roughneck on an oil rig off the coast of Norway. His muscles had ached, and the constant cold had seeped so deeply into his skin, he'd sworn even his molecules had ice crystals growing in them.

But despite the dogged tiredness, he'd used the precious hours meant for sleeping to write about his childhood as if he could purge it from his soul.

It hadn't worked. Not completely. But the publishing world, and then the public, had loved his cathartic musings about his formative years on a struggling, windblown croft surrounded by the ever-present sea. When he'd hit bestseller lists all over the world, the media had billed him as a wunderkind.

Intoxicated by his first success, he'd quickly written a second book about his adventures in Norway. While working on the ice, he'd encountered a pair of orphaned polar bear cubs that he'd rescued from starvation and kept alive until they could be relocated to a zoo. His fans had adored the tale.

With all the dosh he made from his first books, he'd left the roughneck life behind and headed to Glasgow. Then a few years later, he'd moved to the welcome obscurity of London. In a city of over eight million, no one cared if a man chose to sup alone. Since his author photo was taken from the back with him staring out at the sea, no one recognized him. He could eat, drink, and write in peace. Nobody expected him to converse or even to make small talk. After a childhood on a remote island, he'd finally found solitude and peace in the teeming crowds of one of the largest cities in Europe.

But the public didn't like his wry witticisms about city life. Sales from his next two books plummeted. And that had led to the fateful call with his editor a few weeks ago. Magnus could still hear the man's rough Bostonian accent growling in his ear.

People aren't buying your urban jungle crap. You've gotten too acerbic. Too much misanthropy and too little humor. Get back to your roots. Small towns. Living creatures. I know the perfect place for you. It's been all over the internet, a zoo in a place called Sagebrush Flats. It's got the animal angle from your first books, but in a different enough locale so it'll be fresh. Go work there for a season. Write about it. That, that I can sell. The other stuff, I can't.

Because Magnus preferred to keep his current lifestyle and not go back to being a roughneck, he once again found himself in the back of beyond. The idea of shoveling manure again didn't bother him. Animals and their shite he could take. But the human kind? Aye, that was the problem.

Across from him, the bonny blond still beamed. Welcoming. Charming. Sweet. And he didn't believe any of it. She'd plopped her arse down in the booth across from him for one reason and one reason only. Gossip. She wanted to be the very first to meet the hulking stranger so she could blether to her friends about him the following morn. Magnus wasn't a chap who typically attracted the lasses, especially those as braw as the likes of this one.

"I swear none of us bite," the woman joked and waited a beat for Magnus to speak. He didn't. If he did, he knew he'd block on at least one of the words. Unfortunately, the woman stayed. "We're all very friendly."

Magnus longed for a big city with its pubs and cafés where a man could find solitude among millions of strangers. Really, anything but a dusty town where the only establishments open on a Monday night were a pizza take-out shop and a curious American diner-restaurant-bar hybrid called the Prairie Dog Café. It had all the ills of a local British pub and none of the charm. The assortment of old farm equipment and elk antlers tacked to the walls wasn't to Magnus's fancy. Give him an ancient stone building in London with a cheerful fire to chase away the dreich, and he'd be content.

"Come on," the blond insisted as she rose from the table. Magnus shook his head, but the lass didn't listen. She reached forward and grabbed his hand. At the unexpected contact, Magnus jerked back, jamming his elbow hard against the wooden booth. He didn't like being touched, especially by a stranger. He appreciated even less the strange jolt of awareness zipping through him. He didn't want to lust after the dafty woman.

Surprise showed in the blond's leaf-green eyes. "I beg your pardon. I didn't mean to startle you."

Baws. Now it would be all over town that he was a nervous numptie. Anger and frustration whipped inside Magnus like the furious polar winds of the North. Worse, his larynx muscles tightened ominously, and he felt his chest constrict. If he tried to speak, tried to explain that he wanted to be left alone, he'd never manage to force the words out. His neck would stiffen, and his tongue would feel thick and useless as it stuck to the roof of his mouth. He'd be left as helpless as a carp flopping on a trawler's deck. The welcome in those green eyes would turn to shock and then discomfort and finally to disgust or, worse, pity. Within a bloody night, the whole town would know about his stutter. They might even give him a nickname like his schoolmates had.

His cheeks burned, and he was grateful his thick beard hid the redness from the lass's prying eyes. The woman stood there expectantly, clearly waiting for a response.

Magnus grabbed his laptop, the hasty movement upsetting his ale. Quickly mopping up the liquid with one hand, he shoved his computer in his messenger bag with the other. Placing the sodden napkins in a neat pile, he stood up. Although the lass was tall and willowy, his massive frame still dwarfed hers. He expected her eyes to widen at his full height. Most folks' did upon first meeting him. But instead of a flash of leftover primordial fear, he thought he spotted something else entirely…appreciation.

Lust speared him. Strong and heady. It was an attraction Magnus didn't want to feel, especially when it tangled his tongue worse than driftwood caught in a fishing net.

He pushed past the lass. He had no choice but to brush against her shoulder since she was blocking his exit from the booth like an auld fairy stone. As his large body collided softly with her slender one, he swore her heat seared him.

"Wait," the woman said, "I didn't mean to chase you away like a bluetick hound after a possum. Let me at least replace your beer."

Magnus swung toward the lass, no longer caring how rude he'd become. He was either going to make a fool or an arse out of himself. And having been both, he much preferred the second. Asses got more respect than jesters. Even if he couldn't find the rhythm to explain himself, there was one phrase he could always force out.

"Fuck off."

The lass's lower jaw dropped slightly, revealing that she'd understood his deep Orcadian Scots accent. Instead of looking ridiculous with her mouth agape, the lass's perfect pink lips formed a rather seductive O. Not waiting for his body's reaction to that particular observation to become apparent, Magnus stormed from the Prairie Dog Café. As he burst out into the twilight, he greedily turned his face in the direction of the cool evening breeze. The restaurant had been roasting. Although Sagebrush in early January was much cooler than what he'd expected for the desert, the air still felt thin and dry. Aye, he missed the familiar damp of Britain.

Shoving his hands deep into his pockets, Magnus slouched as he ambled down the street. He'd been waiting all day for that ruined draught and a bit of relaxation after a long flight. Perhaps he'd have better luck in the morn at the tea shop on the corner. It looked pleasant with its lavender-painted facade and lace curtains in the windows. He'd checked the menu online. The owner claimed her nan was British, and some of the items sounded surprisingly authentic. It was one of the few things Magnus was looking forward to in Sagebrush. Knowing his luck, it probably would turn out to be the favorite haunt of the blond, although she was probably too busy getting blootered to make it to the tea shop as early as he planned.

"What was that all about?" June's best friend, Katie, asked as she appeared, holding a glass of sparkling grape juice. She had her other fingers spread wide over the slight swell of her stomach. June didn't think Katie even realized that she'd barely moved her hand from her belly all evening. The new mama simply radiated protective affection for her unborn twins. Scientists claimed hormones caused the pregnancy glow, but June believed it sprang from pure love, and Katie had always been a big softie when it came to family.

"That man just told me to fuck off," June said, still unable to shake her disbelief at the man's rudeness. Her atypical feeling of annoyance only spiked when Katie gave an exaggerated snort, her mass of red curls bouncing.

"Josh," Katie shouted over to their mutual friend from college who was in town for the weekend to celebrate her good news. "You won't believe it. Some guy actually told June to fuck off."

"Well, he didn't tell me to fuck off exactly. It was more like 'feck aff.'"

"Suu-uure," Katie said before she took a long sip from her flute of grape juice. "Totally different."

Josh sauntered over to join them, his West Coast designer clothes looking slightly out of place in the sea of flannel and jeans. "What's this I hear about some guy giving June the brush-off?"

"My word, you'd think no one has ever been rejected before in the history of mankind."

"Oh, we all have, June. Just not you." Josh slung an arm over her shoulder in a brotherly gesture. Although he'd moved back to California after college to start his own computer security company, the three of them had remained close. "What did this guy look like anyway?"

"From the back, not June's usual type," Katie said. "Too hairy. Too beefcakey."

"Too rude," June added.

Katie's husband, Bowie, walked over to them and pulled his wife against his side. The two had been married less than six months, and they still basked in the honeymoon glow. June had a suspicion, though, they'd probably be this adorably sweet when they were in their nineties, and she was never wrong when it came to matters of the heart.

"Who's a rude, hairy beefcake?" Bowie asked.

"June's unrequited love." Katie stood up on her tiptoes to brush a quick kiss across her husband's mouth, even though they'd only been separated for a matter of minutes.

June found the couple's affection incredibly sweet. Josh, though, had a tendency to tease them. When she spotted him starting to roll his eyes, she jabbed him in the stomach with her elbow. This was Katie and Bowie's evening, and she didn't want anything to ruin it, even good-natured ribbing.

Before Josh could protest, June said quickly, "Heavens to Betsy, I was just making nice to the man. I don't know why y'all are turning it into a declaration of love. It wasn't as if I was flirting."

At her last statement, all three of her friends burst into uncontrollable laughter. June glared at them. Katie got herself under control first. "June, you flirt with *every* guy. It's how you interact with the entire male population of our species."

"Our species? Have you seen how she gets with the cute animals at Bowie's zoo?" Josh asked.

June popped Josh on the arm, but she couldn't argue with Katie. She was a flirt. "Well, maybe I was flirting just a smidge, but I was only being welcoming to a stranger. Like Katie said, he's not my usual type." June liked her lovers to be as easygoing as herself. A romance should be as delightful and pleasant as sweet jam made from the first spring pickings. It should *not* have the drama and devastation of a fall hurricane, and Mr. Rude seemed to have the personality of a tempest, a tornado, and a tsunami all rolled into one godforsaken storm.

Plus, June liked her men tall, but not hulking. There was nothing like a refined runner's build that looked delicious in a suit or just jeans and cowboy boots. Although hair color didn't matter, she preferred her lovers clean cut with no beard and not even a hint of a five-o'clock shadow.

Yes, June enjoyed handsome, debonair men. She supposed it was from all those classic films she'd watched with her mama. When her father moved the family from one air force base to another, the black-and-white movies had remained a comforting constant. No matter what part of the globe they lived on, Errol Flynn, Clark Gable, and Gregory Peck still possessed those devastating smiles that melted a woman's worries clean away.

In contrast, the scowling Mr. Rude looked like a grumpy Paul Bunyan. Yet, when the man had stood and stared her down with his piercing blue eyes half hidden by a mop of dark-brown hair, she'd felt a thrill clean down to her toes. It hadn't been the smooth pull of attraction. No this—this had been a searing bolt of primal energy. It was as if some elemental feminine instinct had instantly, and explosively, responded to his raw strength.

And there'd been something about his face. True, his unruly hair and beard had obscured his features, but June had always possessed an eye for a person's bone structure. Her second talent after making jam was giving folks a makeover. And if anyone needed her helpful advice, it was Mr. Rude. Oh, he'd never be classically handsome. The planes of his face were too harsh. But with the right hairstyle and a trimmed beard, he'd look arresting, especially considering his cobalt-blue eyes.

But June had no desire to poke that particular bear on his snout by offering fashion tips…well, almost no desire. She did love a good project, and Mr. Rude would definitely provide a challenge.

"Hmmm, he may not be your type, but I'm detecting a classic June Winters glint in your eyes," Katie said.

June smiled airily. "I'm just thinking about how I'd go about taming a wild Scot."

Josh snorted. "That sounds like the title of a romance novel."

"Oooo, I wonder what June's crush would look like in a kilt," Katie added. The brown in her eyes deepened, which always happened when she was developing concept art. Although June generally appreciated her friend's graphic design brilliance, especially when she put it to use helping market

June's two businesses, this time she wished her friend had a smidgen less color in her imagination.

"I can see the book jacket now," Katie said in her normal voice, before she turned it theatrically throaty. "Bulging biceps, ripped chest...hairy legs."

June was just about to retort when Bowie broke into the conversation with something blessedly sensible. As the director of the zoo and a former single dad, he was as solid as granite, a trait June appreciated, especially in conversations like this one. "Wait. Was the guy Scottish?"

She nodded. "With a deep brogue. If my nan didn't listen to Scottish music, I doubt I would have understood him."

"Shit," Bowie said, rubbing his hand over the back of his head. "That was probably Magnus Gray. I hope you didn't scare him off. He's supposed to start work at the zoo tomorrow."

Katie turned toward her husband, her red curls swinging. "June's guy is the mysterious writer who's going to volunteer at the zoo for several months?"

"Unless June's man is visiting Rocky Ridge National Park and was just passing through, but I doubt it," Bowie said. "It isn't tourist season, and we don't generally have a lot of Brits in Sagebrush."

"Dang blast it all," June grumbled, "*he's* Magnus Gray. I was planning to ask if he'd chat with Nan. During the Blitz, her parents sent her to live on the island he wrote about. She's been listening to his audiobooks for years."

The teasing glint left Katie's eyes as she regarded June with a serious expression. "How is your grandma doing?"

June sighed, wishing she had something better to

report. "I'm not sure. She keeps calling me in the dead of night, thinking we had some big kerfuffle and I'm angrier than a tomcat in the rain."

"I know Lou can have his off days," Bowie said, mentioning his eighty-year-old adoptive father who lived with him, Katie, and Abby, Bowie's twelve-year-old daughter.

"I'm worried it's more than just tiredness. This horrible, haunted look comes over her face as soon as the sun goes down. It's like she's constantly fretting about something fierce."

"Why don't you bring her by the zoo?" Katie asked. "The animals always cheer her up."

"We'll give her a personal tour," Bowie promised. "I know how much your grandma loves the baby animals, and the orphaned polar bear cub is due to arrive soon. That's one of the reasons Magnus contacted me. He had some experience with the species when he was a roughneck in Norway, and his editor had heard we'd received a grant from the Alliance for Polar Life."

"His second bestseller was about polar bears," June said. "Nan listened to that one too. She missed the animal anecdotes in his other books, though, so she stopped asking me to download them."

"His email said something about getting back to his roots," Bowie said. "I wasn't going to turn down free labor, especially from someone with his background in caring for animals."

"Why didn't you recognize him just now?" Katie asked.

Bowie shrugged. "I didn't know what the man

looked like. Magnus is very private. I haven't even talked to him on the phone. All of our correspondence was through email. When I researched him online to check out his credentials, the pictures I saw were taken from the back."

"According to Nan, Magnus Gray would make a hermit seem downright sociable. Part of his mystique, I suppose."

"He sounds like an ass," Josh interjected with his typical bluntness.

"My sentiments exactly," June said. "I was just being genteel. Poor Nan. She was tickled pink he was coming to town."

"I don't know, June," Josh teased. "As you always say, if you try hard enough, you can charm a snake."

"I'd rather try my luck with the actual reptile. They have a more pleasant personality, even the rattlers."

Magnus rose before the sun. He wasn't meeting Bowie until ten o'clock, but even years after leaving the croft, he couldn't escape the rhythm of rural life. During his childhood, the responsibility for the farm animals had mainly fallen on Magnus, with his da off early on his trawler bringing in the day's catch. Their Shetland sheep and shaggy Highland beef cows had been fairly self-sufficient, but the milch cows had required his attention before and after school. Once Magnus had finished the morning milking, he'd quickly toss feed in the chicken run before rowing to the larger island for class. In the evening, there'd always be a stone wall to repair or a barn to clean. And that was in the winter months.

Work had only intensified in the spring with lambing, calving, and planting. In the summers, Magnus had helped his da on the trawler, the two of them working in silence with only the sound of the waves lapping against the sides of the boat. Life on the oil rigs had been just as constant and demanding. Magnus had spent long shifts hefting hammers and wrenches as he kept the machinery working.

When Magnus had begun writing full time, he'd found himself fighting a low thrum of pent-up energy. Eventually, he'd buckled and begun lifting weights. In the past, he'd mocked the toonsers who paid good money to work out in sweaty, smelly indoor gyms instead of earning their muscles. And then Magnus had become one of them. But it was either exercise or go absolutely barmy.

As daft as it sounded, a part of Magnus actually looked forward to hauling feed and cleaning out pens again. It would be good to use his muscles for their intended purpose. He just wished it didn't mean dealing with the zoo's guests and all the townsfolk.

Luckily, the streets seemed fairly deserted as he left his B and B. Bowie Wilson had promised him lodging, but Magnus hadn't wanted to bother looking the man up as soon as he'd arrived in town. Instead, he'd stayed the night at the Red Cliff Inn. The place didn't serve breakfast until eight, but at least it had been clean, neat, and, most of all, quiet.

Thankfully, the Primrose, Magnolia & Thistle opened at six thirty. Up ahead, a welcoming glow seeped from a large picture window. Picking up his pace, Magnus could fairly taste the bangers and

tattie scone. The fare on the menu was heavier than the
food served by a traditional British tea shop, but he was
in the States now. He supposed he should be grateful
that a Wild West town like Sagebrush Flats even had
something approaching a traditional Scottish breakfast. Although the name of it—the Hungry Scotsman
Platter—made his hackles rise, he'd order the blasted
thing. As long as a breakfast included black pudding
and beans, he wouldn't quibble over what a Yank called
it. He supposed it was better than the Kilted Southerner,
which was an appalling mix of Scottish and U.S. cooking. Proper white pudding should not be paired with
grits. It just wasn't done.

Magnus pushed open the door, and a little bell
chimed. Two older men with sun-leathered skin and
cowboy hats glanced up at his entrance. Their eyes
scanned him briefly, taking his measure. They might
dress a wee bit different than the old folks back home,
but they were all the same. Magnus bobbed his head
politely. The men returned the gesture. Their assess-
ment of him complete, they returned their attention to
the more important matter of breakfast.

Magnus turned toward the front of the tea shop and
froze. Behind the counter stood the blond lass from
the Prairie Dog Café. She'd wrapped her long, wheat-
colored hair into a comely top knot that drew Magnus's
attention to the graceful lines of her neck. For a minute,
he went utterly doolally and imagined planting his lips
there. Because of his cursed imagination, he could practically feel her shiver in his arms and see those pink
lips part as she groaned. Baws, he'd be sporting a fair
stauner if he didn't stop the direction of his thoughts.

The woman smiled, and her green eyes sparkled with an unholy chirpiness, especially given the early hour. Magnus wondered if she'd divined his thoughts. She did look a bit like a fae creature despite her height. One thing was certain. She didn't look either goosed or hungover—just happy to the point of being mental.

"Hi there, stranger." She grinned broadly. "Welcome to my tea shop."

"Fuck me. You bloody own this place?" His dismayed shock had evidently startled the stutter right out of him. He didn't even block on the *P*, which generally gave him trouble.

To his amazement, the lass's smile didn't turn brittle at his crudeness. In fact, it stretched a little farther northward in pure glee. The barmy hen was taking delight in his misery.

"I sure do. Now how can I help you, Magnus?"

He glowered. How the fuck did the lass know his name? She must have read the confusion on his face.

"We don't get many Scots here in Sagebrush, especially in the winter. When I mentioned your accent, Bowie figured it was you."

Magnus scowled. *Damn it all to hell. And damn the nosy lass too*. Was the whole town gossiping about him now?

"So," the woman asked, leaning across the tall glass counter that showcased various pastries, "what can I get you?"

"I'll be having the Hungry Scotsman P-P-P..." His throat closed up. He couldn't fight the tightness. He stood there stuck on the *P* as he helplessly watched the lass's face. He wondered in those long seconds of horror what her expression would be. Frustrated annoyance like his da? Amusement like his classmates? Pity like the headmistress? Discomfort like the townsfolk? He'd witnessed them all…or so he'd thought.

A light flickered in the lass's eyes as if she'd just solved a challenging riddle. Then she stuck her arms akimbo and delivered a look a mum would give to a lad who wanted to quit football just because his team got mullered. At least Magnus assumed that was the look. He'd never had time to play sports, and his mum had bunked off when the allure of mainland Scotland had grown too strong for her.

"Now why didn't you tell me that you were a person who stuttered?" June asked. "I would have understood, honey. Is swearing one of your avoidances? You don't need to worry around me. Just be yourself. I don't mind disfluency. And people who do can go straight to the devil."

Magnus blinked. The woman made his head spin faster than a weathercock in a gale.

"Disfluency?"

"Do you prefer another term?"

Magnus rubbed his head. He couldn't help it. What he preferred was to be left alone, but it didn't appear the fae lass would grant him that particular wish.

"What one would you like me to use? My brother, August, is pretty flexible about terminology, but I know some people prefer certain words over others."

"Your brother?" Why the hell was she blethering about her sibling?

"He's a person who stutters," the lass said. "I did too

in elementary school, but I've been fluent for years. It's partially why I speak like a southerner. My mama's from Georgia, but I grew up all over the world. But that doesn't mean I use my drawl as an avoidance. It's how I talk naturally, and the slower cadence gives me more control over my rate of speech. The experts say speaking with a fake accent only works for so long, you know."

The deluge of information pelted Magnus like spray from an arctic wave. The woman could drown a body in random facts. She talked funny, and he didn't mean her drawl. She sounded like a bloody medical pamphlet from the National Health Service.

"So?" the lass asked, with an expectant expression on her face. He simply stared back in confusion. A bloke needed a compass to navigate her speech.

"What term do you prefer instead of disfluency?" she clarified.

"I don't give a shite," Magnus said in frustration. Why the hell would he care what she called his damn stutter? He wanted to live free of the bloody thing. Calling it something different would never change how people reacted to it.

"I'm sensing you don't like talking about it."

"Aye, that's right."

She leaned over the counter and said in quiet seriousness, "Ignoring it won't make it go away. My brother tried that for years, but August found it was easier if he just told people up front. He's a JAG officer in the Air Force now."

Was she giving him advice on his own stutter?

Magnus glowered. For once, the blond heeded his look. She straightened, but the welcoming smile returned. What was it about her pink lips that made him think of snogging when the woman herself was nothing but a constant vexation? She had him in a snirl. And he didn't like it.

"So," the lass said conversationally, "what would you like to order?"

Magnus opened his mouth to respond and discovered he'd lost his appetite. The lass had ruined his ale and now his breakfast. "Fuck me."

Without giving the hen a chance to react, he turned and left the tea shop. He'd eat at the bloody B and B.

It wasn't until Magnus was halfway down the street that a realization struck him. He hadn't stumbled over his words once since the lass had started havering about disfluency. In fact, he hadn't even thought about stuttering. Not once. Which never happened. Especially in the company of a stranger. An annoying one at that.

Honey was bored. It was a frequent occurrence, but that didn't mean she liked it. She was a clever, daring honey badger, and she did *not* belong in any zoo. No, she belonged in Africa. She should be running through the bush, killing cobras, robbing beehives, and chasing away hyenas. Not that she had ever *done* any of those things, but she would be very good at them. Very good.

Unfortunately, her skills had been wasted since birth. Her first memories were of growing up in a house, which she'd hated. There were only so many cupboards she could raid. She'd become very good at learning to get into places where the silly bipeds did not wish for her to go.

Honey smiled. That, at least, had been fun, not as exciting as tussling with an apex predator like a lion...but she *had* enjoyed watching her old human's face turn red. The vein on his forehead would do the most interesting things.

One day, people in matching clothes had invaded her old home. They'd rudely placed Honey in a small carrier and lugged her to a vehicle that reeked of other animals. Although she had loved sneaking rides in her old human's car and tearing up the upholstered interior, she had *not* enjoyed the smelly van.

Then Honey had arrived here. The zoo. Her new home had a nice shade tree, and the humans gave her "enrichment" toys...

But there was a monumental problem with her new residence. *Him.*

Honey detested sharing her enclosure, even with her own kind. And Fluffy was especially intolerable. Even his name was ridiculous. Their species was not fluffy, neither in temperament nor in looks. They were mean with coarse fur. No suitable mustelid would go by "Fluffy."

But he had the audacity to act superior to *her*. And she fully intended to prove him wrong.

Chapter 2

JUNE WATCHED IN SHOCK AS THE GIANT SCOTSMAN ONCE again stormed away from her. He slammed the door to the tea shop so hard, she swore the building shook. Poor Stanley Harris and Buck Montgomery jumped at the sound. The two regulars turned toward her, their eyes wide.

"What did you say to make the newcomer go off half-cocked like that?" Buck asked.

"Nothing," June said. "I was just making polite conversation, that's all. Some folks don't have any manners these days."

Neither Buck nor Stanley seemed convinced, and they both loved a good story. "I don't know, Miss Winters," Stanley said, tipping back his cowboy hat in a clear effort to get a better look at her face. "He sure seemed mad."

Buck nodded sagely. "Reminded me of a bull at the rodeo with his privates all cinched up."

Luckily, June was saved from answering by the sudden appearance of her nan. Buck instantly flushed. Everyone knew Clara Winters didn't tolerate swearing or any off-color remarks in her tea shop. June might own and run it, but Clara remained queen.

But instead of her grandmother's hazel eyes lighting with proper indignation at Buck's breach of etiquette, they remained glassy and a little unfocused. With an almost childlike expression, she glanced around the room, looking like a wizened apple doll in a folk-art museum. June's heart squeezed at the sight as worry thrummed through her. Although her nan was in her nineties, until the last couple of weeks she'd been an energetic woman. Even with her petite frame, June's grandmother had always exuded a stalwart stoutness—a steeliness forged during the opening months of the Battle of Britain and refined through years as a military wife. Sure, she required more sleep than she had when June was a child, but Nan still pitched in at the tea shop and helped June create new recipes for her growing jam business. Strangers always thought Nan was in her seventies, which was a compliment considering that was two decades younger than her real age. But lately something had changed, and a brittleness had fallen over June's grandmother like a witch's curse.

"June?" Nan's voice was high...too high.

"Yes, Nana?" June gave a reassuring smile.

The woman blinked owlishly. First confusion and then fear slid over her petite features. She looked around wildly as if she could pull the answers from the air. "I—I don't remember."

"That's okay, Nan." June stepped from behind the counter and led her grandmother to a nearby rocking chair. Thank goodness Owen Harris, Stanley's grandson, had given her a good deal on the gliders he made and sold to tourists. With Nan's flagging energy, June had installed one in the tea shop, the kitchen, and even in the upstairs apartment where June lived. She didn't know how she would have afforded them if Stanley hadn't told Owen that Nan was getting sore using the straight-backed chairs in the tea shop, and Owen had agreed to make the rockers in return for free breakfast for a year. And that is what June loved about small towns—neighbors being neighborly.

June patted Nan's hand before she returned to her station behind the counter. "You just sit there and let me know what your question is when you think of it."

Suddenly, like the sky after the rain clouds departed, her grandmother's face brightened. Her hazel eyes sharpened, and her old aplomb returned. "Did I hear an Orcadian accent?"

June felt her mouth twist into an uncharacteristic grimace. "Yes, Nan, you did."

Her grandmother's eyes sparkled, the overhead fluorescent lights capturing glints of green and gold in her irises. "Was he the young man who wrote that lovely book about the Isles?"

June nodded again. "Magnus Gray in the flesh."

"I'm sorry I missed him, dear. What was he like?"

"Grumpy as the day is long. He's got a temper worse than a wildcat with its tail in a knot."

Nan sighed as she pushed back on the rocker. "I remember his great-grandfather, Rognvald Gray, being a difficult man. He rarely came to the pub, not like the other crofters. His son, Magnus's grandfather, was off fighting in the war, but folks said he was just the same as his da. Liked to keep to himself."

"Well, the apple certainly doesn't fall far from the family tree. The grandson nearly bit off my head just for being friendly. Twice!"

Nan shook her head as she reached for a knitting bag.

June had placed one by each rocking chair. Her grandmother had always liked her projects, and June wanted to keep the woman's mind active. Nan had been skipping stitches and messing up patterns lately, but at least it kept her busy. As long as her grandmother focused on one task, her thoughts seemed to stabilize instead of flitting madly about like a tipsy butterfly.

"In his first books, Magnus Gray had the soul of a poet," June's grandmother continued as she pulled out a skein of yellow yarn. "Some were calling him the next Sir Walter Scott. Then he started writing about the London pub scene, and his prose turned to rubbish. It grew drearier than a hard winter on the Isles."

June chuckled at her nan's description. The elderly British expat had been born and raised mostly in London, but her adolescence in Orkney had sewn a thread of romance into her otherwise staid English soul. June got most of her colorful speech from her southern mama, but she'd learned a thing or two from her gran as well.

"He sure seemed cranky," Buck said, interjecting himself into the conversation as he leaned back in his chair.

Nan clicked her tongue off the roof of her mouth as she cast on stitches to make a scarf, her specialty these days. Soon June was going to have to set up a stand by the counter to sell them. If not, she and her grandmother wouldn't be able to fit anything else into their closets.

"I was hoping I could talk to him about the island,"

Nan said wistfully as she began to knit in earnest. Although her hands didn't fly as quickly as they had even a few months ago, the sureness in her movements brought a little peace to June's soul. It was a reassuring sight, watching her nan work the needles with practiced competency. Her grandmother kept talking as a yellow scarf with twisted cables began to form. "I haven't been back to Tammay since before my Oliver passed away fifteen years ago. He took me there for our thirtieth anniversary. We met on the island right after the war. He was a young American pilot and full of brash Yankee swagger."

"Western swagger," June corrected with a fond smile, just as her grandpa used to.

Nan waved her knitting, but June detected a grin lurking under her gran's feigned annoyance. She'd always done the same to Pop Pop.

"Tell me about living in the Isles," June said, even though she'd heard the stories countless times. Growing up all over creation as an airman's daughter, she'd craved roots. She'd finally found them when she'd visited her nan and grandfather here in Pop Pop's hometown of Sagebrush Flats. The Winters had helped settle the town, even though her branch always ended up joining the military and spending their middle years wandering the world. But a connection with the local history hadn't been the only reason June had always felt at home when visiting her grandparents. It was the tales they would tell. June had loved hearing about her grandmother's teen years in Orkney where she'd lived with a great-aunt to escape the German bombs raining down on London.

This time, though, June had an ulterior motive for

requesting Nan's old stories. Similar to knitting, talking about the past seemed to center her grandmother. As her gran rocked back and forth, her gnarled fingers danced along with the knitting needles, and the words flowed from her lips. Customers came in and out of the store. Some of them listened, some of them didn't. Stanley and Buck returned to their own conversation. June paid attention with half an ear as she handled the morning rush. As she passed Louisa Thompson a poppy-seed scone and Darjeeling tea mixed with milk and honey, June made a vow. She would get Magnus Gray to talk to her nan, even if she had to hunt the man down and truss him up like a prize heifer at the county rodeo.

—⁓—

Magnus arrived at the zoo in a sour mood. Instead of a hearty Scots' breakfast at the Primrose, Magnolia & Thistle, he'd scarfed down weak tea and overly sweet French toast drowned in maple syrup. Unfortunately, he doubted the thin slices of cured pork that the Yanks called bacon would keep him full until dinner.

At least one thing was going his way, though. Since it was the middle of the week in January, the zoo was deserted. Magnus felt his shoulder muscles unhunch as he wound his way through the animal enclosures. Finally, peace. Quiet. Solitude. This was why he'd chosen to volunteer during the winter. That, and he didn't want to haul feed under the desert sun in August.

Gravel crunched under his feet as he followed

the directions the owner had given him to the main zoo building. At the sound, a pack of disgruntled llamas and two camels picked up their heads. Magnus paused, watching the odd-looking animals as they chewed their breakfast. He could write about their snaggletoothed grins studded with straw. There was something endearingly comedic about the two species. They reminded him of cows: same big, liquid eyes, same grinding eating motion, same food. The camelids were knobbier creatures, though, all legs and bumpy knees.

He'd read about the female camel, Lulubelle, on the zoo's website. The animal park claimed she'd been lovelorn until she'd met her mate, Hank. All shite, but the public loved it. According to her profile, Lulubelle was pregnant, but even knowing nothing about camels, Magnus would have noticed she was up the duff with her swollen belly and her lumbering, uneven gait. Glancing between her hind legs, Magnus saw her udder was swollen with milk. Her bairn would be along any time now.

Magnus scratched Lulubelle's woolly neck, and something inside him seemed to slide back into place like a latch on an old metal gate. He'd missed this, he realized. The simplicity of animal husbandry. He'd never felt nostalgic for his childhood. It had been rough, dreich, and devoid of comfort…and not just because of the drafty crofter's cottage he'd called home. Yet something about the mix of hay, manure, and animal scent whispered to him. Balanced him. Perhaps this wouldn't be the hell he'd imagined.

Lulubelle emitted a contented, low, rumbling bray that reminded him slightly of a horse's. Magnus smiled. "You're a fine lass, you are." His stutter never troubled him when he spoke to the beasties. When his da was out on the trawler, Magnus used to blether on and on to the cows and the horses. Aye, they'd been his first audience. If it hadn't been for them listening to his descriptions of his day, he might never have become a writer.

Magnus pulled back to stare into the camel's soulful eyes. They reminded him keenly of Sorcha's, one of his da's Highland cows. He hadn't thought of her in years, but she'd been his favorite. She'd come running up to him whenever he passed the pasture, probably because he'd sneak her treats when his da couldn't see. In trying to bury the terrible memories of his youth, he'd discarded the good ones too. Giving the camel one last pat goodbye, he made a promise to himself. When he returned to London, he was going to find himself a dog.

Walking around the bend, he spotted a bear lounging on a fairly good facsimile of a rock. By the animal's contented expression, he wondered if the structure was heated. He paused for a moment, leaning up against the rail to watch the blissful beastie. By its size, girth, and color, he guessed the animal was a grizzly, and he was partial to any bruin after raising two polar bear cubs.

The massive creature shifted. It turned rheumy eyes in Magnus's direction as it sniffed the air. Magnus grinned at the faint snuffling sounds. The elderly animal was having trouble spotting him, but there was no doubt he'd been scented.

"Good morning," Magnus said, and the bear snorted in response.

"I'm sorry I disturbed your sleep."

A rumbling sound emerged from the grizzly as it tried to settle back down on its rock. It did not appear to be successful. After shifting for several minutes, the animal clamored to its feet with a beleaguered groan. Shaking its limbs, it began to pad around its enclosure.

"I'll bring you a treat if Bowie Wilson will let me," Magnus promised.

The bear did not appear to be impressed. It shot Magnus a rather accusing glance as it lumbered back to its rock. It sank down, this time finding a better spot. With a happy sigh, the grizzly rested its chin on its massive paws.

Magnus smiled at the sight. He lingered a bit longer, enjoying the animal's newfound happiness as he felt his own sense of peace creep through him. Aye, he'd spent too much time away from other living creatures.

"You're here early." The male voice was friendly and vaguely familiar.

Magnus turned to find Bowie Wilson walking up the path. He recognized the zookeeper from his online videos. Magnus had spotted him at the Prairie Dog last night, but he hadn't wanted to bother with small talk. Unfortunately, he hadn't planned on the blond menace.

"Aye," Magnus replied. He could always form that word without hesitation. Through the years, he'd accumulated a library of phrases that saw him through most short interactions. Since Magnus avoided longer conversations, it generally worked.

"I see you've met Frida. She's our grizzly and one of our oldest residents. You probably saw Lulubelle, our camel, too. Since everyone passes by her paddock first, she's become our unofficial greeter. She's also the friendliest animal here, although our capybara, Sylvia, is a sweetheart too." The zookeeper had an easy smile, and his affection for the zoo residents flooded his voice. Magnus could respect that. Through the years, he'd learned that the way a man treated the beasties under his care was a reflection of his soul.

Magnus grunted to fill the silence. He'd learned people generally liked to hear themselves talk. As long as he gave them some encouragement, they'd carry on and never notice he hadn't actually uttered a word.

"I thought we'd start with a tour," Bowie said. "You can get to know the animals, and then we can go over what your volunteer duties will be. You said you don't mind shoveling manure or lugging around feed."

"Aye."

Bowie flashed a broad smile, showing off the perfect teeth that all Americans seemed to have. He was a handsome bloke with black hair and gray eyes. If he wasn't already married, he'd be an ideal match for the tea shop owner. They'd make fair bonny bairns, they would.

"It's great having a male volunteer," Bowie continued, his tone perfectly pitched to be cheerful and welcoming. It was the voice of a man accustomed to dealing with the public. "I appreciate any help I can get, but most of my usual assistants are high-school girls who aren't strong enough for the more physically demanding chores."

Magnus nodded, and Bowie kept talking. "Don't

worry, though. This job won't just be about hauling stuff. This morning, I finally got the call from the Alliance for Polar Life."

Magnus jerked his head in Bowie's direction. He'd worked with the Norwegian branch of the APL when he'd rescued polar bear cubs during his time as a roughneck. When his editor had suggested he volunteer at the Sagebrush Zoo, Magnus had been pleased to learn the animal park had received a grant to care for a cub that was not a candidate for rehabilitation.

Magnus started to say *bear*, but he could sense he was going to block on the *b*. Quickly, he switched the word. "Cub?"

"Yeah." Bowie nodded. "Oil exploration near dens up in Alaska scared off a lot of new moms. APL has too many bears to take care of right now. They're going to send us a female cub who was born late in the season."

Magnus whistled. In the wild, polar bears gave birth between November and December. Since it was early January, the bairn must be very young. Magnus started to say just that, but he felt his throat muscles tighten as he tried to say *must be*, so instead he got out, "She a... wee cub, aye?"

Bowie luckily didn't notice Magnus's hesitation or the slightly incorrect syntax. Instead, the man nodded. "She's about a month old, and the APL is struggling to provide round-the-clock care for all the abandoned young."

Magnus jerked his chin again. The group focused on research and wasn't staffed as a rescue center. Although they'd given him advice on how to care for the orphans he'd found, they hadn't had the manpower to care for those cubs either. Plus, the oil rig had been too far north to easily extract the cubs. The other roughnecks had initially given Magnus a hard time about being a polar bear mum, but eventually they'd all helped. The bairns had become his crew's mascots until they were able to be relocated to a zoo.

"The cub's eyes are open, but she's still pretty young," Bowie said, his voice softening as he spoke of the wee bear before returning to its crisper, more professional tone. "It's going to be intense in the beginning."

Magnus responded with a shrug. He'd taken care of cubs in the middle of the Arctic while working fourteen days straight; he could handle caring for one while doing odd jobs around a small animal park. Hard work didn't fash him. It would only improve his book.

"We're not too big a zoo, but we are growing," Bowie said as he started walking again with the confident stride of a man who ran his own operation. Pride seeped from him as he kept talking. "In the last year, we've gotten some grants, and we're starting to rebuild our reputation for providing care for abandoned young and unwanted exotic pets."

"Aye," Magnus said. He'd done his research when his editor had ordered him to come here.

"Part of it is because of this sweet girl."

Magnus looked inside the pen in front of him. A kidney-shaped creature lounged in a heated pool of water. She looked as content as Magnus felt tucked away in a corner of a pub enjoying a good whiskey.

"That's Sylvia, our capybara who I was just telling you about. She mothers all of our orphans."

Intrigued, Magnus stared at the odd-looking animal. He'd read her profile on the zoo's website. The surreal picture of Sylvia as a flower girl at Bowie and his wife's wedding had drawn Magnus's attention when he'd been clicking through the zoo's web pages, but it was the animal's habit of adopting motherless creatures that had truly intrigued him. Strange how a member of a wild species—and a rodent, no less—could have a greater natural affinity for nurturing than many a human.

Neither of Magnus's parents had shown any instinct for caring for him, their only offspring. His mum might have been the only one to physically abandon him, but his da had been more interested in keeping their live-stock alive than he'd been in raising Magnus. His da's way of parenting was to assign chores and give his son a smack or two if they weren't done fast enough for his liking. And when Magnus had stuttered…

Magnus pushed abruptly away from the fence. He started moving forward, hoping Bowie would under-stand that he wanted to press on. He didn't feel like trying to form words. Luckily, Bowie understood the unspoken signal. They walked in silence until Magnus turned the bend.

"Fuck me."

"Yep, that was pretty much my response when animal control brought them here."

Magnus stared in disbelief at the huge herd of goats milling about their pen. The blighted creatures had eaten every possible living thing in their enclosure, leaving only red dirt behind. Knowing goats, they'd probably tried eating that too. One of the dobbers caught sight of Magnus and stared him down with an evil glint in its

unholy eyes. Although Magnus might have been
feeling nostalgic for the farm animals on the croft,
he'd never miss these cloven-footed devils. They
had a scream like an enraged banshee and a foul
temper to match. One of his da's old billy goats
used to stick his head through the wooden gate just
to eat the same damn gorse that grew in his paddock. His horns would prevent him from pulling his
head back through, and he'd bellow bloodcurdling
cries until someone rescued him.

"There was a man who hoarded them that lived
about forty minutes from here," Bowie said. "No
one else would take them, so we got stuck with the
whole herd."

Magnus grunted. A couple young kids bleated
as they bounced around the pen, their hind legs
kicking into the air as they practiced bucking. They
were deceptively cute.

"Kind?" Magnus barked out. He would have asked
about the breed, but he didn't want to risk getting
stuck on the *b*. The beasties didn't look like any goats
he'd seen before. Their eyes were more prominent.

Bowie chuckled. "Let me demonstrate." He
grabbed the gate and gave it a hard slam. The
metal clanged loudly, but that wasn't what startled
Magnus. It was what happened next. Some goats
toppled onto their sides, their legs stiff and straight.
The bairns and juveniles lolled on their backs, looking like someone had knocked over a taxidermy
display. A few of the adults hopped forward, their
joints locked. Magnus scratched his head as he
watched the odd scene unfold.

"Fuck me."

"They're fainting goats," Bowie said. "They've got a genetic disorder that causes their muscles to spasm when they're frightened, startled, or just overexcited. It doesn't hurt them. They'll be up and running in a couple seconds."

"Odd creatures," Magnus said as he watched the goats scramble to their feet and then bolt as if Auld Clootie himself was after them.

"You can say that again," Bowie said. "They're the zoo's current white elephant. We don't have barnyard animals, but most of the goats were in bad shape, and I couldn't turn them away. I thought I'd make this exhibit a petting zoo, but the children are either scared when the goats flop over, or they try to frighten the poor guys on purpose. I'm still trying to figure out what to do with them."

"Supper?" Magnus offered helpfully.

Bowie laughed and shook his head. "I wouldn't have the heart."

"They'd be tough auld bastards," Magnus said.

"Most likely," Bowie agreed as they walked around the paddock to an equally befuddling sight. The next enclosure looked like an empty ten-foot-deep swimming pool, but with red dirt instead of cement for a bottom. Two separate sheds were erected at opposite ends. Unlike the other pens, this one was relatively barren with only a few balls and other small toys.

"This is the home of our two resident honey badgers," Bowie said. "They make the goats look personable, but we love Honey and Fluffy all the same."

Magnus looked at Bowie questioningly. Orkney did not have badgers, but mainland Scotland did. He'd never heard them referred to as honey badgers, though.

"They're from Africa," Bowie explained, "and they're more closely related to weasels than the badgers you have back in Britain. They've got similar coloration to the true badger but are meaner. They kill cobras...for fun. Their skin is so thick, snake venom doesn't always kill them, but just temporarily knocks them out. They're smart and extremely devious."

Now that would make good fodder for his book. Magnus leaned over the fence as he tried to peer into the shelter. He still couldn't get a glimpse of the beasties.

"Fluffy and Honey are nocturnal," Bowie said, "but don't worry. You'll get a glimpse of them. Honey-badger wrangling will be a big part of your job...and cleaning up their messes. They escape at least once a week."

"From there?" Magnus asked in surprise, jerking his thumb toward the dirt run surrounded by sheer concrete walls.

Bowie nodded glumly. "Yep. They're smart. Too smart. I thought if I found a mate for Fluffy—that's our male—he might settle down. Now, I've got two of them running around, and Fluffy is ornerier than ever. Honey is always pestering him, and I think he blames me. If Fluffy escapes, my daughter, Abby, can coax him back to the enclosure. Honey won't listen to anyone, even though she used to be kept as a pet. Luckily, she normally returns to her den on her own."

"They're not a friendly species then?" Magnus asked.

Bowie shook his head. "Nope. In the wild, honey badgers are solitary, although the cubs do stay with their mother for over a year. The adults only interact to mate. There's evidence, though, of honey badgers getting along in captivity. Luckily, Honey and Fluffy haven't physically fought each other, but they're not exactly on good terms. Fluffy's definitely not happy with the invader to his home."

Magnus glanced back at the small shed in the center of the red dust. He could sympathize with the unseen Fluffy. After all, he had his own meddlesome female to contend with.

Fluffy did not appreciate the intruder to his domain. At all.

He ruled this zoo, not this interloper. Yet Honey insisted on escaping. Every. Single. Night.

Evening was his time to roam. It wasn't nearly as interesting to cause mischief when she'd already beaten him to it. Yesterday, he'd gone to rip open a feed bag to discover Honey had already strewn the contents over the storage-room floor. Having the food readily available had taken all the fun out of eating it…well, *most* of the fun. He was a honey badger with an appetite after all. And although Fluffy would never ever admit it, the female mustelid was slightly—just slightly—better at getting into the cabinet containing the honey-covered larvae.

But *he* was blamed for the mess.

Females, Fluffy had decided, were nothing but trouble.

"I want all the details you know on Magnus Gray," June demanded as her best friend carefully climbed onto a stool in her kitchen.

"Uh-uh," Katie Wilson said, shaking her red curls emphatically as she placed her hands on the slight bulge of her tummy, "I'm just here to try out the jams you said you were making to help with my morning sickness."

June turned and pulled out the batch of jelly that she'd whipped up the night before especially for Katie. A few years ago, she'd started a jam business in addition to her tea shop. She'd been building her customer base slowly, starting at farmers' markets and then local grocery stores. A year ago, the Prairie Dog Café had begun putting her jams on their tables and selling jars at the checkout counter. Just last month, the gift shop at nearby Rocky Ridge National Park had ordered its fourth shipment. Online sales, which had grown slowly at first, had picked up late last summer and hadn't stopped. Between the tea shop and jam sales, she'd had enough money to hire more help both in the kitchen and out front.

In August, June had put her business degree to use and drawn up plans for increasing production. She'd considered applying for a loan to lease a small facility. Then Nan's episodes had started, and June had shelved those ideas until she understood more about her grandmother's condition. Between getting up before dawn to start the baking, managing the tea shop, making jam, and developing new recipes, she was already running in more directions than a long-tailed cat at a square dance. She couldn't take on both a major expansion of her jam enterprise and her gran's health problems. And Nan came first.

Which was why June had lured Katie to her kitchen with the promise of jam. The girl would do anything for a sugary treat, and that was before she'd started eating for three. If June wanted to sweet-talk the grumpiest Scot ever to walk God's green earth, she needed all the reconnaissance she could gather. Despite the man's fame as an author, her internet sleuthing had unearthed only that Magnus was notoriously reclusive. And that she'd already figured out on her own. Right now, her quarry was working with her best friend's husband. If anyone knew anything, it would be Katie or Bowie, and June had been perfecting the art of getting secrets out of Katie since college. Although she could crack Bowie open like a nut too, that would take more time and finesse, and June didn't like to wait.

"So, what did you make me?" Katie asked eagerly as she rested her elbows on the counter.

"I started with fresh mint and ginger," June said. "Then I sweetened it with the honey from Lawson's Apiary. Since it's thoroughly cooked, it won't hurt those little butter beans growing inside you. It needed texture so I studded it with bits of candied ginger."

"Gimme." Katie reached out both hands and wiggled her fingers.

June held the bowl out of reach. "Magnus intel first."

Katie's brown irises went doe-eyed. "You wouldn't keep food away from a pregnant woman, would you?"

"I was raised by a career military man and a southern belle," June replied. "I could strategize before I could walk, and I don't take prisoners."

Losing the sweet look, Katie crossed her arms and gave a mock glare. "You're mean."

"I prefer 'incorrigible.' Now spill."

Katie sighed and leaned back in her chair. "There is nothing to spill. I've barely met the man. Every time I run into him, he just grunts and goes back to whatever he was doing."

June sent Katie an exasperated look. "Sweetie, have I taught you nothing? I need dirt."

Katie's cherubic face softened into pure innocence again. June immediately recognized the look. After all, she was the one who'd perfected it.

"And I need jam," Katie said. "Maybe if my stomach was full I might be able to remember details about Magnus."

June arched an eyebrow. "Is this a ploy?"

Katie's expression remained guileless...too guileless. "Feed me, and you'll find out."

"Hmmm." June relented as she placed the jam on the table and gave Katie a day-old biscuit from the tea shop leftovers. "On second thought, maybe I taught you too much."

"I learned from the best." Katie took a tentative bite of the jam-covered biscuit. Then another. Then an even bigger one. She paused for a moment, chewing thoughtfully before swallowing. Then, in her typical straightforward way, she said, "Well, it doesn't make me want to hurl."

"Now there's a slogan if I've ever heard one," June said. Katie drew all the labels for June's products and helped with marketing.

Katie laughed. "Right now, if there was a line of food products called 'No-Vomit Vitals for Pregnant Ladies,' I'd empty the entire supermarket shelf."

June wrinkled her nose. "I don't think that's quite the image I want."

Katie shrugged and returned to eating. "Talking about questionable monikers, I wish morning sickness only happened in the actual morning. These hormones are killing me."

June patted her hand in sympathy. "But in less than seven months, you'll have two little babies to love."

"That's what I keep telling myself. It doesn't help that I'm showing and it isn't even the second trimester."

"Bowie seems happier than a possum eating a sweet potato."

A fond smile crossed Katie's face. "He's already started turning the attic into a nursery and playroom. It's a good thing we have a full-time volunteer right now."

June rested both her elbows against the counter. She knew she was grinning like a raccoon after it raided the larder. "And about that particular volunteer..."

Katie waved her half-eaten biscuit. "Nope. Not going there."

June sighed. "Katie, I need some way to butter the man up. It would do Nan a world of good to talk to him."

"Why don't you just ask him?" Katie said. "He seems like someone who would appreciate a direct approach."

"See," June said. "Was that so bad? This is exactly the kind of information I need."

Katie put jam on the other half of her biscuit. "So, you're going to walk up to him and ask?"

"Goodness no." June waved her hand. "The man has already bolted from me twice. This requires finesse. What does he like? Maybe I should make him a batch of my scones. Men always like baked goods, even grumpy galoots. What do you think?"

"Ginger-Minted Bliss," Katie said.

June blinked at the non sequitur. "Pardon?"

Katie jabbed her knife in the direction of the jam. "That's what we should call it. I can see the label now. I can sketch a pregnant lady, her hands on her belly, a satisfied smile on her face. What do you think?"

"That you're trying to distract me."

Katie sighed and put her knife down firmly on the counter. "June, you know me. I am good at marketing. I am not good at winding men around my little finger. That's your department."

June exhaled loudly and rested her chin on her hands as she leaned on the counter. "But this man isn't reacting like all the others. The more I try to charm him, the more he runs."

Katie laughed. "Welcome to the reality of most women."

"You're certain you don't know anything?"

Katie shook her head, sending her red curls flying. "June, Magnus has only been in town for a few days, and he keeps to himself. Bowie says he's a hard worker, but he doesn't talk much. He seems to have a natural affinity with animals, if that helps."

"So, you're saying if I were another species, he'd be more inclined to chat with me." June originally meant the words as a joke, but as soon as she spoke, the truth rose up like cream separating from milk. Maybe the Scot preferred animals to people because he didn't have trouble speaking around them. Her brother had always been able to talk to the family dog without any signs of disfluency. Although it wasn't the case for all people who stuttered, August spoke more fluently when he was around people he felt comfortable with.

June grinned. Why, that was it! She just needed to show Magnus that he could be at ease with her and her grandmother. And the only way to do that was to keep running into the man, hopefully with Nan in tow.

"Uh-oh," Katie said, "I know that smile."

June didn't even bother to remove it from her face. "Katie, when is that adorable polar bear cub due to arrive? You know how much Nan and I adore animals, especially the cuddly ones."

"June…" Katie said, a warning note in her voice.

But June kept right on beaming. Winning over a bear of a man might just take one adorable cub and a grandmother who loved the Isles.

Chapter 3

MAGNUS HADN'T EXPECTED AN AUDIENCE FOR THE arrival of the polar bear cub. Yet there the lass stood, like some fae creature come to play tricks on mortals. When he'd entered the maintenance facility, she'd waved like they were best mates at primary school. He'd nodded once, hoping that would satisfy her. It didn't work.

"Hi there," the lass said as she moved from the picture window overlooking the nursery. They were congregated in the hallway so they wouldn't overwhelm the cub. It would be enough for the wee bairn to get accustomed to her new surroundings without a flock of humans looming over her.

Magnus dipped his chin in acknowledgment of her greeting. Part of him wanted to leave, but he didn't want to miss this. An unusual excitement hummed through him. It had been more than five years since he'd last held a cub, and after working with the animals here in Sagebrush, he'd realized how much he missed it. It was hard work raising a bear from a wee bairn but rewarding too. There was something about how they clambered about, searching for a warm place to lie or a spot of milk.

"Did Bowie or Katie tell you the good news?"

Magnus gave a slight shake of his head. The lass

didn't need any more encouragement. She beamed as brightly as the harvest moon.

"I'm going to help with the cub. Well, we will. My grandmother and I."

Fuck. Bowie had mentioned they had some local volunteers. When Bowie had run through the list of names, Magnus had thought the name June Winters sounded familiar, but it also had a natural ring. The lass must have introduced herself at some point, or he'd read it on her tea shop's website.

"Come and meet my nan," June said. She reached forward and grabbed his arm. The contact seared him, the heat sending his heart into an erratic rhythm. He debated about shaking June off, but her grandmother looked up at that moment. A smile creased the older woman's face, and Magnus couldn't simply walk away. His da might not have managed to control him as much as the old bastard had wanted, but some of the lessons had stuck. A man respected his elders.

"Pleased to meet you," the woman said in a posh English accent after June introduced her as Clara Winters. Magnus hid his surprise as he shook the woman's hand. Although he'd read on the tea shop's website that the owner's grandmother was from the UK, it was still jarring for a Yank to have a proper British nana.

"It's an honor," Magnus said carefully. As a lad, he'd spent hours talking to the cows, practicing general greetings over and over. He'd figured out which ones came out the easiest, and he stuck to those. He often felt like he was using a damn script, but it was better than getting mired by a word.

"Your first two books were lovely," the woman told

him. Magnus didn't miss the fact she purposely excluded his later works. He might not appreciate being exiled to Sagebrush Flats, but his editor wasn't wrong. The public considered his latest efforts pure rubbish.

Magnus took the half compliment and bobbed his head.

"Did my Junie tell you I lived in Orkney during the war?"

Magnus froze, suddenly feeling like a vole being stalked by a gull. *Baws*. He was an unlucky bastard. Here he was in the middle of the American desert, and he'd bloody run into someone from the Isles.

Magnus shook his head. He didn't trust himself to speak properly.

The woman's face softened into a fond, almost wistful smile, and Magnus fought back a groan. She clearly wanted to reminisce about a place Magnus had spent years trying to forget.

"I was fifteen when the Blitz began," the woman said, her eyes clouding. "Those were terrible days in London."

Magnus bobbed his head.

"My great-auntie on my mum's side lived in the Isles, and my parents sent me to live with her for the rest of the war. It was a peaceful place even with all the military men running about."

Aye, some people might consider Orkney peaceful—if they lived in a snug cottage in a village or on one of the more prosperous farms and didn't have to work from morning 'til night trying to eke out a living on one of the rockier islands. For Magnus, it had been a dreary existence. A love for the land hadn't sunk into his marrow as it had for his father's people. He was, as his da had always accused him of being, his mother's child. A wanderer.

"I have so many fond memories of those years," Clara continued. "I met my husband in Orkney. He was an American airman stationed there toward the end of the fighting. He was the most handsome fellow I'd ever seen."

June chose that moment to pop into the conversation. "Nan has so many stories about Tammay."

Magnus had to prevent himself from physically reacting to the name of the bigger island next to the small one where his da had his croft. *Shite*. The woman had lived in his hometown.

Clara Winters's eyes appeared almost gold as she turned toward him again. "You captured the isle's beauty so well in your writings. It was like I was back walking on the streets of Grarthorpe and taking tea at the Mary Rose."

Magnus jerked his chin in response. Talking about Tammay made him as skittish as a horse crossing the strand with the tide rushing in. That's why he'd never written about the isle after the first book. He'd meant to bury the place, not resurrect it.

June reached for his arm again. He started to shift away, but she was quicker. Her hand brushed his bicep, lingering just for a moment. The slight touch had a seismic effect. Sensation ricocheted through him, unsettling him. He'd just managed to put himself to rights when June spoke again.

"Why, I have the most wonderful idea! You and Nana

could reminisce about Tammay together! Wouldn't that be heavenly?"

Not quite. More like hell. Unfortunately, Clara's face lit like the sunrise over the North Sea, brilliant and encompassing. "Oh, that sounds lovely," she said.

Magnus was saved from answering when the door to the maintenance facility banged open, and Abby, Bowie's daughter, bounded into the room. She had her da's black hair, gray eyes, and love for animals. Every day, as soon as the bus dropped her off, she'd race to the llama pen to check on the pregnant Lulubelle. In her enthusiasm, the wee lassie never took the time to remove her rucksack. Instead, she'd run through the zoo with the heavy bag bouncing off her back.

As a boy, Magnus had never felt exuberance like Abby's when he'd return to the croft. He remembered rowing back to the small island, each stroke adding more weight to his heart. Aye, he'd loved the animals. They'd made life tolerable. But they'd never given him the joy that flowed so freely from the lassie.

The girl's stepmother, Katie, entered the zoo's maintenance facility at a more sedate pace, but no one could miss the excitement in her eyes. She carried a camera bag slung over her shoulder. Magnus had never seen her without it. She handled the zoo's advertising, and she had a way of turning the most mundane moment into a marketing masterpiece.

"Dad called and said they're almost here!" Abby announced as she bounced up and down like a piece of driftwood during a rough storm. Although Magnus had never possessed even a tenth of the girl's enthusiasm, there was something charming about the lassie's affection for the zoo animals. Despite her high spirits, she reminded him a bit of himself as a lad when the cows and the horses had been his only real companions. His da hadn't tolerated any visitors, and he'd wanted Magnus back at the croft immediately after classes, not that Magnus had received many invitations. His stutter had made his schoolmates uncomfortable. Despite his lack of experience with children, he found himself at ease with Abby. The lassie didn't expect anything of him, except for him listen to her chatter about the zoo.

Abby liked helping out around the animal park, and she didn't mind the smellier jobs. Yesterday evening when she'd found Magnus mucking out the indoor llama enclosure during her daily visit to Lulubelle, she'd picked up her own shovel. She'd talked the whole time, filling the quiet with stories of zoo residents. As a lad, Magnus had worked in silence beside his da, the only sound the constant roar of the wind. Surprisingly, he hadn't minded the lassie's endless commentary. Aye, she had surprising wit and keen observation for one so young. And she was a hard worker. She probably would've pitched in longer if her da hadn't collected her for supper and schoolwork.

"The cub?" Magnus asked. He would've said more, but he didn't want to trip over his words. He'd managed to hide his stutter from everyone but June, and he wanted to keep it that way. Luckily, Katie understood his truncated question immediately.

"Bowie said she's doing well after her flight. She's already taken some formula and is sleeping in Lou's arms during the drive," Katie said, referring to the former owner of the zoo who was a trained veterinarian. "Bowie and Lou have the temperature way up in the truck. Bowie says it's like a sauna."

"What's the cub's name?" June asked.

"She doesn't have one yet," Abby said. She'd stopped bouncing, but her body still seemed to vibrate with suppressed excitement. She pivoted to Magnus, her eyes shining brightly. When she spoke, her words came out in a rush. "Do you know any Scottish ones, Mr. Gray?"

"Sorcha." The name of his favorite Highland cow from boyhood slipped from his lips before he'd had the chance to think or even stumble on the word.

Abby clapped her hands and gave a little jump. "I love it."

Just then, Bowie appeared on the other side of the glass. He paused, holding the door open for Lou. The older man moved at slow pace, his eyes focused on the little bear cradled against his chest. Pure affection lit his lined face as he stared down at the cub swaddled in a fluffy pink blanket. Two sleepy black eyes peeked out from the wrapping. Although Magnus couldn't see much else except for a black nose and two little paws, he could tell the wee beastie hadn't grown her thick coat yet. He spotted a flash of pink tongue before her eyes drifted closed.

Silence fell over the hallway as the cub yawned and snuggled deeper into the fleece. Even Abby had stilled, her mouth frozen in an O. Then she let out a squeak and tucked both her hands under her chin.

Magnus could tell Abby wanted to dash into

the nursery, but being raised around animals, she knew better than to frighten Sorcha. Still, she couldn't seem to stop her entire body from pitching forward in the direction of the wee bear. An uncharacteristic smile crossed Magnus's face.

Beside him, he heard a sharp intake of breath. Turning, he found June staring at the wee beastie, her green eyes sparkling with undisguised, almost child-like wonder. She looked just as enraptured as the lassie. Transfixed himself, Magnus couldn't help but stare. He was a cynical arse, raised by a man who didn't believe in emotions. Americans with their wide grins and generally jolly attitudes always left him a bit befuddled.

And June Winters was luminous. Aye, she was a reg-ular solar flare of delight. But she didn't leave him feel-ing confused. Far from it. The heat she radiated warmed him like a crackling peat fire in the dead of winter.

June swung in his direction. A fetching smile touched her bonny pink lips, with the tips curling even more when she caught sight of him. An unusual glow kindled inside Magnus. In that moment, June's excitement seemed solely for him, and he felt drawn to the lass like an eyebright flower reaching for the spring sun.

Which was absolutely rubbish. Because everyone knew what happened to mortals who had the hubris to approach a solar deity. They either got burned alive or fell on their arses like Icarus. Since Magnus didn't par-ticularly desire either result, he turned and exited the maintenance facility. He'd have plenty of time with the wee Sorcha later, and then he wouldn't have to contend with an audience. Especially one that included a bonny sun goddess determined to drive him utterly doolally.

———

June was fit to be tied. The blasted man had just marched away from her for a third time. At least he hadn't slammed the door. But she figured he probably would have if it wasn't for the little cub yawning in Bowie's arms.

Men did not walk away from June. Especially when she smiled at them. They always grinned right back and sauntered over to her. It just got her dander up that Magnus Gray kept slighting her.

"Nan," June said before realizing her voice sounded as sharp as a freshly honed knife. Modulating her voice, she said in a softer tone, "Nana."

Her grandmother turned, her eyes soft from watching Bowie gently lay the little cub next to Sylvia, the zoo's capybara. Sylvia gently nudged the bear with her snout, and the tiny girl wiggled closer, burying her black nose against the rodent's side. Bowie had explained capybaras were comfortable in a variety of environments, so Sylvia would be able to handle both the current warmth Sorcha required and the cooler temperatures the cub would prefer as she grew bigger.

"Yes, dear?" her grandmother asked.

"I have something I need to take care of," June explained. "Would you mind staying here with Katie?"

"Not at all, but are you certain it can't wait? This cub is all you've been talking about for days."

June patted her grandmother's arm. Today had been a particularly good one for the older woman.

She hadn't experienced a single episode of confusion...
yet. June suspected it was partly due to her nan's excitement over the new polar bear. The older woman looked
more animated than she had in weeks. Color had flooded
back into her cheeks, and her hazel eyes twinkled with
a clarity they'd lacked. But it hadn't been just the cub.
Meeting Magnus had contributed too, which was why
June couldn't delay her mission.

"I won't be long, Nan," June promised as she turned
and headed out the same door that Magnus had exited.
It was still fairly early on a Sunday morning, and the
zoo hadn't opened yet. The wind whipped through the
deserted pathways, and June pulled her coat closer.
Blustery days like this made her wish she'd settled in
Georgia with her mama's family. Generally, she loved
Sagebrush, even during the blistering summer heat, but
she could never get used to the cold.

As she turned the corner of the goat pen, she spotted
Magnus's burly form ahead. He moved like an angry
grizzly, his stride both powerful and lumbering. He did
not wear a coat despite the cold. Instead, he hunched
over, his head bowed into the breeze, his hands shoved
into the pockets of his pants. He was a man who pushed
the world away, daring it to defy him.

And June had never been able to resist a challenge.

"Magnus!" she called.

He stiffened at the sound of his name, his shoulders straightening. Then they slumped right back
down as he continued plowing through the wind. June
narrowed her eyes. The blasted man had heard her.
Even if she hadn't witnessed his reaction to her voice,
she'd yelled loud enough to wake the dead in the next

county over. Several of the younger fainting goats
had even toppled over, their legs sticking straight
up in the air.

June picked up her pace and hollered again.
This time, eight goats hit the ground and three
more hopped forward, their knees locked in place.
Magnus hesitated, giving June just enough time to
grab his arm. She would have tapped his shoulder,
but even with her height, she would have had to
stand on her tiptoes.

He heaved a sigh, reminding June of her grandpappy's dog after it lost its meal to the barn cat.
Slowly, Magnus turned and faced her. As she stared
up at over six feet of glowering male, she wondered why he intrigued her. His personality was as
unpleasant as a thunderstorm in August, but there
was something about him that made her want to see
what happened when he smiled.

Magnus watched her expectantly, his blue eyes
like twin icicles beneath his shaggy hair. His beard
obscured most of his mouth, but she had a feeling
he was scowling as well.

"I just wanted a quick chat," June said. "You
don't need to look like an angry lumberjack."

He blew out another breath, his broad shoulders slumping in unison with the beleaguered
sound. When he spoke, he sounded resigned.
"Roughneck." The word dropped carefully from his
lips, and she could tell he was trying his darndest
not to stutter. Unfortunately, she didn't understand
his one-word response.

"Pardon?"

He wet his lips and started again, his tone slow and careful. "I was a roughneck, not a lumberjack."

June brightened. "Oh! I didn't mean your occupation. You just remind me of Paul Bunyan in your flannel." She started to flick the cuff of his shirt, but he stepped back. His brown eyebrows pulled downward in confusion.

"Who?"

"Paul Bunyan is an old tall tale. He lived in Minnesota and had a giant blue ox as a pet."

Magnus crossed his arms and gave her a hard stare, looking more like a Viking than a woodsman. Considering he'd grown up on an isle in the North Sea, it was probably a more accurate description, not that June planned on sharing it with him. He didn't seem too enamored by the Paul Bunyan reference, and she didn't want to attempt another.

"Did you stop me for a reason, lass?"

"I'm on a mission."

He arched one thick eyebrow. "I don't much like being p-p-p-p…"

Magnus's eyebrow dropped back down as his entire body stiffened. When he blocked on a sound, it wasn't just his articulators that locked up. His head moved slightly to the left as he tried to speak. It wasn't unusual for people with disfluency to develop secondary movements. Often, the unnecessary physical reactions started as a way to control the stutter but then became part of it. June wouldn't be surprised if Magnus wasn't even fully aware of what his body was doing. Her brother, August, hadn't been.

Instead of pushing Magnus or trying to finish the statement for him, she waited. It was hard knowing where to

look when someone experienced a hard block. She
didn't want to stare, but she didn't want to glance
away either. Even though June used to stutter, it
was difficult to know how to react. But she'd had
practice with her brother, so she treated Magnus just
as she would've August. It seemed to work.

Magnus swallowed and finished, "…part of your
mission."

"You're not so much a part of it as the end goal."

June might be mistaken, but she thought the
man colored. His beard covered most of his face,
but flags of red appeared on his harsh cheekbones.
It could have been from the cold, but June didn't
think so.

"Your bum's out the window."

"Excuse me?"

"Didn't your nana ever use that expression?"

June shook her head.

"It means you're talking nonsense."

"Ooo, I like that one," June said. "I just love
folksy expressions, don't you? I started collecting
them in a diary when I was a little girl. Since my
daddy was stationed all over the world, I have hun-
dreds. I make up my own too."

Magnus stared at her, and June sensed he was
debating about making another break for it. Before
he could, she grabbed his arm again. His gaze
shifted toward her hand, and she suddenly became
aware of the coiled heat beneath her fingertips.
Very aware. My goodness, the man had muscles
harder than Georgia granite.

"I need to ask you a favor," June told him as she

slowly removed her fingers from his bicep. He shot her a baleful expression.

June dipped her chin slightly, just like her mama had taught her, allowing her to look at Magnus from beneath her eyelashes as she smiled. Men never failed to respond to that particular gesture, even the most bullheaded ones. However, Magnus's expression didn't change, and a whisper of frustration wound through June. "It's not for me. It's for my nana. She loves hearing stories about Bjar—" she explained.

A flicker of softness flashed in Magnus's blue eyes before they froze over again. "I don't talk about that isle, lass."

All of June's carefully constructed arguments blew from her mind as frustrated anger swept through her. The man was as bullheaded as a groundhog after a fresh tomato. "You wrote an entire book about it."

"It was a purge."

"A purge?"

"An enema."

"Did you just call your bestseller an enema?"

"Aye."

"You are a complicated man, Magnus Gray."

"Nay. Just a simple bloke who likes peace, quiet, and a good tattie scone."

Although June fully believed the man liked solitude and Scottish cooking, she didn't buy his first claim. The reclusive author had depths greater than Loch Ness that hid mysteries even bigger than a fabled sea monster. Although June excelled at charting a person's personality within minutes of meeting them, she still couldn't fathom this man.

"Good day." With that parting salvo, Magnus Gray started to turn and walk away from June for a fourth time in a row. Before he could take one step, however, all hell broke loose in the form of cloven-footed critters.

Honey's nose twitched as she watched the Giant One and the Blond One. She respected the devious spark lurking in the woman's green eyes. And she'd been monitoring the hulking newcomer since his arrival. Unlike the careless Fluffy, Honey knew how to conceal her presence. The Giant One had no idea she'd stalked him for days.

He intrigued her. He was not like most weak-willed humans who craved the company of their own kind. The Giant One preferred solitude, just like honey badgers.

Since her arrival at the zoo, Honey had been watching for suitable adversaries. Although the young female cougars had the speed and agility to keep her reflexes limber, they lacked foresight and cunning. The grizzly was elderly and slow. And the rest of the animals did not interest her. Unfortunately, the human keepers did not provide the same amusement as her old biped. They were too pleasant.

But these two were different. They reminded Honey of bees, full of energy as they buzzed at each other. Yes, these two could sting if properly motivated.

Honey smiled as she scurried up a pole of the

goat pen. With one swift nudge of her nose, she lifted the latch. Hanging on to the gate, she used her body weight to swing it open. The silly goats immediately bolted for the exit.

Honey shimmied back to the ground. The Giant One was busy tripping over the horned creatures, but the Blond One stood upright. As Honey scampered away, she made sure the female spied her. It was time to make her presence known. After all, what was the point of starting a game if her opponent didn't know she was a player?

Chapter 4

MAGNUS WAS NOT SURE WHAT HAD HAPPENED. ONE moment he was arguing with the barmy lass, and the next, he was surrounded by a blasted herd of bleating, screaming goats. He'd just started to pivot away from June when two kids darted between his legs. The blighted things must have mistaken him for some sort of shelter as they twined about his ankles. Caught off-balance, he felt his massive frame sway. He couldn't right himself without stepping on one of the cloven beasties. And, as much as goats annoyed him, he didn't wish to crush them under his weight.

Twisting his body, he managed to avoid the wee bastards, but he ended up crashing to the gravel path with a painful thump. Since Magnus couldn't use his arms to brace his fall, his back collided with the ground, knocking the wind out of him. As he lay gasping like a landed sea trout, one of the wee devils climbed on his chest while the other started eating his hair. Magnus could only lie there as he tried sucking air back into his lungs.

Suddenly, June appeared in his vision, her blond hair hanging around her face like a golden curtain. For once, mirth didn't sparkle in her bonny green eyes. To his surprise, real concern shone there instead. If he hadn't met her already, he'd say she looked like an angel hovering over him.

"Are you okay?" she asked. "You hit the ground pretty hard."

He would have reassured her, but that would have required oxygen. Her mouth twisted, and she reached down and lifted a bleating goat off his body. That helped, marginally. Using his eyes, he gestured to the one chewing his hair. She removed that one too. "You just breathe easy now, you hear?"

He had no choice but to listen. As he sprawled spread-eagle on the ground, the lass stood guard, a squirming kid under each arm. A couple adult goats tried to clamber on his body, but June shooed them away. It was odd, he thought, having someone watch over him. His da would have called him a muckle nyaff and left him in disgust for tripping over his own feet.

Finally, Magnus could breathe again. He slowly raised himself on his elbows and then almost plopped right back down. The manky goats were all over the path. How the hell had they escaped?

"A honey badger let them out," June explained.

Magnus swung his gaze toward her in disbelief. A honey badger had caused all this? What would possess the wee beastie to open the pen?

"By its size, I think it was the female, Honey. I saw her darting away just after you fell."

"Baws." Magnus finally managed.

"If you're okay, I'll go put these two critters back in their home before we get the rest," June said, lifting the kids in her arms. They bleated loudly in protest. Magnus nodded. As he heaved himself to his feet, June dropped the two bairns back in the paddock.

Sighing heavily, Magnus took after two of the goats.

They screamed like banshees and darted away.
Magnus swore. He hated chasing the slippery wee
devils. Give him a cow or even a pig over these
bastards.

"I don't think we need to run them down," June
said.

He swung toward her, irritated. He doubted
she'd done much farming. "How do you propose
we get them back in the pen then, lass?"

She smirked, that gleam back in her green eyes.
"Strategy."

Then, she reached down and grabbed a metal
feed bucket hanging from the corner of the pen. She
smashed it against the steel gate, the sound ringing
sharply through the air. The fainting goats toppled
and hopped everywhere, and Magnus had to admit
it made corralling them easier. Aye, the lass was a
clever one even if a pain in the arse.

She grabbed the wee ones, while he hoisted the
adults. They had to bang the gate a few more times,
but they managed to quickly clear the path of goats.
When the last bleating bastard was dumped back in
its home, Magnus turned to regard his unexpected
helper. The cold and the exertion had brought color
to June's cheeks, making her bonnier than ever.
She was as fair and delicate as the fae folk in the
German tales, and just as devious. And something
about her made Magnus wonder what the price of
kissing a fairy would be.

Too steep. Much too steep.

"Thank you. I b-b-best be going now."

June grinned at him, and he felt an unwilling

tug in the vicinity of his heart. "We make a good team, don't we?"

He grunted.

"You know how you can thank me?" she asked, her voice bright and eager. "You could talk to my na…"

Magnus leaned toward the lass, and, for one mad moment, he almost pressed his lips against her pink ones. He was close enough to feel the puff of her breath. Her eyes widened ever so slightly, and he could see anticipation and awareness swimming in those green depths. To his surprise, she didn't push him away. She stood there, just as frozen as one of those daft fainting goats.

"Not going to happen, lass," he said. He wasn't sure if he was talking to her or to himself or whether he was referring to snogging or chatting with her nana. The disappointment that flared in her emerald depths echoed the surprising twinge inside him. Magnus didn't heed the sensation, though. Instead, he turned on his heel and headed to the supply shed to start hauling feed for the day.

It wasn't until long afterward, when he was mucking out the llama shed with Abby chattering next to him about the new baby polar bear, that a thought struck him. Except for that one long block, he'd barely stuttered in June's presence. Had scarcely thought about it even. Which never happened.

The next morning, Magnus woke to the sounds of a hungry cub. Rolling off the surprisingly comfortable air mattress, he stood with a yawn. Walking while stretching, he headed over to Sorcha. Bowie had offered him accommodations about twenty minutes out of town, but

Magnus had opted to stay at the zoo. He didn't mind being around the animals, and the other lodging was directly behind Bowie's in-laws, which meant neighbors. Bowie hadn't argued with Magnus's decision, especially since it meant more help caring for the new arrival.

Magnus had made the right choice. It had been a productive evening. He'd started a blog like his editor wanted. Already, he was getting responses, mostly from readers who were glad he was writing about animals again.

When he entered the nursery, the capybara lifted her head. Sorcha was too busy rooting for milk to notice his entrance. Although the cub's eyes were open, she was still a wee thing, her movements clumsy and hesitant. Her little legs splayed in all directions as she nosed the fleece blanket. The hungry squeaks grew in volume as Magnus headed over to the counter to prepare a bottle. Working quickly, he wrinkled his nose at the fishy smell of the cod-liver oil mixed into the already rich formula.

Once the milk reached the appropriate temperature, he carefully scooped up the beastie. The bear squirmed, still searching for its mother's teat. Magnus chuckled softly as Sorcha's mouth closed over one of his gloved fingers. She sucked eagerly.

"That'll do you no good," he chided her softly as he nudged the tip of the bottle against her black lips. The bear quickly latched on to the rubber nipple. Slurping sounds filled the nursery as Sorcha gulped down her meal. The capybara gave a huge sigh and settled her massive head back down on the blankets. Content that her charge was being well cared for, her dark, almond-shaped eyes drifted shut.

"Aye," Magnus told her softly. "Get your rest while you can. You're a good mum."

When Sorcha finished her bottle, Magnus let her suckle a little longer. Polar bear cubs loved to suck, and if they didn't get the need satisfied, they'd latch on to their own feet and leave the pads raw.

When Sorcha's eyes began to drift closed, Magnus gently placed her beside the capybara. The cub instinctually burrowed into the older animal's warmth. Sylvia lifted her massive head to nuzzle the wee beastie before returning to sleep.

"She's amazing with orphans, isn't she?"

At the quiet whisper, Magnus turned to find Bowie standing in the doorway. The zookeeper's gray eyes were soft as he watched the slumbering capybara and cub. It was strange, working with someone who cared as much about animals as Magnus did. His da had considered affection for livestock foolish. In his mind, the creatures under a man's dominion were merely a duty and a means to making a living, nothing more.

The wee bear chose that moment to sigh gustily. Its little belly, already rounded with milk, heaved with the effort. The capybara's ear twitched as if listening for any signs of distress. Hearing none, Sylvia made her own contented sound.

"Aye," Magnus said, answering Bowie's question about the rodent.

"I'm able to take over cub-watching duties for a few hours." Bowie's voice stayed low in deference to the sleeping animals. "You can go back to bed if you want."

Magnus shook his head sharply and carefully spoke one of the lines he'd used to avoid stuttering in front of his da. "I'll go feed the animals."

Bowie nodded. "Breakfast will be served in two hours up at the house if you want any."

Magnus had no intention of spending his mornings cooped up in a scullery with Bowie's family. Even though he found he didn't mind the young lassie's chatter, he appreciated a peaceful start to the day. There was something calming about spending the sunrise surrounded by the sounds of waking animals and the smell of dirt and hay.

Magnus shook his head again. "I'm fine."

"Okay," Bowie said. Magnus dipped his chin in response as he left the nursery and headed down the hall to the supply room. It didn't take him long to heft the feed bags into the zoo's first-generation side-by-side. His father would have scoffed at the vehicle that looked like a golf cart and an American pickup truck had produced a child. Although Magnus felt a bit absurd wedging his burly body into the driver's seat, it made moving feed easier, and the zoo, small as it was, dwarfed his da's island croft.

Magnus worked quickly, enjoying the quiet emptiness. The land was different than Orkney, drier and less varied, despite the mountains in the distance. It was jarring to see the red dirt beneath his boots instead of grass, black mud, and rock. He missed the tangy smell of the ocean and the sound of the waves crashing against the cliff. But the sense of solitude was the same. Instead of being marooned by a blue-green sea, he was surrounded by dust and sagebrush.

He finished his morning rounds at the grizzly's enclosure. Frida was snoring softly, her head on her favorite rock. Following the proper protocol, Magnus slipped a dish of red meat and berries into her enclosure. Her nose twitched once. One eye popped open. Her snout wiggled again. Then the other eye appeared. With a slumberous sigh, the huge beastie lifted her massive body. After giving her head a good shake, she ambled over to the pile of food. She inspected it with her massive paw, turning it over.

"Does it suit?" Magnus asked.

The bear gave one more giant sniff and began to eat greedily. Magnus grinned at the bear's enthusiasm and leaned against the fence to watch. "Aye, I see it does."

Frida ignored him. Her interest remained focused on her food.

"There's a new arrival," Magnus told her. "A wee bear named Sorcha. Bowie said he might introduce the two of you since you tolerate the manky honey badgers. He hopes you'll be best mates."

Frida took the last bite and grunted her dismay. She swung around, her snout in the air as she tried to scent more food. With her rheumy eyes, she needed to rely on smell more than sight.

"That's all, lass," Magnus told her. "Bowie said you were on a diet."

The bear emitted a grumbling growl. Looking downright fashed, the bruin lumbered back to her rock. Then with a beleaguered sound halfway between a grunt and a growl, she plopped on the ground. Within seconds, she fell asleep.

Chuckling softly, Magnus pushed back from the fence. Checking his watch, he realized it was too early to head to the Prairie Dog Café, and he did not want to attempt June Winters's tea shop. The zoo still hadn't opened, and Magnus decided he could do with a spot of quiet. Finding a bench near the prairie-dog enclosure, he settled down to watch the little creatures dart in and out of their holes. He'd never seen the like, and their antics amused him. When the wee beasties caught sight of him, a couple stood on their hind legs and called out a warning to their brethren. In a flurry of scampering feet and raised black-tipped tails, the whole colony took cover. Holding his large frame very still, Magnus watched as the rodents slowly remerged one by one. He'd write his next blog about the peculiar animals. Already, descriptions had started to form in his mind.

Just then, his mobile rang, the sound breaking the morning stillness. The prairie-dog sentries chirped the alarm once more. A slow smile drifted across Magnus's face as they dove into their burrows. He waited another ring until he pulled out his mobile. Glancing down, he noticed his agent's number. Curious, he swiped to answer the call. Lauren's crisp voice instantly filled his ears. "Hi, Magnus, I am sorry to call you so early in the morning, but Mitch had another suggestion."

Baws. Just when he'd thought he'd pleased the man with his blog. "It was not to his liking." Magnus would have said more, but he didn't want to risk mangling his words. Neither his agent nor his editor knew the extent of his stutter. He was sure they'd caught a vocal tic here or there, but he'd been careful around them for years.

"No, he loved it. He's over the moon about the comments you're getting already," Lauren said quickly. "He just wants more."

Magnus started to ask what his editor wanted, but his throat stiffened and his tongue felt like a great magnet adhered to the roof of his mouth, so he waited for his agent to fill the silence.

"He'd like you to vlog."

Dread, as baltic and bitter as the arctic wind, swept through Magnus, chilling him from the inside out. He would have repeated the word *vlog*, but he knew it would come out *v-v-v-v-vlog*.

"Now, it is up to you," his agent said, "but I agree with him. You need to be more accessible to readers, especially since your books are almost memoirs. Your fans want to feel like they know you."

Magnus pressed his fingers against the bridge of his nose and rubbed. He could not speak on camera, even if it was a recorded piece he could edit.

"Will you do it?" Lauren asked. "It has a lot of potential, and Mitch seemed very enthused with the idea."

Did he really have a choice? Mitch had indicated he had to fight with the editorial board to get this book accepted, and Lauren hadn't finished negotiating the terms of his contract. And Magnus wanted this book to do well. Mitch was the one who'd helped propel his first bestseller to success, and Magnus had learned to trust the publishing veteran's expertise.

"Aye," Magnus said. "I will."

He didn't bloody well know how, but he was used to slogging through all kinds of shite. Other people with stutters ended up with careers in movies, television, and talk radio. He could do a manky vlog. Somehow.

He ended the call and stared at the prairie dogs chittering away again. If he wrote out his lines ahead of time and practiced, he'd manage. He could show more footage of animals doing cute and amusing things. People always found that to be pure magic.

"Well, at least I know now I'm not the only one who puts a scowl on your face," June said.

Magnus turned to find the annoying blond carrying a brown bag and a takeout cup wrapped in a cardboard sleeve. *Baws*, the woman was bringing provisions now. Was she planning on making the zoo her damn home?

"If you're about to tell me a frown is an upside-down smile or some other pish like that, hold your wheesht." It struck him, once again, that he had less trouble speaking around the lass. It made no sense, but that was the way of it.

"I actually just ducked out of the tea shop to bring you a tattie scone. You said you liked them yesterday. I have tea too."

Magnus eyed the brown bag with a mixture of longing and suspicion. He hadn't eaten, and the thought of a hot meal caused a low rumble in the pit of his belly. But he didn't know what the lass would demand in return.

"I d-d-d-don't take bribes." His voice caught on

the *d*, but June's expression didn't change. To his surprise, she didn't look away either. As he gazed into her grass-green eyes, he found himself sliding easily into the next sound.

When he finished speaking, June shook the bag and plastered a sweet, guileless smile on her face. "I'm just being neighborly."

"We're not p-p-precisely neighbors."

"We live in the same small town, so I say that makes us neighbors," June told him cheerfully as she placed the food on the bench next to him. The smell from it made his stomach clench.

"I'll just leave it here, and you can eat it if you want or toss it in the trash. It's yours. No strings attached."

For once, the dafty woman turned to leave him in peace. But no sooner had she started to disappear around the bend than Magnus heard himself calling her name. She turned expectantly.

"I need your help." To Magnus's surprise, the words poured from him with surprising ease. He'd been raised by his da to live self-sufficiently. A man didn't go asking for help like a peedie bairn. He took care of himself without pleeping.

June smiled, a true one and not a self-satisfied smirk like he'd been expecting. "What can I do for you?"

Magnus paused, and not because he was worried about stuttering. He might regret what he was about to offer, but there was no other way. He spoke more fluently around the lass, and she'd said she'd stuttered in the past. Perhaps, she knew a trick or two to help him. "M-m-y p-p-p-publisher asked that I do a vlog about the zoo."

Understanding immediately fell over June's face. She

plopped down on the bench next to him, her face serious as she studied him. "Does your publisher know about your stutter?"

Magnus shook his head. "Nay."

"Is this something you want to do?" June asked. "I never minded public speaking, even back when I stuttered. My grandmother from Georgia always said I was born with the gift of the gab."

Magnus shook his head. "Growing up it was just my d-d-da and me on this peedie isle off T-T-T-Tammay."

"I remember reading that in your book. No one else lived there, right? A hurricane hit the island in the nineteen fifties and destroyed most of the homes?"

"Aye. The Great Storm of 1953. There was one a year earlier in '52 as well. Life was hard on B-B-Bjaray during good times—still is. It's rockier than the other islands in Orkney. Folks got weary of rebuilding and just moved to T-T-T-Tammay, Kirkwall, or south to Scotland. M-my d-da's folks were the only ones who stayed."

"I remember it sounded so lonely and isolated the way you described your daddy's croft. I shivered every time I listened to the narrator describe it in my nan's audiobook."

"Aye. M-m-y d-d-da didn't talk much, so we mostly lived in quiet."

"Was he a person who stuttered too? It can run in families. My uncle on my mama's side stuttered, and so did Grandpappy Horne."

Magnus couldn't help but snort at the idea of his da stuttering. His father would sooner cut out his own tongue than have it tangle around itself the way Magnus's did. "Nay. He just liked *tsàmhchair*. I've gotten used to it myself."

"*Tsàmhchair*?"

"It's Scots Gaelic for solitude," Magnus answered.

"*Tsàmhchair*," June said, rolling the word over in her mouth like a child would a boiled sweet. She repeated it with a faint smile curling her bonny lips. She leaned back and said it a third time before she turned to him. "I like it. It's very musical."

"Aye." Despite his stutter, Magnus had always loved words, loved the way they sounded in his head or on other people's lips. He supposed that was why he'd become a writer. On paper, he could play with words, paint with them, control them.

"Do you speak much Gaelic?"

"Nay, only a wee bit. My Orcadian ancestors would've spoke Norn, which was derived from Norse. M-m-my m-m-m-mum's folks came from the Highlands, and I can remember her speaking some Scots Gaelic. I've always thought it was a musical language, so I taught myself a little more. B-b-b-b-back in my roughneck days, I worked with some Glaswegians, and I lived in Glasgow for a time, so I use their slang as well."

June didn't react to his hard block. He supposed she was used to listening to her brother. It was odd, talking to someone who just accepted his way of speaking. Growing up on the Isles and then working in the Arctic, he'd never met another person who spoke with a stutter. He supposed he may have unknowingly bumped into someone who did in London, but he didn't socialize. He had too much of his da beaten into him.

"So, what do you need my help with?"

Magnus watched her, knowing this would cost him. But there was no other choice. "If you'll tape my v-v-vlog, I'll t-t-t-talk to your nana."

June beamed, and before he could guess her intent, she flung her arms around his shoulders and gave him a quick peck on the cheek. He froze at the unexpected contact. He wasn't accustomed to being touched. His da had never believed in showing affection, physical or otherwise. Generally, Magnus didn't like another person's arms about him. It felt like a trap, and he'd lived in one for too long. But with June, it was different. He didn't feel like fleeing or even shaking her off. Something as soft as goose eider whispered through him, calling to parts long a-slumber.

Still touching his shoulders, June pulled back to look at him. "Thank you. Thank you. Thank you! You don't know how much this will mean to her. To me."

"Why is it so important?" he asked.

To his surprise, her eyes grew as cloudy as the winter sky over the North Sea. "Nana's been having difficulties lately."

"D-D-D-Difficulties?"

June worked her plump bottom lip with her teeth, drawing Magnus's attention there. The lass was worried about her nan, and he was thinking about snogging.

"...so she tends to get confused, especially in the evenings. She still seems to have good short-term memory, but she looks so lost sometimes."

Aye, the hen was talking about her grandma. That settled his thoughts down. He forced himself to focus on her words rather than her bonny mouth. "Do you think she has Alzheimer's?"

June shook her head, her eyes glittering like green emeralds with a sheen of tears. "No. I took her to see the local doctor a few weeks ago, and he didn't think her symptoms fit. He told me it was just part of getting older, but I'm still worried. I might take her to a specialist in the city, but until then, I want to keep exercising her mind. She loves talking about Tammay, and your first two books are some of her favorites. She listens to them over and over. If you could talk to her while we're watching Sorcha, it would do her a world of good."

Magnus sighed. He couldn't blame the lass for trying to help her nan. And it wouldn't be too hard talking to an auld woman about the good old days. If she was like most, he'd just have to say a grain here and a grain there, and she'd be off reminiscing. With any luck, he'd mostly be listening, and if he was with Sorcha, he could focus on the peedie beastie rather than his own memories.

The bigger problem was spending more time with the fae lass. She seemed to be weaving a spell around him, and if he didn't mind his emotions, he might find himself well and truly cursed.

Honey sighed as she watched the Giant One and the Blond One talk. They were civil, polite...and utterly boring. She missed the sparks shooting from their eyes. Now, they just reminded her of the Black-Haired One and his mate.

Quietly, Honey slunk away. She would have to

figure out a way to incite them. For now, though, she would stick to annoying Fluffy. She darted into the maintenance facility, making sure her claws did not make too much noise on the floor. Growing up in a house had taught her how to sneak around the bipeds' spaces. Within minutes, she'd reached the end of her quest: the supply room.

Ignoring the sacks of feed, she headed straight toward the treat cabinet. Climbing up, she used her sharp claws and nose to open the door. Quickly, she withdrew the sticky bee larvae. Despite the rumble in her belly, she did not eat her pilfered booty immediately. Instead, with her tail low to the ground and the bounty carefully secured in her mouth, she scampered back to the enclosure. Unlike her, Fluffy could not access the sweet morsels.

When Honey dropped the larvae onto the dirt of their enclosure, Fluffy showed his teeth and growled. Honey just flicked her tail and hunkered down to eat. Fluffy tried inching closer, but she slashed out with her claws. He jerked away and then did something entirely unexpected. Instead of trying to fight her like any self-respecting honey badger, he merely watched…longingly.

Pathetic. The creature had spent far too much time with the bipeds. He had lost his wildness.

Yet, when Honey stood up and headed toward her den on the opposite side of the enclosure from his, she might—just might—have left a treat behind. Accidentally, of course, because she never would have left one voluntarily. That was something the silly humans would do.

Watching a burly man feed a tiny, squirming cub played on a woman's heartstrings like a virtuoso who'd sold his soul to Beelzebub. June hadn't expected the giant Scot to be so gentle with the small polar bear. The man's whole demeanor changed from fierce Viking to cuddly zookeeper. And, as sure as rain during a wet spring, did it ever look sexy on him. Even with his beard, she could see his broad, easy smile as he let the little cub gnaw on his gloved fingers. Sorcha made happy whirring chirps as she chomped down. Her black eyes shone with delight, and Magnus chuckled. The sound was deep and low, and it rolled over June like a balmy wave, leaving ripples of pleasure in its wake.

"You give the peedie beastie a bottle like this," Magnus instructed in his soft, sexy accent as he gently positioned the cub across his knees. "Her puggy should be supported at all times. You don't want to hold the bear in your arms like a wean, or she could get food into her lungs."

"Does 'puggy' mean stomach, and 'wean' mean baby?" June asked. It struck her that Magnus had less disfluency when concentrating on his furry charge.

"Aye," Magnus nodded. One of his massive hands wrapped around the bear's tummy, applying pressure as he placed the nipple in the cub's mouth. Sucking sounds echoed through the utilitarian room as Sorcha greedily attacked the bottle. Her paws paddled eagerly in the air, and June's heart just melted. This would be perfect footage for Magnus's vlog. Since she'd brought Nan to talk with Magnus, June had an obligation to uphold her end of the bargain she and Magnus had made just the day before.

Although the zoo owned professional camera equipment, June didn't want to disrupt the scene. Instead, she reached into the pocket of her jeans and pulled out her phone. Magnus didn't notice, but June's grandmother looked confused. Nan was having an off day, which was why June had brought her to see Sorcha. Sometimes, when her grandmother's mind seemed foggy, she viewed technology with suspicion.

June gave Nan a comforting smile and kept shooting the scene. Unguarded like this, Magnus would definitely win back the hearts of his former fans...at least the female ones. Who could resist watching a tough, muscular man coo over an adorable cub? It was as tempting as an apple tart topped with whipped cream.

Magnus turned, his eyes narrowing when he saw she was recording him. She flicked the video off and returned her phone to her pocket. "For your vlog."

Understanding dawned in his blue eyes, and he nodded curtly. Although his hold on the cub remained tender, hardness had returned to his face. He was an extremely private man, June realized. She'd always had trouble understanding why some folks sought solitude. She loved people: Old, young, rich, poor—it didn't matter. As much as she'd longed to stay in one place and form lasting friendships as a child, she hadn't minded constantly meeting new people. Humans, with all their quirks, simply fascinated her.

"Do you think Sorcha will be tired after her bottle?" June asked.

"She may want to explore a wee bit," Magnus said. As if in agreement, the cub emitted a squeaking chirp. Magnus chuckled, and June felt her insides go as gooey as chocolate chip cookie dough. There was just too much dang cuteness in the room.

"Aye, you hear that? That's the bairn letting us know she's ready for a tussle." Magnus smiled again, and June decided the man really did need to trim his beard to show more of his grin. There was just something magnetic about the Scot when he stopped his fierce scowling.

Magnus placed the little tyke on the floor. Sorcha immediately tried to clamber around, even though she couldn't lift her belly yet. Instead, she wiggled, using her paws to propel her almost as if she was taking a swim. June cooed. She couldn't help it.

"Why, isn't she the most adorable little mite?" June turned toward her grandmother and froze. The woman sat stiffly in her chair, a fearful expression on her face. Sorcha chose that moment to wiggle in Nana's direction. Her grandmother opened her mouth and emitted a hideous shriek. The bear cub froze, its half-lidded eyes trained on June's gran. The capybara, who'd been snoozing in the corner, lifted her head.

Magnus started to rise, but June was faster. She dashed to her grandmother's side as quick as a cottontail with a bluetick chasing it. Right now, she felt just as scared as the poor rabbit, except for her, the danger wasn't easy to determine. "Nan, what's wrong?"

The woman grabbed June's forearm. Her fingers gripped with bruising force despite their delicateness. June didn't yank away. She just patted her nan's hand gently. "It's okay. It's just a bear cub."

"It's going to eat me!" Nan shrieked, her voice unnaturally high and not at all like her usual cadence.

Magnus crouched by her grandmother's other side. To June's surprise, he took the older woman's hand in his, using the same gentleness he'd displayed with the cub. "Sorcha's just a peedie thing."

Nan swung her gaze between the two of them, her hazel eyes slightly wild. She was clearly not convinced by his words. Magnus continued, saying, "I'll protect you if Sorcha tries to hurt you."

That seemed to satisfy Nan. "My Oliver would have protected me too."

"Oliver was my grandfather," June whispered, grateful that Magnus appeared to be calming her gran.

Magnus gave June a slight nod, but he kept his focus on Nan. "Aye, you met him on T-T-Tammay."

"Yes," Nana said slowly as if coming out of a stupor. "Yes. Yes, I did. He was a fine-looking young man. All the girls on the island thought he was the most handsome of the Yanks. The men were so dashing in their uniforms, although I'd always preferred the Coldstream Guards in full dress until I met Oliver."

"And where did your great romance begin?" Magnus asked.

"The Selkie's Strand," her grandmother said, naming the pub that June had heard about for years. Although June had never visited it, Magnus had painted such a vivid picture of the place in his books that an image sprang to her mind. The ancient, whitewashed stone inn stood by the sea, right off the docks. Inside, the smell of old peat fires mixed with the salty tang of the ocean and years of whiskey spills. The heavy wooden tables bore scars from years of use. One or two locals always occupied the chairs by the bar, no matter the time of day. June had always planned to visit one day with her grandmother, but she wondered now if she'd waited too long.

"Aye," Magnus said. "The auld folk still talk about the ceilidhs they had during the war with all the young men on the island. They say there's never been the like since."

A slow half smile broke across Nan's face. Some of the cobwebs still lingered in her hazel eyes, making them appear more brown than green, but the fear had vanished. "Those days were both wonderful and terrifying. It was lovely, having all the young folks around, but we never forgot the boys were there to catch the German U-boats and to protect the convoys and the fleet stationed in the Scapa Flow."

"M-M-M-My d-d-d-da always avoided the Flow when he was out on his trawler. All the tourist ships and divers m-m-made him crabbit."

"There were no tourists in Tammay when I was a girl," Nan said. "What do the islanders think of them?"

Magnus lifted his shoulders and shrugged. "M-M-M-Many are happy. It gives some folks a way to make a living, and it's brought back the old crafts. B-B-Best of all, there's new people to keep the *clishmaclaver* interesting."

A soft whisper of a smile drifted across Nan's face. Relief tinged with joy seeped through June. Her grandmother was looking more like herself. June swore color had even returned to her cheeks, and her eyes had definitely sharpened.

"Oh yes," Nan said. "The islanders loved gossip,

although it wasn't too different from our neighborhood in London. But the details they would find noteworthy!"

"Aye," Magnus said, and suddenly switched into different pitched voices, his Orcadian accent thicker than ever. "'Did you hear, Auld Jack Marwick painted his auld gate blue?' 'Ach no, what color blue did he?' 'Sky blue.' 'As in when the sky is shining, or when a storm's a-blowing?' 'When the sun is out.' 'What kind of a deeskit nyaff does that? You cannot tell if it's open or not!'"

Nan actually gave the tiniest of chuckles, a rarity after an episode of fearfulness. June sent Magnus a grateful smile as she carefully directed Sorcha to worm her little body in another direction. Magnus bobbed his head in acknowledgment before he turned back to her grandmother.

Nan reached out and patted Magnus's hand. "That's precisely how the villagers spoke. I can just imagine what they say about the Yanks, Aussies, and English who come on holiday."

"Aye. Every ferry carries a fresh tale, but there are some folk, like m-m-my d-d-da, who wished we were left in peace."

"He sounds like your great-grandfather, Rognvald Gray."

Magnus's face darkened at the sound of his ancestor's name. "Aye, the Grays of Bjaray have always been pure bastards."

Nan must have been feeling much more like herself. At Magnus's cussword, her silvered eyebrows pulled down, and she looked every inch an English rose in high dudgeon. "Watch your language, Mr. Gray. You are in the presence of two ladies."

Magnus didn't appear either chastised or annoyed by Nan's dressing-down. His face remained stormy, but his anger didn't appear directed at June's grandmother. "Aye, but we are. We're pure rotters. Every last one of us."

June watched Magnus carefully. She'd checked his first book out of the local library after he'd asked her for help with his vlog. The way he'd described growing up in virtual silence with his daddy had clung to June's heart like a burr. She'd flipped through the pages, scanning them with fresh eyes. His writings had always possessed a haunting quality, but on reexamination, they took on an even greater poignancy. Loneliness saturated the pages, and June had begun to ache for the little boy growing up in such isolation, no matter the beauty of the landscape surrounding him.

"Oh, I wouldn't say that," Nan protested.

Magnus laughed, the sound as barren and harsh as the sea cliffs he described in his writings. "Did you ever meet a Gray?"

Nan nodded. "I saw your great-grandfather from a distance once. I was visiting some friends on Bjaray and saw him plowing his field with horses."

"Aye, and I bet he didn't wave, but turned his b-b-b-back."

Nan gave a reluctant nod. "But he was busy."

"A Gray is always b-b-busy," Magnus said, and June detected a thread of bitterness in his voice.

"Did you know your great-grandpappy?" June asked.

Magnus shook his head. "Nay. He was in the grave years before I was born. Grays don't live long."

"Is your daddy still alive?" June asked.

Magnus's eyes instantly became as shuttered as a house before a hurricane. He rose to his feet. "It's time for Sorcha to p-p-p-put her head down for a wee kip."

Magnus stooped to pick up the little bear who'd been busy inching over the floor and trying to pull herself up and over the enrichment toys Bowie had left littered about the room. Magnus had told June it was good for the cub to try clambering over different surfaces. In the wild, the cub would've been preparing to survive on the ice floe with her mama by now.

Magnus picked up the bear, cuddling her close to his chest. He leaned his head near Sorcha's as if sharing secrets. June listened closely, and she detected the faintest strains of "Dream Angus," an old Scottish lullaby her nan had sung to her years ago. Unexpectedly, tears stung June's eyes. Normally, old memories typically brought joy. This time, though, she couldn't escape the feeling it would soon be her caring for Nan instead.

Magnus placed the cub next to the capybara. The little bear instantly snuggled against the massive rodent's furry heat. She yawned and rested her chin on the capybara's haunch. The rodent nuzzled the cub before snuggling into the nest of blankets. Within moments, both animals fell asleep.

Magnus carefully stepped away from the two. With his attention on Sorcha and Sylvia, June took the opportunity to study him. She had not lied several days ago when she'd called Magnus a complicated man. For all his bluster and claims to be a rotter, he'd rushed to her grandmother's side when she'd needed help. June had a feeling Magnus would have talked about Tammay even without their deal. He'd wanted to distract her nan from her fear, and he'd done so admirably.

Magnus wasn't like the men who normally captivated June. Yet something pulled her to him. And, June thought, as she watched the huge rodent cuddle a baby bear, if prey could comfort predator, perhaps it wouldn't be too farfetched for two polar-opposite humans to decide to explore an attraction.

Chapter 5

"YOU WANT ME TO DO WHAT?" MAGNUS ASKED, staring at June in disbelieving horror. Surely, he had not heard the barmy woman correctly.

June nodded, her pink lips spread into a wide smile as if she hadn't just insulted him. She had come to help him, Bowie, and Katie get an enclosure ready for Sorcha. Since polar bears required rather complex exhibits to stay stimulated, they had decided to start early. June Winters, with her designer blouses and high-heeled shoes, didn't seem the type to move dirt to install a large pool. She'd shown up looking like a fresh-scrubbed farm girl ready to pose for a travel magazine cover with tight jeans, pink wellies with chickens on them, and a formfitting plaid jacket. To Magnus's surprise, though, she turned out to be surprisingly handy with a spade. Unfortunately, she seemed equally easy with her advice.

"I swear it will improve your vlog's viewership," June drawled.

"It is not your concern," Magnus snapped. *Baws*. He'd only asked the lass for help two days ago, and he certainly hadn't requested grooming tips.

He swung his gaze toward Katie and Bowie for assistance. Both of them wore old Carhartt jackets and sensible jeans. Their muck boots, as Bowie called them, were plain green with no fancy patterns. These were people who Magnus understood.

Katie gave him a commiserating half smile as she lifted one shoulder in a helpless shrug. "June's a natural makeover artist. She can't help herself."

Bowie didn't say anything. Instead, he studiously kept his attention focused on the tip of his shovel. He looked like he wanted to use it to dig a hole to escape the situation. Magnus could sympathize with the zookeeper. Greatly.

"You wanted me to help you," June pointed out. "I am only making a recommendation."

"I am not cutting off my bloody beard."

June sighed, looking like the very soul of patience itself. He growled. The lass had gone completely doolally.

"I didn't say to shave it off," June said. "I mentioned a trim."

Then, before Magnus could duck away, the lass stood on her tiptoes and reached up to push his hair back. "You have very striking features, and it would make you more approachable if people could see your face. Isn't this about connecting with your audience?"

Get up, Assie Pattle. Stop blethering to the coos; you sound like a bampot. You're late again, you dobber. Quit your stuttering, you nyaff. You don't want people knowing that you're a deeskit idjit, do you?

His da's voice sprang up like a sudden squall, threatening to blow Magnus down and drown him in memories. He reared away from June so suddenly that he startled her into taking a few stumbling steps backward. This was why he didn't get close to people. He'd had a lifetime of his da telling him what to do and how to be.

Laying his shovel slowly and deliberately on the red

dirt, Magnus turned and stalked away. He would find another chore to do until the dafty hen left. Perhaps he'd work on the honey badger enclosure. The wee beasties kept escaping.

Magnus had just passed the otters when he detected the tread of footsteps behind him. His body went as taut as a dinghy's mooring rope at high tide. To his surprise, it was Katie's voice he heard next.

"Magnus, wait," she called. Since the woman was carrying twins, he obeyed. She rushed over, puffing slightly. "You walk really fast."

Magnus gave a curt nod, hoping he didn't appear too rude. He liked Katie well enough. Unlike June, she was friendly without being overly familiar.

Shooting him one of her grins, Katie placed her hand behind her back and drew in a long breath before she began. "I'm sorry about June's pushiness."

"She's n-n-n-n-n-not your responsibility," Magnus said.

Katie's expression turned rueful. "Well, I am the one who invited her today, and I am her best friend. She can be intense sometimes."

Magnus sent her his driest look. June possessed the force of a winter hurricane.

"She means well," Katie continued quickly. Unlike her friend, she didn't drag out her words. "She really does. June is remarkably impervious to criticism, so she doesn't always understand how her words might sound to someone else."

"I wish she'd leave me in peace."

Katie laughed, the sound as buoyant as her red

curls. She reminded him of an Orcadian lass in that moment. "I think you're the first man ever to say that."

That Magnus didn't doubt. June had a face as pretty and rare as the Scottish primrose.

"Aye," Magnus agreed.

A solemn honesty replaced Katie's mirth. "She really is good at figuring out the best look for people. Back in college, she gave me a makeover. It might sound shallow, but I found confidence for the first time in years. I was bullied back in high school, and June helped me get past that. I owe a lot to her."

Magnus grunted. Katie was a bonny lass herself, but in a subtler, earthier way. June, however, was as bright and incandescent as the northern lights dancing across the sky…and just as unpredictable.

"She did the same for our friend Josh. I swear he has more designer clothes than she does now, but he was a classic geek when she met him. He credits her with helping him get the poise to run his own cybersecurity business. And don't tell Bowie I said this, but Josh is smoking hot. He always looks like he's ready for a *GQ* photo shoot."

"What if I d-d-d-d-don't want to pose for *GQ*?" Magnus asked.

Katie lifted one arm for a shrug. "Then that's not the look for you, but I don't think that's what June is trying to do. She has a knack for helping you find your own style—something that suits you even if at first it surprises you. She can read people well…although she can't always understand why people aren't as naturally self-possessed as she is. It's like she can divine everyone's strengths, but not their vulnerabilities. In June's opinion, people don't have weaknesses, just character quirks that make them unique. I think that's why people tend to like her so much."

Just then, Magnus heard June calling his name. Katie lowered her voice and said, "Go easy on her. The more June pushes, the more she cares about you."

Now that surprised Magnus. He doubted very much that the lass had any feelings for him. He was her latest pet project; that was all. Hadn't Katie all but admitted June liked fixing people? And Magnus was perfectly happy with himself as he was.

Katie leaned even closer. "I'm not sure if June even knows this, but I think she has a crush on you. I've never seen her like this with another guy. Give her a chance."

"Why are you t-t-t-t-telling m-m-m-me this?"

"Because I think you like her too," Katie replied with a surprisingly impish smile that he would expect to see on her stepdaughter, Abby. Without giving him a chance to respond, she turned on her heels and headed back the way she'd come. Before he could process Katie's claims, she disappeared, and June barreled into view. God save him from American women. He'd thought deciphering the Orcadian lasses was difficult, but the Yanks were an even greater mystery despite their brazen straightforwardness.

Magnus crossed his arms. "I like my beard the way it is."

June studied him, her green eyes penetrating. Magnus thought of what Katie had said about June detecting the strengths in people. He wondered for a moment what she saw in him.

"No, you don't," June said finally.

"Do not tell me what I wish or do not wish."

June's eyes burned brightly, reminding him once more of the aurora borealis. "You use your facial hair to hide."

Magnus opened his mouth to deny it, but the truth smacked him with the force of a cow's kick to the gut. *Aw, goat's baws*. She was right.

"You don't wear your hair or beard like a Viking berserker because you like the look. You do it to tell people to fuck off. You want to appear tough and a little wild, so people will leave you alone. Correct me if I'm wrong."

Magnus glared at the lass. The fact she was right and was pointing out truths about himself annoyed him.

"You want to sell books, right?"

He nodded reluctantly, knowing conceding that point would cost him.

"Well, the hermit vibe is no longer working for you, Magnus," June told him matter-of-factly. "People want to get to know you, and they can't with all that hair hiding your smile, and something tells me you've got a beautiful one."

Magnus snorted. "I have an ugly mush."

Confusion clouded June's eyes. For once he'd succeeded in unsettling the lass instead of the other way around. "Mush?" she repeated.

"Face. I think Americans call it a mug."

June cocked her head to the side, examining him. It felt as if she was trying to shave him using her eyes.

Firmly, she shook her head. "No. No, you don't. On a child's face, your features would have been as harsh as lye soap, but you've grown into them just fine."

Heat suffused Magnus's cheeks. He didn't know how to respond to June. She managed to both flatter and insult him. Katie's words rushed back to him, *I think she has a crush on you.* His flush flamed even hotter. There'd been women, aye, especially back in his roughneck days. Lasses who didn't mind a woolly-bearded man like himself sharing their beds. But all they'd been to each other was a warm, willing body, looking for some comfort and release, nothing more. None of the women had fancied him as a person. He'd been as interchangeable to them as they to him. He supposed if he'd wanted, he could have found a good woman and settled down, even before he'd become a bestselling author. But not with a lass who looked like June Winters.

"I'll not go clean-shaven," Magnus said.

By her grin, she knew she'd already won. "A bit of scruff will be perfect on you. Women love a little mystery."

Magnus snorted. "I want to sell books, not sex."

"Honey, sex sells everything."

"You're not going to let this be, are you?" Magnus asked.

Her pink lips curled even more. "Nope."

He sighed. When Magnus thought about it, the lass did have the right of it. He hadn't chosen his hairstyle because he particularly liked it. His facial hair had provided protection from wind and ice when he worked on the oil rig. It had been easier to maintain and less fuss. He'd noticed when he'd moved to Glasgow and then to London that it kept people from asking too many questions. A wild

look demanded respect and instilled instinctual trepida-
tion. But according to his editor and agent, he needed to
appear charming, not menacing.

"What do you have in mind, lass?" Magnus asked.
He had no bloody idea what hairstyle would look best.
His da had always said it was no use spending money to
go to the barber on Tammay. He'd cut Magnus's hair,
and Magnus had trimmed his da's. When Magnus had
worked as a roughneck, he'd worn it at the length that
allowed him to cut it himself. He'd never seen a reason
to change that until June's prodding.

But the expression on the lass's face made Magnus
further doubt his decision to change his looks…even if
the delight in June's bonny green eyes did trigger an
unusual thrill deep inside him.

Two days later, June realized she'd been wrong. Under
all his shaggy hair, Magnus wasn't merely striking. No.
He was even more devastatingly compelling than she'd
suspected. The stylist she'd recommended in the nearby
city had done wonders. Although Magnus still sported a
full beard, it had been shaped and trimmed to highlight
his rugged features, instead of obscuring them. The stylist had left enough of Magnus's unruly curls to balance
out the harsh planes of his face, giving a charming twist
to his new look.

Pausing in the middle of the zoo's path, June pressed
her hand against her heart. "Don't you look like a long,
tall glass of cool water."

Magnus blinked. His blue eyes seemed electric now
that they no longer had to fight against all that hair. June

felt a pang in her heart that sent desire spiraling through her body like a firecracker lighting up the July sky. My, my, but the man had a powerful effect on her senses.

"Is that a compliment or an insult, lass?"

"Compliment, at least from where my mama grew up. Ooo, your readers are going to looove your videos now!"

Magnus scowled. With his beard trimmed, he looked even fiercer. To June's surprise, a shiver slid through her, but it wasn't from fear. Goodness, her mind must be going as soft as taffy if she found his brooding nature attractive. Yet something deep and feminine inside her just thrilled at the sight of him in all his surliness.

"We should get started." Magnus ended the conversation as he pushed open the door to the maintenance facility. June followed, admiring the man's backside. She'd never paid attention to it before, which was a little surprising considering how many times he'd walked away from her. And, good heavenly days, did the man have a fine posterior! He might not be like her typical lovers, but June was starting to think she was more than ready for a change.

When Magnus entered the nursery, Sorcha froze, her black eyes studying him in confusion. She was obviously having difficulties reconciling his familiar scent with his new appearance. With a happy trill, she finally accepted him without his mass of hair. As quickly as her unsteady legs would allow, she slithered and crawled around her playpen, squeaking the whole time with utter joy. In response, Magnus's face broke into a welcoming grin as he crouched down to greet the little cub and Sylvia. June's heart went as soft and gooey as a melted chocolate bar.

"I think someone has a little crush on you," June observed.

Now that Magnus's beard was trimmed, his fair Scottish complexion did little to hide the fierce blush creeping over his skin. "Aye," he said, his voice a low rumble that reverberated through June, "that's what I hear."

June glanced at Magnus, not quite understanding his response. The heat in his blue eyes seared her. Her throat thickened as her body went pliant with molten desire. A mere look had never managed to kindle this much lust. Her lips parted, and Magnus's scorching gaze focused there. The fire flickering in his cobalt irises matched the one blazing inside her. He stood up slowly, and June's body went taut with anticipation. Her heart pumped faster, sending the flames higher. If he didn't kiss her soon, she'd burn up like dry tinder in autumn.

Magnus's lips dipped close to hers, and she could feel the puff of his breath. Despite the warmth roaring through her, she shivered. His large hand reached up, cupping the back of her head in a tender grasp. She inhaled, practically tasting his kiss.

Then, just as Magnus's mouth began to brush against hers, a loud squeak ricocheted through the room. It was as effective as a fire hose. Magnus sprang back, and to June's surprise, a look of alarm flashed across his face. He hadn't wanted to kiss her, she realized with a shock as stinging and as unpleasant as a real one from an electrical outlet.

Magnus's face went blank and then softened as he glanced down at the floor. Still in a fog, June followed the direction of his eyes. With beseeching black eyes, little Sorcha playfully tried to bat his leg through her playpen. She clearly wanted to cuddle.

Magnus lifted the cub into his arms, and June swore the little bear sighed in contentment as she snuggled against him. June knew with complete certainty the man would know how to make *her* purr. Quite happily. But from his reaction to their near kiss, it didn't seem likely that he'd try.

"We should b-begin filming," June said, the crispness in her own voice surprising her. She never talked sharply. Never. She'd even stumbled over the word *begin*, which hadn't happened in years. During her childhood, *b*'s had given her trouble, but she rarely had difficulties with them now.

"Aye," Magnus said, although he didn't appear happy about it.

"I assume you want to start your vlog series with Sorcha," June said. My, my, when had she begun to sound so officious? She sounded like a general ordering a forlorn hope.

Magnus nodded.

"Let me get the video equipment. I know where Katie keeps it," June said. When she left the room, she still felt off-kilter and not in a good way. Magnus was attracted to her but didn't want to be, and that knowledge ate at her like ten possums after a single ear of corn. She needed to discuss this development with Katie.

When June returned to the room, the taping didn't

go well. At all. The instant Magnus spied the camera, his whole body visibly tightened. He had one hard block after another. She could see the tension in his neck as he tried to force out his speech. Like before, his head jerked as though he could physically push the words from his lips.

She knew better than to tell him to relax. Managing a stutter was a complex process, and hearing someone diminish it into a simple command was as irritating as fleas to a stray. Uninformed suggestions had never helped June as a child, and they still drove her brother crazy.

Unfortunately, June found herself low on patience. Magnus's tension mixed with her own, making a very bitter brew.

Magnus finally shook his head, his blue eyes dark. He didn't want to continue. June hid a sigh and flipped off the camera. She didn't need her talent for reading people to sense the frustration and disappointment rolling off Magnus. She needed to stop stewing over his rejection and focus on her part of the bargain. The man had asked for her assistance, and she'd accepted. He hadn't promised anything other than to chat with her nana. He'd done that. Now it was her turn.

"What techniques did your speech pathologist teach you?"

Magnus gave her an annoyed look. She fought back an unusual swell of frustration. "I'm just trying to help," she said, unable to prevent her voice from rising slightly at the end.

"T-T-T-T-Tammay has less than five hundred souls. What makes you think a speech pathologist would be one of them?"

Surprise and empathy burned through her atypical annoyance. "You never had any speech therapy?" Even with her father bouncing the family from military base to military base, her parents had always made sure she and her brother received the best instruction on managing their disfluency.

Magnus's expression turned even drier. "Does m-m-m-my d-d-d-da slapping me upside my head to stop my stuttering count?"

Ice sluiced through June's veins. An image ripped through her of a young Magnus standing in front of his father. The boy was vainly trying to force his throat to work properly as desperation darkened his blue eyes. Across from him, his daddy began to ball his hand into a fist. June's brain yelled for her to stop as a chill invaded every inch of her body. Surely, a parent wouldn't be so cruel.

"Are you being serious, Magnus?"

He didn't respond verbally, but she read the truth in his face before he expertly shuttered his expression. This was a man who knew how to cloak his feelings. June started to reach out to touch him, but he flinched. She worried her bottom lip as she debated how to handle the revelation. She was a talker, and when she had a problem, she worked through it verbally.

"Do you want to chat—"

"No," Magnus bit out the word so fast that even with his Orcadian accent, it sounded harsh and clipped.

June shut her mouth. Her instinct was to push, but her usual tactics didn't appear to work with

Magnus. If she tried to pry more out of him, he'd dash off again. And she didn't want that.

"You said you don't stutter as much around me," June said. "Do you know why? Maybe we can use that to help you."

Magnus looked at her balefully. "You do not want to know."

June crossed her arms. She might have decided not to probe into his past, but she was going to help him film the videos. "You have to give me something to work with, Magnus."

Magnus copied her stance. Since he had more than several inches on her, she had to admit he did it better. She did not, however, back down. Next time, she was going to bring sweets. There wasn't a human alive who couldn't be tempted by her jam. Everything in life went better with preserves.

"Have it your way," Magnus said. "I think it's because you rip my knitting until I'm fair boiling, and I forget about stumbling over my words."

June's nana didn't use too many Scottish idioms, but her grandmother had always muttered about knitting being ripped when she was madder than a puffed toad. June had even borrowed the expression a time or two, but she hadn't expected that answer from Magnus. She'd naively thought he stuttered less around her because he found her presence comforting due to her own experiences with disfluency. The real truth caused an unusual flicker of hurt to knife through her. She generally didn't give a fig what people thought. If someone didn't like her, there were plenty of others who did. But Magnus…he mattered. Surprisingly so. Even if June could not quite figure out why.

"Well," June said, plastering on a smile to hide the sting, "that's interesting."

Magnus looked surprisingly contrite. "Sorry, but that's the way of it, lass. It could also be because you don't try to rush me, and you don't seem uncomfortable when I get stuck on a word."

June forced herself to let go of her hurt. Years ago, when kids had teased her because of her stutter, her mama had said, *Junie, some people have a lot of hate in their hearts. Don't let them put it in yours. Instead, try to give 'em love. If that doesn't work, honey, there are just some folks who are too broke for fixing. That's their problem, not yours. Life will be happier if you just learn that one truth.*

"I was always the opposite," June said. "When I got as angry as a wet hen, I couldn't get a word out."

Magnus studied her, his blue eyes searching. She resisted the urge to shift under his scrutiny. She was accustomed to doing the analyzing and not the other way around.

"Is that why you smile so much, lass?" Magnus asked when he finally spoke.

June's lips parted. An odd feeling swept through her, almost as if she'd flown out of her body and was staring back down at herself. "I suppose you're right. I never really thought about it."

One corner of Magnus's mouth lifted upward. The lopsided smile added a touch of softness to his stern features, and June felt an answering tug in her own heart. She wondered what the man would look like with a full grin.

"I've never met anyone as jolly as you. I swear

your smile could b-b-b-badger the storm clouds into hiding."

On the surface, the words sounded like something a lover would whisper. But Magnus didn't say them as a compliment…more of an observation. There was a tiny thread of affection in his voice, the kind one would have for an eccentric aunt. And June had no trouble detecting his exasperation.

"Do I baffle you, Magnus?" she asked.

He laughed then, his chuckle deep and loud. It bounced off the walls, startling both Sorcha and Sylvia. The little bear jumped and then lost her balance. She landed with her short legs splayed in all directions. The capybara used her sizable snout to help the cub regain her balance.

"Aye, lass," Magnus said, "you baffle me."

"You baffle me too," June admitted, "and that's unusual for me."

"I am a simple m-man, June. You are trying to m-make me more complex than I am."

June shook her head. "No. I don't think that is it. You're as layered as two onions growing together."

"You're looking too hard, lass."

"Maybe you aren't looking hard enough," she countered.

"There's no use arguing," Magnus said.

June nodded in agreement. There wasn't. She was right, though. The stubborn man just wouldn't admit it. She glanced at the camera. "When's your deadline for posting?"

"Th-Th-Th-Th-Three days. I told my editor and agent I needed t-t-t-time."

"I think we should call it quits for today and try again tomorrow," June said. There was no use forcing it. Magnus was too frustrated. Back when June stuttered, her favorite speech therapist, Miss Sue, always knew the right time to take a break.

Magnus scowled. "Aye. Not that it will be much different."

June reached out and patted his hand. His eyes flitted down, and he watched her action as if it was something foreign to him. She'd thought about what he'd said about his da and wondered whether he'd received much physical affection growing up. If she remembered correctly from his first book, he'd mostly mentioned his father and rarely his mother. June had some recollection the woman had abandoned the family, but she wasn't sure. If that was the case, Magnus would've had no place of refuge, no comforting words when his daddy struck him for stuttering.

"You'll do fine," June said. "It doesn't have to be perfect either. A little bit of disfluency wouldn't be bad."

Magnus looked as if he wanted to protest. But before he could speak, Bowie popped his head in the doorway. He was breathing hard, and his lips were pulled into an atypical frown. Shoving his hand through his sweat-soaked black hair, he asked, "Hey, Magnus, sorry to interrupt, but would you be able to give Lou and me a hand? We're trying to apply salve to one of the llama's legs, and I'm having trouble holding her still."

"Aye," Magnus said. "June and I were finishing up anyway."

As soon as the men left, June headed for her tote bag. She'd brought her copy of Magnus's book from the library in case she had some time alone with the cub. Nan was at the house with Abby and Katie, and June had volunteered for at least another hour. With Sorcha playing happily on the floor, she had time for research.

Although stuttering wasn't triggered by a traumatic event or caused by a horrible childhood as many people believed, that didn't mean understanding Magnus's past wasn't important in figuring out what approach would work best with his personality. And this wasn't the only digging June planned on doing. She still had her old notebooks from speech therapy, and she was going to try to chat online with her brother to see if August had any suggestions. June wasn't looking for a way to fix Magnus's disfluency, but she wanted to help him control it enough to allow him to vlog comfortably.

June flipped through the passages until she came to the one she'd vaguely remembered.

> Bjaray, at times, seems formed by the very winds that buffet the small isle—a speck of resilient life in the middle of an endless howling roar. The barren beauty of the land seeps into a man's soul and either soothes him or drives him mad. My mother fled, following the blowing gale, the power of its force greater than her desire to stay with her husband and squalling bairn—or so my da always claimed. She left before my fifth birthday, leaving behind the memory of a smile as faint as the smoke from a long-dead peat fire.

The poetic words ensnared June. Magnus wrote with all senses, weaving descriptions that sprang from the page and captured the reader. June had always found his work romantically bittersweet. Now, it triggered an ache so deep it almost pained her. The beauty remained, but sadness had crept into his work, deepening the sense of isolation until it threatened to overwhelm June.

She wondered what it would be like growing up abandoned by one parent and irrationally punished by the one remaining. June hadn't experienced a bad bout of disfluency in years. But she remembered. It had felt like her throat and mouth had betrayed her. It was very easy to feel trapped and alone in those moments. But her parents had always supported her, and June had found friends who understood when she needed time to speak. But Magnus, living on an island with just his father and farm animals, hadn't received that love. He'd done it alone…but he wasn't by himself any longer.

Not if June could help it.

Perching unnoticed on the cabinets, Honey watched the Blond One slowly turn pieces of bound paper. Humans were dull creatures. She did not understand how objects could fascinate them for hours.

Honey turned with a sigh and used her nose and claws quietly to push open the window. She had learned the trick while living in a house. Using the downspout to reach the ground, she scurried through the zoo. She found the Giant One and the Black-Haired One fighting with a llama, while the Gray-Haired One held a noxious-smelling tube in his hand. Although Honey generally found herd creatures particularly insipid, this one was kicking and spitting as the bipeds chased it. Watching the big humans run amused her. They did not have the grace of a honey badger. They skidded wildly when they turned, churning up mud. The llama brayed.

Finally, the Giant One managed to catch the knobby-kneed animal by its midsection. More spitting occurred. The human shook his head as some landed in his hair, but he did not let go. Honey smiled. She'd been right. He *did* have some honey badger in him.

The Gray-Haired One narrowly missed a kick to the face as he applied goop on the llama's leg, but he only chuckled fondly and then made soothing sounds in the back of his throat. The llama ignored the elderly biped and continued to protest as he wrapped white material around its limb. When the Gray-Haired One finished, the humans released the camelid back with the herd and then left the enclosure.

Honey sighed. That was not nearly enough entertainment. She would just need to make her own.

Chapter 6

HONEY HAD ESCAPED. AGAIN. MAGNUS'S SIDE FELT damn near bursting. He'd been chasing the damn whalp for hours. Every time he passed the honey badger enclosure, he swore that the male, Fluffy, laughed at him. *Bloody nuisances. Both of them.*

Bowie had left Magnus in charge while he drove his wife into the city for her obstetrician's appointment. The two had been more excited than a couple of oystercatchers with a bucket full of mussels, and Magnus didn't want to ruin their day with a telephone call. Abby was the best at badger wrangling, but the lassie was at school. Magnus knew Lou would help him, but he didn't think it was good for the eighty-year-old to dash around the zoo, and someone needed to watch Sorcha. He'd debated letting the wee devil exhaust herself instead of chasing her like a bloody nyaff, but she might decide to chomp down on one of the zoo patrons.

Although the zoo closed soon, June was coming to help Magnus with the video. Even if he did catch the blighted beastie, Magnus smelled like a rookel of rubbish and probably looked like it too. He'd need to bathe before he was fit to appear on any video.

Just then, as he rounded the corner, Magnus caught sight of the wee rascal. He dashed forward. Honey darted to the left and then the right. She almost slipped past him, but he managed to get his hands around her middle. Carefully, he hoisted the beastie into the air. Although her legs spun wildly, Magnus swore she grinned.

"Cheeky bastard."

This time, he definitely spied a flash of white, jagged teeth. "You're a clever one, you are."

Honey chittered as if in agreement as Magnus carried her back to the enclosure. After he placed her inside, he scanned the pen but could not determine how the creature had escaped. He sighed, locking the gate behind him. Hopefully, she'd stay…this time.

Fluffy watched with interest as the Giant One deposited Honey back into their pen. Had she actually made a mistake? Had the human caught her? Maybe she wouldn't act so smug now.

Then, Fluffy saw it.

Her toothy smirk.

The minx had planned to be captured. Fluffy was sure of it. She must be toying with the bipeds.

A grudging respect for Honey rose inside Fluffy. He hated to admit it, but he could learn from the wily female. She had a diabolical streak even wider than his own.

And, truth be told, he'd been softening toward her ever since she'd left him the honey-covered larvae… although he would never admit she'd given it to him.

A few minutes later, Fluffy smiled as he watched Honey build a ramp from the mud in their cage. Deciding to be kind, he went to help. She hissed at first and then relented. With the two of them working, they quickly finished her escape route. Honey swished her tail in his direction before she scampered away.

———∿∿∿———

Magnus dashed back to the maintenance building and headed straight toward the shower. He had to admit he appreciated the Yanks' love of convenience as he turned on the spray. This was faster than a bath, even if not as pleasant. He'd just finished scrubbing his body when he heard the crash, closely followed by a scream. June's scream.

Only taking enough time to wrap a towel firmly about his waist, he ran from the room. He paid no heed to the trail of water he left as he pounded around the corner.

"Oooo! No, you are not getting away again, you little minx!"

June's voice. Magnus would recognize her drawl anywhere. By the sounds of it, Honey had escaped again. Magnus shot down the hall. It had become personal. He was going to capture that peedie whalp and check the enclosure more thoroughly. Hell, he'd build a glass ceiling over the whole area and make a giant terrarium if that's what it took.

Magnus barreled at full speed toward the supply room. Both the honey badgers were constantly invading it, and the crash had definitely emanated from that direction. He'd just rounded the corner when Honey darted between his legs, chittering madly. He went to grab the beastie, his fingertips skimming the top of her coarse fur. Before he could lower his hands to get a more solid grip, June emitted what he could only classify as a battle cry. Her yell, though, quickly turned panicked.

Magnus lifted his head to discover June skidding toward him. Her arms pinwheeled in the air in a desperate attempt to gain traction. Magnus quickly glanced at the floor and saw it was slick. From the scent, he guessed the honey badger had knocked over the cod oil Bowie had ordered for Sorcha.

"Sweet heavens to Betsy, I can't stop!"

Magnus barely had time to release his tentative hold on Honey before June crashed into him with bruising force. Although he outweighed her by more than a few pounds, his crouched position had him at a disadvantage. He could have kept his own balance if he'd rolled her over his shoulder, but that would have pitched her into the wall. Unlike her slender form, his massive body was built to take an impact. Grabbing June the best he could, he used his bulk to cushion her fall.

When she landed at an angle, spread-eagle on top of him, he could only pray his towel hadn't slipped...or fallen off completely.

June had expected to slam into a concrete-block wall. Smashing into Magnus—a wet, practically naked Magnus—felt almost as hard, but so much more interesting. As she lay feeling the strong planes of his body, she debated how to extricate herself. She'd fallen splayed over him at an odd angle, preventing her from easily pushing herself off. She didn't want to risk jamming a knee or poking an elbow into a vulnerable part of his anatomy, and considering his state of undress, wiggling away didn't seem advisable either. Although June wouldn't mind a glimpse of a naked Magnus, she didn't want to embarrass him by knocking off the towel precariously draped over his waist.

She'd caught only the briefest glimpse of his body as she'd careened toward him. Even with her concentration focused on stopping herself, a part of her had appreciated the glory that was Magnus Gray in the almost nude. His beautifully sculpted muscles perfectly suited his large frame. A woman could spend an entire day exploring the ridges of his chest and abs. Of that, June had no doubt.

Even through her clothing, she could feel the lines of his muscles pressing against her. Her body basked in the glorious sensation as liquid lust pooled inside her. She wanted to squirm against him but held back. She didn't want to accost the man. Not that his body wasn't reacting to hers. His hard length pressed insistently against her, and it took all her concentration not to respond to the instinctual invitation.

Instead, she kept the rest of her body perfectly still as she twisted her head to glance at Magnus's face. His eyes were pressed tightly shut.

"Are you okay or did you get the wind knocked out of you again?"

One blue eye popped open, then the other. "I'm fine, lass."

June smiled. "I seem to have gotten us in a bit of a pickle."

"Aye."

"I'm not sure the best way to climb off you."

"I can fix that." Then, in one fluid motion, Magnus hoisted her into the air. As she levitated over his body for a second, she took the moment to appreciate the sight of him stretched below her, all glorious straining muscle. Magnus possessed the beauty and perfection of a fine sculpture…with a thousand times more sensuality. When he deposited her gently on the floor, she instantly missed his warmth.

"Thanks," she said.

He nodded brusquely and carefully pushed to his feet, his hand gripping the towel to keep it in place. *Pity*.

June started to stand herself, but no sooner had she begun to rise than her feet slipped again. What in tarnation had that little rascal knocked over? It was slicker than a banana peel on a freshly waxed floor. June pumped her arms again, hoping this time she'd find better traction. Just as she thought she'd fall on her rear, two strong hands snaked around her waist. But as soon as Magnus righted her, her sneakers squeaked ominously, and she began to slide dangerously. Without thinking, she automatically wrapped her arms around Magnus's strong torso. And that…well, that triggered a very different instinctual response. She reveled in the sensation of his warm, wet flesh. The contrast between his smooth skin and the coiled strength sent a thrill of delight skipping down her spine. Before June could stop herself, her hands danced across his back, and she felt his muscles bunch and tighten.

She glanced up then. The tension in Magnus's jaw had nothing to do with irritation and everything to do with need. His blue eyes practically burned into hers.

She wanted him. Wanted him inside her. Wanted to

feel his delicious weight against her. Wanted to experience his shudder as he climaxed.

Her mouth grew so dry, it felt like she'd inhaled sand. She swallowed. Hard. Then wet her lips. Magnus's eyes flashed as a groan—deep, guttural, and consuming—escaped from him. It echoed the desperate desire billowing inside June.

The lass was trying to kill him.

Bewitched, Magnus watched as June's tongue licked her plump lower lip. He wanted to taste her. All of her.

She felt so good against him, her body both slender and lush. He yearned to touch and taste and bury himself deep inside her softness. He could have resisted. If his upbringing had taught him anything, it was how to deny himself, how to live without.

But then she'd glanced at him with those green eyes, and he couldn't let go. Not when he spied need swirling in those emerald depths…a need mirroring his own. A lass had never looked at him like that. Then again, he'd never experienced this level of primal lust either.

Magnus prided himself on being a deliberate man. He did not trust strong emotions in any form. For all of his da's quiet stillness, the man had moments of blinding rage when he reacted without thought or reason. And the villagers all said his mum's folks knew only how to live in excess. They drank too much, danced too hard, loved too easily, and fought too violently. Her family had never displayed more than a passing interest in him, and for that, he'd felt grateful.

But one emerald glance, and Magnus's carefully constructed caution drifted away as easily as autumn leaves floating on the tide. He didn't think. Didn't consider the consequences. He just dipped his head and tasted the tempting sweetness of her lips.

Sensation exploded, ricocheting through his body. Need kindled into blazing passion. It consumed him. Instead of slaking his desire, the kiss only fueled its dizzying madness. He'd never experienced anything of its kind. It was heady and freeing, like he was rushing through the sea on a racing boat, the wind full in his face as he sliced through the waves at full tilt.

He pulled June close, her clothes already damp from his skin. That knowledge only fueled his lust. His mouth covered hers, and he drank like a man marooned for days with no water. It was mental and magic all at the same damn time. He'd spent his whole life trying to avoid people, and now he couldn't get close enough to this one fae lass.

———————

If Magnus's strong arms hadn't been banded around her back, June would have melted to the floor faster than a Popsicle in August. Heavens to Betsy, the man could kiss like the devil. And his body…his body was as deliciously decadent as warm pecan pie topped with French vanilla ice cream. And she wanted a bite. Or maybe two.

For once, June's mind had stopped thinking. She just felt. Like ingredients to a good jalapeño jam, sensations swirled through her, spicy and hot with a hint of sweetness. And just like the jelly, Magnus's kisses warmed her belly, leaving her craving more.

Her hands moved along the strong planes of his back to rest in his dark-brown curls. Their softness warred with Magnus's toughness, and she reveled in their silkiness.

Magnus held her slightly off the ground to make up for their height difference, causing her breasts to press against his hard chest. The wet fabric of her shirt molded to June's skin. She felt almost naked but didn't mind. She wanted no barriers between them. If it hadn't meant breaking the embrace, she would have pulled off her shirt and tossed it aside.

As if sensing her need, Magnus slid her down the length of his body. She made a sound in the back of her throat that turned into a cry when she felt the insistent ridge of his erection. He groaned too, his body bent over hers. A thrill pulsated through June at the feel of his powerful form surrounding hers.

"Is everything all right in there?"

The sound of Lou's voice had the effect of an upended water bucket. Magnus thrust her away with such suddenness, she almost slipped again. He held her at arm's length, his chest heaving as he drew in harsh breaths. His intense blue eyes seemed to bore into her. June watched as the passion in them turned into shock and then dismay.

He hadn't wanted to kiss her this time either, June realized with a sharp pang that punctured her bubble of bliss. The man had simply lost control, and that obviously unsettled him.

Although June wasn't particularly pleased that

she'd almost jumped a man with Nan and Lou only a couple of doors away in the maintenance facility, she didn't feel any of the regret registering in Magnus's eyes. Hurt welled within June as sudden and as intense as the previous lust. She didn't know how to deal with it, so she shoved it deep inside and smiled.

"Thank you for breaking my fall twice," she said. "Landing on you was sure better than hitting the floor or the wall."

———※———

What the hell had he just done? Magnus stared at June in disbelief. He never lost his internal balance. Never.

"Steady on" was his motto. His creed. His sanity. It had carried him through childhood and the darkest period of his life. It had propelled him to leave Bjaray and finally to find some degree of peace. Yet one unguarded moment with the lass, and his emotions were churning faster than a deadly waterspout, ready to suck in an unsuspecting sailor.

Aye, the lass was dangerous for all her sweetness.

She lived in the sun, and Magnus dwelled in the mists. She'd try dragging him into the brightness if he got too close, and he preferred the shadows. He knew them and could avoid their lurking specters.

June was the kind of woman who'd burst into a man's life, rearranging it. When he left Sagebrush, he'd be forever trying to shove everything back into place. Living alone meant living in peace.

June smiled merrily. He had no idea how the lass could go from kissing with the passion of a selkie reunited with her long-lost lover to a jolly mate. Based on her enthusiastic participation, she'd clearly felt some attraction, but it had not shaken her. Not like him. Maybe she was used to the dizzying madness, or perhaps she had not felt it as keenly as he had.

While Magnus tried to pull himself together, June glanced over her shoulder and shouted, "Magnus and I are right as rain, Lou. One of the honey badgers just knocked over the supplies, and I slipped on something oily."

"The sound scared your grandma," Lou said, his voice studiously even. "You might want to come here."

Magnus watched the brightness fade from June's face and worry take its place. The sight bothered him. Greatly. He may not share the lass's unending zest, and it might even exhaust him at times, but he hated watching it drain away. He might be off his head, but he wanted June's grin back, and acting even more doolally, he wanted to be the one to put it there.

After quickly pulling on clothes, he followed June into the nursery. Her nan had a wildness about her face as she sat in a chair by Sorcha. Lou had moved to Clara's side, his stance the same protective one he used when treating an injured animal. He bent slightly over her, his hand resting gently on her shoulder. It was apparent he was trying to give her support without frightening her more. Her eyes were round and slightly unfocused, and her hands shook as she nervously played with the large buttons of her coat. Clara Winters normally appeared so proper, but the vitality seemed sucked from her, leaving her as fragile and delicate as a dry leaf

June rushed to her grandmother's side and grabbed her hands, just as she had during the last spell Magnus had witnessed. "It's okay, Nana. I'm here."

Clara ripped one of her trembling hands from June's grasp and lifted it nervously toward her throat. "That beast was after you."

"Nana, it was just a little ol' honey badger. It couldn't do me any harm even if it tried."

Clara remained unconvinced, her eyes slightly unfocused as they watched June with almost palpable doubt. "It is fierce and has nasty teeth."

"But it's no bigger than a speck, Nan," June said at the same time Lou patted the elderly woman's shoulder.

Her grandmother shook her head, her voice shaky but utterly serious. "It can grow, Junie, eighteen feet high."

"Now, Nana," June said patiently, "you know that's not true."

A stubborn look fell over the elderly woman's face. Magnus exchanged a glance with Lou over both women's heads. Concern swam in the older man's eyes. June needed help, and Lou's presence wasn't enough to distract her nan from her fears. Magnus gave the veterinarian a quick nod as he moved forward.

"Clara, do you remember me?"

Her gaze flitted over his, sharpening momentarily before going fuzzy again. "You're the writer fellow."

"Aye," Magnus said as he drew up a chair next to

the elder Winters's. "We both used to live in
T-T-T-Tammay."

The woman thought about this for a moment and
then nodded. "Yes. I remember."

"Did you do a lot of rambling there?"

"Yes." She nodded. "I would go with my girl-
friends, Dotty and Peg."

"Aye, T-T-T-Tammay is a good place for a stroll,
especially in the gloamin'. If you walk quietly enough,
you might catch sight of a pine m-m-marten."

A small smile drifted across the woman's face.
Beside Magnus, June visibly loosened the tension
she'd been carrying in her shoulders. She shot
Magnus a grateful grin. A swell of triumph rushed
through him. Aye, he was becoming a fair numptie.

"I remember spotting a pine marten when I was
a girl," Clara said. "They were very rare."

"Aye, the wee beasties are still scarce in the isles
and the Highlands," Magnus said. "Conservation-
ists are trying to bring them back, though. They've
been reintroduced in mainland Scotland. There's
hope they'll reduce the invasive gray squirrel
population."

June's grandmother nodded, but Magnus could
tell the woman was only half listening. He'd succeeded in distracting her, or so he'd thought.
Suddenly, her face tightened, and she gripped her
granddaughter's hand so hard, her knuckles grew
white under her papery skin. June, for her part, did
not even wince under the pressure. She just patted
her grandmother's arm, and Lou gave Nan's shoulder another comforting squeeze.

"There it is. It's going to eat us." With the hand not clinging to June's, Clara pointed a shaking finger in the direction of the doorway. Magnus turned to see Honey watching them, her little nose twitching, oblivious to the problem she was causing.

Lou started forward, but Magnus knew the elderly man had no chance of catching the peedie bastard. Magnus bolted from his own chair. Honey emitted a call of panic and started to scurry away. He, though, had endured enough of the wee blighter's trickery. He snagged the beastie under its belly and lifted the snarling tube of claws and fur into the air. June's nana screeched, and Lou moved as quickly as he could to Magnus's side despite his slightly uneven gait.

"I'll take her back to her enclosure," Lou said. Although the words were meant for Magnus, the veterinarian's attention was directed toward Honey. He spoke in the low, almost melodic tone that he used to soothe upset animals.

"Are you sure?" Magnus asked as he held the hissing creature away from him. He didn't fancy getting bitten.

Lou nodded as he carefully disengaged the honey badger from Magnus's hands. The fact that Honey didn't manage to sink her teeth into the veterinarian's thumb proved the man's skill. "Stay with Clara. You're good for her. Your tales bring her mind back into focus."

Magnus nodded and retook his seat as Lou ambled from the room with his growling charge. June shot them both a grateful look as she kept patting her grandma's arm. "It's okay, Nana. Lou is taking Honey back to her home."

"It will eat him."

"Now, Mrs. Winters," Magnus said. "That blighter

is not much bigger than a peedie pine marten. He can't hurt Lou."

Clara shot him a look that told him she considered him a bampot for the observation. Magnus ignored her censure. "Did you ever see t-t-t-tammie norries on your rambles?"

"Of course, I saw puffins," the woman snapped, using the English word for the birds rather than the Orcadian one. "They're everywhere on Tammay."

"B-B-B-Bjaray as well," Magnus said, keeping his voice calm. "I remember m-m-my d-d-d-da always trying to scare them away from the croft. He didn't like dealing with all the shite they left."

Clara frowned. "They did shit a lot."

June made a sound halfway between a choke and a splutter. Magnus cast a glance in her direction and found her red-faced, holding back laughter and tears. He supposed she'd never heard her nana curse before. Mrs. Clara Winters didn't seem the type for foul words, but he knew even the primmest auld folk sometimes started swearing when suffering from dementia.

"But they are b-b-bonny birds with their orange, black, and yellow bills," Magnus said.

"Their eyes always reminded me of a mime's face paint," Clara said with an air of final authority on the matter. Magnus suppressed a smile. He didn't think the woman would appreciate it.

"Aye. I can see that."

"They made me laugh," Clara said. "Whenever I felt sad, my Oliver would plan a picnic near the cliff where they nested."

"'Tis a sight to watch them b-b-bobbing on the rocks, their chests puffed out like they're on their way to meet the queen."

Clara smiled softly, and Magnus thought he saw a glint of a tear in June's eyes. Before he thought better, he reached out and squeezed the lass's upper arm. She sniffed and sent him a glance that caused his entire soul to freeze. No one had ever looked at him like that. Like he was wonderful. It pleased him as much as it unsettled him. He did not want people relying on him, wanting things from him, but earning such an expression from June? Watching those grass-green eyes of hers darkening into emerald…

Aye, he was a fair numptie today. A fair numptie.

Trying to understand Magnus Gray was like finding her way in a cave with a faulty lantern that kept flickering off and on. Dark. Twisty. And, sometimes, unexpectedly wonderful.

The man acted gruff and closed-off, but he turned into just the sweetest thing around her nan or the animals. And *that* Magnus? The kind-hearted man with the low chuckle? She wanted him as much as she did the brooding, passionate one, maybe even more. He seemed like his true self in those moments, unguarded by his grumpy exterior.

But *this* Magnus—the happy, pleasant one—didn't want her. And June only had two strategies when people pushed her away. She either shoved right back, or she let the person be. But she didn't want to walk away from Magnus, and bullying her way into his good graces didn't appear to be working.

She needed a new plan. And for once, she wasn't coming up with one.

"I don't think we'll be able to film right now." Magnus inclined his head toward her grandmother.

June nodded. Magnus spoke the truth, but that didn't make June feel less wretched. She'd promised to help the man, and here he was talking to her nan instead of filming the video.

"I'm sorry. Katie will be home all day tomorrow. Why don't I stop by then and leave Nan at the house with her?"

"Where are you taking me?" Nan asked, her voice pitched too high. June's heart clenched so hard it felt like a giant was squeezing it. Helplessly, she patted her grandmother's hand. The gesture didn't seem to do a bit of good, but June didn't know what else to do.

"You're going to visit Katie later, Nana," June said. "Don't you want to hear all about her babies?"

"They're here?"

The confusion in her nan's eyes and voice caused June's heart to twist. Tears stung the back of June's eyes, but she forced them back. "No, Nan, the babies are still in her belly, but she went to the doctor's today. She had a sonogram, so there will be lots of pictures. You'd like that, right?"

Her nan nodded slowly. June turned to Magnus. "Does that work for you?"

"Aye, lass," he said, his voice as soft as a kitten's fur. Then he turned to her grandmother. "Did you ever see the northern lights dance across the sky? When I was a wee lad, I imagined it was fairies having a ball."

June settled back down and listened to Magnus and her nan talk about Tammay. Instead of paying attention to their words, she focused on the times that Magnus stuttered and the times that he didn't. If they couldn't film the video right now, she could at least try to figure out how he could better manage his disfluency. She had a call scheduled with her brother early the next morning, and it might help if she could describe Magnus's blocks. No two people stuttered the exact same way. Figuring out how a person moved their throat, lips, tongue, jaw, and even chest was one of the first steps.

Magnus claimed she angered the stutter right out of him, which she supposed made sense. The more people thought about their disfluency, the worse it could become. Perhaps Magnus's irritation distracted him. But he seemed more at ease when speaking with her nan. He didn't have many hard blocks. To help Magnus, June needed a way to make him feel more comfortable in her presence. Unfortunately, her usual tricks didn't work on him, and she was plumb out of ideas.

~~~

"Let me get this straight," Katie said, her brown eyes wide. "You're coming to me again? For advice? On men?"

"Yes," June said. "I've already answered that twice. I told you, I'm short on time. Magnus has a deadline for his vlog."

"June, you don't take recommendations. You give them."

June crossed her arms and stared Katie down. "I brought you an entire basket of jam, including the mango chutney you've been begging for."

Katie shook the wicker container in June's direction. "Let me explain your normal MO. You ply me with jelly, wait until my mouth is full, and then sneak attack me with unsolicited advice. You do not bribe me for suggestions... At least you never did until you met Magnus."

"But I need help. I'm at my wits' end with this man."

"Juuuune, I already told you I don't know much about him. And I am not spying for you."

June waved away Katie's protests. "I'm not asking you to do that. The thing is, he sometimes looks at me like I'm a burr stuck on his clothing. I'm not used to that."

Katie placed the basket of jam on the table and sighed. She selected one, popped open the lid, and then pulled out a spoon. Sliding the open jar in June's direction, Katie gestured for her to sit.

"Am I this bossy?" June asked.

"Yes. Now, sit and eat."

June shrugged and dug her spoon into the jelly. Katie had picked Sunset Delight, a lemon and orange curd inspired by Nana's old British recipes and one of June's favorites.

"June, you told Magnus, in public, to cut his hair and trim his beard. In *public*, June." Katie delivered June a hard look that almost made her squirm. Normally, she was the one giving advice, and it felt odd to have those roles reversed.

"Well, he needed it," June pointed out. "And I was right, wasn't I? Isn't he just the handsomest thing you ever saw now?"

Katie groaned and rested her head on the granite tabletop before lifting it again. "That is beside the point."

"He asked me to help make his vlog. I was doing just that."

Katie rubbed her forehead. "June, he wanted you to videotape him, not give fashion tips."

June thought about that for a moment. "I didn't mean any harm. Do you think I insulted him?"

"Yes."

"Truly?"

"I love you, June. I really do. But you can be a little pushy at times." As Katie spoke, she squeezed her thumb and forefinger together.

June took a huge bite of the Sunset Delight. The sweetness really did help when listening to friendly criticism. "I just like fixing things that need fixing, that's all."

"But some people don't want fixing,"

June sighed heavily. "Magnus keeps telling me the same thing."

An affectionate smile drifted across Katie's face. "Maybe you should listen."

June dug into the lemon-orange curd. "But he *did* ask me to help with the video."

Katie sat down on the stool next to her friend. "Then do that, but don't try pushing your way into other areas of his life. Just because he's asked you to assist with his vlog doesn't mean he wants you to change everything about him, including how he naturally talks."

"I'm not trying to 'cure' his disfluency," June said, wanting to make that clear. "I just want him to realize his stutter doesn't have to be a burden. It's part of him, and that's okay. I don't think anyone ever told him that.

other, and you change each other for the better. I think that's why you like Magnus. Nobody has ever challenged you. He does. And if you let him, he may just add something to your perfection."

"*Hmmph*," June said, but only in jest. Katie's words made sense, even if they frightened the dickens out of her. June liked being in control. She liked fixing things. Making things right. It made her feel vulnerable to think about someone doing the same with her.

"Look at it this way," Katie said. "After more than a decade of friendship, you're finally coming to me for advice. Maybe Magnus is already changing you, and it's not so bad, is it?"

"Well…" June teased, and Katie bumped her shoulder with her own. June shot her best friend a smile. "I suppose it's not so bad."

"See," Katie said.

And June did see. A little. Falling in love had always been easy for her. Pleasant. Like a dip in the local swimming hole on a fine summer day. Warm. Relaxing. No drama. But it had never been real. And it had never lasted long. Each romance had melted away like cotton candy, leaving behind only a trace of sweetness.

A relationship with Magnus wouldn't be like that. It would have storm clouds. And it would take her to places she didn't know. To things that weren't familiar. Was she ready for something like that?

~~~

"Now d-d-don't this beat all," August drawled. At

his exaggerated accent, June narrowed her eyes. His link to the internet was slightly choppy, and his smug face froze momentarily on her screen. August didn't have as deep a southern intonation as June, so she knew he was taunting her like a wildcat with a chipmunk.

"We don't have time for sass," June said as soon as her brother regained connection. "I have a lot of questions."

"Well, that's just it, June Bug," he said, using their mother's nickname for her, "you've never come to your b-b-baby brother for advice, and I'm a lawyer."

"Your degree is so new it's still got peach fuzz on it."

He rolled his eyes, and the image froze. June debated about taking a screen shot, but the picture cleared. This time, her brother looked more serious. "So, what's your question?"

"I have a friend who stutters," June answered. "He grew up on a remote island and didn't receive any speech therapy. He's a writer, and his editors want him to do a vlog. I'm trying to help him."

"Of course, you are," August said, but he sounded more fond than teasing.

"Do you have any advice?"

August tipped his chair back, clearly considering her question. "It's a little hard when I've never met the man."

"I know, Aug, but I've got to start somewhere," June said, and then gave her brother the best description she could of Magnus's disfluency. Her brother leaned toward the screen again and listened closely. Even with the graininess of the connection, his green eyes looked serious.

"You know how b-b-bad it got for me in high school?" August asked.

June nodded. Although she'd been at college or in

Sagebrush, she'd heard from her mama all about her brother's struggles with bullying. "Yes."

"It was college and ROTC that turned things around," August said. "I had an instructor tell me to purposely stutter on words that I didn't have difficulty with and to maintain eye contact. It got everything out in the open."

"And that helped?"

August nodded. "T-Tremendously. There's a book that a lieutenant with disfluency told me about, *Self-Therapy for the Stutterer*, by Malcolm Fraser. It's available for free on the Stuttering Foundation's website. It helped me more than some of my speech pathologists. You might want to read it and give it to your friend."

"Thanks, I will. You're a peach."

August grinned, and his green eyes lit with amusement. "I still can't believe you actually asked me for help. I'm definitely bragging to Mom and Dad."

June ignored him. If she didn't, they might bicker through the rest of the call, and she didn't want that. It was hard getting in touch with her brother. "How are you doing?"

"Great," he said. "I'm getting a lot more experience in JAG than I would've at a law firm."

"So, you're still enjoying it?"

He nodded. "Oh yeah."

June watched him as a mixture of bittersweet pride filled her. The military ran strong in her family, and she didn't doubt that her brother would become a career airman. She wished his job didn't take him all over the world, but she couldn't deny he loved the work he did. He wasn't like her. She wanted stability; he wanted adventure.

They chatted only a little longer before he needed to go. After June hung up, she stretched and then bent right back over the computer. She had more research to do before meeting Magnus.

Chapter 7

"YOU WANT ME TO STUTTER ON PURPOSE?" MAGNUS stared at June in disbelief. She nodded eagerly, reminding him of an excited puffin after it sighted a school of sand eels.

"Why would I do that?" he asked in utter surprise.

"I've read up on it, and it's not uncommon. It gives you control. I called my brother, August, and he says it really helps him."

"Are you off your head, lass? I asked you to reduce my stuttering, not to tell me to snirl my words. I can do that all on my own. Thank you very much." At least June had his blood running so fast, he forgot to be careful with his speech, and he could talk more freely. Unfortunately, Magnus knew as soon as she dragged out her camera, his throat would grow thicker than a medieval fortress's outer walls.

June bit her lip, distracting him. He watched, mesmerized, as she pulled it between her straight white teeth. The lass had him spinning in so many directions, he felt like a top whirling on the deck of a storm-tossed trawler. One minute she had him fighting equal parts anger and confusion, and the next moment lust was pumping through his veins. Aye, June was going to send him straight to Bedlam.

"I've been told recently I can be a bit pushy," June said.

Magnus stared at the lass dryly. Calling her a "bit pushy" was like calling the entire North Sea a wee puddle. "I can see their point, lass."

She glared at him and then continued, "So I'm trying to hold back my opinions, but this is important."

Magnus crossed his arms. The lass appeared earnest, and he didn't recall anyone trying to help him, really help him, with his speech. His schoolmates had mocked him. His teachers had told him to relax and stop trying so hard. And his da had tried to shake or slap the stutter out of him. None of those methods had helped.

"All right, lass, explain how you think this will work."

"Because it lets the audience know you stutter—"

"But I don't want them to know. When people hear me, see what my m-m-mouth and b-b-body do, they judge me, even if they don't mean to. You know that."

"Yes, but the rest of the video will prove those assumptions invalid. Just think of the inspiration you could be to kids who stutter and to other adults."

Magnus snorted. "What if I don't want to be an inspiration?"

June gave him a hard stare, her green eyes alight with passion...and not the sexual kind. She looked like Boudicca, ready to do battle against the Romans.

"Your disfluency is part of you," she said, "and there's nothing wrong with showing a little in your video."

He watched her in disbelief. Old taunts played in his head. *M-M-M-Mangle M-M-Mouth M-M-Magnus. Ma-Ma-Magnus. You're blethering like a deeskit nyaff again, son. Hold your wheesht if you can't talk like a normal bloke. Stop letting your tongue get all snirled up, you bulder.*

"Your problem is you're not connecting with your readers. This will humanize you. Everyone has difficulties they struggle to overcome. You'll give them something to identify with, even if they don't have disfluency."

Hell, the lass was making some sort of sense, not that Magnus particularly liked it. He'd been the village idjit as a child, and he had no desire to become an international one as an adult.

"Give it a try," June said. "If you don't like it, I'll delete the video. I promise. Cross my heart and hope to die. You can watch me get rid of it. I swear."

Magnus hesitated, but the lass had already watched him stumble over his words for an hour yesterday. Although the woman could be dictatorial, she seemed to be an honest sort, and he trusted her to delete the recording if he asked.

"We stop when I say we stop."

"Understood," June said and flashed him one of her most brilliant smiles. "You won't have regrets, I promise."

He was not so sure, but he nodded anyway. "So how do I go about this?"

"Try a short introduction," June said. "Pretend you're just chatting with me at a coffee shop. Tell me that you stutter and throw one in on purpose. Don't use a word you usually block on, though."

June walked over to where the zoo's professional camera was set up on a tripod. As she adjusted the equipment, Magnus stared into the lens. He doubted this would work, but with only another day left until his deadline, he had no choice.

"Try looking at me and not the camera," June said as she stepped to the side of the tripod. "It's important to maintain eye contact."

Taking a deep breath, Magnus stared into June's grass-green irises and did something he'd never done before. He didn't try to hide the way he naturally talked, didn't try to fight it, didn't worry about his words trapping him.

—⁓—

As June watched Magnus, a smile drifted over her lips. His speech wasn't perfect. Far from it. But it was better than yesterday. Much, much better. And the more he spoke, the more he began focusing on the subject matter and not on forming syllables. He tussled with Sorcha as he reminisced about the cubs he'd raised before. Then, gradually, as Sorcha pounced on his knee, he began to speak like he wrote. Boldly. Colorfully. Sensually. She felt drawn into his tale, drawn into him.

Katie would need to edit the video to make it smooth enough for listeners to follow. There were a couple places where Magnus had a hard block, but overall, June hoped he wouldn't mind showing most of his moments of disfluency. It would be a compelling piece.

"How did I sound, lass?" Magnus asked as he concluded.

"As they say on your side of the pond, 'brilliant'!" June said. "How did it feel to you?"

"Not b-b-b-bloody b-b-brilliant," Magnus said. But he didn't scowl, which June took as a sign of success.

"Do you want to watch it?" June asked.

He nodded reluctantly and moved to stand next to

her. Although he did not touch her, June's entire body reacted to his nearness. Her nerve receptors seemed programmed to sense the exact type of heat he radiated. As she pressed Play, she could feel his breath on her cheek. She wanted to turn in to the caress of air, to press her lips against his, but she didn't. The man didn't truly want her...not yet.

But she still couldn't stop her awareness of him. Her whole body tingled with suppressed desire. No man had ever triggered such a reaction with his mere breath. She wondered what it would be like to fall into bed with him. How would it feel to fan this smoldering heat and passion into a bonfire?

She imagined his body above her, beneath her. When he came inside her, would his massive frame tremble? Would his blue eyes glow in intensity, or would they darken in satisfaction? She thought of him gazing down at her as he entered her and then of his eyelids squeezed tight as his orgasm shook him.

Her own body grew rigid with need. June swore her breath had started to come out in puffs. Firmly, she forced herself to stop thinking about the man naked. Instead, she concentrated on the video. In replay, it was just as good as she thought.

"What do you think?" June asked when it finished.

Magnus stepped back, looking thoughtful. "It wasn't as b-b-bad as I'd believed."

"A couple places could use some editing, but Katie is good at that. And most videos require some tweaking."

Magnus nodded sharply and shoved his hands into his pockets. "Aye."

"Is it something you'd feel comfortable posting?"

He paused. "I am not sure, lass."

Just then, Sylvia bumped against him. June swore the capybara had more intuition than some humans. Magnus smiled down at the rodent and patted her on the head. Sylvia sighed and then moved off to settle down on the bed of blankets that she currently shared with Sorcha.

"I think your readers will love it," June told him. "You've developed a real bond with Sorcha, and it shows. It's adorable watching you two tussle."

"There will be more than one comment on my stuttering. People will complain I should have fixed it."

June didn't answer right away. She didn't have jam handy for this conversation, but she knew one way to make Magnus feel comfortable. Walking over to the corner where Sorcha was now trying to climb over her toys, June plunked down and patted the floor. Magnus followed suit. She handed him a frayed rope, and the little bear immediately began to play tug-of-war.

"Magnus, you *will* get mean, nasty comments. The internet is full of ignorant trolls. Even Bowie has received negativity for his videos, and his posts are so popular he's been on two different talk shows. Most of your feedback will be positive."

Magnus focused on Sorcha as he jerked the rope back and forth. The cub made a playful growl, one that she would have used in the wild when roughhousing with another cub or her mama.

"I don't really have a choice," Magnus said slowly. "My d-d-deadline's tomorrow, and the video's better than I'd hoped."

He looked up, his blue eyes locking onto hers. "You

were right, lass. Stuttering on p-p-purpose helped. Thank you."

Triumph, as warm and sweet as hot fudge on a sundae, slid through June. She'd always taken pleasure in helping people, gratitude or not. But hearing the appreciation in Magnus's low voice started a flutter deep in her belly that formed into a bubble of joy.

"You're welcome."

When Magnus spoke again, his voice was low and deep. "And you were correct about eye contact as well. You have b-b-bonny eyes, lass. They remind me of fresh grass in the spring."

Warmth spread through June. Men had complimented her green irises before, but never like that. June tried to remind herself that Magnus was a writer, and he knew how to wield words. But still she couldn't stop the rush of emotion swirling through her. Swallowing, she asked in a surprisingly even voice, "Would you like me to be with you when you post it?"

Magnus paused, glancing at the cub. He waved his big hand near Sorcha's snout, allowing the little girl to lunge at it. The polar bear caught his fingers in her paws, and she began to happily gum his thumb. June waited patiently, even though it just about killed her. Finally, Magnus spoke.

"Aye, lass, you can join me."

Magnus sat stiffly in front of his laptop as he wondered why he'd foolishly agreed to have June present when he uploaded the video. He did things alone. Always.

His da, for all his reclusiveness, had always required a companion. Someone to assist with the chores. Someone to make breakfast. Someone to control.

But Magnus was a true loner. He'd always preferred the croft when his da was out on his trawler. He'd learned self-sufficiency early on, and it suited him.

So, it galled Magnus that not only had he agreed to June's presence, but a part of him welcomed it. Gladly. Having her sitting next to him, feeling her arm pressed against his, made all of this easier. Not easy. But easier.

The video was more professional than he'd imagined. Aye, it wasn't perfect. His stuttering was evident. But with Katie's editing, it felt smooth if not quite polished. An odd sense of pride had crept through him when he'd watched it a second time. He'd done it. Something he'd never thought he'd accomplish. And he owed much of it to the lass beside him.

But making the video, as hard as that had been, paled in comparison to uploading it to his author's website. Magnus was normally not a feartie, but the idea of stuttering, even voluntarily, on such a public forum caused his innards to turn baltic. Memories, long buried, clawed for escape from their icy tomb.

June's hand suddenly rested on his knee. Delicate. Warm. And strangely safe.

"Are you ready?"

"Aye," he lied and reached forward. Before he could stop himself, he clicked the mouse, sending the video hurtling into cyberspace. There was no retracting it. A pit formed in the depth of his gullet. He would have felt less exposed if he'd posted a picture of his naked arse.

"How are you feeling?" June asked.

Magnus grunted and sent an email to his publisher and agent with a link to the video. There, he'd done it. He'd met their accursed deadline.

June beamed. "This calls for a celebration."

She reached into the ridiculously large bag that she insisted on calling a purse. His scorn evaporated when she withdrew Highland Park whiskey and two shot glasses. Magnus raised an appreciative eyebrow. It had been distilled in Orkney for over two hundred years.

"My grandfather's favorite," June explained.

"Mine too," Magnus said as the lass poured them both shots.

"He got a taste for it when he was stationed in Tammay," June explained. "It's become my whiskey of choice when I'm not drinking bourbon."

"D-D-Damn Yank," Magnus scoffed.

She poked him. "When a woman has a drawl thicker than molasses and drinks Kentucky bourbon, she is *not* a Yankee. She is a *southerner*."

Magnus raised his glass to her. "Very well, Miss Scarlett O'Hara."

"You mock, but I make a mean mint julep. Both in drink form and as a jam that tastes delicious with lamb."

He swiftly grabbed the bottle of Highland Park and held it to his chest. "Not with this whiskey, you don't."

She laughed. The sound was as bright as the sun

sparkling on a calm sea. It seemed to flow through him, washing away the doubt pooling inside him. He'd never teased a lass like this…or laughed with one.

But a chuckle formed deep in his chest and came rumbling out. It felt good, being with June.

"You play nice, now, or you're not getting the next thing in my purse."

"B-b-bloody hell, how much do you have stowed in there?"

She ignored him and pulled out two scones and a jar of preserves. "No celebration is complete without my jam. This one is called Apricot Delight. It's one of my favorites."

Sweet, decadent flavor exploded in Magnus's mouth as he took a bite. The lass could cook. He hadn't had a scone this good since he left Tammay, and certainly none in the States had ever come close to being this delicious. And the jam was pure magic. Light, fruity, with just a hint of cloves for contrast. He closed his eyes, savoring the tastes, letting them blend in his mouth. When he opened his eyelids, he found June looking at him, her eyes once again the color of emeralds.

"I could watch you eat my food all day long," she said, her voice husky.

Magnus felt a hot blush stain his cheeks. He swallowed. He yearned to lean forward, to capture her lips with his. But he didn't. A relationship with June would never work, and he didn't need the pain…or more memories to bury.

He pulled back, and he thought he might have detected the faintest glimmer of hurt in June's eyes. Before he could look closer, the lass busied herself with rooting in her muckle bag again.

This time, when she reached inside, she pulled out something covered in wrapping paper with a bow on top. He stared at it warily. He couldn't recall the last time he'd received a present. His da had normally forgotten his birthday and had never been one for celebrating the holidays.

"It isn't much. It's not even new," June explained, "but I wanted you to have it."

Slowly, Magnus reached forward and accepted the gift. Feeling almost as awkward as he had when posting the bloody video, he ripped off the paper. To his surprise, a book of children's poetry fell into his lap. He raised his eyes to June in confusion.

"It was mine," she said. "From speech therapy. I used it to practice reading in a mirror. The poems are silly, but I think it's one of the reasons I have so little disfluency today. Growing up, I couldn't keep a lot of my stuff since we were constantly moving to different military bases. But this I kept. I even took it to college."

Magnus shook his head and extended the anthology to her. It humbled him that she had offered it to him, but he could not take her childhood treasure. "I cannot accept this."

She wrapped her fingers around his and gently pushed her gift against his chest. Her eyes had returned to their gentler grass green, and she said simply, "You need it."

He realized rejecting the gift would insult her, so he gave a brusque nod and closed his fingers around the book. She grinned. A gossamer softness slipped through Magnus and seemed to settle in the very core of his being. His body, against his will, leaned toward June, pulled to her like the tide under the thrall of the moon.

Before his lips could graze hers, his mobile rang. His agent. He fished it from the pocket of his trousers and lifted it in June's direction. "I b-b-better take this, lass."

She nodded and, in typical American fashion, flashed him two thumbs up. He nodded in response before answering.

"Magnus, that was amazing," Lauren said. "The readers will love it. But I didn't know you stuttered."

"Aye," Magnus said.

"You should have told me. We could've talked to Mitch if you didn't feel comfortable with the vlog."

"It needed to…" Magnus paused as he felt his throat begin to close over the word *be*. Any other time, he would have switched to a different word. But he saw June give him a nod of encouragement. If he could post a video of himself stuttering on the internet, he could trip over a word or two while talking to his agent who he'd known for years. Magnus swallowed and allowed himself to speak naturally: "…b-b-be d-d-done."

Just then, he heard a ping on his mobile indicating a waiting call. Pulling it from his ear, he glanced down to see his editor's number. "M-M-Mitch is calling me," he told Lauren.

"Go. Take it. Keep up the good work."

"Aye." Swiping with his finger, he switched over. His editor's Boston accent immediately boomed through the mobile's speakers.

"I just watched your video. It was great, compelling. Everything your last books have been needing," Mitch said. "Have you considered talking about your stutter in the next one?"

"You want m-me to write about it?" Magnus asked, not quite sure how that made him feel.

"Yeah," Mitch said. "It's good stuff for the kind of introspective work you do. Readers would eat it up."

Still, Magnus wasn't convinced, and Mitch must have noticed his hesitation because he added, "Just think about it."

Mitch said his goodbye shortly after that. Neither of them was one for blethering once the real business was complete. When Magnus returned the mobile to his pocket, he found June watching him. Although he hadn't used the speaker feature, his volume was high enough that she'd apparently heard every word.

"What your editor suggested might not be the worst idea in the world."

Magnus cocked his head, regarding her. Given the success of his first vlog entry, he was beginning to realize he shouldn't dismiss her ideas outright. She wasn't a nyaff, just a wee bit overenthusiastic.

"And why is that, lass?"

"You told me once your writing was like a purge. Maybe it would help you to work through everything surrounding your disfluency. When you're done, you'll be left with only your own perspective of your natural speech patterns, and not what everybody else has been telling you to feel and do for years."

Magnus stared at June, surprised by her insight. Her words not only made sense; they appealed to him. He liked the notion of ridding himself of the rubbish surrounding his stutter. The lass had the right of it. A purge would do him good.

"I also brought you this," June said as she pulled out a stack of papers held together with a black clip.

"That really is a wizard's bag," Magnus said.

She ignored him. "It's a printout of a self-help book on stuttering. My brother recommended it. It's written by a cofounder of a major company who also experienced disfluency."

Magnus tried not to show his skepticism as he said gently, "I d-d-don't think anything will cure my stutter, lass."

"This book isn't about curing it," June said. "It's about you having control over it."

Control. Now *that* Magnus could respect. He reached for the papers. "Thank you, lass."

She nodded toward the stack. "There are a lot of steps in there, none of them easy, but you have the determination."

It was odd, being complimented about something personal. He'd grown accustomed to praise about his writing, but not about himself. He nodded stiffly, staring down at the sheaf of papers.

"I'm willing to help you as much as you want. One of the first steps is analyzing your disfluency. We've got plenty on tape, and we can watch it together if you want."

Magnus bobbed his head again and lifted his eyes toward hers. "I'd like that, lass."

She smiled softly, "So would I."

—◆◆◆—

That evening, after June had left and Bowie was watching Sorcha, Magnus found himself alone. He started leafing through *Self-Therapy for the Stutterer*. The steps it laid out were rigorous, but he'd handled intensity before. When he finished the first read-through, he reached into the old trunk Katie had loaned him and pulled out the book of children's poetry. Not wanting Bowie to overhear, Magnus grabbed a penlight and slipped out into the empty zoo. The wind blew, sending tumbleweed careening down the paths between the exhibits. Ignoring the bite to the air, Magnus hunched over and headed toward Frida's enclosure. The grizzly lifted her chin at his approach. Although she had access to her indoor den, she'd chosen to lie on her heated rock again. When he sat down on a nearby bench, she let out a rumbling sound. Magnus chose to interpret it as a greeting.

Glancing around to make sure no one but the animals could hear, he switched on the penlight and flipped open June's anthology and began to read aloud. He tried to keep his tongue and jaw loose as he attempted to speak with the lightness the self-help book recommended. Frida quickly fell asleep, her soft snores filling the air. Magnus lowered his voice as he flipped the page. The poems were silly, meant to amuse bairns. But as he read them, he felt his mouth quirk upward, finding himself helplessly charmed by the playful verses…much like his reaction toward the woman who'd gifted him the book.

Chapter 8

TWO WEEKS LATER, JUNE WAS JUST FINISHING CLEANING UP the tea shop for the day when her phone rang. Seeing Katie's number, she answered. "How are you feeling, honey?"

"Good," Katie said. "The morning sickness hasn't been too bad today. Your jam seems to be helping."

"We need to get your testimony for Ginger Minted Bliss on the website."

Katie laughed. "I'm not sure how persuasive that would be since I'm a part owner of your jam business."

"Honey, I think any woman suffering from morning sickness would try just about anything safe and natural."

"True," Katie admitted, "but enough about me. I was calling on behalf of another pregnant lady. Lulubelle is in labor. You said you wanted to be here for the birth of her calf."

"Why, of course!" June said. "After all, I was present at her first meeting with Hank."

"Do you want to drop your grandmother off with my parents? Mom says she doesn't mind, and Lulubelle is still a long way from delivering. There's no one at my house since Lou is down at the paddock."

"Already? Won't that be a lot of standing for him?" The veterinarian was an active man, especially for his age, but he was still eighty years old, and June had a feeling camel births weren't a quick process.

Katie sighed. "Lou can be stubborn, especially when an animal's welfare is at stake. Bowie's helped the llamas during labor, but this is his first camel birth. Lou wants to be on hand in case something goes wrong. Luckily, Magnus is helping too since he's had a lot of experience delivering calves and foals."

"Let me check with Nan first to see if she's up for visiting the ranch. At least it's familiar since she used to visit your grandparents out there." Although June didn't watch her grandmother 24/7, she didn't like leaving her alone for long stretches of time. She worried what would happen if Nan spiraled into one of her spells with no one around to help her.

"You can tell her that my mom's happy to have the company. She's even pulled out old photographs of our grandparents together. She thought your nan might enjoy that."

When June hung up the phone, she immediately found Nan, who was still knitting in her rocking chair at the front of the shop. Fortunately, her grandmother seemed thrilled with the idea of visiting the old Hallister homestead. Today had been a good one, and she didn't seem overwhelmed by the drive or change of scenery. Even with her gran's cooperation, it still took almost an hour before June finally arrived at the zoo.

She found everyone at the pen Bowie used when he wanted to separate one of the llamas from the rest of the herd. Lulubelle was lying down and breathing heavily. Bowie crouched by her side, talking to her in a reassuring tone. Someone had pulled up a chair for Lou. The older man leaned forward, resting his elbows against wooden slats of the stall as he watched the camel closely through the opening. June could tell the veterinarian wished he could leap off his chair and vault over the rails to assist. Instead, he settled for monitoring the whole process with eagle-eyed intensity.

Positioned off to the side, Katie stood behind her tripod as she filmed the birth. Like Bowie and Lou, her entire focus remained on the camel. Although June knew Katie cared for each of the critters at her husband's zoo, her friend had a special spot of affection for Lulubelle. The camel had been the first to welcome her when she'd started volunteering, and Katie had been instrumental in finding the old girl a mate.

Abby sat next to Magnus on the top rung of the stall. The preteen swung her feet back and forth. Boredom showed on her pixie-like face, but other than giving June a welcoming wave, she didn't move from her perch. Observing the early stages of a camel's birth probably wasn't the most exciting activity, especially for a kid with Abby's energy level. But nothing, not even tedium, could tear the girl away from one of the animals that she loved.

June took up a position by Magnus. As she settled down next to him, she noticed the lines of his body were coiled for action. The man truly cared about animals, and for once, he wasn't hiding his emotions. He looked up at her approach and then turned his gaze back to Lulubelle.

"How's it going?" June whispered quietly, bending close to him. One of his curls framed his ear perfectly, and she resisted the urge to touch the silky strand.

"She's just entered the last stages of labor," Magnus

said quietly, his entire attention zeroed in on Lulubelle. "The b-bairn should be here soon."

Although June had come to watch the birth of the camel, she found her eyes drifting more than once in Magnus's direction. His intensity fascinated her. His early books had been filled with his wonder for all living critters, and one particular passage she'd read recently sprang to mind. She remembered it because she'd emailed an excerpt to Katie, knowing Bowie would enjoy it.

> Growing up on a croft crystallized in me the responsibility a man has for the creatures placed in his care. It is an instinct we carry in our souls passed down from our ancient forebears who set down their spears to build the first crude corrals.

What woman wouldn't feel a touch swoony after reading that? June had never thought the salt-of-the-earth type would appeal to her, but an elemental part of her simply reacted to Magnus's steadfastness.

"Shit," Bowie said suddenly, his voice uncharacteristically worried. The thread of concern in his voice sent dread spiraling through June. She'd never seen the zookeeper flustered before...no matter what trouble the animals had caused. "Lou, you better take a look at this."

Beside June, Magnus stiffened, clearly on alert too. Lou rose stiffly from his chair, but as soon as he was on his feet, he moved rapidly despite his unsteady gait. With a grunt, he bent to check on

Lulubelle. When he straightened, his face looked grim. "We may have to turn the calf."

At Lou's pronouncement, Magnus jumped from his perch and landed in the birthing stall. Within seconds, he joined Bowie and Lou. "Breech?"

The two other men nodded solemnly. All looked worried. Magnus turned toward Bowie. "Have you done this?"

"Not with an animal this big," Bowie admitted, rubbing the back of his head. A muscle in the side of his cheek twitched, and June could tell he was clenching his teeth. "Lou can walk me through it, though."

"I turned calves on the croft. Foals too," Magnus said, his stutter nowhere to be heard.

Bowie and Lou exchanged a silent glance before Bowie nodded. "Okay. If it comes to that, you can take the lead."

The minutes seemed to drag as Lulubelle's breathing became more labored and erratic. Even knowing very little about animal husbandry, June could tell the camel was struggling. A horrible mix of terror and exhaustion filled the animal's large brown eyes as she strained her massive body. Lou patted and comforted Lulubelle with his soothing voice, but her fear did not noticeably dim.

Finally, with a silent communication between the three men, Magnus began the long, brutal process of turning the calf. June had never watched anything like it. Magnus fought almost as hard as Lulubelle. It took both gentle precision and brute strength to adjust the calf's position. The process wasn't quick. It wasn't easy. And it wasn't without cost to both man and beast.

Sweat dripped down Magnus's brow. June could see his back muscles bunch and pull under the flannel fabric of his shirt. His face showed the strain, and his arms trembled under the force, but still he fought to save both mother and baby.

Finally, he stepped back, and the calf began to appear. Time sped up as near-tragedy transformed into the miracle of birth. The calf soon rested on the ground, tired and trembling. It lay in a tangle of long, gangly limbs, its small mouth opening in the faintest of rumbling cries. The sound stole June's heart. A relieved smile broke over Bowie's face as he quickly stepped forward to towel off the little camel. With a matching grin on his weathered face, Lou heaped praises on Lulubelle as she clambered to her feet.

Breathing heavily, Magnus sat back on his haunches, his hands resting on his thighs. Tiredness and joy mixed in his face as he watched mother and calf. When Bowie finished taking care of the baby, he walked over to Magnus and gave the man a hand up. Magnus took it.

"Thanks," Bowie said, his voice rough with gratitude. "I owe you."

Magnus shook his head. "It needed d-d-doing."

June's heart squeezed, and she felt a bit of herself fall in love with the Scot. How could she not after that herculean display of strength to save two struggling animals?

"You did good," Lou said, clapping Magnus on the shoulder. He bobbed his head in acknowledgment, red flags appearing over his cheekbones. Compliments clearly didn't rest easy on him, but Magnus didn't insult Lou by rejecting his praise. Instead, he gave another nod and then walked stiffly over to gently pat Lulubelle. He spoke in low tones, but June could hear him praising the new mama. Lulubelle stretched her long neck to nuzzle his hair. Although the camel always acted affectionately, the gesture seemed deeper. June couldn't shake the feeling Lulubelle knew Magnus had saved her and was showing gratitude.

The new mama then headed over to her baby, inspecting it with her snout. The calf wiggled, already attempting to rise. It bleated with the effort. Lulubelle rumbled softly to her little one, the sound sweet and homey.

Abby made an *oooo* sound as she clasped her hands together under her chin as if she would explode if she didn't try to hold in her joy. She gave a little bounce of excitement. Swiveling toward her father, she announced quietly, "This is the most adorable thing I've ever seen!"

The fact that the preteen still managed to speak softly despite her enthusiasm showed how much time she spent around animals. Bowie chuckled and ruffled his daughter's hair. "The calf is pretty darn cute."

After giving her husband and stepdaughter a fond smile, Katie sidled up to June and whispered, "Bowie says a newborn calf can stand within two hours. Isn't that incredible?"

June nodded as she kept her eyes trained on the little baby camel. It looked so small and tiny lying next to Lulubelle. Skinny too.

With gentle patience, Lou checked the vitals of both camels, even though June knew the elderly man's muscles must be killing him after sitting for so long. Although his movements were stiff, he worked fast. A satisfied smile stretched across his face when he finished and moved back to the fence rail. Bowie and Magnus followed suit, allowing mother and calf the opportunity to continue to form a deep connection.

"I'd best be having a bath," Magnus said quietly before he ducked from the barn and headed outside. June slipped after him.

"Magnus?"

He turned without stiffening like he had in the past when she'd followed him. Instead of annoyance, she just saw confusion. "Aye, hen?"

"What you did back there... It was amazing."

Color rose in Magnus's cheeks again, and she wondered why any attention, let alone praise, made the man so visibly uncomfortable.

"I've done it many t-t-times afore, lass. Just not with a camel. T-T-T-Turning a breeched animal is part of living on a croft."

"It doesn't make it less incredible. Without you, Lulubelle and her calf wouldn't be here."

"Bowie would've managed."

June wasn't so sure. Although Bowie was strong, he hadn't grown up around large mammals, not like Magnus had.

June studied him closely, wishing she could understand him better. How could such a caring man have become so isolated? His gruffness was both a fortress and a weapon. If anyone tried to breach his walls, he cut them down before they could reach his inner keep. And there he stayed, alone and cut off.

"Why is it so hard for you to accept a compliment?" June asked softly.

Magnus's eyes shuttered, and he opened the door to the main zoo facility. "I haven't done anything to d-d-d-deserve it."

June let him go inside alone. The man was clearly exhausted and covered in filth. It wasn't fair to keep him from his shower. But as soon as he was out of earshot, she said softly, "I think you have."

―――~~―――

There was nothing like witnessing new life, Magnus thought as he watched the wee calf make another attempt to stand. Her mother hovered anxiously nearby, using her head to nudge and guide the peedie camel. The bairn managed to get her front legs up, but as soon as she tried to raise her hind ones, her forelegs folded at the knees. Her rear stuck in the air, her hooves splayed out to keep her back half upright.

"I think we should call her Knobby," Abby proclaimed, her voice bright with the unabashed joy that only a child could display so freely.

Lulubelle chose that moment to snort. Loudly. Abby giggled. "I don't think Mama likes that one. I guess it isn't dignified enough. You haven't named an animal yet, Miss Winters. Would you like to?"

"Do you want a good southern belle name?" June asked.

"Why not?" Bowie said with a shrug. Like Magnus, he'd sneaked off briefly to take a shower, and his wet hair stuck to his head. He must have been just as tired as Magnus, but his face shone with the same energy as his daughter's. It wasn't difficult to see the source of the lassie's love for animals.

"Savannah," June suggested. No sooner had the word crossed June's lips than the wee bairn finally stood. She held her position for several seconds before her wobbly legs collapsed. The whole group chuckled softly, not wanting to frighten the calf.

"I think she likes it," Abby said.

"Savannah it is," Lou pronounced, and the wee camel struggled to her feet for a second time.

They stood in silence for a little longer before the group started to drift away. Bowie left first to check on Sorcha. Katie then nudged Abby, reminding her that she hadn't started her homework. Abby made a couple protests, but Katie held firm. The preteen relented and followed her stepmother from the barn. After they left, Lou creakily walked back into the birthing stall. Magnus debated about helping the older man crouch down to check on the camels, but he didn't want to embarrass him. June made a move to assist, but she must have thought better of it too. Lou managed well enough on his own. When he was satisfied that mother and calf were doing well, he said his goodbyes and headed back to the house.

June lingered, obviously as enthralled with the peedie calf as Magnus. As she stood beside him, he noticed her sway slightly and then yawn. Magnus narrowed his eyes. It was not terribly late in the evening, but the lass must get up early in the morn to start the baking for her café, and she'd been standing on her feet for over two hours watching Savannah's birth.

"You all right, hen?" Magnus asked.

June nodded as she smothered another yawn. "Four o'clock in the morning is showing on me, that's all. I'd better go soon and pick up Nan, but I want to stay just five more minutes."

She looked so tired standing there that Magnus acted without thinking. He stepped next to her and pulled her close, so she could lean her weight against him. She nestled into his body like it was the most natural thing. Pressing the back of her head against his chest, she gazed up at him. "Thanks."

"'Tis nothing, lass. You're a slight thing."

Her mouth curved into a soft smile tinged with affection. Magnus almost dipped his head and captured her bonny pink lips with his own, but June returned her gaze to the camels. She sighed and wiggled closer. Tenderness whispered through Magnus like gentle snowflakes after a blizzard's end. He only felt this content when sitting by a fire sipping whiskey and reading a good book. And he'd never experienced peace like this while in the company of another person. It was the kind of quiet that seeped into a man's soul and slowly washed away the day's worries.

Neither of them spoke as they watched Lulubelle fuss over her baby. Savannah managed to nurse on unsteady legs. Despite her wobbliness, she greedily drank the colostrum, the nutrient-rich milk that would help ensure her health and survival.

"It's beautiful, isn't it?" June said, her voice full of wonder.

"Aye. A m-m-man can never grow weary of a sight like this."

"You must have witnessed a lot of births growing up on a farm."

"Aye, but it never stops being m-miraculous," Magnus said.

June shifted. Although she still kept her body pressed close to his, she tilted her head to gaze at him. A smile drifted across her lips. Slow. Sweet. Tempting.

A huge sigh from Lulubelle broke the spell the lass was weaving. Magnus turned with June to watch the camel settle down with her calf. Within minutes, the pair drifted off to sleep. June yawned and pushed herself upright. "I'd better head out now. Nan will be wondering where I am. She's having a good day, but I don't want her getting scared."

Magnus nodded. "All right, lass."

"I'll see you tomorrow."

"Aye, see you in the m-m-morn."

Magnus followed June with his eyes until she disappeared from sight. Although it wasn't too baltic tonight, his body instantly missed her warmth. *Aw, baws.* Truth be told, he craved her presence. And Magnus didn't like that. He didn't want to feel this incessant need for another.

And it wasn't just sexual. It went deeper than that.

He'd lived his whole life independently. He dreaded ending up like his da, a permanently beelin' arse because a hen left him. But June? June made him want. Made him long. Made him feel things he didn't wish to.

Magnus knew he should stay away from the lass. But he couldn't. It wasn't just that she kept popping up everywhere like a mole in a vegetable patch. *He* didn't want to avoid June anymore. Which wasn't like him. At all.

Aye, his head was full of mince, and it was all the lass's fault.

---~~~---

The next morning, June woke in a good mood. Unlike many people, she didn't mind rising early. She supposed it was left over from childhood. Her father hadn't believed in sleeping in…or in letting the rest of the family do it either. June's mama always claimed the military was bred into him, and they should be grateful he didn't insist on playing the reveille each morning. Even as a teenager, June hadn't minded, not like her brother, August. She enjoyed waking before dawn and feeling a sense of satisfaction at what she could accomplish while most people lay abed. And, even as extroverted as she was, there was something magical about the quiet before the sun broke over the horizon.

Humming to herself, June bustled about the kitchen. She breathed the scent of yeast as she placed dough in the mixer. Sometimes, she'd knead by hand, but she rarely had time anymore. Her mama had taught her to cook, but it had been Nan who'd shown June how to bake. She used to spend her summers in this kitchen while she learned what it took to operate a tea shop. She'd found her place here, in this very room. While other kids dreamed of fancy careers, she'd always known she'd take over Nan's business, not that her grandparents had ever pushed her. No, it had always been June's own dream. Growing up rootless, she'd wanted a place to call home, and this was it. Plain and simple.

June had just finished putting the baked goods in the display cabinet when the door chimed. Stanley Harris and Buck Montgomery walked in already bickering. June hid her smile as she pretended to buff out a smudge on the display case. She could set her clock by those two men. And that's why she loved small towns—the familiar rhythms that kept the heart of the community beating.

By the time the men reached the counter, June was already getting their standard order ready. The old cowboys never changed. Stanley liked egg, cheese, and ham on a bagel with black coffee, and Buck liked her version of a Scottish breakfast and took his coffee with two sugars and a helping of cream. Neither drank tea.

The men only paused their argument long enough to greet June. Then they were back debating the best ointment to use on a hoof infection. June shook her head fondly as she finished their orders. No sooner had she set their plates in front of them than Lacey Montgomery walked in. She wore her park ranger's uniform, her chestnut-brown hair pulled into a ponytail. She greeted Stanley and her grandfather, Buck, before heading to the counter.

"What would you like?" June asked.

"The clotted-cream crepe and a coffee to go," Lacey said. "Oh, you know what, add a sausage to it."

"Big day?"

Lacey nodded, her ponytail bobbing. She wasn't a very tall woman, but the energy she exuded more than made up for her lack of height. "It's the start of my wolf survey."

"How's the reintroduction going?"

Lacey beamed. "Great! I'm hoping we get a lot of wolf pups this spring. It's mating season now, so part of my study is to see how their normal patterns of movement change."

"Are you still having trouble with Clay Stevens?" June asked. Unlike in some communities, most of the ranchers near Sagebrush Flats had embraced the reintroduction of wolves to Rocky Ridge National Park. And their acceptance had everything to do with the woman standing in front of June. Since her mama ran the Prairie Dog Café, the whole town had watched Lacey Montgomery grow up. According to town tradition, she'd had been talking to anybody and everybody about how the park needed wolves ever since she did a project on *Canis lupus* in first grade. When Lacey's parents had lost big in an investment scheme and her papa had a heart attack, the whole town had pitched in to help send her to college to become an ecologist. But there was one man who didn't approve of the wolf pack…or Lacey, not that anyone listened to his bellyaching. Even though Clay Stevens's maternal line had owned a huge spread to the north of town since pioneer days, he was still a no-good city slicker.

Lacey rolled her eyes. "Clay's trying to organize another protest at the next town-hall meeting. The last one fizzled, but he keeps trying. He insists on calling the pack Lacey's Wolves. It's starting to feel personal. You'd think it was *my* father who scammed the entire town, not *his*. I swear if anyone is a big, bad wolf, it's him."

June laughed. "Good way of putting it."

"So how about you?" Lacey asked. "I hear you have

your own bad-tempered male to deal with." At her question, both her grandfather and Stanley perked up. The older men turned in their seats, not even bothering to hide their interest.

At the mention of Magnus, a sweet warmth crept through June. She thought of his combination of strength and tenderness last night when he saved Lulubelle and Savannah, and of the way he'd held her afterward. It had been good standing there, feeling Magnus's body against hers as they watched Lulubelle nestle her new baby. Despite the quietness of the moment, it had been powerful. Something had stolen inside June and hadn't left.

"Magnus Gray's not so bad," she said.

Buck snorted. "He's like a grizzly with a sore tooth."

"He was just having a bad day, that's all," June countered.

"Folks are saying he's stormed away from you twice," Stanley said. "Me and Buck here saw it once with our own eyes."

June shook her head. "You're making too much of it."

Buck snorted. "Something must be wrong with him, treating a pretty girl like that. Men of my generation, we know a thing or two about how to act around a lady."

"That you do." June smiled at Buck. His weathered face lit up.

Lacey rolled her eyes again. "Grandpa, stop flirting with June, or I'll never get my breakfast."

"She's flirting with me!" Buck protested, but

both he and Stanley returned to their own conversation. They'd moved on to a perennial favorite—debating the best way to rope a steer. June quickly finished Lacey's order. Another customer came in and then another. It wasn't until over an hour later that June had time to glance down at her watch. When she saw the time, worry niggled. Nan should have come by now. It wasn't like her to be this late.

June poked her head in the kitchen and told her assistant that she had to run over to her grandmother's for a second. She dashed out the back door of the tea shop and hurried up the steps to the wraparound porch surrounding Nan's home. Silence greeted her when she unlocked the door and poked her head inside. Panic clawed at June. Trying to stay calm, she bolted up the stairs, not caring that she sounded like a stampeding buffalo.

When she reached the top, she heard a low groan coming from her grandma's bedroom. Talons of ice stabbed into June's heart as she yanked open the door. Her grandmother lay in bed, her mouth agape as she stared at the ceiling. When June drew close, the woman turned her head, her eyes glassy with fear and confusion. The horror in them deepened into pure terror. "The devil is coming. He's going to drag me to hell. The rats are already here."

Chapter 9

JUNE TYPICALLY EXCELLED IN A CRISIS. LIFE AS A military brat had taught both organization and control. Her father had been deployed to war zones, and so had her brother. She'd grown up learning how to internalize fear and make it productive. When things went topsy-turvy, she stayed calm and logical by focusing on what needed to be done.

But this time. This time, her brain didn't cooperate. At all.

June tried to reach for Nan, but the woman shrank back, shrieking in utter terror. "You're going to kill me! You're here to kill me."

"No, Nan," June said, trying to center the turmoil spinning madly inside her. "It's me, June. I'm here to help."

"No, you're not," Nan said, her voice high and wobbly. It was simultaneously a child's and an old woman's. "You look like June, but you're not. You're here to murder me!"

June's heart shattered. To her horror, tears threatened to fall. She took a breath. Tried to think. But nothing had prepared her for this.

She reached for her phone. Her family lived scattered around the world. They couldn't help. Not immediately.

June started to dial Katie's number, but she

stopped. She'd retained enough reason to know she didn't want to drag Katie into this right now. She would insist on accompanying June to the hospital, and June wasn't about to bring her pregnant friend there. Plus, Katie's morning sickness was awful right now, and June doubted she could handle the car ride.

Although June had plenty of other friends in Sagebrush, her index finger swiped past those numbers. Instead, she pressed on the name most recently added. Magnus Gray.

———∽∾∾∽———

Magnus stood watching Lulubelle and Savannah when his mobile rang. To his surprise, as soon as he saw June's name, a smile drifted over his face. True, he'd just been thinking about the lass, but he wasn't prepared for the jolt of pleasure.

"Hullo," he said.

"M-Magnus?"

At the fear in June's voice, he gripped the phone. "What's wrong, lass?"

"It's Nan," June said. "She's…she's not right. I think I need to t-t-take her to the hospital."

Magnus stepped back from the stall and headed in the direction of the Victorian. "I'll be right there, lass. Do you want me to bring Katie?"

He heard June swallow hard. Although she said she no longer had a stutter, her concern seemed to have caused it to resurface.

"N-No," June said. "Katie's morning sickness is so bad right now, and I don't want her babies exposed to hospital germs."

"Do you want me to drive you?"

"Yes. Yes, p-p-please. The ambulance will take too long."

"I need to t-t-t-tell Bowie that I'm leaving. You live above the tea shop, aye?"

Magnus heard a watery sniff on the other end of the line. When June spoke, she sounded a wee bit more collected, but her voice still shook. "Nana's in the building behind. We're in her bedroom. The back door's unlocked."

"D-d-don't fash yourself," Magnus told her. "I'll be there as fast as I can."

Danger. Honey could smell it. Normally, she thrived on the scent. Her pedestrian life—first as a pet and now as a zoo resident—had allowed for little peril.

But this was not the same as attacking a cobra or a lion.

This was *not* exciting.

She had not liked the look on the Giant One's face when he'd rushed past their exhibit twice. He had looked grim. Angry humans were amusing. Sad ones were not.

Beside her, Fluffy chittered softly. He too had picked up on the sudden tension swirling through the air like smoke before a deadly wildfire.

Honey glanced his way. Perhaps Fluffy had more true honey badger in him than she had suspected. Honey didn't know why, but she found herself sidling in his direction. He glanced at her, his black eyes steadily watching hers. Then he shifted...as if

making room for her. Their kind did not cuddle. Ever.
Yet, somehow, Honey found herself pressed against the
male. But they weren't snuggling. Certainly not. That
was only something silly herd animals and humans did.

———

As soon as Magnus opened the back door to Clara
Winters's house, he heard the older woman scream.
Worried, he dashed up the stairs. When he burst into the
room, she shrieked even louder.

"He's here. The devil is here!"

"It's just Magnus, Nan," June said. "You know,
Magnus. He writes those stories you like so much. The
one about Tammay and the other about the polar bears."

June reached for her grandmother's hand, but the
older woman snatched it back. She curled toward the
wall, watching June with the eyes of a hunted, wounded
animal. June's face crumpled. Magnus's heart clenched
as he saw the normally bright lass fighting to hide her
tears. He wished like hell he'd been able to bring Katie
along. He was never one for emotions, and the air was
heavy with them. But June had called him, and she
needed his help. So, Magnus drew in his breath and
cautiously made his way to the bedside.

Not for the first time, he cursed his bulk. He was built
to intimidate, not to cajole. No wonder Clara thought
him Auld Clootie.

June glanced in his direction. She bit her bottom lip
so hard it turned white. "I'm sorry," she said quietly.
"She thinks I'm the devil too."

"I've been called worse."

June's grandmother made a keening sound that

reminded Magnus of an injured lamb. Although he had little experience with soothing humans, he had plenty at settling animals. Without thinking, he began to sing softly. He picked an old tune, "My Love's in Germany," one June's nan might recognize. It was a quiet song about a young lass waiting for her lover to return from war. Although it was originally written about Scottish mercenaries long before the nineteen forties, he imagined it had been sung during the war at the Selkie's Strand.

Clara Winters uncurled slightly. "I remember that one. Dot and Peg used to sing it."

Magnus switched into another. He'd never had trouble with stuttering when singing, not that he did it much in public. He'd gotten blootered a couple of times during his roughneck days and belted out a few ditties, much to the delight of his coworkers. Growing up, he used to croon to the animals, especially when one was sick or hurt. It had passed the time, especially during the short winter days when he'd felt trapped by the low light and howling wind.

As Magnus crooned to June's nan, he didn't feel as self-conscious as he would've thought. He was too focused on calming her. He could feel June's gaze, steady and warm. Magnus didn't turn in her direction for fear of disturbing her grandmother. Clara's breathing, although still shallow and erratic, became less frenetic. The woman's eyes drifted shut, and sleep finally claimed her.

"Something's not right, and I don't mean just the devil bit," June said, her voice watery. Magnus glanced at the lass and saw she still fought to hold back her tears. Unaccustomed to giving comfort, he awkwardly slung his arm around her slim shoulders. Her body curled into his as she stared down at her nan. Magnus followed her gaze. The older woman's jaw had gone slack in sleep. "She shouldn't have fallen asleep that quickly...not after being so frightened."

Magnus nodded. "Aye."

"Do you think you could carry her to my SUV?"

"Aye, lass. She's naught but a twig."

Magnus carefully lifted Clara and prayed the elderly woman stayed asleep. Despite his assurances to June, the steps were narrow and twisted in the middle. Even with her slight weight, if Clara fought him, it would make the process difficult and dangerous. Although she stirred, she was too puggled to fully wake. Her dazed eyes fluttered closed again as Magnus carefully navigated the steps.

June led him to her SUV parked in a garage between her nan's house and the tea shop. He gently placed Clara in the back seat, and June immediately busied herself with making her nan comfortable with the items she'd grabbed from the woman's bedroom. Magnus didn't offer to help. He figured fussing gave June something to do, something to focus on. Patiently, he waited as she placed a pillow behind her grandmother's head and tucked a quilt around her. When June was satisfied, she handed him the keys, and the two of them silently climbed into the vehicle.

As he pulled onto the main street and headed east, June pulled out her mobile. She glanced over at him. "Would you mind if I made some calls? I need to let my family know."

"Do whatever you need to do, lass."

Magnus focused his attention on the road to give June her privacy. Although her voice sounded strained, she kept it remarkably steady as she spoke with her parents. When she finished sending an email to her brother, she made a forlorn sound, halfway between a sigh and a sob. Magnus's heart twisted.

"My parents will be here as quickly as they can, but there's no direct flight, so it'll take time. My brother's deployed so he definitely can't make it. I don't even know when he'll read my message," June told him, her voice wobbly.

Magnus nodded. Silence fell, and he heard another watery sigh from June. He reached for the radio, desperate to distract her. It was a long drive to the hospital.

"What music do you like, hen?"

"Anything." The word came out as soggy as undercooked bread pudding. Magnus quickly flicked to the station with the strongest signal. It was American country, not his favorite, but it was music. He glanced over at June. She'd curled her body toward the window, and the sunlight illuminated the tracks of silent tears on her cheeks. An ache spread inside Magnus like lichens growing over the cliffs. Without thinking, he reached over and laid his massive hand over June's delicate one. She instantly turned her palm to rest against his as she laced their fingers together. He squeezed but didn't let go.

"Thank you," she said softly. "For coming."

"It was no b-bother, lass."

—◊◊—

When they finally reached the hospital, the staff immediately took Nan into triage. Then the waiting began. Nurses and doctors flitted in and out. All around her, June could hear the terrible sounds of the ER. The constant beeping of machines. The groans of other patients. The squeak of shoes accompanied by the sound of wheeling gurneys. Through it all, Magnus stayed by her side. His solid presence helped steady June as the rest of her world threatened to fissure around her.

Nan lay so still, looking like a rag doll under the white hospital blankets. Her mouth was still agape, her skin almost gray in its paleness. A phlebotomist came and drew blood. The ER doctor examined her. Someone came to wheel her away for a CT scan. Magnus reached over and took June's hand. His fingers were thick. Strong. Despite his career as a writer, they were callused, and there was something comforting in that, something honest.

"Are you hungry or thirsty, lass? I could bring you something from the canteen."

"No, I'm fine," June said. Her stomach sloshed with guilt and worry. Nothing would stay down even if she tried.

The orderly brought her grandmother back, and still they waited. When her parents called from the airport for an update, June could tell them little. Finally, the doctor returned. June gripped Magnus's hand. Part of her wanted to know Nan's diagnosis. The rest of her dreaded to hear it. It was awful. This not knowing. But the knowing might be worse.

"Your grandmother's had a severe sodium drop," the doctor said. "We're still running tests, but we're going to admit her. We'll need to bring her sodium levels up slowly. We believe she's also experiencing a urinary tract infection, and we're sending a sample to the lab to be cultured."

June nodded. She should be asking questions, finding out more. But her mind refused to cooperate. She felt like a child again, dropped into yet another foreign country, another base, another new life. The doctor kept talking, and June did her best to absorb everything, but her head just buzzed. Magnus seemed to be listening intently as he sat next to her, his shoulder wedged against hers, his hand still wrapped around her fingers. She focused on his warmth and his strength, instead of the yawning hole inside her.

The hours slipped together, both rushing and trickling by. Her grandmother was moved to an intensive-care step-down unit a few floors up. There was paperwork to complete and more questions about her grandmother than June could answer. The medical assistant bustled in and out as she worked to make Nan comfortable. Next came the nurse who hooked her grandmother up to more machines. Doctors came. A cardiologist. A psychologist. An internist. A neurologist. A urologist. Information flew at June. Nan did have a urinary tract infection. Her sodium levels were going up too fast, so they were going to cut back. The doctors recommended a spinal tap. An orderly was taking her for an MRI. Questions were asked. How long had Nan experienced confusion? What medications did she take? Did she live alone?

The light left the sky and then returned. June's brother managed to contact her, and her parents called from yet another airport. Katie phoned, worried. She wanted to come to the hospital, but June ordered her to stay home. Katie only relented after she talked to Magnus.

It was afternoon the next day when June's parents finally arrived. As soon as she saw her mama, all the tears she'd been holding back burst forth like the Great Flood. Her mom held her tightly and rocked her as her dad, ever the officer, took charge.

As June hugged her mother, she tried to battle the guilt consuming her. She, who had always excelled at whatever she tried, had failed. She hadn't taken care of her nan. She should've taken her to a doctor in the city weeks ago. If she had, none of this would have happened. None of this.

───✧───

Magnus had learned long ago it was nigh impossible to disappear into the background with a broad, six-foot-plus frame. But it had never stopped him from trying. He stood in the corner of the hospital room, wishing for a way to extricate himself without calling attention to his presence. June and her folks deserved their privacy, and he had always felt as useless in family situations as a palm tree growing in the Arctic. But June had unfortunately run to her mother, and the two were embracing in the doorway. With his bulk, he could never slip past them.

Her father's gaze fell on him almost immediately. Magnus nodded sharply. The older man's eyes narrowed

as he sized him up. Although Magnus was an inch
or two taller and more than a few pounds heavier
than the former military man, he resisted the urge
to shift his weight from foot to foot like a peedie
lad called into the headmistress's office. The man's
lean frame was ramrod straight, and he exuded a
lethal confidence that time behind a desk hadn't
dulled. *Shite*, Magnus and June were barely even
snogging, and he was sweating harder than he did
after unloading a lorry full of feed.

Although June's da was shorter than Magnus,
he was still tall, and she must have inherited her
height from him. In all other aspects, she looked
like a copy of her mum. Same willowy build. Same
blond hair. Same bonny features. Same wellspring
of emotions.

The nurse bustled in. June's da fired off questions, and finally June and her mother moved
from the doorframe. Magnus muttered something,
grabbed his bag, and slipped from the room. He
headed to the small waiting area where he'd found a
coffee machine earlier. The stuff was pure rubbish,
but he poured himself another cup. He preferred tea
and generally hated the bitter American brew, but
he'd been awake for more than twenty-four hours.
Even with her family here, June still needed him.

He stretched and rolled his shoulders. The lass
thought herself responsible. She hadn't said as
much, but he'd seen it in her face as plain as a
tammie norrie's bright-orange beak. June needed
rest. Perhaps with her parents here, she'd finally
leave her nan's side. She hadn't even gone down to

the canteen for food. Instead, he'd brought it back, but she hadn't eaten much.

Settling down in a chair, Magnus first called Bowie to let him know he'd be at the hospital at least a little while longer. As soon as he hung up, he pulled out his laptop and began to write. After about a half an hour, he headed back to Clara's hospital room. It was time for June to get some sleep.

At his entrance, June and her parents looked up. Something caught in his chest at the sight of the lass. Even puggled—her eyes bleary, her normally perfect blond hair mussed, June was a bonny woman. But while she normally bubbled with energy, a weariness clung to her, and the urge to protect, to soothe roared through Magnus. He'd never experienced the like for another human. Aye, he'd felt responsibility for an orphaned lamb or a sick calf, but June was no sheep or cow. This was deeper, more demanding, this primal need to care for her.

"You n-n-n-need to rest, June," Magnus said, too focused on persuading her to take a break to worry about stuttering in front of her family.

June shook her head. "I'm fine, Magnus. You can go on home if you need to. You've been such a big help. I don't know how I would've gotten through this without you."

"You're deeskit, lass," Magnus insisted, using the Orcadian word for tired.

June's mom turned toward her and patted her hand. The gesture reminded Magnus keenly of June herself.

"June Bug, your friend is right. You're plumb tuckered out. Your daddy and I can handle things while you get some shut-eye."

June Bug. The name suited her perfectly. Magnus might even have smiled if he hadn't been so worried.

Unfortunately, June shook her head resolutely. "I don't want to leave Nana."

"We can stay at the hotel next door," Magnus said and then looked directly at June's da. "In s-s-separate rooms."

The man's expression remained neutral. June's didn't. Her bonny mouth pressed into a stubborn line. "I'm not going anywhere."

Over her head, her parents exchanged a look of concern, and Magnus saw the first crack in her da's military bearing. When he spoke, his voice was paradoxically gruff and gentle. "You're not going to do anyone any good if you collapse."

"I'm not going to collapse." June crossed her arms.

Just then, her grandmother groaned. She shifted in the bed, muttering something about fire consuming her bones. A hush descended. Tears welled in June's eyes, and she pressed her hand against her mouth. The lass was exhausted, despite her protestations.

"June," her da said in a quiet, commanding tone, "you need sleep. If anything happens, your mother and I will call you. Immediately."

"But—" June started to say before her da interrupted.

"Go to the hotel. That's an order, June Bug."

She glanced over at her mom, who gave her a sad smile. "Your daddy's right, June. A body's got to rest."

June's gaze next fell on Magnus. He didn't speak. He just extended his hand to help her up. She sighed heavily but accepted his offer. He pulled her gently to her feet. As they walked toward the door, she turned back to her parents. "Y'all will call me the moment y'all learn something or if she takes a turn. Y'all promise."

Both her parents nodded, and June finally left the room. Magnus followed her closely. The lass held herself stiffly. Too stiffly. She reminded him of a finely spun glass ornament. One wrong tap, and she could shatter.

—∿∿—

June felt like a wraith drifting aimlessly as she walked beside Magnus. Once they'd exited the hospital, he'd placed his warm hand on her back to guide her to the hotel. Folks passed, laughing, talking. Horns honked in the distance. A truck whizzed past. People jostled her as they hurried along.

Normal. Their world was normal, and June's was falling apart.

Guilt gnawed at her. She'd known her grandmother didn't seem right. True, June had taken her to the local doctor, but she should have pursued it further and taken Nan to a specialist.

Her throat thickened uncomfortably. She could feel the flood of tears inside her gaining strength. But she would not break down. Not here. Not on the street. She would wait until she was alone.

She responded to the slight pressure on her right shoulder and entered the revolving door of the hotel. Feeling hollow, she trailed after Magnus as he made his way to the reception desk. He booked two connecting rooms while June stood there, thinking of her gran's empty hazel eyes.

A sob bubbled up from deep within June, but she ruthlessly shoved it down. She thought of her nan—her real nan, the one June had known all her life. Her nan was tough, determined. She'd taught June that a lady never displays ugly emotions in public. June would *not* shame her grandmother.

She straightened her shoulders and managed to smile at the hotel staff. She kept the grin on her face as she rode the elevator with Magnus. Somehow, she even nodded politely at an elderly couple who got on after them. Magnus handed her an electronic key card when they reached their rooms. Try as she might, June couldn't get it to work. Frustrated, she jiggled the handle, resisting the urge to kick something.

Magnus appeared at her side. He gently removed the card from her hand and swiped it. He held open the door, letting her enter first. She walked into the room and just stood in the darkness. Magnus flipped on the light and removed her purse, along with the bag she was carrying of new clothes her mother had bought her at the airport gift shop. Magnus placed both satchels in the closet and turned to face June.

"Are you all right, lass, or do you want m-me to stay?"

June felt her face crumple. She flung her arms about Magnus, burying her head against his solidness as she sobbed. His strong arms enveloped her, his rough hand gently caressing her hair. "They're taking good care of your nana. Do not fash yourself."

"It's my fault!" The words burst from her along with an even stronger torrent of tears.

"There's no truth in that, lass," Magnus said as he rocked her.

"Yes. Yes, there is." June pulled back to thump her hand against her own chest. "She is my responsibility! Mine!"

Magnus shook his head and cradled her against him once more. "You took her to the doctor. What m-m-more could you have done, hen?"

"I should have demanded a blood test. Taken her for a second opinion. Done something else! She wasn't right. I *knew* she wasn't right."

"The doctor said they didn't know why her sodium d-d-dropped or how long she's had her infection," Magnus said. "She is old, June."

"I—"

"Do not go blaming yourself. There is no good in that. I know."

"But—"

Magnus cut her off by hoisting her in the air. She clung to his neck as he carried her over to the king-size bed. Instead of laying her down, he climbed onto the bed, so that she sat on his lap. He sighed and stroked her hair.

"When I was a lad, I blamed m-myself for m-my m-m-m-mum leaving."

That statement shocked the protest straight out of June. She shifted her body to gaze up at his blue eyes. She saw truth there, and a maturity that comes with making peace with a body's own personal devils. But underneath it all, she thought she glimpsed vestiges of old hurts and doubts.

"Oh, Magnus!"

"It m-means nothing to me now," he said, "but you cannot go accusing yourself of things that cannot be helped."

"But I should've…"

"'I should've not cried so m-much as a b-b-bairn. M-maybe it was my stutter. If I only would've…' Thoughts like that are a fungus, lass. They grow roots into your soul and infect it. Do not let them take ahold of you."

June pushed through her own pain to listen to Magnus's. "You weren't to blame. No matter why your mama left, it was her decision."

"Aye, lass," Magnus said. "And your nan is in the hospital because of a disease, not because of you. It is fine to feel sad and worried, but you cannot fault yourself. It helps no one, and your nan wouldn't like it."

"I'm so scared," June said as another sob hit her. "What if her mind never comes back? What if she's trapped in terror?"

Magnus pulled her even closer and rested his chin on the top of her head. "It will not be like that, lass. One doctor said they can give her medicine to calm her fears."

"What if she's never my n-n-nana again? What if…?"

Magnus stopped her with a soft, quick kiss. "Och, lass, she'll always be your nan."

June reached for him then. Reached for his solidness in a constantly shifting world. Reached for the comfort he could give. Reached for the escape he represented.

Her lips hungrily met his. She didn't know all she was demanding, but she instinctually knew he could provide it. His mouth opened under her assault as he gave her what she needed.

It was a hot, messy kiss. Lust ripped through June's already rioting emotions, sending her spinning wildly. She yearned for Magnus's heat and his strength, craving the explosive power he stirred inside her. It was like a drug that could chase away the pain. She wanted to forget.

Pushing Magnus's chest to nudge him down on the bed, she reached with her other hand for the buttons on his shirt. She needed to feel him. All of him. The skittish energy that had bounced inside her since she'd walked into her grandmother's house demanded release. A release only he could give.

Magnus broke their kiss. June let out a frustrated sound, which caused him to groan. "I know, lass. I know. But this isn't right. You aren't yourself, and I'll n-not be t-t-taking advantage."

"Maybe I don't want to be myself right now," June said stubbornly.

That triggered a low chuckle from Magnus. He lay back on the bed, propping himself up on his elbows, his shirt halfway unbuttoned. The position further pulled at the fabric, revealing his toned chest and just a hint of his six-pack. At the sight, liquid desire pooled inside June. Unfortunately, she didn't have much time to appreciate the sight before Magnus climbed to his feet. "Get some sleep, lass, and then we'll see what you want."

Sweetness stole through June, tempering the maddening passion. She smiled at Magnus as she tried to balance herself after losing all equilibrium. "I didn't know you were such a gentleman."

Magnus gave her one of his rare smiles as he lifted her into the air and gently placed her on her feet. "Nay, I am merely an honest crofter."

"Maybe too honest."

To her shock, he bent and kissed her forehead. He pulled back, surprise darkening his blue eyes. Before she could comment, he jerked his head in the direction of the bathroom. "Have a bath, lass."

"Are you saying I smell, Magnus Gray?" she teased, feeling a little more like herself although she missed his touch.

A half smile appeared beneath his neatly trimmed beard. "Warm water soothes all manners of ills, hen, especially after a long day. And you have had several of them all together."

"I suppose I can't interest you in accompanying me." She plucked at the collar of his flannel shirt. Now that he stood, it no longer gaped open, but she could still see a swath of his chest.

Affection glowed in his blue eyes as he ruefully shook his head. "I'm afraid I must say no tonight."

"Oh well, you can't blame a girl for trying," June said. But Magnus was right. A shower would do her good. Although it wouldn't be nearly as satisfying as sex with him, it wouldn't leave any regrets either. When she and Magnus finally came together, she didn't want it to be because she needed to forget. She wanted it to be because they both wished to remember.

Chapter 10

Magnus felt his shoulder muscles uncoil as the bathroom door shut. The lass had nearly killed him. He'd never experienced this much need for a woman. He'd wanted her so badly, his body nearly shook. But this wasn't the right time. June wasn't ganting for a night of fun. She was looking for a way out of the pain, and he'd be a manky bastard if he took advantage.

She wasn't herself. He'd watched her closely as they'd walked to the hotel, and she'd moved as stiffly as a sleepwalker. The spark that was June had been banked. He'd lived in numbness long enough to recognize it in others. And with a lass as vibrant as June, it wasn't hard to detect.

Magnus didn't want her returning to an empty hotel room after her bath, so he settled into the sole armchair, opened his laptop, and started typing. Unlike with his last couple books, the writing flowed from him as easily as it had in the beginning of his career. But this story was different from his debut. That had been about purging the past. Nor was the current manuscript an adventure like the second memoir. This book was quieter, and to his surprise, more humor crept into his vignettes. A playfulness permeated his tales about little Sorcha, Frida, and the prairie-dog colony. Writing had always been a need for him, an urge to put words on paper. But lately it hadn't been about just filling an instinctual demand. Instead, he'd taken more delight in the process.

And while sitting in the hospital, with his shoulder pressed against June's, he'd started to include a few passages about his stutter. It had felt strange typing those words and watching them appear on the screen, yet not terrible. Not like he would have imagined. Perhaps he'd drawn strength from June's silent courage as she'd held herself together while her grandmother lay so still across from them. He had never imagined a hospital as an ideal writing location, but it was a place of extremes. A place of birth and death. A place where a man, faced with the fragility of life, found himself contemplating his own.

Magnus heard the water turn off, and he tried not to imagine June standing in the shower with beads of water clinging to her. Her body would be warm from the hot spray, her muscles pliant. He imagined pulling her against him, feeling her soft, smooth skin.

Baws. He had a fair stauner now. Aye, no denying it, he wanted the lass with a fierceness he'd never experienced before.

He managed to shift his laptop just in time to hide his erection when June walked back into the room. She wore pink flannel pajamas covered in cupcakes. That should have dampened his lust, but instead he only noticed how cute her toes looked peeping out from under the ridiculous ensemble.

June smiled. "I know they're old-fashioned, but I've always loved a pair of jammies. My mama found these at the airport. Aren't they just the most darling things?"

Magnus jerked his chin in reluctant agreement.

They'd look absurd on any other adult, but on June, they held a kittenish sex appeal. Neither observation seemed appropriate, though, especially when June was so pleased with her mum's purchase. She needed something silly, something comforting, and Magnus would not ruin it.

"If you're ready for sleep, I'll head to my own room," Magnus said.

June nodded and sat down on the edge of the massive king-size bed. She smiled, but it didn't have the brilliance of her normal grin. She looked a little lost, and Magnus's heart wrenched. He didn't want to leave the lass, he realized, and not just because she looked forlorn. For a man who loved privacy, June's presence had become unexpectedly but undeniably important to him.

Bending down, Magnus brushed a kiss against her forehead. Again, not like him at all. He wasn't a tender man, at least not when it came to humans.

"*Caidil gu là*," he told her softly.

"What does that mean?" she asked.

"Sleep until day," he translated.

"Magnus?"

"Aye?"

"Thanks. For everything."

"It was nothing, lass."

"I couldn't have gotten through this without you." June's green eyes glistened in the dim light, and Magnus felt an answering pang deep inside himself.

"Aye, hen, you could've. You're a strong woman, June Winters."

Her smile turned shaky, and she bobbed her head. He turned to leave, but as soon as his hand touched the doorknob, he heard his name again. He turned to see June watching him, her eyes wide and earnest.

"Can you stay, Magnus?" she asked softly. "I don't want to be alone."

Auld Clootie himself couldn't have dragged Magnus from that hotel room. If June needed him, he would stay. He nodded, and in three strides, he returned to her side. Cupping her cheek in his hand, he gazed down at her bonny face. Even tired, exhausted, and dressed in those ridiculous pajamas, she was a braw lass.

"Would it be all right if I had a bath first, hen? I'm manky."

She nodded, and he headed to the bathroom. He showered quickly, then toweling himself off, he reached into his bag where he'd stuffed one change of clothes. He normally wore only boxers to bed, but that didn't seem appropriate tonight.

When he reentered the room, June had dimmed the lights, leaving only the one by the bedside on. She lay on her side, tucked under the covers, but she'd left plenty of room and even pulled back the duvet for him. He stopped, riveted by the sight. It was so welcoming. His heart, which had been receiving a workout these past few days, ached again. But this was a different kind of pang. A sweet one. A comforting one. A dangerous one.

June shifted then and glanced over her shoulder. Her eyes were bleary, her face tight with strain. "I can't sleep. My mind's going faster than a runaway locomotive chasing down a mountain."

And with that, the familiar twinge of pain

returned. He crawled into bed and drew her close. He
brushed a kiss on her temple. She sighed and snuggled
in to him, the soft curve of her bum brushing against
his boabie. Lust speared him, but he battled it back.
Unfortunately, that allowed the softer need to take hold.
He'd never yearned like this before. Ever.

Fluffy cocked his head as he studied Honey. She did
not seem her normal self lately. First, she had cuddled
against him, and for the last few days, she'd made no
effort to escape their enclosure. He wondered if it had
anything to do with the disappearance of the Giant One
and the Blond One. Honey seemed to delight in harass-
ing the two bipeds.

Fluffy did not like seeing Honey out of sorts, so he'd
formed a plan. When Honey disappeared into her den,
Fluffy dashed to her food dish and snatched a piece of
meat. Honey's head instantly popped into view. Turning,
he scampered out of their enclosure, and she followed.
He headed to the nearest garbage can where he dropped
the food.

She skidded to a stop and watched him suspiciously.
When he didn't move, she slowly approached and
snatched the meat. Before she could dart away, Fluffy
knocked over a garbage can. Honey started at the clang.
Then she smiled her toothy grin.

That evening, they knocked one can over after
another. They did not leave a single one unturned.

When they returned to their enclosure, they did something honey badgers rarely did...they snuggled against
each other instead of immediately going their separate

ways. Fluffy smiled. Sometimes, it was good to have a partner in crime.

———⁓———

June woke in a circle of warmth. For one wonderful moment, she simply luxuriated in the feel of Magnus's body pressed against hers. Then, all too soon, her memories crashed into her like a landslide. She jerked into a sitting position, jarring Magnus awake.

He groaned and rolled over. "What time is it, hen?"

She glanced at the clock. "Three."

"Go back to sleep. We'll go see your nan first thing in the morn."

She flopped back down, but despite the fact she'd barely rested in days, sleep evaded her. Instead, she thought about her nan's eyes...and the empty terror there. A sob tore through her. Although she tried to muffle it with her pillow, the bed shook from its force.

She felt Magnus's hand on her shoulder. He made a low murmur in the back of his throat as he rolled her against him.

"Magnus?" June asked softly.

"Aye?"

"I want to be with you."

"It's your grief talking, lass."

"Yes"—June wouldn't deny that—"but not the way you think. It's not like before."

His whole body went stiff. "What do you m-m-mean?"

"I'm making the decision with my head," June said. "It's not so much to escape as it is to hold on to something good."

"Are you certain, hen?" Magnus's voice sounded taut, like a bowstring being drawn back.

She nodded. "And it is *you* who I want. There's something about you, Magnus. You have this amazing quiet strength, and I need that right now."

Magnus's breath caught noticeably at her words. His rough fingers brushed against her cheek as he pushed back a tendril of her hair. "I'm not one for small towns, lass."

"And I'm not planning to leave Sagebrush, but I'm not asking for forever, Magnus. I'm asking for tonight."

He swallowed, and in the dim light seeping through the crack in the curtains, she watched his throat work. "Are you absolutely sure? This is what you desire?"

His chivalrous streak touched her. She had no doubt he wanted her, not with the evidence digging into her thigh. And, even in the semidarkness, his eyes fairly glowed as they hungrily watched her.

She didn't answer his questions with more words. Instead, she brushed her lips against his. He groaned. Deep and low. The sound curled inside her and settled low in her belly. She deepened the kiss. In response, he slanted his mouth over hers as he eased her back onto the bed. Already she could feel the pressure of his weight, and her body thrilled at the contact. His mix of power and tenderness made a heady elixir, and June wanted nothing more than to get drunk on it.

Her fingers sank into his unruly curls, and she marveled at their softness. He framed her face with his hands as he slowly and thoroughly plundered her mouth.

A kiss had never consumed her senses like this. Her whole body hummed like a tuning fork, and they'd barely started.

And still Magnus did not break the kiss. He seemed content to drive her slowly mad with his tongue and lips. She moaned against him as her body instinctually rose to meet his. He lowered himself, allowing her to feel his bulk. But aside from that concession, he kept his mouth firmly locked on hers.

He kissed with a fierce tenderness that managed to possess her more than any crushing demand ever could. She swore he coaxed sensations from every cell until she was saturated with pleasure. His musky scent filled her nostrils. Both their breathing grew labored as his chest pressed against hers.

Just as June felt pulled as tautly as a fiddle string ready to snap, Magnus's lips left her mouth and trailed along the side of her throat. His caress remained unhurried, his tongue darting out. Licking. Teasing. Enticing.

June began to writhe as glorious need sparked through her body, her nerve endings sizzling with anticipation. Her body yearned for him. A moan escaped her lips. Finally, his hand slid under the flannel of her pajamas and captured her breast. She whimpered as Magnus circled her nipple with his thumb, his rough calluses at odds with the gentleness of his touch. With his other hand, he unbuttoned her top. When he fumbled, she moved to help him. As soon as he pushed the fabric aside, she yanked at his T-shirt. He rose on his knees to strip it off. He didn't reach for his fly, though. Instead, he sank back down, his mouth closing over one of her nipples, his hand over the other. If she'd thought he'd been thorough with her mouth, it was nothing like his attention to her breasts.

Helpless against the pleasure pulsating through her at an erotic tempo, she clung to his back. Her fingers slid over his taut muscles. They bunched and extended as he altered his position to better explore her body. His skin felt like warm silk and just as decadent. Near his shoulder blade, June unexpectedly brushed against a hard, rough patch. Scar tissue. Her hand lingered there as she wondered about the old hurt. Magnus's tongue curled around her nipple, teasing it gently. A spear of lust shot straight to her core with sizzling accuracy. She forgot about his shoulder in the explosion of pleasure and need.

He moved his attention lower as he hooked his finger around the elastic waistband of her pajama bottoms. He pulled them down in one swift motion. Rocking back on his heels, he stared at her in wonder. Watching him cockily, she reached over and flicked on the light. She wanted to see his eyes as they ran over her naked length.

He did not disappoint. The blue in his irises darkened into a cobalt so deep they practically glowed. She basked in his admiration.

"Aye, you're a bonny lass, June Winters. A very bonny lass."

She smiled and ran her hand down his muscular chest, loving the feel of his ridges. There was so much beauty in the sheer, raw power of his body. If she had Katie's artistic talents, she would sketch him like this. Instead, she settled on memorizing the image of him on his knees, straddling her, his eyes burning, his muscles glistening with sweat.

"You're not so bad yourself," she told him. The glint of surprise and doubt in his eyes shocked her. How could he not be aware of his own magnetism?

She reached for his fly. "It's my turn for the full show."

He obliged her, quickly shucking his pants and then his boxers. When his erection bobbed free, she didn't try to hide her interest. That part was as big as the rest of him. She reached out and stroked his length with one finger. At the contact, his eyes fluttered shut, and she could see the tendons flex in his neck.

"I'm ready for you," June told him.

Magnus drew a shaky breath and then said, "Nay, lass. Not yet."

Then he bent his head and licked her, his thumbs stroking her inner thighs. She cried out as wave after wave of pleasure coursed through her. He entered her in one smooth stroke. She gripped his strong shoulders as he began to move, slow and steady. The delicious friction sent sparks spiraling through her. Her fingers dug into Magnus's skin. She began to buck against him, demanding him to move faster, harder. Instead, he maintained his teasing rhythm, until their breaths came in short staccato huffs.

Finally, he began to pump in earnest. Their bodies slid against each other. One of his large hands massaged her breast, heightening her pleasure as he supported his weight with his other arm.

She came first, the glorious sensation reverberating

through her already sensitized body. She'd never experienced an orgasm this powerful, this deliciously complete. As she lay gasping, trying to absorb the sheer pleasure rioting through her, Magnus threw back his head. And as he exploded inside her, his body shook. June used the last of her strength to gather him close so she could feel his massive frame tremble against her slighter one. She'd fantasized about this, but the reality was more intensely erotic than she'd even imagined.

A smile drifted over June's lips as she lay under Magnus, fully and utterly sated. This round had been about her. The next one would be for him.

———ᵥᵥᵥ———

Magnus propped himself up as he watched June luxuriate under him, a pleased expression on her bonny face. Her green eyes had gone soft and languid as she studied him from under her eyelashes. Moving as slowly and deliberately as a sleepy gray seal, she reached up and traced shapes on his chest with her index finger.

"Ooo, I liked that, Magnus Gray," she purred, her voice as thick and sweet as honey from the Lowlands.

Satisfied male pride coursed through him. He'd set out to give June pleasure and to relax her. It appeared he'd succeeded admirably at both. Not that it had been a hardship. June made love like she did everything—openly and honestly, without restraint or subterfuge. She hadn't tried to hide her body's natural reaction to his touch. Instead, she'd let him witness every sensual gasp and moan. It had nearly driven him to lose control, but he'd managed to hold back until pleasure had saturated both of them.

"Good," Magnus told her.

Suddenly, a wicked gleam lit her hazy green eyes, and her smile curled into a naughty grin. Her hand skimmed along his chest, dipping lower until she cupped him. Her gaze still locked on his, she began to fondle him, her fingers lightly brushing his boabie in an erotic dance. Generally, he never allowed a woman to play with him for long. Even in intercourse, he didn't like to be touched, except for the main event. With June, though, he couldn't get enough of her caresses.

His arms began to shake from the exertion of holding himself up and from the havoc her touch was playing with his nervous system. Unable to maintain his position, he rolled them both over. A cheeky look flashed over June's face. In one fluid movement, she sat back on her heels, giving him a full view of her lovely breasts. They were the perfect size to hold in a man's hand. Pert and bouncy. She was a braw, lush lass, every bit of her.

Between the sight of her glorious body and her long exploration of his cock, his boabie began to stir. She grinned with a confidence that charmed him as much as her body aroused. The lass was magic. Pure magic.

"Somebody's waking up," she said.

"You're pure t-t-temptation, hen."

He'd never stuttered while boffing, but then again, he normally didn't do much talking in bed. To his surprise, the verbal slip didn't puncture the haze of pleasure surrounding them. June just looked delighted by his comment, and he reached up to cup her face. Tenderness swelled inside his heart. He couldn't get his fill of this lass, even with her naked body astride his, her hand around his cock.

"Get ready," she said.

He brushed his hand down her back, feeling the delicate curve of her spine. "For what, lass?"

She gave him a saucy wink. "For this."

Then that bonny pink mouth closed around his prick. He moaned aloud. His eyes threatened to roll back in his head, but he did not let them. He'd dreamed about making love to June for too long not to watch. She kept her eyes trained on his, her boldness nearly driving him mad. Lust darkened her irises, and they shone like gems. Without a trace of self-consciousness, she did not break their gaze as she licked and teased him. His hands fisted into her soft, blond hair, and despite the mad want coursing through him, he made sure to keep his grip light and gentle.

Och, the lass was going to slay him with her mouth. When he could no longer withstand it, he allowed his eyelids to drift close.

"Lass," he said between gritted teeth.

"Yes, darlin'?"

"Would you like to ride?"

She laughed then. The sound was bright, and triumphant peace stole through him. After all she'd been through the last few days, he'd managed to coax a little mirth from her.

"Why, yes! I think I would."

He lifted her, settling her on him. She gasped and then wiggled. He forced his eyes open. A slow smile drifted across his face as he watched her adjust to his girth. She moved experimentally at first and then faster. He placed his hands on her hips, feeling the soft swell of her bum as she guided them both into oblivion. It was frighteningly easy…surrendering to this lass.

Afterward they snuggled together, both breathing heavily. She curled into him, fitting perfectly as he draped his arm over her side. It was strange, lying so close to another human and not feeling trapped. Instead, a peace slipped through Magnus.

Sleep claimed the lass, but he remained awake. He carefully lifted his head to check on her. June even slept with a slight smile on her face. At the sight, Magnus couldn't help but grin. Even in the midst of her sorrow, she exuded a lightness that the darkness inside him craved.

He reached over and flicked off the light. As he settled back down, June nestled close. When her body slid into place, she sighed deeply in her sleep.

"*Caidil gu là*," he whispered softly.

He still didn't drift off immediately. Instead, he lay thinking about the trust in the lass's embrace. Even though he'd revealed more of himself to June than he'd ever shown to any woman, he'd still held back. But June hadn't. Not in the slightest. She possessed such an open heart. But he never would. Something was broken inside him that would never be fixed. Reclusiveness ran in his da's family, and Magnus had taught himself never to need another.

He just hoped he didn't hurt June. He wouldn't want to dampen the light that made her unique.

Chapter 11

THE DAYS BLENDED TOGETHER AS JUNE PRACTICALLY LIVED at the hospital over the next week. Katie had driven up despite June's protests. She had, at least, listened to June and hadn't entered the hospital. Instead, the two of them had eaten lunch. It had been one of June's few escapes from the endless waiting and worrying.

Their other best friend from college, Josh, had called from San Francisco several times. He'd offered to fly out but decided to wait until her folks left and she needed more help. She'd told him it wasn't necessary, but Josh had reminded her that Katie and she were the only family he'd ever had. If there was a crisis, he'd be there. And, he'd pointed out, Nan had always baked his favorite pie when he was in town.

With August deployed, he couldn't come, but he'd promised to head to Sagebrush the next time he had any leave. June had tried to place her laptop on Nan's hospital tray so her gran could video chat with August, but that had only frightened the elderly woman. She'd glanced at June, her hazel eyes wide with confusion, as she'd asked if it was a bomb and did June know how to defuse it?

Her grandmother had become combative with the nurses and swore they meant to kill her. She calmed slightly with family members in the room, so June and her parents had taken rotating shifts. June felt as worn down as an old grinding stone, the friction chipping away at her little by little.

What made it all bearable was Magnus. He'd become a surprisingly constant presence. Although he'd driven back to Sagebrush a few times to help Bowie and to temporarily close up the tea shop, he'd always returned. Today, he'd brought her videos of little Savannah and Sorcha along with more of her clothes.

June was lying next to Magnus on the hotel bed, her head resting on his shoulder. Using his free hand, Magnus swiped his phone to pull up a clip of the little camel. Despite the sorrow clinging to June, she found herself laughing as the calf tried to suckle the phone. Gums, lips, and one giant brown eye filled the screen. First came sucking sounds and then frustrated grunts of disappointment.

"She has her mum's brains," Magnus said, and June lightly bumped him on his shoulder.

"That's not nice, darlin'," she scolded. Unconcerned, Magnus shrugged and selected another video.

In this one, Abby appeared first. She held the phone with one hand as she waved with the other. Her voice was bright and filled with the endless energy of youth. "Hi, June! Sorry to hear about your nana. Sorcha and I miss both of you. So does Savannah."

"The lassie insisted on sending you a m-m-message," Magnus explained as he paused the clip. "She's got a soft heart."

"She takes after her father," June said.

"Aye. He's a good man."

Magnus restarted the recording, and Abby's voice again filled the hotel room. "You *have* to see what Sorcha's doing now." The camera panned the zoo's nursery, and the little bear crawled to the camera, her movements steadier and more confident than before. She batted the cell phone with her paw. Her black pad covered the screen, and then her nose appeared. At the sound of Sorcha's snuffles, June chuckled again.

"She's as curious as a cat after a bird," June said.

"Aye," Magnus agreed. "We're p-p-planning on introducing her to Frida soon. There's a risk, and she's just a peedie thing, so Bowie is only going to let Frida smell and see her. Since the grizzly tolerates the honey badgers, he's hoping she'll take to Sorcha. The wee beastie needs the companionship of other b-bears."

"Will you tape the meeting for your vlog?"

"Aye, lass. I was hoping we could record the audio t-together, even if we have to do it here at the hotel. Katie said she could layer my voice over the video."

It struck June then that Magnus would have had very little time to do his vlog in the past week. Plus, she hadn't been there to help him. "Heavens to Betsy, I just realized I haven't thought about your videos for days. Did you record one this week?"

"I asked Bowie to guest star for m-me," Magnus said.

"I'm sorry I haven't been able to help."

"Don't fash yourself. I told my agent and editor it was a family emergency. Since I don't have any myself, I thought it was a fine time to use that excuse."

June turned toward him in surprise. Even though they currently shared a hotel room and had begun sleeping together on a regular basis, she realized she knew very little about Magnus aside from what she'd read in his writings. Despite being first-person accounts, his memoirs actually revealed very few details about his life outside of his interaction with the animals and the environment.

"Have you cut all ties with your daddy then?" June asked. Although she believed in families sticking together, in this case it might be best if Magnus didn't have contact with his father.

Magnus stared ahead, studying one of the innocuous but inoffensive prints that hotels hung in guest rooms.

"M-my d-d-da made it clear that I was as good as d-d-d-dead to him if I left the croft. As you can see, I left."

Magnus spoke the words without any feeling, but his stutter had noticeably worsened. June reached for him, almost expecting to find his skin as cold as his words. It wasn't, but he didn't turn at the contact either. There was a hollowness in him, and in this moment, it threatened to swallow June too. She didn't like to see him in pain, and she had a feeling Magnus's calm demeanor hid a black hole full of hurt.

"He's never tried to reach out to you then, even with the success of your books?"

Magnus's laugh was bitter and short. "Nay, lass. But I'm m-m-m-much better without the b-b-b-b-bastard in my life. He's not the forgiving sort, and he wasn't that p-p-p-p-pleasant of company to b-b-b-b-begin with."

"Was it hard? Growing up on an island alone with him?" June asked quietly, dreading the answer, but needing to hear it.

"Aye, lass." Magnus turned to face her again, his blue eyes still dead. "But I d-d-d-don't want to t-t-t-t-talk about it."

"Talking sometimes helps."

The laugh he gave was short and bitter. He brushed his hand along her cheek. "Lass, I know you like to b-b-blether, but havering never fixed a problem."

"What about your mama?" June asked.

Magnus stiffened, his body taut. "I have not spoken to her since I was a p-p-p-p-peedie laddie. I h-h-h-hardly remember the woman."

"Has she tried to contact you?"

Magnus glanced away, but not before she saw the answer in his face. She reached out and brushed her hand down his bicep. "What did she say?"

"I wouldn't know, lass. I never open her letters."

"She sends letters, not emails?" June asked in surprise.

Magnus shrugged. "We're a bit old-fashioned on T-T-T-Tammay. It is not unusual."

"But she doesn't live there anymore," June pointed out.

When Magnus spoke, she could hear a thread of frustration in his voice. "Aye, but she was raised there. It's a place that gets in the blood and stays there even if her folks originated from the Highlands."

"Maybe she sent the letters so you would know who the sender was," June said. "It could be she wanted to give you the option of reading them or tossing them."

Magnus turned back to June, his eyes not lifeless anymore. Deep emotion burned inside them. He might have resolved things with his father, but not with his mother. "I don't give a shite, June. I don't want to argue with you either. Can you just let it be?"

She would. For now.

"Okay."

The blue fire in his eyes immediately banked. Instead, a fond smile drifted over his features. "You fash yourself too much, lass."

Then he turned and kissed her before returning to type on the laptop perched on his legs. He was on a writing streak… At least that's what he claimed. Much to June's annoyance, he wouldn't let her take a peek at any of his work.

Settling back against the pillows she'd arranged behind her back, she reached for the paperback she'd picked up at the hospital gift shop. But she couldn't concentrate on the words. For once, though, it wasn't because of worry for her nan. She was thinking about Magnus.

No one should live without family. No one. It just wasn't right. No wonder the man kept his emotions bottled up tighter than a good bourbon.

His daddy sounded like a terrible person, but she wasn't so sure about his mama. It wasn't right to abandon a child, but maybe the woman had thought she had no choice. What if she'd tried to see her son, but his daddy wouldn't let her? Magnus had said he was the unforgiving type.

June spared a glance at Magnus. He looked so stoic, sitting there, tapping away at his keyboard. Although Magnus was one of the kindest men she'd ever met, he had a stubborn streak wider than the

Mississippi during the spring melt. He wouldn't pardon mistakes easily either. But that only hurt him.

June thought about those unopened letters from his mama, and she couldn't help but wonder what they contained. Maybe they could have helped Magnus. He said he'd blamed himself for her departure from Tammay. Although he'd said he'd made peace with her leaving, he'd never actually said whether he still believed he'd chased her away. Maybe his mama's words would ease some unresolved pain. Maybe the woman felt as alone as her son.

June straightened. She needed to do some digging on Magnus's mama. She didn't like to see things broken that could be fixed. And it would give her a nice distraction from worrying about her nan.

Honey heard a snuffling sound outside her burrow. It was Fluffy. She debated about chasing him away.

His nose appeared at the opening to her den. She lifted her head and debated. With one swift strike of her claw, she could send him yelping back to his own sleeping quarters.

But he had been amusing lately, and she hadn't minded the times they'd fallen asleep pressed against each other. She had not experienced any other fun since the Giant One disappeared along with the Blond One. Perhaps Fluffy was not that bad.

Fluffy's eyes came into view next. He looked hopeful. Honey watched him carefully, but she did not snarl. Instead, she moved to allow him to enter her burrow. It was time to allow him to stay the night. She was ready for a new adventure.

———∿∿∿———

"In the wild, adult b-b-b-bears, especially the males, are known to kill cubs. It is one of the many d-d-dangers a young polar bear faces after she leaves the den with her m-mum. Now our wee Sorcha here isn't that old. She's about two months old and isn't even steady on her legs. Yet she's about to meet a full-grown b-b-bear who isn't her m-m-mum. And it's not even a polar bear but a grizzly…"

"Ooo, I like that," June said as she hit the pause button on her tablet, which they were using to record Magnus's voice. Later, Katie would synthesize his narration with the footage of the bears' meeting. When June also paused the silent video playing on Magnus's phone, the image on the screen froze, leaving a bright-eyed Sorcha staring up at them. The little tyke had certainly become more alert since June had seen her over a week ago. "But the meeting went fine, right?"

"Just watch, lass," Magnus said with a smile. "You'll miss the whole experience if I give away the end. And you're interrupting my narration."

June scowled. "It isn't polite to keep a lady in suspense."

"I'm a writer, June. That's my way."

"Well, then hurry up and finish."

"You're the one who stopped m-me. I was going along fine."

June lightly bopped him on his arm and realized abruptly how normal she felt. Only Magnus could tease her into momentarily forgetting the worry clawing at her. Although antianxiety medicine had helped with Nan's terrors, her grandmother remained in a haze nothing penetrated. Slowly, her body had fought off the UTI and her sodium levels had returned to normal, but *she* hadn't.

"Och, lass, there you go worrying again," Magnus said. "Just listen to the tale." Leaning forward, he turned on both the video and the recorder. Little Sorcha continued to explore her carrier as Magnus and Bowie transferred her to Frida's den. Her tiny claws grabbed at the sides, scraping and testing it. Then she stuck her snout through the opening, her black nose wiggling. Satisfied with the scents she detected, she began to gum the metal.

Then, a loud snuffling sound came from the outdoor enclosure. The cub froze in midchew, her black eyes huge. The camera panned upward to show Frida sniffing at the closed gate separating her outdoor enclosure from the indoor facility.

"As you can see, we took p-p-precautions during this original meeting. If Frida t-t-tolerates our young cub, it will give Sorcha the chance to interact with another bear and learn important skills. Even though Sorcha won't return to the wild, socialization is still important to her well-being. Sagebrush Zoo doesn't have another p-p-p-polar bear, but they are a subspecies of grizzlies like Frida. In fact, the two types of bruins have successfully b-b-b-bred and produced offspring. But will this elderly beastie accept the wee whalp?"

Frida sniffed the air ominously, and June clutched at her neck. She couldn't stand the tension. She turned off both devices.

"I feel like a bug trapped in a web watching a spider approach," June said. "What happens?"

Magnus chuckled and laid his hand over hers. "Are you a feartie, June?"

"No," she said indignantly.

"Just watch."

She sighed and sank back against the headboard. Magnus restarted the video, and June leaned forward. Bowie and Magnus cautiously moved the cub's crate closer to the gate. Frida turned in their direction, her muzzle sticking through the metal bars as she smelled Sorcha's scent. Her less rheumy eye latched onto the little bear. She stilled. Then she began to claw and dig at the gate while making a noise halfway between a growl and a moan. When that didn't work, she pushed against the steel grate with her large body.

"Is she trying to reach Sorcha to attack or take care of her?" June asked, forgetting to turn off the recorder. Realizing her mistake, she clasped her hand over her mouth. Luckily, Katie would be able to edit out her exclamation, but she hated disrupting Magnus's voice-over, especially when he was doing such a good job.

The elderly bear soon exhausted herself. Instead of wandering back to her favorite rock, she lay down with a sigh, her eyes trained on Sorcha. The camera zoomed in on her face, and June couldn't stop her *aww*. The affection and protectiveness in Frida's eyes were undeniable.

"The zookeeper, Bowie Wilson, considered this meeting a success. We will still proceed carefully as we work to introduce these two b-b-bruins, but it seems for now Sorcha may have a bear m-m-mum after all, and Sylvia, the capybara, can get some well-earned relaxation before a new orphan arrives at the zoo."

Magnus finished, reclining back in the bed. June clapped her hands. "Oooo, I love it, Magnus. Your fans will just eat it up."

"So will my editor."

June paused as she reached forward to touch Magnus's bicep. She was trying her darndest not to push him about his disfluency, but she *had* promised to help him. They'd grown closer—much closer—in the past couple weeks, and he'd become more relaxed in her presence. She hoped that meant he'd let her help him more.

"Would you like to work on your stuttering?"

Magnus paused, his blue eyes flitting to hers. He seemed to wage an internal debate before he nodded solemnly. "Aye, lass."

"I have a file of our first attempt to record your vlog," June said, pulling it up on her tablet.

"And why is that, lass?"

"I promise I didn't look at it. I kept it in case it would come in handy. Think of me like a coach going over old plays."

"You can't help but help people, can you?"

June shook her head. "It's who I am."

"Aye, it is," Magnus said with a soft grin. "Well, if you're going to m-m-make me view that shite, put it on."

As the video played, June laid her hand over Magnus's. Self-analysis wasn't easy for anyone, and she knew his disfluency made him uncomfortable. Each time he watched himself during a hard block, he visibly winced.

"I d-d-didn't know I jerked that b-b-b-badly,"

Magnus said as he scowled at the screen. "M-m-my d-d-d-da always did say I looked like a numptie."

Pain for Magnus lacerated June. She was beginning to form an intense dislike for his father. His daddy might be the one person June could actually hate, and she didn't believe in that emotion. Knowing any attempt at comfort would only conversely make Magnus *un*comfortable, June spoke matter-of-factly. "It's not unusual for people with disfluency to develop secondary behaviors. August used to tap his thigh with his finger, and I remember my speech pathologist telling me not to pull my ear."

"So, I need to keep myself steady then, lass?"

"It would help," she said. "Do you want to say one of the words you usually block on? There's a mirror right across from us so you can see what you're doing."

Magnus complied, and they both watched his articulators carefully. She wasn't trained in speech pathology, so it was harder for her to pick up on the subtle tensions in his body. Flashbacks to her own therapy sessions popped into her head as she remembered trying to understand what she was doing when she spoke. It was challenging, being so in tune with her speaking habits.

"I think I hold my chest tight, and my tongue gets snirled against the roof of my mouth," Magnus finally concluded.

"I remember my speech pathologist telling me to focus more on the sides of my chest out at the ribs. If you concentrate on the sternum, you're not drawing in enough breath."

"I'll try that, lass."

"Do you think this helped?" June asked, feeling uncharacteristically nervous.

"Aye, lass, I do," Magnus said.

—⁓—

"So, there's no instruction manual?" Bowie asked Magnus the next day as he stared at the box of parts spread on the floor of June's tea shop.

Magnus shook his head. Perhaps he should have bought a new stair lift rather than finding a used one on the internet. The doctors planned to release Clara Winters in a couple days, and June was worried about maneuvering her grandmother up and down the narrow flight of stairs leading to June's flat above the tea shop. Instead, she and her da were planning on setting up a room for her nan in the sizable pantry off the scullery, which meant June was planning to sleep on the floor.

Magnus didn't like the idea of June bunking down in a sleeping bag each night, even if she was going to buy a piece of foam to put under it. That's why he'd purchased the stair lift without telling June. If he'd asked, she never would have let him pay for it. His royalties were just sitting in the bank, and he was a man of simple tastes. His only luxury was his small London flat, and he didn't even live in a very posh neighborhood.

He'd told June and her father he'd move the boxes from the back room and put them in the attic with Bowie's help. The two of them had already done that, since June's nan would need a place to sit during the day. Along with hanging light-blue curtains on the small window, they'd even put a fresh coat of paint on the walls, which Katie had picked out. Now, they were tackling the stair lift…or at least trying to tackle it.

Magnus shifted through the supplies once again. Nothing. He shrugged and pulled out his mobile. He looked up the manufacturer's website. Luckily, they had instructions and a handy video. He held the phone out to Bowie and said, "Looks easy enough."

Bowie raised an eyebrow. "If you say so."

Magnus chuckled. He'd been doing a lot more of that lately. He blamed June. "T-t-t-try keeping an old tractor from the thirties running in the dreich climate that is B-B-B-Bjaray."

"Dreich?" Bowie asked.

"D-D-D-Damp," Magnus explained. He'd gotten accustomed to June understanding his slang. Normally, he tried to limit it around the Yanks.

"Remind me to have you take a look at my old truck," Bowie said with a smile.

Magnus snorted as he grabbed the tape measure from the floor. "I've seen it. Even I'm not that good."

"Har. Har," Bowie replied.

The installation went surprisingly smoothly. Magnus liked working with the other man. Although Bowie wasn't as quiet as Magnus, he wasn't a talker either. They made an efficient team with Magnus mostly directing and Bowie helping. When he'd screwed in the last bolt, Magnus stood and wiped his hands. He glanced at Bowie. "Do you want to give it a go, or should I?"

Bowie bent a little and gestured toward the seat like a maître d' at a high-end restaurant. "Be my guest."

Magnus sat down and pressed the button. As expected, the chair moved at a glacial rate, but it got the job done. Magnus rode it up and down a few times, but couldn't find any glitches. Satisfied, he brought it back to the bottom and climbed off.

"So, you learned how to do all this stuff back on the farm?" Bowie asked.

"And as a roughneck," Magnus said. "Anything that b-b-broke, we fixed. The wind in the Arctic will freeze your arse off in a second, so you learn to be quick."

Bowie was quiet as they both packed away their tools. When the zookeeper lifted his head, his expression was serious. "It's nice what you're doing. It will mean a lot to June and Clara."

Magnus nodded brusquely and then concentrated on organizing his wrenches neatly in his toolbox. His da had been a meticulous man, and Magnus had learned early to return everything to its rightful place. The simple task also gave him an excuse not to respond to Bowie's compliment. Praise had always made him as uneasy as a guillemot protecting its nest from circling gulls.

When they finished the job, Magnus made one quick sweep over the stairs to make sure they hadn't missed anything. He flicked off the light. Bowie exited first, and Magnus locked the back door with the key June had given him.

When he turned, he found Bowie studying him. "So, you and June, huh?"

Magnus froze. He hated personal questions, but Bowie didn't seem like he was pressing for gossip to spread like manure in spring. Instead, it felt like something a friend would ask. Magnus glanced at Bowie sideways, debating whether to answer. He was a Gray, and Grays were notorious loners. His school-mates had never accepted him. The silent laddie from Bjaray with a hermit for a da and a mum who didn't care enough to stay. The whole isle of Tammay had considered him an odd sort from a long line of odd sorts.

When he'd signed on as a roughneck, he'd learned to live in close quarters. He'd gotten along well enough with his bunkmates, but he'd never become one of them. He'd kept to himself, clicking away at his keyboard when he wasn't working. They'd called him the Scrivener and mostly let him be. Since then, he'd lived alone. First in Glasgow and then in London. He hadn't wanted or needed companionship. Now, June had wormed her way into his life. After spending the last week sleeping with her, he couldn't deny they'd formed some sort of relationship.

And now this. This gesture of friendship from Bowie. He'd brushed off overtures like this before. He should now. After all, he wasn't planning on stay-ing in Sagebrush, and he didn't want to become any more embroiled in this village than he already was.

But he found himself nodding in response to Bowie's veiled question. "Aye. June and me."

<hr />

June felt as nervous as a possum treed by a bluetick hound. They were finally bringing her nan home. They'd hired a transport service, which had cost a penny so pretty it could've won a beauty contest, but her grandmother was too weak to ride in the car.

Although Nan had stopped talking about hellfire and the devil, her mind was still as mixed up as scrambled eggs, and it broke June's heart.

As much as she wanted her grandmother home, June worried something fierce. In the hospital, her nan had a battery of nurses and aides to care for her. In another week, it would be only June. That was as much vacation as her daddy could take from his civilian job at the Pentagon, and her mama needed to return to her job as a director of a charity for at-risk youths. Her friend, Josh, promised to come in a few weeks, but although June would appreciate his support, he wasn't the nurturing type. His specialty was computers, not people. And there was no telling when August would manage to visit.

But as June kept reminding herself, she had Katie, Bowie, the townsfolk, and, most surprisingly of all, Magnus. The man had stuck by her side the whole time— a steady rock as the foundation of her world had cracked. Even now he sat beside her in the SUV, his hand resting on her thigh as they followed the medical transport van that carried her nan and her parents. He always seemed to sense when she needed his silent support. June was a talker, and so was her mama. She was accustomed to hashing out her problems, but there was something undeniably comforting about Magnus's quiet strength.

He glanced over as they turned off the main highway into town. "Are you doing all right, lass?"

She sucked in an unsteady breath. "It's going to be hard. It was difficult watching Nan lying on that hospital bed, but it's at least a place where people who are sick go to heal. Back home...I just think it's going to hit me harder."

There. June had finally put words to the tension simmering inside her since the doctors had mentioned her grandmother would be released. June hadn't quite found a way to define it before. Understanding the emotion made it a little easier to handle.

Magnus patted her leg, but he didn't try to placate her. She liked that about him. He didn't dismiss her feelings. He just offered her his steadying presence. That, more than any false assurances, grounded her.

When they pulled up to the tea shop, tears stung the back of June's eyes as she spotted the sign hanging in the window that read: *Welcome home, Clara & June!* She did love this town. Magnus leaned close and told her, "Katie's doing."

"I love it," June said as she unbuckled her seat belt. But as she reached for the door handle, the enormity of the situation slammed into her. A sob escaped her throat, and those pesky tears dripped down her face.

Magnus gently turned her in his direction. Using his callused thumb, he brushed away the wetness. "You are a strong woman, June Winters. So is your nan. You'll both get through this."

June nodded, sniffing back more tears. He was right. She could manage. Taking another deep breath, she turned and resolutely opened the door. She straightened as she exited the car and marched straight into the tea shop. It would take a while to bring her grandmother into the house from the transport van, but she needed to make sure the place was ready. She knew Katie, Bowie, and Magnus had prepared the pantry, but she wanted to make sure everything was in place.

She walked through the main room, trying not to notice how empty it felt for this time of day. The chairs were all pushed under the tables, the display case bare, the blackboard behind it blank. She swore the place even smelled musty after being shut up for a week.

June moved quickly, and not just because Nan needed her. She practically charged through the kitchen and had just started to pass the stairs to reach the back room when she spotted it. The chair lift.

More tears filled her eyes. She turned to Magnus wordlessly. He'd done this. She *knew* it.

"B-B-Bowie helped," Magnus told her. "We installed it three days ago."

She stood on her tiptoes and touched his cheek, his beard bristly against her palm. "Thank you," she whispered, and then she kissed him. Soft and sweet. His hand rested on the small of her back, warm and steady. She pulled away and finally managed one of her trademark smiles. What was it about this man that made her feel so good when everything else was going so wrong?

"It was nothing, lass," he said. "I like t-t-t-tinkering. It was no t-t-t-trouble."

June knew Magnus didn't accept compliments easily and noticed his disfluency had increased. Gently, she held his face and forced him to stare into her eyes. She let her warm gratitude show. "I love it, Magnus. It will mean so much for Nan and me. We would've been like sardines stuffed into that back room."

Beneath the discomfort in Magnus's eyes, she spied warm pleasure. Leaning forward, she sneaked another kiss…this time on his nose. His eyes widened with surprise.

"I'd give you a better one, but we don't have the time, darlin'." She patted his cheek one last time before heading to the back door. When she opened it, the driver of the transport was helping her grandmother down from the van under the watchful eye of June's parents. Both men assisted Nan up the steps and into the tea shop. Although her gran could walk, she remained unsteady and weak.

When her grandmother entered, she looked around in confusion. "Why are we here? I thought I was going home."

June reached forward and squeezed her grandmother's hand. "You're going to stay with me for a while. Won't that be fun!"

Nan appeared entirely unconvinced, and June tried not to take it to heart, but she felt a little twinge anyway. She'd been getting better, though, at accepting her grandmother's unfounded doubts and criticisms.

June's dad patted his mother's shoulder as he led her to the comfortable armchair that Magnus and Bowie had moved from Nan's house. "June is going to take good care of you, Mum."

Nan brushed her hand over the fabric of the armrest before she allowed her son to ease her into a more comfortable position. She'd lost weight during her hospital stay, and she looked frail and a little lost perched in her wing chair. There was an innocent look on her face as she watched them owlishly. "I am cold."

"I'll get a blanket," June said brightly. Too brightly. Using the task as an excuse, she turned quickly, hoping no one saw the sheen of tears in her eyes. She grabbed a warm afghan folded neatly on a nearby rocking chair. It was Nan's favorite, and another torrent of tears threatened to fall as June realized Katie must have remembered and instructed the guys to place it there.

Once covered up, her nan promptly fell asleep, her mouth agape. The blanket slipped, and June watched as her father gently rearranged it. June turned before she started bawling like a newborn and woke her nan.

Slipping from the small room, she found Magnus waiting for her in the kitchen. He watched her, his blue eyes solemn and supportive. "Has she settled in, lass?"

June nodded. "Yes. She's asleep already."

"That's good, right?"

She nodded, but the tears started to bubble up again. Before they spilled over, she walked straight to Magnus and buried her head against his chest. It felt so good, holding all that coiled strength. He didn't say anything, but he brushed his large hand over the back of her head, the gesture undeniably tender. Magnus could convey more in a caress than most men could in a thousand text messages.

Her parents exited the back room, and Magnus pulled away. He was shy about touching her around her parents. Considering the newness of their relationship, that didn't surprise June. But over the past few days when she'd really needed his strength, Magnus had always given it.

With her grandmother in the hospital, her parents hadn't asked her too many questions about her new beau. They'd just accepted his presence. June knew her mama had a million, though. Once her grandmother got settled, her mother was going to corner June. Not that she minded. Despite the distance between Sagebrush and DC, she chatted with her mother every day on the phone, and they'd always talked about relationships.

She'd rarely talked to her dad about boys. But she'd never forgotten what he'd told her after her first breakup when he'd found her crying in her room. He'd looked at her and said matter-of-factly in his gravelly voice, "June, that boy was only a stepping-stone in your life. He helped you grow, but it's time you moved on to another. If you keep standing still, you'll never find your path. And one day, you'll meet a man who isn't a stepping-stone, but a cornerstone."

That advice had steadied June through the years. Her friends always told her she had the healthiest outlook on dating, and she credited her daddy's wisdom.

Her father hadn't spoken to her about Magnus, nor had he made a big deal about grilling him. Unlike the stereotypical, strict military dad, he trusted June to make her own choices, especially when it came to men. But although her daddy hadn't given his opinion, she sensed his silent endorsement. After all, June didn't know what son wouldn't approve of a man who'd pitched in to help his mum, even if that man was also dating his daughter.

But that didn't stop Magnus from acting as nervous as a chicken with a hawk circling overhead when her daddy caught them touching. June found it sweet—this bashful side of Magnus. Since he otherwise seemed so stoic, so in command, she liked watching him shift from foot-to-foot like a teenage boy about to take a girl to the prom.

"Daddy," June said, pulling her father over to the stairs, "look what Magnus installed."

"Wilson helped," Magnus said. His voice was stilted, and June knew he was doing his darndest not to stutter. She also didn't miss that he'd switched to Bowie's last name to skirt the plosive *b* sound. Luckily, her daddy understood. June's brother, August, used to do the same thing until he stopped relying on avoidances to hide his disfluency.

Her father bent to inspect the installation. He jiggled the chair with that officious shake all men seemed to employ when checking out equipment. He grunted in approval and started playing with the buttons. He rode the chair for a complete circuit and then gave Magnus a curt nod. "Looks good. How much do we owe you? These things aren't cheap."

Magnus shook his head. "I got it on Craigslist, so I didn't pay full price."

"I looked there too," her father said. "I was planning on getting one before my wife and I left town. They're still steep, even used."

"Don't worry about it. M-m-most of my royalty checks sit in the bank. I don't have family myself, and I'd like to spend it on a fellow islander from T-T-T-Tammay…and for June."

A look passed between the two men. Finally, her father gave another stiff nod. "All right, then."

Magnus visibly relaxed, and June sensed something had changed between the two. By letting Magnus pay for the stair lift, her father had given him tacit approval, and Magnus knew it.

They adjourned to the tea shop where they could hear June's grandmother if she called. Magnus excused himself to head back to the zoo, and June's mama volunteered to keep watch over Nan while June and her daddy made sure they had the upstairs apartment properly set up.

As June rushed back and forth between the tea shop and her nan's house, she thought back to what Magnus had said. She couldn't imagine living alone like he did with no family. Even when moving from military base to military base, June had always had her parents and brother. When Nan had collapsed and June hadn't had any close relatives nearby, she'd never felt so alone and vulnerable.

But that…that was Magnus's reality. His everyday existence.

And that tore at June's heart.

Magnus deserved family. Any man who would remain with her in the hospital day after day after day had a true a capacity for love. And the knowledge he lived in such isolation destroyed June.

With Nan back home, June needed to do more research on Magnus's mama. So far, she'd only learned through genealogy sites that her maiden name was Mady Budge. It was a start. Although June could never repay the man for all he'd done for her family, maybe she could help him reunite with his own.

Chapter 12

MAGNUS CHUCKLED AS SORCHA SQUEAKED AND PULLED ON the ear of the stuffed animal he'd purchased a few weeks ago from the hospital gift shop. He'd been looking for a trinket for June when he'd spied the stuffed grizzly bear. It looked a bit like Frida, so he'd bought it along with a necklace for June. The little bear had immediately taken to the toy. Although her back legs still dragged occasionally when she crawled, the wee beastie was growing feistier by the day. In the wild, it would only be a couple more weeks before she would emerge from the den with her mum.

"Are you ready for your visit with Frida?" Magnus asked. The little cub turned her black eyes on Magnus and let out another high-pitched squawk. She bumbled over to him and used her teeth to pull at his sleeve. The wee whalp loved fabric.

"Aye, you need a bear to play with," he told her as he gently lifted her up and placed her into the carrier. Bowie and Lou wanted to wait until Sorcha was at least three months old before placing her in the same enclosure with Frida. Although the elderly bear seemed intent on mothering the wee cub, they didn't want to risk Sorcha getting hurt. If Frida suddenly attacked, no one could stop three-hunrdred-and-thirty pounds of enraged bear, especially not the fifteen pound Sorcha.

Right now, they took Sorcha for evening visits after

the zoo closed for the day. They kept the two separated, but it gave the bruins a chance to learn each other's scent. The daily meeting had become one of the highlights of Magnus's job. Abby had been begging to join them, but Bowie wanted to limit the number of distractions. And Magnus knew the zookeeper didn't want his daughter anywhere near the bear enclosure if Frida attempted to attack the wee bairn. Even with the gate separating the bears, watching a full-grown grizzly charge could be a terrifying thing. If the lassie screamed, it would make the situation worse. Even though Frida hadn't shown any signs of aggression, Bowie was still proceeding slowly with the bruins' introduction.

Magnus whistled happily as he and Sorcha entered the indoor facility. He removed the blanket he'd draped over the crate. Although Sorcha no longer needed the nursery as warm as she had upon her arrival, she wasn't ready for the chill of a high-desert winter. Bowie had made sure that Frida's indoor shelter was set at sixty-five degrees Fahrenheit, which translated to approximately eighteen degrees Celsius. Even after a month and a half of living in the States, Magnus still had trouble adapting to the American measurement system.

Frida must have already smelled Sorcha because she appeared at the opening to her shelter. As she had the last few days, she immediately lay down and pushed her snout through the space between the bottom of the gate and the ground. Although Magnus was not a cuddly sort of bloke, part of him wanted to pet the massive beastie's head. However, since his profession required his fingers be on a keyboard and not in a bear's stomach, he didn't get too close. Instead, he rested his back against the wall as he watched the bears interact.

At the sight of the bigger bear, Sorcha began to squeak enthusiastically, and Magnus grinned at the sound. "Do you hear that, Frida? The peedie cub wants to have a play. Are you up for a wee scuffle?"

A giant claw slid under the gate. Aye, the bear did want to tussle. Magnus had no doubt that the grizzly would be gentle with the cub, but he understood why Bowie and Lou wanted to proceed cautiously. Frida was a wild animal, and there was no telling how she'd react when Sorcha was no longer on the other side of the metal grate.

As the bears regarded each other, Magnus pulled out his tablet and mobile. He'd begun to use Sorcha's and Frida's playtime as a chance to practice the tips from *Self-Therapy for the Stutterer*. One of the tasks was to practice in front of a mirror while phoning stores to request information. Magnus made it a little more high-tech with the use of his tablet's camera. Focusing the lens on himself, he dutifully rang several places and asked questions about the merchandise. Over the past week, it had become slightly easier. *Slightly*.

When Magnus finished his self-assigned task, he leaned back to regard the bears. "June sends her love."

Both ignored him. Frida remained focused on Sorcha, while the peedie bruin had turned her attention to playing with the metal sides of her carrier.

"She wishes she could visit you, but she can't leave her nan," Magnus continued. He was worried about June and her gran. Even with her folks still in town, the lass seemed as worn down as a four-hundred-year-old front stoop. "It would do them both good to come to the zoo. June's been wanting to see you and wee Savannah too. With her parents leaving the next morn, I don't think the lass will have time to pop by for a long while."

Sorcha made a plaintive sound, and Magnus glanced at his watch. It was getting near feeding time. Hoisting the crate, Magnus said to Frida, "It's time to say goodbye."

At the sight of the cub being lifted, the elderly bear emitted a sound between a growl and a whine. Magnus ignored the protest. "Don't fash yourself. I'll watch over the bairn."

Frida clawed at the ground beneath the gate. Ignoring the grizzly's dramatics, Magnus turned from the facility. As he left the building, he peeked under the blanket to check on Sorcha.

"You're such a peedie thing. I wish I could take you to June's tea shop myself," Magnus said as the cub stared back at him with dark eyes framed by fluffy white fur. Her coat had grown thicker, preparing her for life outside the den. Although the hibernating animals emerged in late spring, they entered a world still encased in ice, and they followed the floes north to their hunting grounds.

"Even if you're built for adventures, we cannot take a risk with you. You're very important, you know. As tough as you bears are, there's only a grain of you left, and we don't want to lose a single one of you."

Sorcha appeared unimpressed. Magnus dropped

the blanket over the carrier as he made the short trip back to the nursery. He lifted the cub from the crate. The wee lassie snuggled into his arms, her powerful jaws opening into an adorable yawn. Her teeth had already started to erupt, foreshadowing the mighty predator she'd become.

"Och, all the visiting has made you wabbit," Magnus said. Laying the cub down next to Sylvia, he headed over to the counter to mix up the cub's evening meal. Combining formula with wet cat food, he scooped the contents into a syringe. After carefully measuring the amount so he could record what Sorcha ate, he squirted a little in a dog bowl. As soon as he laid the dish on the ground, the little cub scrambled to her feet and padded across the mats Bowie and Magnus had placed on the floor to give her more traction. Her pink tongue darted out of her black-lipped mouth as she greedily scarfed down the food. Impatient, she licked the end of the syringe, ready for more.

Once the little bairn had her fill, Magnus gave her a bowl of water. Sorcha started to dunk her entire head into the dish. Chuckling, Magnus pulled her back. "Now, lassie, we've had a talk about this. You're not ready for swimming just yet."

When Sorcha finished drinking, she wandered back over to Sylvia. With another adorable yawn, she flopped down on the capybara. A contented look drifted over the wee bear's face as her black eyes closed. Aye, she was a cute whalp. Sylvia lifted her head to check on the cub, but soon joined her charge in slumber. Leaving the two animals in peace, Magnus turned to leave. He grabbed the carrier on his way out. As he lugged the crate to the supply closet, an idea hit him like a sudden spray of salt water.

He couldn't take Sorcha to June's tea shop, but she wasn't the only baby animal in residence. He needed to ask Bowie for permission and to make sure the zoo had the right permits, but the idea could work.

------ww------

June was about to hand a spiced chai latte to Mrs. Mabel Saunders when a buzz stole over the tea shop. Even Nan noticed the excitement as she straightened in her rocking chair. June's parents had left the night before, and this was the first time her grandmother would be spending the entire day with June. During the last week and a half, her parents had stayed upstairs with Nan since crowds overwhelmed her. But they'd brought her down to the shop every day to get her accustomed again to the noise and people. Although they'd tried to build up her tolerance by gradually increasing the length of Nan's stays, June still worried.

She hadn't mentioned her concerns to her parents, though. They were already feeling guilty about leaving her alone to care for Nan. Although they'd discussed relocating her grandmother to DC, June didn't like that idea. Sagebrush had become home to Nan over the decades, and she took so much pride in the tea shop. Plus, both of June's parents worked away from the house. Sure, it would be a struggle for June to watch her grandmother while running two businesses, but it wasn't impossible… At least that's what she kept telling herself.

They'd also briefly considered placing Nan in a personal care home either in Sagebrush Flats or in

DC, but June had immediately rejected the idea. Poor Nan's mind was as fuzzy as a freshly picked peach, and living in a strange place would only confuse her more. Although Nan was still nervous, her terrors had lessened since she'd come home from the hospital, and June didn't want to make any decisions that might cause her grandmother to backslide. If the time came when June couldn't give Nan the care she needed, then she and her parents would make the necessary call. But not now. Not yet.

Last night, she'd confided her worries to Magnus as they chatted over the phone. In his typical fashion, he hadn't said much, but what he did add had possessed the poignancy only a writer could deliver. *June, your nan lived through the b-b-beginning of the Blitz. That forged a strength of spirit that cannot be daunted.*

"Now that isn't a sight you see every day," Buck observed, jarring June out of her reverie.

Stanley turned around to wave at June. "You've got to see this. Clara too."

June turned to exchange a look with her nan, before remembering her grandmother wouldn't understand how to respond to nonverbal communications anymore. Instead, June switched to a smile as she headed over to the rocking chair. "Nan, would you like to take a look?"

"Do I have to?" Nan appeared downright grumpy at the prospect.

"You might enjoy it." June kept her voice bright. Nan scowled, but she allowed June to help her up. When they reached the large picture window, June gasped in delight. Outside her shop stood three camels. Magnus and Abby sat astride Hank, with Lulubelle and Savannah following behind. Despite the glass separating them,

Lulubelle seemed to sense Nan's approach because she swung her massive head and stared straight at the older woman. June swore the animal gave her grandmother a silly grin as she batted her dark eyelashes. Wondering how her gran would react, June turned her head. Joy shot through her as she spied a smile on Nan's face.

By the time Magnus had dismounted and helped Abby down, a crowd had gathered. Locals mixed with college students in town for budget ski vacations. With the preteen's help, Magnus tied the camels to the hitching post June had bought at an antique store and installed in front of her tea shop for some Old West ambience. Although a couple of local ranchers used it for their horses, no one had ever tied camels to it.

Leaving Abby with the camels, Magnus pushed his way through the growing throng, or rather, he moved forward and people immediately stepped back at the sight of his bulk. He opened the door, his eyes focused on June with an intensity that made her shiver.

"Since your nan couldn't come to the zoo, I'd thought I'd b-b-bring it to her."

She smiled. "You sure did. How did little Savannah do with the walk?"

"As long as she's following after her mum, she's fine," Magnus said. "Do you think your nan would like to come out and see the p-p-peedie camel?"

June nodded. "Just let me get her coat. It's a bit brisk outside for her." She turned to Buck and Stanley. "Can you watch over her while I go upstairs to grab her things?"

The men nodded, and June dashed off and gathered up her grandmother's warmest peacoat and hat. It wasn't too terribly cold outside, but Nan chilled easily. As soon as June had the elderly woman suitably bundled, Magnus made his way back into the shop and helped the two of them navigate the crowd. When he'd safely escorted them to the camels, he hurried back into the shop for her grandmother's rocking chair and favorite blanket.

"Isn't this awesome!" Abby bounced on her feet. "When Magnus told Dad about his idea, I begged to come. Since it's Saturday, Dad agreed. You should've seen everybody's faces when we rode through town. I even saw five of my classmates!"

June laughed at the girl's excitement. "Well, y'all certainly surprised us. Isn't that right, Nan?"

Her grandmother didn't answer. Instead, she glanced around the crowd, her eyes large and frightened. Concerned, June gave her hand a reassuring pat. Luckily, Magnus returned with the chair. No sooner had June arranged the throw around Nan than Lulubelle bent her head to greet the elderly woman. Although June worried the huge animal might scare her grandmother, Nan just smiled softly. Lulubelle carefully nuzzled the ninety-year-old as if she understood the older human required gentleness. Savannah followed her mother's example and started to nose June's grandmother as well. Magnus tightly held the lead rope in case the little girl became too curious.

The tourists in the crowd pelted Magnus with questions. Where did the camels come from? What was the one-humped species called again? How old was the baby? What were their names?

With her typical enthusiasm, Abby tried to answer, but her voice got drowned out. Magnus did his best to ignore the situation, but June could spy the tension in his shoulders. He detested crowds, and this one had begun to press in on them. She gently laid her hand on his shoulder and bent close to his ear. "Why don't you try speaking to them?"

The look he sent her could have melted metal. She ignored his bluster. After all, she'd seen behind it. "This would be great for your vlog, darlin'. I'll start taping. I just have my camera phone, so it will be rough. But that'll just add to the atmosphere. We could call the episode, 'Taking the Zoo to the Streets.'"

Magnus looked dubious, and June gave him a little nudge with her shoulder. "It could be fun."

He snorted. "For you p-p-p-perhaps."

"Just give it a shot, honey. If you need me to take over, I'm right by your side. I've been around the zoo long enough that I'll be just fine fielding questions."

"I always stutter in crowds," Magnus admitted quietly.

"Try doing it on purpose like before. Then you'll get it over and done with."

Magnus frowned. She could see the doubt swirling like rain clouds in his blue eyes. She reached down and squeezed his hand. It was her turn to give support.

"You've got this, Magnus. I believe in you."

———

June was a modern Mary, Queen of Scots. One look from her grass-green eyes, and the lass could bewitch men. But she had the intelligence of Queen Elizabeth I—a deadly combination to be sure.

Magnus felt her slight hand press against his. Over the past few weeks, he'd become accustomed to her touch. It had become as familiar to him as the smell of gorse mixed with sea and the gentle low of cattle. And it had the same steadying effect.

Yet it was the fire in the lass's gaze that blazed through Magnus's blood. He'd never had someone look at him the way June did, never had someone believe in him. And it didn't feel superficial. Aye, there was a steadfastness in June's certainty. She truly thought him capable of speaking to a crowd this size.

In defiance of his own doubts, he found himself nodding and turning toward the throng. Despite all of his practice with June and the bears, he hadn't gotten to the stage of purposely stuttering in public, unless he counted the vlog. The self-help book had recommended going to stores and similar places to get desensitized to his blocks, but he hadn't been able to force himself to do that yet. It was hard enough stopping himself from switching word choices when he felt himself begin to tense.

June squeezed his hand once more before she released it to train the camera on him. He didn't have to be perfect, Magnus reminded himself. June had taught him that. And Magnus knew if he failed, June wouldn't judge him, not like his da. But he would disappoint her if he didn't make an attempt.

Magnus took one more breath and began, purposely stuttering on the word *camel*, which never gave him trouble. "These c-c-camels came from the Sagebrush Zoo."

"What are their names?" asked a little girl clinging to her mother's hand.

Magnus reached up and patted Lulubelle. At the gesture, the camel made a contented sound, and the crowd laughed. Not at him. Not at his stutter. At the camel.

Magnus felt himself relax...marginally. "This lass here is Lulubelle."

He reached over and patted Hank next. The male camel gave him a sidelong glance, which triggered another round of chuckles. "Hank is the zoo's m-m-male." Magnus turned to Savannah. When he brushed his hand over her woolly head, the little calf playfully butted him. The crowd let out a collective "Awww."

"And this wee lassie is Savannah." At the sound of her name, the peedie camel gave a little skip. More sounds of affection filled the air, and Magnus felt an even greater sense of ease.

A peedie lad who'd been sucking his thumb removed his finger and pointed at Savannah. In a loud, high-pitched tone only a toddler could achieve, the bairn cried, "Baby!" The crowd chuckled again. The child looked particularly pleased with himself as he stuck his finger back in his mouth.

"What do camels eat?"

"All variety of things," Magnus said. "For a special t-t-treat, we give them alfalfa hay, which horses and coos also fancy."

"Ooo," a lass in her early twenties called out, waving to him, "I love your accent. It's so sexy. Are you from Scotland?"

Magnus's tension flooded back. His throat began to tighten as his tongue stuck to the roof of his mouth. He managed an "Aye," which caused the hen and her two friends to squeal. Loudly.

"What part of Scotland?" the lass's friend asked.

"Do you ever wear a kilt?" The third hen fired off her question so fast Magnus wouldn't have been able to speak even if his throat hadn't felt like rubbish.

"Are you single?"

The trio paused then and stared at him expectantly. A thin sheen of sweat covered Magnus. He never wanted to talk about himself, and the lasses' aggressive interest made him as uncomfortable as a sea trout pulled from the water.

He felt June's hand on his bicep. Warm and steadying. He turned in her direction and found her smiling brightly at the women.

"Magnus is from a tiny island in the North Sea called Tammay," June said. "He doesn't own a kilt, although it is one of my life goals to see him in one. And, sorry, ladies, but he's currently all mine, and I'm not one for sharing."

Disappointment gleamed in the hens' eyes, but the rest of the throng laughed again. Some of the pressure inside Magnus eased, but he knew he'd lost his speaking rhythm. June kept her grip on his arm as she scanned the crowd. "How would y'all like if I went inside and brought out a treat for these lovely camels? I might not have alfalfa, but I do have some nice Granny Smiths I use for making my famous apple butter."

The crowd cheered, and Magnus shook his head fondly. Only June could command a group with such ease. With a few sentences, she'd managed to make the lasses simmer down and distract everyone's attention from him.

"Would you like to help me cut up the apples?" June asked Abby quietly. The girl nodded eagerly. Turning to Magnus, June whispered, "Watch Nan." Then she darted into the shop with Abby following close behind. Fortunately, the people began to talk among themselves, but Magnus saw June's grandmother shift uncomfortably. She gazed up, her hazel eyes clouded again. "Where'd Junie go?"

He reached down and patted the auld hen as he'd seen June do. "She went inside to get apples for the camels. I'll watch over you."

That seemed to satisfy Clara. She gave him a little nod and turned her attention back to the animals. June came bustling out of the shop with a bowlful of diced fruit. Everyone clamored to be the one to feed the camels, but June selected the wee lassie who'd first spoken and two other children. Abby showed them how to hold the treat properly so the beasties wouldn't accidentally nip the children's fingers. The little girl from the crowd giggled as Lulubelle gently suctioned the apple from her hand.

"That tickles!" she said as she turned to Magnus, a bright smile on her already cherubic face.

"Aye, lassie, it does."

"Thank you!" she told him. "This is the best day ever!"

Magnus glanced up at June. Although he wouldn't classify this as the best day ever, he'd spoken to a large group, something he'd never dreamed of doing. But the lass had made it possible. He didn't know how. After growing up under his da's constant control, he despised when people tried to tell him what to do. But June? June could cajole him into anything. As much as Magnus appreciated today, June's ability sometimes left him uneasy—as if he was in danger of losing the peaceful independence he'd nearly died to achieve.

—⁓—

Honey was bored. Bored. Bored. Bored.

The Blond One had not appeared for days, and the Giant One's grumpiness had vanished. She had tried a game of chase yesterday, but he hadn't lost his temper. Not once. It had been the dullest romp through the zoo.

Honey needed an adventure. Slipping from her enclosure, she headed toward the house where the humans made their den. Finding a nice spot in the bushes, she waited for an opportunity. In her old home whenever she needed a bit of excitement, she would sneak into one of the vehicles.

After an hour's wait, the Red-Headed One finally emerged. Honey silently trailed the biped to her car.

As Honey watched the woman open the door, she smiled. This would be fun.

—⁓—

There was a honey badger in June's kitchen. In. Her. Kitchen! And June swore that the little rascal was grinning at her. Broadly. It was definitely taunting her. The little devil waited, its black eyes staring unblinkingly at June. As soon as she dove in its direction, it scurried away. This time it scampered right through the middle of June's legs.

June didn't know how many health code violations were being broken right now. It was one thing to have a caravan of camels outside her shop. Their visit yesterday had drawn in the tourists. A snarling, foul-tempered honey badger could only attract trouble.

At least Nan was asleep in the back room and blissfully oblivious to the chaos. June's assistant had already fled, but, thankfully, not before the woman had put in a call to the zoo.

Honey must have slipped unnoticed into Katie's car and then into the tea shop. Katie had only stopped in for a second to drop off nutrient shakes for Nan. No matter what June whipped up for dinner, her nan wouldn't eat properly. June had tried making her grandmother's favorite dishes, but even that didn't coax her into taking more than a few bites. When June encouraged her to attempt a little more, Nan claimed she had trouble swallowing, even though she could consume food just fine. They'd even checked at the hospital for a physical reason for her loss of appetite. Unfortunately, or maybe fortunately, Nan's diet difficulties were all in her mind.

And that was the heartbreaking reality with disorders affecting the brain. They were typically not as immediately lethal as physical ailments, yet they slowly and devastatingly weakened the body. They were often difficult, if not impossible to diagnose. After a battery of tests and a team of doctors, Nan's illness remained unknown. Yes, they knew about the sodium drop and the UTI, but it didn't explain her grandmother's continuing symptoms that didn't present like classic Alzheimer's or dementia.

So here June was, watching her nan slowly fade. Not knowing why. Or the timeline. Or what was going to happen next. Or whether there would *be* a next.

It was wearing. Her parents had left less than a week ago, but June still felt an overwhelming exhaustion she'd never experienced before. She'd always been the one with the endless energy. A firecracker, her maternal grandpappy had called her. But she felt as burned out as a sparkler after the Fourth of July. Her grandmother had an endless list of demands. When she wasn't asking for something, she was regarding June with suspicion. There were times when June saw a flicker of her old nana, and often that hurt the most. The only time June had time to herself was when her gran was sleeping.

And now, during one of those precious naps, a honey badger was hell-bent on destroying June's kitchen and her two businesses along with it. As if sensing the direction of her thoughts, the little devil stared straight at her as it deliberately stood up on its hind legs. The minx turned and scaled the bottom cabinets, using one of the oven handles for leverage. June gave a battle cry and lunged at the weasel.

"Oh, no you don't. You're not putting your dirty paws all over my counters, and you're certainly *not* getting into my preserves."

She swore the little imp winked. June's cry certainly didn't stop its upward crawl. As her hand grazed its coarse fur, the creature turned its head to snarl. Its sharp, dagger-like teeth came perilously close to June's fingertips.

She didn't care.

With an agility fueled by frustration heaped upon frustration, June yanked the critter off her counter, ignoring the scrape of its talons against her expensive stainless-steel oven. The honey badger twisted, trying its best to claw and bite. It hissed worse than a goose after a chunk of bread. June didn't give a fig. She hissed right back. Precisely at that moment, both Magnus and Bowie walked into her kitchen.

———

Magnus never knew what to expect when he entered June's tea shop. The woman was like a kaleidoscope, always bright and constantly changing. Nothing, however, would have prepared him for the scene before him.

June stood in the center of her normally pristine scullery holding a snarling Honey. The mustelid violently bucked its body in a futile bid for freedom. Fangs flashed, and claws pinwheeled.

Despite the beastie's ferocity, June remained undaunted. Instead of stepping back or dropping the whalp, she leaned forward. Her lips curled back like the honey badger's, but instead of sharp gnashers, she revealed a row of perfect pearly whites. The guttural sound that emerged from June was elemental.

Bowie leaned toward Magnus and murmured, "Part of me wants to laugh, but most of me is afraid to."

"I wouldn't," Magnus advised quietly.

Woman and beast turned in their direction. Both froze. The honey badger recovered first, arching its long body. June maintained her hold, and the rest of her seemed locked into place. Although Magnus was the last thing from a jolly fellow, he felt mirth swell inside him like a hot-air balloon. With effort, he managed to tamp it down.

"Do you need h-help, lass?" Magnus asked, this time the hesitation in his voice coming from suppressed amusement and not his stutter. June must have recognized the difference since her expression turned as dry as a stale oatcake.

"No, I'm just as right as rain over here," she said.

Bowie stepped forward and relieved June of her furry burden. Honey did not appreciate the transfer. She thrashed even harder, her head twisting like a snake's. Bowie gave the creature a surprisingly fond smile. Magnus would've wanted to strangle the wee blighter.

"How'd you get here?" Bowie asked Honey. He was greeted with a prolonged growl.

"It must have stowed away in Katie's car," June answered. "She dropped off some nutrient shakes earlier today."

Bowie frowned at Honey. "Is that so?"

"Bowie," June said, her drawl even thicker than normal, "if y'all don't get that varmint out of my kitchen this instant, honey badger pie is going to be on the menu."

"Yes, ma'am," Bowie said and then started toward the exit. He didn't even take time to turn around as he spoke to Magnus. "I take it you're staying."

"Aye."

As soon as Bowie and the wee devil departed, Magnus turned his attention back to June. To his utter horror, her face crumpled. In a very un-June-like fashion, she slumped into a chair and buried her head in her arms. Deep, heaving sobs echoed through the utilitarian scullery.

Baws.

Cautiously, Magnus moved forward and rested his hand on her back. The contact seemed to make her cry harder. Still, he didn't pull back. June wasn't like him. She didn't crave solitude when she was hurting. She needed people.

He didn't try asking what was wrong. June was a natural talker, and she'd tell him when she was ready. Instead, he just stood there, stroking her hair, letting her know she wasn't alone.

Finally, she stopped and raised her head. Streaks of tears marred her bonny cheeks, but she was still a braw lass even after all her crying. She sniffed and swiveled in her seat, clearly looking for a tissue. Magnus spied two dry dishcloths and handed her one.

She glanced up at him. "This doesn't seem very sanitary."

"Lass, there was a honey badger in your scullery."

June gave a resigned shrug. "This towel is going directly into the wash."

"I can do that for you."

Her lower lip started to wobble again. June lifted a shaky hand to her mouth and pressed it there. Magnus placed his hand on her shoulder. "There's no harm in grieving, lass."

June shook her head. "I've got to be strong, Magnus. Nan needs me."

Magnus scowled as he studied her. Although her

green eyes appeared bright, he could see faint lines of tension surrounding them. Aye, her whole face looked pinched and a little peely walley. Maybe he'd been wrong. Maybe the lass did need prodding in order to open up to him.

"You're always telling me to talk about it," Magnus said.

She gave a watery laugh and plucked at the second dishcloth. "I'm not used to being the one who needs to unload."

Magnus pulled up another chair. "I'm better at listening than at blethering."

June sighed, the sound weary and sad. "I feel like a piece of candy at a taffy pull. I'm being yanked in so many directions, I don't know which way to go. I love Nan, I really do, but this isn't easy."

Magnus reached over and rubbed her back. "You're doing a fine job, lass. A fine job."

She teared up again and nodded jerkily. "But it's hard, especially at night. I'm getting no sleep. She's constantly getting up. I think she's lost all sense of time."

"Would it help if I stayed here t-t-tonight, lass?" Magnus asked. As he blocked on the *t*, he realized he hadn't stuttered for most of the conversation.

"But the zoo—"

"Bowie doesn't need my help at night anymore," he said. "And he did fine without me when your nan was in the hospital."

Finally, June nodded. "It would be nice. Having your company again. I've missed you."

It was odd being needed. Aye, his da had tried to keep him on the croft, but the auld man hadn't really wanted Magnus himself. He just couldn't stand being alone with no one to order about and to help with the chores.

But June?

June desired *him*. And that both alarmed and pleased him.

"I won't be around as much," Magnus said as he supervised Sorcha's evening visit with Frida. Both bears ignored him. Sorcha was too busy chewing on her teddy bear, and Frida's entire focus was on trying to get to the cub.

"I'll be bringing your food," Magnus said. "Don't fash yourselves about that, but I'll no longer be sleeping here. I'm moving in with June and her nan."

He paused then, half expecting the animals to turn their bright eyes in his direction. To him, the news seemed as powerful and transformative as a Pangaea-rending seismic shift. However, the bears didn't even sense his tension. Instead, Sorcha executed a half pounce and bit her toy grizzly straight on the nose. Frida watched the younger bear intently.

Magnus sighed. Maybe the beasties were right. He was being overly dramatic. He wasn't proposing to the lass. She knew he was moving in for practical reasons. Neither of them had made promises or spoken of a future. He was simply helping a mate, not bargaining away his freedom.

"She's finally asleep," June said quietly as she slipped into bed beside Magnus. She didn't know why she bothered to lower her voice. She'd removed her grandmother's hearing aids, and Nan couldn't detect a sound.

Magnus placed his laptop on the nightstand next to him and started to turn off the light, but June laid her hand on his bicep. He stopped, his gaze locking on to hers. "Aye, lass?"

She smiled—and it felt good. She hadn't been doing enough of that lately. "I'm not planning on going to sleep right now."

He scowled, and she wanted to kiss away his frown.

"You need your rest, lass."

June winked. "I need you more."

Red crept over his cheeks, but June could tell her words pleased him. He reached out to cup the back of her head. She adored when he did that. It made her feel safe, cherished even.

"Are you sure, lass? I'm not expecting it t-t-tonight."

"Well, I sure am," she said as she tugged at his T-shirt. "I've missed you these past couple weeks. Have you been thinking about me?"

"Aye, hen," Magnus said, his voice as rich and thick as maple syrup, "all the time."

"Then, I think it's high time you showed me some of those thoughts."

"Do you now?"

She nodded, and Magnus lifted his head to capture her lips. His kisses possessed the same lyrical quality as his Orcadian accent. Soft, tender, deep.

June shivered, and she felt Magnus's smile. He rested

his forehead against hers as he spoke, his voice a low rumble. "I haven't even gotten started, lass."

Then he flipped their bodies. She emitted a muffled squeal of surprise before she reached up to circle her arms around his strong back. "I sure am liking the beginning, though."

He gave one of his rare smiles. "As am I."

His mouth covered hers. She gasped, and he took advantage of her intake of breath to deepen the kiss. Sweet heat swept through her like warm jam. Ooo, a girl could get used to this. She sighed and pulled him closer. He obliged, letting a little more of his weight press against her. Her body melted. Craving more, she arched in to him. He moved to nuzzle the side of her neck as she ran her hands up and down his biceps. His muscles were taut from the effort of holding his massive frame perfectly above her slender one.

"I just love the feel of you," she whispered in his ear before giving the lobe a playful nip.

He lifted his head to stare down at her. His eyes had darkened into cobalt, and the electric-blue hue sent delicious chills skittering up and down her spine.

"M-me too, lass. Me too."

"I swear some primal part of me just dances in delight whenever I feel you."

Magnus emitted a bark of startled laughter. "I didn't know primal parts danced."

"Oh, they do, Magnus. They do."

"Och, lass, you're a rare one."

"I know," she said smugly as she lifted her head slightly to kiss his nose. She always loved his surprise at the gesture. Magnus Gray was a man who needed more tenderness in his life.

He grinned at her, and her heart flopped over in her chest like a hooked trout. She'd never seen him so... happy. And that, in turn, made bliss bubble inside her.

Magnus had never felt like this. Aye, he'd experienced contentment while sipping whiskey at his favorite pub, but not cheer. Now it flowed through him like a mountain brook in spring. Pretty soon he'd be beaming like a numptie, and for once, he didn't care. He chuckled, and the joy seemed to explode inside him, so he tried it again.

June's eyes shone like emeralds. "I love hearing your laughter."

"You make it easy, lass." He was so comfortable, his tongue didn't even tangle on the cursed *ma* sound.

June's expression turned serious as she reached up to stroke his hair. Gentle. Soft. Tender. "You're a wonderful man, Magnus Gray. I hope you know how special you are."

Something fractured inside him...or maybe it opened. For once, he didn't have words to describe the sensation. It overwhelmed him, like a swollen river unable to contain the floodwaters after a levee broke. He couldn't fight the current. He didn't even try. He allowed it to sweep him along as he captured June's mouth.

He poured his torrent of emotions into the kiss, but it wasn't wild or frenetic. It was slow and powerful. Everything felt heightened. His blood pounded harder than waves beating against a sea stack, his need for June drenching his senses.

Reveling in the satiny smoothness of her skin, Magnus skimmed his hand over her body. When he brushed his fingers over her breasts, she gasped. Galvanized by the sound, he lifted his mouth from hers to tease her nipple. She made a soft sound in the back of her throat, and sweet insanity consumed Magnus. He used his tongue, lips, and fingers to coax a symphony of sighs and moans from June, each one more enchanting than the last.

She began to writhe beneath him. His boabie jerked in response. Magnus ignored his body's instinctual command, but not hers. He trailed his mouth down her belly, tasting the salty sheen covering her skin. When his mouth closed over her, she sucked in her breath, her hips bucking. Stroking her inner thighs, he teased and licked. When she cried out, the sound echoed through him and sent his heart thumping even faster.

He wanted to be inside her, but he didn't give in to temptation. Not yet. He wanted to hear more of her siren calls. He wanted to taste her sweetness. He wanted the absolute madness of it all.

His mouth still on her, he reached with his hand to stroke her breast. She gave a sharp sound of pure pleasure. Magnus would have smiled in triumph if it hadn't meant breaking the rhythm of his strokes. June was close, and he wanted to watch her crash over the brink.

His patience was rewarded. She lit up like the London sky on Guy Fawkes Night. Her bonny pink lips separated ever so slightly as pleasure suffused her face. A tender ache spread through him, reaching so deep it almost hurt. Aye, she was as gorgeous as an arctic sunrise casting its yellow-gold radiance across the frozen land. And just like the ice floes, Magnus felt illuminated by her glow.

She opened her eyes, and her emerald gaze latched onto his. Despite the passion racing through him, his entire body stilled. June could weave a spell stronger than any fae creature in all folklore.

She reached for him, her hand gently running through his hair. He leaned into the caress, kissing her palm. He'd never been a tender man, but he was with June. He couldn't help it.

"You, my darlin'," June drawled, "are beyond amazing."

Then she cupped his cheek and guided his mouth back to hers. He felt as alive as a seal spiraling through the waters of the Scapa Flow. With his mind pure mince, he allowed June to nudge him onto his back. She climbed on top of him, her movements as alluring and seductive as a selkie emerging from the sea.

She bent her head to kiss his chest, her hair a curtain of fine blond silk. One of her delicate hands slipped down his body to cup his stauner. He was already on the brink, and her touch nearly caused him to lose himself. Somehow, he managed to maintain a shred of control, and it didn't take long for June to reward his efforts.

She teased him, first with her fingers and then with her tongue. "Lass, I cannot..." he said, his Orcadian accent thick even to his own ears.

June arched one golden eyebrow in clear challenge. "Then don't."

Her bonny pink lips closed over his tip, and he was

undone. For the first time in his life, Magnus let go and allowed another to lead. Pleasure tore through him with such an intensity he thought for a moment it might rip him apart. And it didn't end with the explosion. As he lay panting, his blood humming in his ears, he felt her touch. Gentle. Sweet. Devastating. He'd never allowed anyone to explore his body as she did, but he could not stop her. Instead, he basked in her caresses, relishing the feel of her hair brushing his flesh as she pressed her lips against his chest and neck.

"You're p-p-pure m-m-magic, lass." Magnus breathed out as he summoned enough energy to run his hand down her delicate spine. He had no idea how June could both arouse and relax him. Fuck, he didn't even fash himself about his stutter.

In response, she nibbled the skin by his ear, her fingers tangled in his curls. She kissed his brow next and then the tip of his nose. Time slipped away as they lay together, touching and gently teasing. When June took his earlobe gently between her teeth, his boabie began to stir. She paused over him long enough to deliver a cheeky grin before working her way down his throat.

He groaned and lifted her as he sat up. Positioning her on his lap, he pressed a kiss against her temple. "There, lass. Now we can pleasure each other."

She ran a finger down his sternum. "Ooo, I like the sound of that."

Magnus had never been with a woman like this. There was a depth to their lovemaking…a rawness that had nothing to do with roughness and everything to do with need. He forgot to hold himself apart, to keep his soul locked down so no pain could touch it. When they finished, they collapsed together. June instantly snuggled against him, her soft bottom pressing against his prick. Instinctually, his arms wrapped about her, and she covered his triceps with her hands. She sighed then, the sound deep and contented.

"I could get used to this," she said, her words ending on a yawn before she drifted off to sleep.

And that's when it struck Magnus with the force of a cannonball. He agreed with the lass. He could become accustomed to lying next to her, and that terrified him to his core.

He once again felt like a sailor of old, lured by the song of a beautiful sea witch. Just like an enchanted seafarer, he'd forgotten himself. He'd made himself vulnerable and let June inside. He'd begun to need her when he'd always promised himself he'd never rely on another. Aye, he was under June's thrall, and it remained to be seen whether she'd lure him straight onto jagged rocks.

Chapter 13

"THANKS FOR STICKING AROUND A LITTLE LATER today," Bowie whispered as they watched Frida sniff Sorcha. The little bear didn't seem intimidated by the grizzly's massive frame. She just stared up at the larger animal, her black eyes alight with amusement.

"I wouldn't have wanted to miss this," Magnus told him and Lou, his eyes trained on the bears. He stood between Bowie and Lou as they watched the two beasties greet each other inside Frida's exhibit. So far, the meeting had gone perfectly, but nervous energy still coursed through Magnus, and he could feel it roll off Bowie and Lou as well.

With the short attention span of all babies, Sorcha turned away from Frida and began exploring the new exhibit. Frida followed behind the wee cub. With her poor eyesight, she stayed close to Sorcha. The close supervision didn't bother the polar bear. Oblivious to her newly acquired nanny, the whalp scrambled over one of the fake rocks. She reached the top but had trouble with the climb down. She slipped and slid a few inches. When she hit the uneven ground, her own furry feet tangled her. Somersaulting backward, she let out a high-pitched squeal.

Frida's ears twitched, and she instantly ran over

to check on her new charge. Gently, she nosed the wee bear, helping Sorcha stand. Lou emitted a low whistle, pitched so it wouldn't startle the animals. "Would you look at that?"

"It's pretty incredible," Bowie said quietly.

"Who would've thought a geriatric grizzly would take such a shine to a baby polar bear?" Lou said, shaking his head. "I admit I wasn't sure about this idea of yours, Bowie, but it turned out well. Real well."

"Watching them together is amazing," Magnus added as Sorcha started to climb on Frida's back. The old grizzly didn't seem to mind being used like a jungle gym. She just lay down, letting the peedie beastie tug at her fur.

Bowie smiled fondly at the two creatures. "I didn't doubt Frida for a second. Despite her massive incisors and sharp claws, she's nothing but an old softy."

"June would love to see this," Magnus said.

"Why don't you bring her by?" Lou asked as he rested his forearms against the fence rail. "I could sit with Clara up at the house."

Magnus shook his head. He'd thought about that already. "I don't think it would work. Clara gets d-d-distressed easily, and she's not ready to leave June's flat or the tea shop."

"Katie's mentioned her mom is willing to watch Mrs. Winters," Bowie said. "She's just having trouble convincing June to leave her grandmother. Maybe you can persuade her?"

"What m-m-makes you think I can when Katie can't?" Magnus asked. The two women were closer than two sheep huddled against a gale.

Lou chuckled at the question, his eyes twinkling.

"I think you may have a special sway over our Miss Winters."

Magnus wasn't so sure. June might have woven her fae magic about him, but he didn't think she was caught in the same trap. Aye, the lass cared for him, that he didn't doubt. But June was a woman who loved easily and generously. She was like a fairy, flitting through life tending to people like they were flowers in her garden. But she remained unchanged, always searching for that one soul who needed a little extra care.

———∿∿∿———

"My word, y'all have gotten far with Sorcha's exhibit!" June said as she peered over the construction site. Katie's mom was watching her gran, and Magnus had convinced June to take a trip to the zoo. She drew in a breath of air, letting it fill her lungs. Although part of June couldn't help but fret about Nan, Magnus had been right. She'd needed time away. Lately, she'd been feeling more cooped up than a chicken stuck in a henhouse.

"The grant money p-p-paid for professional labor," Magnus said as he leaned against the chain-link fence that prevented curious onlookers from getting too close, "but Bowie's d-d-determined to make the dosh go as far as possible, so we're doing most of it ourselves."

"Ooo, I definitely think we should do a vlog of you helping. Something that makes your muscles bulge. Your female fans will love it!" June ran her hand over Magnus's bicep, and he instantly colored.

"I d-d-d-don't know, lass."

June had made the suggestion half in jest, but she began to warm to the idea like a biscuit baking in the oven. "You know, the more I think about it, the more I like it. This takes you back to your roots. Your first books were full of physical labor. People will love seeing you get as dirty as a hog in a mud bath."

Magnus scratched the back of his head as he considered her words. "We've d-d-done most of the digging. We've excavated the pool area and laid the foundation for the inside facility. Bowie said he wanted to d-d-do some framing soon, though."

"That would be just perfect! Plus, we can get a video of you walking around the site and explaining what you've already completed. Katie can work her editing magic and add pictures of Sorcha. After all, you need to have a cuteness factor." June bumped their joined hands against Magnus's thigh, and he grunted at her joke.

"Speaking of Sorcha, I cannot wait to see that little cub again," June said. "Do you think she'll recognize me?"

"You're a wee bit hard to forget, lass."

June winked at Magnus, and his flush returned. "Why, Magnus Gray, are you saying that I'm unforgettable?"

Something flitted over his face. Before June could interpret the emotion, it vanished like a wisp of smoke from a barbecue fire. An unusual sense of unease slipped through June. Something felt off, but she couldn't quite figure out what. She had no earthly idea why her words would've upset him.

"Aye, hen," Magnus answered, his voice more solemn than June would've liked.

She was just about to question him when they turned

a bend, and June caught sight of Frida's enclosure. Little Sorcha was climbing on the ancient grizzly. The older bear lay patiently, her head resting on her enormous paws as the little tyke tugged on her ear with her teeth. At the sound of their approach, the cub turned her head. She let out a squeal of joy and promptly lost her balance. There was a flash of black pads as Sorcha rolled head over heels down Frida's flank.

When the little bear landed, she lay stunned for just a moment. Then she scrambled to her feet, shaking herself off. She immediately began loping in their direction, her black eyes sparkling with excitement. Magnus used a key to unlock the zookeeper's entrance. They stepped inside a small building that served as Frida's indoor home. There was a lock-out area built inside the indoor facility that doubled both as a gate to the external enclosure and as a separate space where they could keep Frida if they needed to perform any medical treatment. Because the lockout had two separate doors, it helped ensure safety of both the bear and the zoo employees. Keeping the internal gate closed, Magnus used a chain to open the one that led directly into the enclosure. He called Sorcha's name, and the little cub immediately scrambled into view.

June laughed at the polar bear's enthusiasm. "Somebody's crush hasn't diminished."

"She knows who brings her food," Magnus said as he released the gate leading into the outdoor enclosure before Frida could enter. When it was secure, he opened the inner door, and Sorcha bounded out. With a squeal, she leaped at Magnus's feet. Chuckling, he bent over to tussle with the little critter. Sorcha made the most adorable sounds as she attacked Magnus's gloved hand. The bear had grown bigger and stronger since June had last seen her. Although the cub seemed as enthusiastic as ever in her play attack, June noticed Sorcha didn't bite or claw too hard.

"Do you want to feed her?" Magnus asked. June nodded, and he handed her a food dish. At the fishy smell, June wrinkled her nose.

"Is this chopped-up fish?" she asked.

"Aye. Cod. It's her favorite. I think it's Frida's influence."

"How so?"

"Grizzlies are known for catching salmon, but polar bears have more access to meat. In the wild, they hunt seals. If a whale washes up to shore, they make quick work of the b-b-blubber and muscle."

June made a face at Magnus's description. "That's disgusting."

He shrugged. "They're bears. What do you expect?"

"Cuteness."

Magnus laughed as he gestured toward Sorcha scarfing down her food. "They're not all like this peedie one here."

"Is she still getting milk?"

Magnus nodded. "In the wild, they nurse for over a year."

"I didn't know they stayed with their mamas that long."

"Aye, for about two-and-a-half years. There's a lot to learn about being a p-p-proper bear."

Sorcha looked up, her mouth ringed with particles of food. She made a squeaking sound, prompting a grin from Magnus. "Don't fash yourself, Sorcha. Frida is making sure you know what to do."

The cub went back to eating. It didn't take her long to finish her meal. Magnus released her back into the enclosure with Frida.

After they left the exhibit, June reached for Magnus's hand. When her fingers touched his, he jumped. She glanced at him in confusion. "Are you afraid of a little PDA? The zoo's closed for the evening, darlin'."

"PDA?"

"Public displays of affection," June amended.

Magnus's gaze fell on her, his eyes dark and solemn. He didn't speak for a moment. Although June couldn't read the emotions swirling in his blue depths, she sensed an internal debate. When he spoke, his voice was as soft as velvet. "A-A-A-Afore you, I've never held someone's hand. That's all."

That's all. *That's all!* June tried not to stare at Magnus in disbelief. "Never? What about your parents?"

"I suppose I might have clutched onto my m-mum's hand when I was a peedie lad, but not that I can remember. M-m-my d-d-da wasn't one for it. If I'd reached for his hand, he would've thought me a nyaff."

"But surely there's been someone," June said, her mind not able to process that Magnus had never experienced this most basic of human affection. "A girlfriend?"

Magnus shook his head. "Just you, June. Just you."

Before June could respond to that revelation, a rumbling bray broke into their conversation. Lulubelle came running up to the side of the fence, a goofy smile on her face. Savannah made the same sound in miniature as she pumped her skinny legs to keep up. Hank followed more sedately.

"Why, hello," June drawled as she reached to pet Lulubelle's neck. The camel sighed in contentment. The old girl did love her pats.

Savannah poked her head through the fence and nuzzled Magnus's hip. He chuckled, low and deep as he scratched the calf's fuzzy head. "You know where the treats are."

He reached inside his pocket and broke off a piece from an alfalfa pellet. Placing it in the palm of his hand, he held it out to Savannah. The little camel gobbled it down and turned adoring brown eyes in Magnus's direction.

Hank shifted before craning his long neck over his daughter. He grunted at Magnus in clear demand. June laughed and patted the male. "Somebody's feeling left out."

Magnus gave Hank the rest of the pellet, which, of course, meant Lulubelle wanted one too. After he fed the older female camel, the baby bumped her large nose against his pocket. He rubbed her side and shook his head. "That's it, lassie."

Savannah blew a raspberry and looked mournful. June reached forward and brushed the camel's thick wool. "It's okay, sweetheart. I'm sure Magnus will give you more tomorrow."

"Aye. You know you're my special girl."

"Why, darlin'," June said, popping him on his shoulder, "I thought that was me."

Magnus colored again, and June hid a smile. Now that the Scotsman had finally stopped scowling, it was fun flirting with him. He possessed an inner sweetness that seeped out every time she teased him.

"You know how you can make it up to me?" June asked and then looped her arms around his neck and pulled him close. "A kiss."

"I can do that, hen."

It was a tender embrace—the knee-melty kind that turned a girl's heart into mush. For all his toughness, Magnus had the softest lips. He brushed his thumb over her cheekbone, and she shivered at the feel of his calluses. She sank into the magic of his kiss It was after hours, so there was no chance a zoo visitor could wander across them.

That's when she heard it...the chittering. She and Magnus both broke the embrace and simultaneously turned in the direction of the disturbance. A honey badger sat directly in the middle of the path. June glared at the animal. *Honey*. The little minx wasn't even bothering to hide. She just stared at them boldly, her long body deceptively relaxed.

"She's taunting us," June said.

"Aye."

"Do you think we should chase her?"

"Nay." Magnus framed June's face in both his hands and captured her mouth with his. June tried to relax back into the kiss but couldn't. She could feel Honey's black eyes boring into her. Magnus suddenly pulled back.

"Baws!"

"You feel it too?"

He nodded, and they both swiveled toward the rascal. The honey badger shifted her body, so she faced away from them. Then she looked over her shoulder, her little face expectant.

"Do you think we'll get any peace unless we give in?" June asked.

"Nay."

She sighed. "We might as well make this fun." She reached out her hand to Magnus. He stared at it.

"Won't it feel like we're peedie children playing on the village green?"

She winked. "That's the point, darlin'."

He shrugged and wrapped his warm fingers around hers. Her heart pitter-pattered like a teenager's. At the sparkly sensation, she laughed and tugged his hand. She hadn't felt this free since Nan went to the hospital. As they took off at full speed, she heard Magnus's chuckle join hers.

That night, June lay in Magnus's arms as she listened to his steady breathing. Over the past week, the sound had lulled her back to sleep when she'd woken, worrying about Nan. But this time, she wasn't fretting over her grandmother. Her conversation with Magnus had stuck with her. It broke her heart he'd never held hands. She couldn't imagine the isolation he'd endured as a child.

Unable to fall back asleep, she carefully lifted Magnus's arm and rolled from his embrace. He grunted, and she pressed a kiss against his cheek. At the touch, he settled, a faint smile on his lips. June sat there for a moment, just staring at the hard planes of his face in the wan moonlight. His features had become so beautiful to her despite their harshness. She gently stroked his curly hair, careful not to wake him.

He wasn't at all like she'd first thought. Underneath his gruffness lay a wellspring of tenderness. It was no wonder he'd formed such a hard shell to protect himself. Otherwise, he wouldn't have survived childhood with his father. He deserved a family who loved him, and June was determined to see if at least one member still did.

Quietly, she slipped from bed and opened her laptop. She checked her inbox and smiled when she spotted a message waiting there. Through genealogy websites and some social media sleuthing, she'd tracked down a woman on Tammay who she believed to be a cousin of Magnus's mother. She clicked the file open and grinned. *Bingo*.

She scanned the short note, and her excitement started to bubble. The cousin didn't have Mady Budge's contact information, but she'd remembered a few Christmas cards coming from a suburb of Glasgow called Bearsden. She wrote it stuck in her mind because she couldn't imagine Mady living so close to a big city and because it had a natural ring to it. June leaned closer to the monitor and thanked the British for their quaint village names. Skimming further, she read that the cousin thought she'd heard Mady had moved back to Orkney about a year ago and settled in Kirkwall, but she wasn't certain. It didn't matter to June whether or not Mady's relative knew her exact location. With these additional details and social media, it wouldn't take long now to find Magnus's mother.

Magnus watched as Clara Winters's eyes finally drifted closed. He rose quietly from the armchair that June's father had placed in the room. The older woman was sleeping peacefully, but she'd been jumpy since sunset. Magnus could see June fraying like an old quilt, so he'd sent her to fiddle with new jam recipes. In the past two weeks, he'd learned cooking calmed her nerves. Luckily, her grandmother accepted his presence so June could find relief. The lass was working too hard nursing her nan while also keeping two businesses running.

Knowing even a screaming banshee wouldn't wake Clara, Magnus quietly set up his latest gift, a video baby monitor. June needed more freedom of movement, and she was afraid of leaving her nan alone. Carrying the video screen with him, he headed down the steps.

The smell of fried streaky bacon hit his stomach. Although he still preferred a healthy slice of ham for breakfast, he had started to admit the American version held its appeal, even if he didn't completely understand the Yanks' fascination with it. They even dipped the meat in chocolate.

As soon as he stepped into the scullery, June jerked her head in his direction, her eyes wide with concern. "Is Nan okay?"

"Sleeping like a bairn," Magnus answered as he held

out the monitor. She reached for it and then lifted her eyes toward him. They were the color of a spring meadow with the sun shining on it.

"Oh, Magnus, you shouldn't have."

"It's better than going off your head worrying about what she's doing."

"But these are expensive," June protested.

He leaned forward and brushed his mouth against hers. "Just accept the gift, lass."

"It's wonderful," June said.

"And if she calls for you, just press this button, and she can hear."

June threw her arms about his neck, her slight weight pressing against him. In response, his arms wrapped around her slim waist, and it struck him how familiar the feel of her body had become.

"I love it, darlin'." Thank you," she whispered and kissed him. He drank in the smell of her lemon-scented shampoo as their lips slid softly against each other. She tasted faintly of tart fruit, sugar, and smoked meat.

"New recipe?" he asked as they pulled apart.

She nodded as she headed to the stove to stir the large pot sitting there. "It's bacon-cranberry jam."

"Ah, it tastes a bit like lingonberries," Magnus said.

"So my nan says," June said as she dipped a spoon into the mixture. She pursed her bonny pink lips to blow on it, and he felt himself harden. She'd done the same to the tip of his boabie just last night.

Oblivious to the spell she was casting, June popped the lukewarm jam into his mouth. "Tell me what you think."

He ate slowly, giving himself time to savor each flavor. The first time June had fed him one of her new creations, he'd gobbled it too quickly, and he'd disappointed the lass when she'd started asking questions. He'd learned that when he answered her, he needed to speak like a writer.

"So, what's the verdict?" June asked as soon as he swallowed.

"Good," Magnus said. "T-T-Tart but smoky. What's it called?"

"Not sure yet. Katie always comes up with the names. I don't know how she does it. She takes a bite, closes her eyes, and *voilà*, she sees the perfect label. I think it's part of our success. Our products are just flying off the shelves at the national park and the local supermarket."

Magnus leaned back in the chair. "Have you thought about expanding, lass?"

June sighed. "It was in the works before Nan got sick, but it's on hold now. I've got enough frying pans in the fire. If I put on another, something's going to get burned."

Magnus frowned. He didn't like the idea of June delaying growing her business. She was talented and smart. He had no doubt she could handle increased production. Her jams would sell. She had a knack for combining unexpected ingredients and creating something that was pure magic.

"Have you thought about getting help with your nan?" Magnus asked. "Your idea for jams to soothe morning sickness is brilliant. You could make a lot of dosh selling them over the internet."

She exhaled before reaching for a ginger root. As she spoke, she sliced it rhythmically. When June worked on new recipes, she preferred to do her cooking the old-fashioned way. "My parents and I looked into hiring a part-time caregiver, but it gets pretty expensive very quickly."

When Magnus spoke next, he kept his voice gentle. "Have you considered nursing care, lass?"

June paused in cutting. Magnus thought he spotted tears in her green eyes, but she blinked them away. Resolutely, she pressed down on her knife. "It's always an option, but I'm not ready to make that decision. She's improved by being home, and I don't know how she'd react to a strange place. I've got things under control."

Magnus didn't agree. June couldn't sustain this pace. Even when her nan didn't call her, June wasn't sleeping well. She was working as hard as he had during his roughneck years, but he'd had weeks off at a time. She didn't. A body needed rest, or it just collapsed.

What Magnus didn't know was his place in all this. Aye, he'd begun sleeping with the lass on a regular basis, and he wasn't such a numptie as to believe that was all that brewed between them. For the first time in his life, he'd entered a real relationship, even if that made him damned uncomfortable. He had no prior experience, and occasionally he felt like he was climbing one-handed up a steep sea cliff, the rocks slick beneath his fingertips.

He wasn't like June. He didn't give advice. He'd lived his whole adult life trying to avoid entanglements. Now, he was caught as firmly as a sea trout in a trawler's net.

He added milk and sugar to his tea and sat down across from June. She'd begun to finely dice the ginger. He stirred his drink and debated about how much to say. When he did speak, he kept his words measured.

"June, you cannot go at full t-t-tilt all the time. Humans aren't built like that."

She put down the knife. Placing both hands on the counter, she raised her gaze to meet his. This time, he had no trouble spotting her unshed tears.

"I know," she said in a small, very un-June-like voice, "but I'm not there yet. Josh is coming to town to help for a few weeks, and Katie's mom offered to lend a hand. I'm holding on right now, and I'll figure something out."

Magnus rose from his chair and quickly strode around the table. He opened his arms, and June instantly snuggled against him. He kissed the top of her head and then rested his chin there. "Just mind on to care for yourself, lass."

She nodded with a sniff, and Magnus could feel his shirt grow wet from her tears. They stood there for a long while, neither of them saying anything. It felt strangely natural, comforting June.

––––––

June woke the next day feeling more like her old self than she had since Nan's hospital stay. Josh was due to arrive in two days, and she always loved when the irreverent Californian was in town. His dry humor never failed to amuse her.

But her college friend's arrival wasn't the only thing brightening June's mood. Her talk with Magnus last night had loosened something inside her. It felt good to unburden her inner worries. She hadn't wanted to admit to her parents how much she'd been struggling. They'd insist on flying out and either placing her grandmother in a home or taking her to DC. And June didn't want that.

She still didn't have a solution, but she felt better just acknowledging the problem. She'd figure out a way to fix it because that's what she did. She always found a resolution for thorny situations, even when others couldn't. She'd get through this.

Beside her, Magnus yawned and stretched. She took a moment to appreciate the movement of his muscles. Nude, he stepped out of the bed and bent to pull on his boxers and pants. June raised an appreciative eyebrow at the sight of his tight rear. When he stood up, he caught her looking and flushed.

"Morning, darlin'," she said, walking around the bed to press a kiss against his lips.

"*Madainn mhath*," he greeted her in Scots Gaelic, his eyes as bright as hers. She'd never dated another morning person, and she liked it. Neither of them needed scads of coffee before they could communicate, nor did her energy level threaten to cause him to dive right back under the covers.

"What are you planning today?" June asked him as he shrugged into a T-shirt.

"Bowie and I are going to work on framing Sorcha's enclosure," Magnus said. "Katie is going to film it. When your mate Josh comes to town, I thought you could help me with the audio when I give a tour of the exhibit."

"That sounds like a plan." June pulled her hair

into a ponytail and checked the time. "I better head downstairs and get baking."

Magnus nodded and grabbed his laptop before settling into the armchair June kept in her bedroom. "I'll get some writing done afore your nan wakes, and then I'll head over to the zoo."

"I'll have your tattie scone waiting for you," June promised.

"And tea?"

"And tea." She smiled as she leaned across the bed to give him another kiss.

Humming happily, she headed down to the kitchen and dove right into her morning work. There was nothing quite like the delicious smells accompanying bread making. Although she loved experimenting with jam, baking always comforted her. The precision it required enforced a familiar rhythm. As a child helping out in the summers, June had grown to love the routine. She could picture her grandmother kneading dough as she hummed along to the sounds of Big Bands. Nan had loved her music. Unfortunately, her hearing aids made it less pleasurable for her nowadays.

June inserted her earbuds. Although she didn't have many of the old crooners on her playlist, she had a couple. She liked to mix it up more than her grandmother: pop, some Celtic, swing, R&B, classical. Magnus had recently introduced her to some Scottish bands whose music she'd just downloaded.

The morning passed quickly. After Magnus left, June tried out the baby monitor. He'd bought her the most expensive option, which included a watch-like screen that strapped to her wrist. It worked like a charm. Nan could remain in the back room and snooze instead of having to sit wherever June was working. And June didn't have to worry about her grandmother getting into trouble. The other day, she'd caught Nan trying to eat a paper napkin, and she'd worried about letting her out of sight ever since.

She spent the afternoon making jam as her grandmother rocked in her chair. June had tried to interest the older woman in knitting, but the activity only frustrated her. Instead, June simply talked to her. Because of her antianxiety medicine, Nan kept nodding off, but June didn't mind. As long as her grandmother seemed peaceful, June was happy.

Magnus returned home at dusk carrying a bag of food from the Prairie Dog Café. June breathed in the scent of fries and hamburgers. "My, my, does that smell good."

Magnus chuckled as he distributed the food. "Americans and their grease."

"As opposed to boiling away the taste."

"Better on the arteries."

"I don't know what to do," Nan said suddenly as she stared blankly at the food.

June suppressed a sigh. Unfortunately, this had become a common routine. "You just need to eat it, darlin'."

Her grandmother eyed the sandwich like it was a toothy gator ready to snap. "Too much. I can't chew all that."

June reached for the burger. Removing it from the bun, she cut up the meat and put it on a smaller plate. She'd read big helpings could confuse people with dementia. Although Nan hadn't been diagnosed with that particular disease, June still found the information useful. Her grandmother looked glumly at her plate but began to eat mechanically.

Magnus told them about his day. Evidently, Honey had opened the llama gate just after the zoo's closing. Although most of the herd had stuck together, a few had broken away. Bowie's daughter, Abby, had pitched in to help, along with Katie and Lou. Savannah had proved the hardest to corral. Evidently, the little camel treated the whole episode as a game. She'd only returned to the pen for a drink of milk. Magnus showed them the video Katie had posted to the zoo's website. Even Nan smiled at the animals' antics.

After dinner, Magnus and Nan talked while June prepped for the next day. When she finished, she got Nan ready for bed. Magnus came in to read to her grandmother, allowing June to head to the shower. She took a long one, letting the hot water beat the day's stress from her body. When she entered the master bedroom, she found Magnus unpacking his knapsack and laying out his clothes. It struck her that he should just move his belongings from the zoo to her house, but June didn't believe in casually inviting a man to live with her. A question like that required finesse, and finesse required jam.

"Would you like to try my new creations from last night?" June asked. "I was thinking about going downstairs and grabbing some."

"I'd never say no to your cooking," Magnus told her as he settled into the bed with his laptop.

She hurried down the steps and grabbed a couple leftover scones and her two new jellies. Returning to the bedroom, she sat cross-legged at the foot of the bed as she split open a pastry. "Which do you want first? The bacon jam or the apple-ginger? I have to warn you the last one has a hint of apple cider vinegar."

"Vinegar? In jam? That's an odd one, hen, even for you."

"It's for the pregnancy line. I wanted to include one for heartburn relief."

"I'll start with the b-b-bacon jam."

"Coward."

"Aye."

June slathered the scone and handed it to Magnus. He took a bite, and she watched him savor it. She fixed her own pastry with the apple-ginger concoction before she made her first move.

"It's been nice, having you here. I know Nan loves when you read to her."

Magnus nodded and ate off another healthy chunk. June smiled. "Since you've been sleeping over every night, I was wondering if you'd like to store your belongings in my closet. I could give you a drawer too. That way you won't be dragging your knapsack all over creation."

Magnus choked on his scone. He thumped his chest and straightened. June frowned as she reached for his cup of tea, which had been cooling on the nightstand. He accepted it and took a big gulp. She watched as he swallowed.

This was *not* going as she'd planned.

He regarded her with watery eyes. "I'll th-h-h-h-think about it, lass."

She wanted to push. She hated waiting for answers, but she held back. His stutter had worsened, and she knew she'd made him uncomfortable. She was trying very hard not to demand too much. Magnus was as skittish as a newborn colt, and she didn't want him galloping off.

―――⁓―――

"So, the lass asked me to move into her flat above the tea shop," Magnus told Sorcha and Frida as he leaned against the fence. He'd just brought the little cub for her daily ramble in the grizzly's enclosure. The polar bear was happily toddling through the exhibit, while the older bruin lay on the ground. Frida raised her head at Magnus's voice, but Sorcha ignored him as she clambered over the rocks.

"I won't be here forever," Magnus continued. Sorcha chose that moment to swivel in his direction. Her black eyes looked as soulful as a wee seal pup's. Despite the gale brewing inside him, Magnus chuckled softly. "Not you too, Sorcha. One hen asking me for more than I can give is enough."

Sorcha turned back and took a flying leap at a bright-red ball. Batting it first with her paw, she then chased it. At the movement, Frida shifted with a grunt, inching closer before lying back down to watch the younger bear as carefully as her rheumy eyes would allow. When the peedie bruin got close to the edge of the exhibit, which dropped to form a moat below, Frida lumbered to her feet and growled. Sorcha froze. The old bear herded the cub back to safety. When the grizzly tried to lie back down, Sorcha decided it was time to roughhouse. As the whalp climbed over the elderly bruin and tugged at her fur with her teeth, Frida heaved a huge sigh that bounced off the rocks surrounding them.

Magnus could sympathize with the animal's resigned exasperation. Right now, he felt yanked in more directions than a Shetland pony fighting its lead. He didn't mind helping with June's nan. Obligations had never bothered him. The endless chores hadn't driven him off the croft. Part of him had enjoyed the rhythm of rural island life. Even hard work had never fashed him.

But he'd hated the expectations. The demands. The sense of someone else dictating his life.

Without thinking, Magnus rubbed the back of his head. He felt the scar. A ridge of puckered skin that should lie smooth and flat. His hand moved to his shoulder and skimmed the hard patch there too.

He growled. At himself. At June. At his da. He didn't know. Maybe all three.

He ripped his fingers away and clutched the rail of the exhibit. Frida growled playfully at Sorcha. The little bear made a sound in the back of her throat as she pranced in front of the grizzly. Frida lifted a paw and gently bopped the younger bruin. In response, Sorcha attacked the bear's massive leg.

Magnus exhaled slowly, forcing his rioting blood to calm. What June offered made sense. He was all but living at the tea shop, and she hadn't cajoled him into coming in the first place. He'd offered. The lass needed help, and he wouldn't abandon her or her nan.

Only a nyaff would keep dragging his belongings back and forth. The only time he spent in his room at the zoo was when he shoved his knapsack inside in the morning and then grabbed it in the evening before heading to June's. She was right to offer him space for his things, and he shouldn't be a bawbag about it. She'd said nothing about making the arrangement permanent. Hell, she hadn't even offered him a key.

"So, what do you think?" Magnus asked the bears. "Should I move my shite into her flat?"

Both animals ignored him this time. Frida had rolled onto her belly, and Sorcha had climbed on top. The two were snarling at each other. Even Frida appeared to be enjoying herself. A faint smile drifted over Magnus's face.

"Och, what good are the two of you?" Magnus asked as the bears continued their play.

If he stored his clothes at June's, he needed to make it clear he wasn't changing his ultimate plan. As soon as Magnus finished gathering fodder for his next book, he was returning to London. Immediately. And June would understand when he left. She wasn't his da.

Fluffy watched Honey curiously. She'd been acting odd lately. Very odd.

Although he'd watched her release the llamas yesterday, she had not been escaping as much as she normally did. Instead, she spent her time digging, even though they each had a perfectly good den.

And when she did leave, she returned with dry sagebrush and grass instead of yummy treats. Any food that she did collect, she gobbled right up. She didn't even taunt him.

Something had changed. Fluffy just knew it.

"Where should I stow this, lass?" Magnus asked as he hoisted an old British Army duffel in addition to his trusty knapsack. At the sight of the larger bag, June felt her lips curl into a smile. Magnus was moving his stuff into her rooms. She'd been right not to push him last night.

"I can clear you some space in one of my drawers and my closet," June said.

Magnus shook his head. "I'll be keeping my belongings in my holdall."

"I don't mind giving you room for your things, darlin'," June said. "It's no fun living out of a suitcase."

He shrugged. "I'm used to it. It'll make packing easier when I go back to London."

A whisper of unease slipped through June's happiness. It wrapped around her heart and settled there. She swallowed, but it didn't make the uncomfortable feeling disperse. She wasn't used to feeling like this...at least not anymore.

As a small child, she'd hated when her family inevitably relocated to a new base. Each move meant saying goodbye to all her friends. And it had hurt. A lot.

She vividly remembered crying in the closet, her knees tucked against her chest. In her seven-year-old mind, she'd thought if she hid there and sobbed long enough, her parents would relent. Her mama had found her and crawled in next to her. Stroking June's hair, she'd pulled her close and said, "June

Bug, I know it's hard to go, but think of all the memories that you're taking and the ones you're leaving behind for folks here to enjoy."

So, June had always focused on that. When she arrived at a new place, she put all her effort into making her time there special. Then, she'd have something to tuck away and bring with her when she left. She worked hard to give people good memories of her too. She supposed that's why she always fixed things even long after she'd put down a whole system of roots in Sagebrush Flats.

June had gotten used to people sticking around. This was the kind of place that pulled people back like boomerangs. Katie had returned after being away for over a decade. Although June knew Magnus was just passing through, she'd gotten lulled into the comfort of their routine. He seemed to belong here. In Sagebrush. At the zoo. With her.

But she had learned long ago that she couldn't make people stay, no matter how much she wanted to. So instead, she'd do what she always did. She'd absorb as many memories as she could, and she'd make sure Magnus took plenty with him.

But it would hurt like the dickens when Magnus returned to London. He'd become a part of her, and it was going to feel as if something had been yanked from her soul. But she'd patch it up. She always did.

And she wanted Magnus to depart whole. She hated the thought of him going back to Britain alone. There was only one way to fix that problem: She needed to speed up her search for his mother.

"You want me to go to a party?" Magnus asked as June made bread dough with her mixer. It was his day off, and her assistant hadn't arrived yet. He'd thought he'd have a relaxing morn sipping his tea as she buzzed about him, but he'd gravely miscalculated.

"Yes. It would be so much fun!"

"Your bum's out the window."

June turned from measuring flour. "My bum is certainly in the window. Everyone loves a party."

"I don't," Magnus said. "And that's not how you respond to that phrase."

June smiled and planted a kiss on the tip of his nose. Normally, he found it charming. Now, it made him feel itchy, like the hen was trying to manipulate him. He didn't like that. Ever since he'd moved his bags into her flat two days ago, he'd felt restless. He didn't want to get trapped again, and he hoped he hadn't voluntarily stepped into an inescapable cage.

"It's to welcome Josh back to Sagebrush, and I'm having it right here at the tea shop. All you have to do is walk downstairs."

"I'm not a local. I don't need to be greeting him."

June's eyes had gone as green as the summer grass, and Magnus felt a pang when he gazed into them. *Baws*. He was going to give in, even if he didn't like it.

"I need a night out, Magnus. Katie's mom agreed to watch Nan, and I can relax and get away from everything."

Magnus sighed and took another swig of tea.

He would've made it stronger if he'd realized they'd be having this conversation. Hell, he might even have mixed up an Irish coffee. "Why don't I just watch your nan, lass? I can even read her some of my new work." Which he never let anyone see before he handed it over to his publisher.

"But I want you to be there." Instead of sparkling like emeralds, her eyes had become as rich as jade. *Baws.*

"Fine, lass. I'll come, but I won't be liking it."

She gave a happy sound that reminded him of an excited puffin. She flew around the island counter to give him a hug and a peck on the cheek. He grunted.

"You can practice being more open about your stutter and using the post-block technique in public!"

"Now that sounds like a party game," Magnus said dryly. "Cocktails and prolongation fun." June, of course, ignored his sarcasm.

"You're doing such a good job going into the stores here at Sagebrush. I think this would be perfect!"

"If you say so, lass."

"You won't regret this," she promised. "After all, it's one of my parties. You'll have a grand old time."

That, Magnus very much doubted.

Chapter 14

"So, what's new in Sagebrush?" Josh asked as he sipped the latte June had just made him. Before she could answer, a group of female ski tourists entered the tea shop. They were a smidge or two older than the college students Sagebrush Flats normally attracted, which put them in their midtwenties. When the women spotted Josh's tall frame, the three tried covertly to give him the once-over, but neither June nor Josh missed their glances.

Josh smiled smoothly as they approached and raised his cup toward them in a salute before taking another drink. "You ladies have come to the right place. My friend here serves the best tea and coffee in town."

If Katie had been with them, she would have rolled her eyes, but June played right along. She gave the most nonthreatening grin. She never minded being Josh's wing-woman. After all, she was the one who'd taught him the art of flirting. The poor man had possessed absolutely no game when she'd met him in college. Magnus was practically a Casanova in comparison.

"Josh," she drawled, "you just give a girl the nicest compliments." Then she leaned toward the women and pretended to whisper conspiratorially. "He has to. We've been friends forever. But he is right. I do serve the best tea and coffee in town. Just don't tell Karen Montgomery. She runs the Prairie Dog Café, and she'd skin me alive if she heard me. She wins on burgers, but only 'cause I don't make them here."

The group laughed politely, but June knew they'd already dismissed her, which was her intent. She leaned back and let Josh do his thing. Hiding a smile, she pretended to clean the spotless counter.

She didn't blame the women for their interest. Josh was classically handsome, and his auburn hair gave him a roguish charm. Thanks to her tutelage, he dressed impeccably. Although he'd ditched his suit for Sagebrush, he wore crisply pressed chinos and a cashmere turtleneck under a taupe suede jacket. It was hard to believe he'd once dressed in only a couple T-shirts and an ill-fitting pair of jeans that had made his lanky body look like a blue string bean.

After June took the women's orders, Josh flirted some more. By the time she had their food ready, the brunette was texting him her number. Josh flashed one of his debonair smiles as the women departed. He turned back to June, and she shook her head.

"You can dim the wattage, Romeo. That grin won't dazzle me."

He leaned over the counter and winked. "But I learned from a master."

She patted him on the head. "And you have done well, young Jedi."

He chuckled as he returned his phone to his pocket. "It's 'young Padawan,' but the *Star Wars* reference is appreciated."

"It's fashionable now, darlin'," June said.

"I wish it had been in high school," Josh said. "I would have been the most popular guy with my Darth Maul light saber. I saved for over a year to buy that thing."

"I'm not so sure that's a status symbol, honey. Even now."

"You're probably right. Hard-core fans are deeply divided on *Episode I*," he said with a shrug before he changed the subject. "So, my original question still stands. What's been going on with you and Katie?"

"Katie has graduated from nausea into constant hunger mixed with heartburn. I can barely keep her in jam." June paused for a moment and gave her old friend a sly smile. "And I've shacked up with a man."

Josh dramatically clutched at his heart. "No!"

She reached over the counter and batted his shoulder. "Don't go mocking me now."

"So, who is it?" Josh asked.

"Magnus Gray."

That succeeded in getting a real reaction out of the Californian. "The woolly Scot?"

June nodded.

"You're shitting me."

June shook her head. "I'm not. And you better watch your language, or Nan will make you wash your mouth out with lye soap."

Josh ignored her threat. "The writer? The guy who actually walked away from the Great June Winters?"

"The very one."

Josh whistled and then bobbed his head. "Once again, I bow to the master."

June sighed. "I wouldn't bow too low. He isn't even unpacking his stuff. He told me when he left his duffel bag in my closet that he's still planning on going back to London. That's why we're having a party in your honor tomorrow night."

Josh blinked and then shook his head. "You're going to have to walk me through that again. I'm out of practice following June Winters's logic. I swear it's harder than advanced calc."

June bopped his shoulder again.

"You know," he said as he rubbed his arm, "if you keep doing that, I'm going to turn black and blue. I'm a redhead. I've got skin like a peach. A white one."

"If Katie catches you saying that, she'll give you a bruise."

"She's got the hair and the temper, but not the complexion," Josh said.

June rolled her eyes. "I swear you have the focus of a gnat. I have no idea how you managed to make millions."

"Money is a great motivator."

June gave him a mock glare, and he dropped his hand from his bicep. "Okay, you were saying something about a party?"

"I want Magnus to leave with good memories, so I thought I'd have a party and invite some of my favorite people. You're my excuse."

"Gee, thanks."

"You can bring your tourist and her friends."

Josh paused and then grinned. "Okay. Now you're talking."

"So, it's all settled?"

"For me, but I don't know about your Scot. He doesn't seem the partying type."

"I'm not planning a big, boisterous event," June said. "I'm just going to have some close friends over—"

"And some random strangers," Josh interjected.

June glared, and he held up his hands in mock surrender. "Hey, I'm not complaining."

June sighed. "Josh, I really want to make Magnus's time in Sagebrush memorable."

Josh for once sobered, his snark gone. "Maybe just being with you is memorable, June. Did you ever think of that? Not everyone's a social butterfly."

June patted the side of his face. "Aren't you just the sweetest?"

"I'm being serious, June. It's like when you dragged Katie and me to parties back in college when we just wanted to play video games."

"Says the man who now hobnobs up and down the California coast."

Josh took another swig of coffee. "That's business, June, and power. It gets old fast."

June studied him closely as her fix-it radar started to tingle. "Are you happy, Josh?"

He paused with his coffee cup halfway to his lips. Bringing it back down to his side, he shook his head. "Uh-uh, June. I know that look. No meddling."

"But if you're dissatisfied with your life—"

Josh gave a bark of amused laughter. "June, we can't all be as deliriously bubbly as you."

"I am not deliriously bubbly," she protested.

Josh gave her a sidelong glance before speaking with a high, exaggerated drawl. "'Josh, dahlin', problems are just bunches of lemons waiting to be made into lemonade.'"

June batted him again. "I don't use clichés." She paused, considering. "Well, at least not bad ones."

"Enough arguing," Josh said. "Tell me more about your moody Scot."

June sighed. "I like this one, Josh. I really do."

Josh studied her. "He doesn't seem like your normal type."

"He's not," June admitted, "but he's just the sweetest man."

"Are we talking about the same grump who told you to, and I quote, 'Feck off'?"

June looked around the tea shop. The only patrons were Stanley and Buck, and they were too engrossed in their own conversation to pay attention. With her voice lowered, the two old-timers couldn't hear if they tried.

"He lived on a small island with only his da growing up, so I think that's why he doesn't like crowds. I'm trying to change that." Tracking down Magnus's mother would help too.

Josh cocked his head and studied her. "Juuuune, what aren't you telling me?"

June shrugged nonchalantly. "What makes you think I'm hiding something?"

"You have that look you get when you're about to meddle."

"I don't meddle. I fix things," June said.

Josh snorted. "That depends on your point of view. What are you planning to do to the poor man?"

June swung her eyes around the tables and chairs again out of an abundance of precaution. When she spoke, she dropped her voice even further. "I'm in the process of tracking down his mother. He doesn't have any family to speak—"

"What the hell, June!"

Buck and Stanley's heads popped up like prairie dogs. *Drat*. Both men swiveled in their direction. Josh went to speak, and June waved at him to keep his voice low.

"June, I'm telling you right now. You don't want to do that."

"Shh," June hissed. "This isn't the place to talk."

Josh crossed his arms as he used his considerable height to tower over her. "You brought it up."

"But you're the one who drew the attention of Sagebrush's biggest gossips."

"Fine, but don't do anything stupid until you've had a chance to talk with me. Believe me, you're going to want to."

Magnus sat at one of the tables June had left up for the party. Around him, people chatted. June stood in the thick of it, her bonny lips open in a hearty laugh. The sound tinkled in his direction, washing over him. She was in her glory, a brilliant, shining sun holding the gathering together, giving it life. Aye, she was a braw lass, and he could watch her for hours.

He took a drag of the craft IPA that June's friend Josh had brought from California. It was hoppier than Magnus liked, but it wasn't rubbish either.

He saw June grab the elbow of her friend and then tip her head in his direction. Magnus barely suppressed a groan. The hen had shown a surprising amount of restraint by not forcing him into the middle of the festivities. It seemed his reprieve had ended.

Josh made his way over to Magnus's table, two beers in hand. He slid one in Magnus's direction before sitting down. "June thought you might need another."

Magnus snorted. "M-m-m-more like she thought I needed the company."

Josh didn't react to Magnus's block, so he figured June must have prepared him. Hell, she'd probably sent her friend over so he could practice stuttering openly.

The man laughed easily at Magnus's comment. "That's June for you."

"Aye," Magnus said, and an awkward hush fell over them.

"June tells me you're a writer," Josh said.

"Aye, and you?" Magnus asked even though he already knew the man had started his own IT security company. Listening to the Californian explain his job would be better than talking himself.

"I build firewalls and shit like that. When they don't work, I hunt down and stop hackers," Josh said. "It's like being a bounty hunter without any blood, guts, or danger."

Magnus snorted in amusement, but it wasn't long before another wave of uncomfortable silence hit. Magnus took a sip of beer, and Josh drummed his fingers on the table. June glanced in their direction and made an encouraging motion with her fingers.

Josh turned to Magnus again. "I think that means we're to keep talking."

"Aye."

Josh paused and then gestured toward Magnus with the neck of his beer bottle. "So, I see June's been working her magic on you."

"Come again, now?" Magnus asked as protective rage roared through him. Was the manky bastard referring to the fact June was sleeping with him?

Josh chuckled. "You can relax. I wasn't talking about that. June's like a sister, and the less I know, the better. I was referring to your new look. You're less hairy than the last time I saw you."

"I thought Americans weren't b-b-b-blunt," Magnus said.

Josh laughed again and took a swig of beer. "I'm a bit of a douche. Ask Katie or June or, better yet, Bowie."

Magnus gave a short nod. He wasn't sure if he liked this man, but at least he wasn't boring. Unlike ceilidhs, American parties didn't have much entertainment other than drinking and blethering. If Magnus had to pass the time with someone, Josh wasn't the worst bloke.

"June's good at it," Josh said.

Magnus turned to him in confusion, and Josh clarified. "Giving people makeovers. Hell, you should have seen what I looked like before she got her hands on me. I was a mess. Katie too, but don't tell her I said that."

Unease slipped through Magnus. Although he'd cut his hair and trimmed his beard at June's suggestion, he didn't like the idea of her molding him into someone different. And he liked it even less if he was just part of a pattern. Katie had also mentioned to Magnus that June was good at makeovers.

"Yep," Josh said, oblivious to Magnus's tension. "Our June likes her projects."

"P-p-p-p-projects?"

"Back in college I was a complete dork, not just a geek or a nerd, but a certifiable dork. I had trouble talking to anybody, let alone girls. Katie…Katie was easy. She was like me, a geek. June was Katie's roommate, and June took pity on both of us. She changed both of our lives, but especially mine. I had shit for confidence. I never could've gotten clients if it hadn't been for June. Plus, I look a hell of a lot better."

A cold, sick feeling twisted through Magnus. Luckily, he'd learned early to hide his emotions. Josh seemed to have no idea of the maelstrom he'd stirred up.

"Did you d-date?" Magnus asked, pleased with how steady, how normal his voice sounded even with his slight stutter.

"June and me?" Josh leaned back in his chair. "Naw. She intimidated the crap out of me when I first met her, and then she became like family. She's got a big heart. She can't come across a problem and not try to fix it. It can drive you batshit crazy, but she's normally right in the end."

Was that what Magnus was to June? Just some damn problem? A fucking project?

It made twisted sense. Lasses as bonny as her didn't shag ugly munters like him. All her poking and prodding didn't mean shite. She was just trying to repair him like some broken-down tractor.

—⁓—

"I think that went well." June sank into one of the chairs across from Katie. Bowie had his arm slung around his wife's shoulder, while Josh sat next to June. Everyone else had left, and Magnus was upstairs watching Nan.

"Except for when the friend of Josh's date brought along Clay Stevens," Katie said.

June sighed. "I know. I thought Lacey Montgomery was going to spit nails."

"Well, Clay is a bit of a dick when it comes to her wolf-rehabilitation project," Bowie pointed out.

"Isn't he the son of the guy who scammed the town?" Josh asked. "Sagebrush's Bernie Madoff?"

June nodded. "Lacey's parents lost their life savings, and her daddy had a heart attack right after."

"Shit," Josh said. "No wonder she can't stand Clay Stevens."

"At least they steered clear of each other tonight," Bowie said.

"I don't know," Josh said. "The fireworks might have been interesting."

"You are incorrigible," June said.

Josh gave her a shit-eating grin. "Yep, and I've got no plans to change."

"Thanks for talking to Magnus," June said. "I hope he had a good time. He seemed distant when he went up to sit with Nan."

Bowie shrugged. "He's a quiet guy, June. I wouldn't read too much into it."

Josh rolled his eyes. "June's got it in her head

she should track down his mother, which I think is a shitty idea."

Bowie's body stiffened, and he turned to level his gray eyes on her. "Didn't he say in his books his mother abandoned him?"

June nodded. "But we don't know why she left. She may have had a good reason. His daddy sounds like a horrible, horrible—"

"I don't care how bad his father was, June, or even if his mother felt she had no choice," Josh said. "Magnus is not going to appreciate you digging into this."

"Josh is right," Bowie stated stiffly.

"But—"

"June," Katie broke in softly, her brown eyes concerned. "I think you may want to listen to the two former foster kids on this. Some hurts go beyond fixing."

"Still," June continued to protest.

"Fuck, June," Josh said, "you're going to make me go there."

"Go where?" June asked in confusion.

"My mom left me at a bus station when I was six," Josh said. "If any woman who I dated tracked her down, I'd never speak to that person again."

Shock washed over June as she studied one of her closest friends in the world. "I thought you ended up in foster care because your mom was dead."

Josh shook his head. "I let you think that, June, because I was afraid you might pull a stunt like this."

Unbelievably hurt, June swung her gaze toward Katie. "Did you know?"

Josh answered for her. "I swore her to secrecy, so blame me if you're going to get pissed off."

"I see," June said shakily. She pushed back from the table, feeling as unsteady as a landlubber during a squall at sea. She was the duct tape, the one people came to with their problems. People didn't hide things from her. They didn't exclude her.

"June," Katie said, her chair squeaking as she clamored to her feet, her hand supporting her pregnant belly. June could see the sympathy in her friend's cherubic face. Katie hadn't meant to hurt her. Neither had Josh. But they had.

June plastered on a smile, because that's what she did. She smiled. "It's okay, really. I understand. I do like to stick my nose in other people's business. I get that."

"Fuck, June," Josh said as he stood as well. "I didn't mean to hurt you."

"Then what did you mean, darlin'?" June asked, keeping her voice soft and steady...sweet, even.

"You said you really like this guy, and I don't want you to blow it. And if you do this, you will. Hands down."

June swung her eyes toward Bowie. He'd also risen and looked like he was trying to fade into the wall. "What do you think?"

He swung his gaze toward Katie, and June stepped forward. "I'm not asking your wife, honey. I'm asking you."

Bowie rubbed the back of his head, his gray eyes steady. "Magnus is an intelligent man, June. He's got money and resources. If he wanted to track down his mother, he would've done it."

"And how would you feel?"

"You want the honest truth?" Bowie asked.

"Yes."

Bowie sighed, long and hard. "If my mom was still alive, and Katie contacted her without my knowledge, I'd feel like a camel had kicked me right in the heart. It's difficult putting a past like that behind you, and this could undo a lot of things he worked hard to resolve."

June sank back into her seat. "I screwed up, didn't I?"

Her friends rejoined her at the table. Katie reached forward and grabbed her hand.

"Not necessarily," Josh said. "How far have you gotten in your search?"

"I emailed her last night," June said in a small voice.

Her three friends exchanged glances. June gave an uncharacteristic groan and dropped her head to rest it against the scarred wooden table. She wasn't used to feeling like this. Except with Nan's health, she never second-guessed herself.

"Maybe you have the wrong person," Katie said gently as she patted June's hand.

"Or she won't respond," Josh added.

June lifted her gaze to study them. "What if she does? What if she wants to talk to Magnus? Would I have a right to keep that from him?"

"Well," Katie said, "I guess you'll have to wait and see what happens. You'll know what to do."

"Clearly, I won't," June said glumly.

"We'll all be here," Katie promised.

"I might need y'all," June admitted, not realizing how soon that would be.

About an hour later, June finally made her way up to her rooms above the tea shop. She found Magnus asleep in bed. He had Nan's monitor on the nightstand, his laptop resting on his stomach. Realizing he must have dozed off while writing, June gently removed the computer. She snuggled down against him, but sleep evaded her.

June was not accustomed to guilt, and the nasty emotion threatened to chew her up from the inside out. The longer she cuddled next to Magnus, the worse it got. Unable to withstand it, she slipped from their bed and padded to her computer. Powering it up, she debated what to do. Maybe she should email the woman and say it was all a prank. It might not be the most genteel solution, but then June would never know if she'd contacted the right person. Then she'd have nothing to confess to Magnus.

Sighing, June opened her account and saw it: an email from Mady Budge. A sick feeling sprang up in her heart and crept through the rest of her body. Swallowing against the pressure, she scanned the note. She read it twice and then collapsed against the chair.

She'd found the correct Mady Budge, all right.

June glanced over at Magnus. He slept so peacefully, so quietly. He'd done so much for her and her nan, and she'd wanted to give him something in return. Instead, if Josh and Bowie were right, she may have just triggered a tsunami designed to destroy his well-ordered life.

June checked the time. It would be morning in the UK. Mady Budge hadn't said much in her message. She'd just confirmed she was Magnus's mother, and she'd be willing to renew contact if he wanted. But Magnus was a famous author. His first books had remained on the bestseller list for weeks. The woman might be more interested in money than a reunion. And June needed to know this critical fact. Because somewhere in her sleeplessness, she'd arrived at the inevitable conclusion. She had to tell Magnus. Now that Mady Budge had contacted her, June had no choice. She'd messed up, but keeping quiet would only compound her mistake. This, June realized too late, wasn't about her. It was about Magnus.

But if she was going to reveal this to him, she wanted all the facts. Dangling a half answer in front of him seemed worse than the whole truth…even if it meant telling Magnus that his mother just wanted to take advantage of his success.

June grabbed her phone and headed downstairs. Feeling uncharacteristically nervous, she dialed the number Mady had provided. The first ring seemed like it would never come, but it was only the delay of a transatlantic connection. Finally, she heard a voice on the other line.

"Hullo?"

June swallowed and then dug for her normal confidence. She charmed people. That's what she did. She could handle this. "Hello, is this Mady Budge?"

A long pause. "Aye."

"This is June Winters. I'm the woman who emailed you."

An even longer hesitation. "Aye."

June rubbed her temple. The woman may have left before Magnus's formative years, but there were already striking similarities. She just hoped the lady wouldn't hang up.

"I have a confession to make," June said. "Magnus didn't know I contacted you."

Silence, but no click of the phone.

June took a breath and continued, "I am sorry to put you in this position, but I wanted to talk to you personally before I admit to him what I did."

"No m-m-m-m-matter," the woman said. At her disfluency, June squeezed her eyes shut. Mady Budge sounded so much like her son. She even blocked exactly the same way on the *m*. Then again, both *Magnus* and *Mady* started in a similar manner, and people who stuttered often had difficulties with the first letter of their name.

"I thought that m-m-m-might be the case," the woman said. "I don't blame him. I shouldn't have left like I did."

"Why did you?" June asked gently.

The woman didn't speak, but June could tell she was trying. June leaned her head against the cool wall. She'd meant to heal a family. Instead, she'd just dug at old wounds.

"I couldn't take him with m-m-m-me," the woman said, and June believed her. "I had no education, no skills, no m-m-m-money. I m-missed him. Every single day."

June stared at the clock on the wall, watching the little hand tick the seconds away. She needed to know if the woman was telling the truth, and June knew the only way was to open up herself.

"Ms. Budge?"

"Aye?"

"I was a first-rate fool to start this, but it's like a raging bull now. There's no stopping it. I contacted you because I care for your son. There's a hole inside him that's wider than the Atlantic, and he doesn't deserve that. Do you know how he's spent the last few weeks? He's been helping me care for my nan. She's elderly and gets confused something fierce. He sits with her and tells her about life on Tammay. He hates talking about his boyhood home because he was so unhappy there, but he does it because she lived on the island as a girl during the war and it brings her peace. Your son doesn't deserve more hurt than he already has. So, what I'm asking is...do you really want a relationship with your son? A real one?"

"Do you love my son?"

June squeezed her eyes shut as the truth hit her. She did. She loved Magnus Gray, and she was about to lose him. "Yes."

"But you're going to t-t-tell him what you did even if it might m-m-m-make him leave?"

"Yes. It's what's best for him."

"I love my son too," the woman said, and June noticed she spoke without a hint of disfluency. Mady let the words hang in the air, giving them time to float there, cementing their importance. When she spoke again, her stutter returned. "I loved him since he was a p-p-p-peedie b-b-bairn, and he grabbed my finger. But I wasn't strong, not like you. I m-m-m-made the only choice I could. Staying on with his d-d-da would've killed m-me, but I'm not that feartie anymore. I'll not bother him. I've lost that right. But if he wants anything from m-me—anything—I am here."

"Thank you," June said. "I'll tell him when he wakes up."

"Aye," Mady said, and then paused. "Good luck, hen. What's for you will not go past you."

After Mady hung up, June stayed in the kitchen for a long time, just staring at the walls. She didn't sit in silence very often. She normally hated it. To be honest, she didn't like it now. But she needed it. Maybe if she'd thought before galloping ahead like a racehorse, she wouldn't be in this pickle.

When she heard Magnus stirring, she slowly got to her feet. Realizing her shoulders were bent forward, she straightened. June Winters did not slouch. She didn't avoid problems either. She faced them. And she wouldn't start flinching now…even if her heart felt heavier than wet Georgian mud.

Magnus woke slowly, which was unusual. His mind sought the protection of sleep, but his body had been trained since childhood to wake before sunrise. With a groan, Magnus rolled over. Concrete thoughts had yet to form, but he felt a sense of loss.

His eyes slowly opened and focused on the empty swath of bed. June should be lying there, her eyes closed in slumber, a half smile on her bonny lips. But she wasn't.

Magnus's memory came crashing back and, with it, an even greater sense of unease. His conversation with Josh still plagued him. He hadn't talked to June about it yet. Part of him wanted to retreat, but he found he could not. He needed to speak with her.

Perhaps their relationship wasn't just about her trying to fix him like a bloody piece of rusted farm equipment.

He stood up, the floorboards cold beneath his feet, but he didn't bother with socks or slippers. He was used to drafts much worse than this. After all, he'd grown up in a centuries' old crofters' but-and-ben. Still, the chill bothered him more than usual. Perhaps it was waking up without June's warm body tucked against his.

He wondered if she'd made it to bed last night with her mate being in town. Magnus was just about to go look for her when he heard her tread on the stairs. He started forward but froze when she appeared in the open doorframe.

The lass looked stricken. He rushed to her. "Your nan?"

June shook her head. "No, but you may want to sit down."

He paused. Thick and deadly, dread pumped through him. He hadn't felt the sensation in years, but it tasted familiar. After all, it had been his constant companion growing up.

"What is it, lass?"

June swallowed. Then she lifted her chin and held his gaze. "I tracked down your mother."

—⁓—

Everything inside Magnus froze. He couldn't think. He just stood dumbfounded like a bloody bleating sheep, except he wasn't making a sound.

June gave him a timorous smile, her bonny pink lips quivering ever so slightly. But he felt nothing beyond a baltic wind sweeping through the hollow inside him. June and her light had started to fill that emptiness, but that vanished with her words. Hell, the brightness had been leaking from him ever since Josh had hinted Magnus was the latest in a long line of projects.

"Magnus, say something," June pleaded softly, her green eyes luminous in the dull light from the lamp.

But Magnus couldn't. And not because of his stutter. He simply had nothing to say to her.

"I know it was beyond stupid." June wet her lips. "I had this fool notion I could fix things for you. I sense a loss deep inside you, and I didn't want you to leave Sagebrush without helping you resolve it."

So Magnus's fears were right. He had been nothing but clay to June...and a sad, pathetic lump at that. A lump that wasn't even complete.

Anger and betrayal sliced through him. He'd lived his whole childhood being beaten and slammed into a shape his da desired, like an ingot on a forge. He'd almost traded his life to escape, but this time was worse. This time Magnus feared he'd have to barter his soul.

He walked over to the closet and began to pull out his holdall. Fingers touched his shoulder, and time blended together. It wasn't June's hand he felt, but his father's meaty one. He flinched, his body tensed for a blinding blow.

When it didn't come, he whirled around, and his bag practically knocked into June. He caught it just in time, but she still jumped back. He saw fear flash in her eyes, but it wasn't enough to cause him to simmer down. He might be a manky bastard, but he didn't care. He couldn't stay in the flat any longer. Walking over to the nightstand, he grabbed his computer and shoved it in his knapsack.

"Magnus…" June spoke his name softly, like she was addressing a feral dog. He ignored her. His days of being cajoled had ended.

Hoisting both bags over his shoulder, he headed out the door. Despite his anger, he remembered to tread quietly. He didn't want to rouse June's nan. Magnus had reached the back door, his hand on the handle, when he heard June call his name again. By the sound of it, she was standing directly behind him. He didn't turn around.

"Magnus, I think we should talk." He could hear the tears in her voice, and he almost relented. And that? That enraged him even more. The lass had gotten inside his head, something his father had never achieved.

He turned the knob and yanked open the door. He heard the fall of footsteps behind him.

"You need to know your mother loves you, Magnus, even if you don't contact her. She wanted you to know that."

Magnus stiffened as fresh pain ripped through him, threatening to cut him to pieces. His whole life he'd been numb, but June had taught him to feel. And this? This was agony, worse than the physical pain of taking a shovel to the head and a bullet to the shoulder.

He walked out the door into the darkness. The whole time, even as he spoke, he kept his eyes trained on the horizon, even though he didn't see a glimmer of light. "Fuck off, June."

~~~

June had no idea how long she stood in the kitchen after Magnus left. She couldn't move. The pain was too great.

She didn't even have righteous anger to sustain her. She'd done this. She'd driven him away.

She didn't cry. Not yet. All her energy went into absorbing the blow. She didn't understand how to handle the emotions pounding in her heart. Guilt. Regret. Hurt.

June simply didn't know what to do. Because she, the ultimate fixer, had broken something beautiful. And, for the first time, she had no idea how to repair it.

———

Magnus walked straight to the zoo. He hadn't put on a coat, and he welcomed the chill lingering in the air. It gave him a semblance of calm, which he needed to deal with Bowie. Magnus had never been clear on how long he planned on staying. After all, he was working for free.

But not anymore. He had no intention of remaining in Sagebrush Flats any longer than it took to make his goodbyes.

He stepped through the quiet zoo. At this hour, even the animals were abed. Well, most of them. The honey badgers—the nocturnal peedie buggers— were probably awake and causing mischief.

Magnus put his bags down in his old room by the nursery. He tried lying down, but sleep danced out of reach. Instead, he kept seeing June and her bonny pink smile. He growled and punched the air mattress. It gave a sad sound and started to deflate. Magnus scowled at it. Evidently, he'd be giving Bowie money for a new one.

Sighing, Magnus rose to his feet and headed back outside. He needed to say goodbye to Frida anyway.

—⁓—

Honey twitched her nose as she watched the Giant One stomp into the darkness. He was angry, but not a fun angry. His eyes did not flash, and his face had not turned interesting shades of red. No. Instead, he seemed sad and quiet.

Human melancholy, Honey decided, was boring.

She scurried into his room. Swiveling her head, she scanned for mischief. When her gaze fell on the large bag, she gave a toothy grin.

She bounded over and sniffed. It reeked of the Giant One. Perfect.

With her claws and incisors, she managed to get inside. Material spilled out. She pounced on it, tossing the articles into the air and then playing with them. This wasn't as fun as attacking a snake, but reptiles were not readily available.

Honey paused in her mayhem. Although it was an unusual thought, she realized Fluffy would enjoy this. Leaving the semidestruction behind, she hurried into the night. She slunk past the Giant One as he talked to the grizzly. Fluffy did not appear to be in the enclosure, but she found him playing chase with the two female mountain lions. When he caught sight of her at the edge of the other animals' enclosure, he immediately left his game to follow her. She led him straight into the maintenance building.

When he spied the pile of human clothing, he skidded to a stop. Then, he immediately pounced. Honey joined him. She had not had this much fun in weeks. And it wasn't just because the Blond One was not at the zoo. Honey had been feeling very peculiar lately, and she couldn't seem to stop herself from preparing a burrow.

Chapter 15

"I'M LEAVING," MAGNUS TOLD FRIDA. AT THE SOUND OF HIS voice, the old bear raised her head. With the darkness, the grizzly didn't appear to see him. She sniffed the air instead. Clearly catching his scent, she heaved a huge sigh and rested her chin on her massive paws.

"You'll have to find another mate to blether with," Magnus informed Frida. The beastie nonchalantly flicked an ear.

"I'm serious."

Frida emitted a low rumbling sound, and Magnus leaned against the fence. He wished he could pat the old girl like one of his da's cows.

"I won't be coming back, so this is truly goodbye."

The grizzly ignored him, and despite everything, Magnus felt his lips slowly form into a half grin. "The silent treatment will not work. I can't stay here any longer."

Frida shifted and then grunted. The old bruin most likely wanted Magnus to stop talking so she could go back to sleep. But he didn't leave. Bowie wouldn't be awake yet, and Magnus didn't want to be alone with his thoughts.

"I know it's as sudden as a blast of wind," Magnus continued, "but there's no helping it. It's time for me to return to London. My editor and agent might not be pleased, but I have clips I haven't posted yet. And I've got enough for a book."

Frida rolled over and began to writhe to scratch her back. It was part of the bear's morning routine. She must have figured Magnus wasn't going away. He'd have to give her a treat for the inconvenience.

"You'll be in the book. Little Sorcha too. But don't let the fame go to your furry head."

Frida snorted and lumbered over to a large rock. She rubbed against it. Magnus found himself giving another half smile. "That itch isn't going away, now, is it?"

The bear emitted a contented sound before dropping to the ground. Magnus couldn't make out her features in the dark, but he imagined she wore a pleased expression on her old face. Magnus heaved his own sigh. He wished he could solve his problems so easily.

He heard the tread of footsteps behind him. Turning, he spotted Bowie walking under one of the security lights. Magnus glanced at his watch. It was still early for the zookeeper to be out and about. As the man came closer, Magnus could see his solemn expression.

"You know," Magnus said simply.

"Yeah. June just called Katie." Bowie joined Magnus at the rail. For a moment, neither spoke. It was Bowie who broke the silence. "I know what June did was—"

"I don't want t-t-t-to talk about it," Magnus said sharply.

"Okay," Bowie said easily enough. They were quiet again, and Magnus found he didn't mind the other man's presence as much as he'd thought he would. It was good, not being alone. And he blamed June for that weakness.

Minutes passed before Bowie spoke again. "So, what's your plan?"

"I'm leaving at first light."

Bowie didn't respond immediately; he just stared thoughtfully into Frida's exhibit. "I'll miss having your help around here. It's been great, and I appreciate all you've done, especially with Sorcha and Savannah."

"Aye. I'll m-miss the p-p-p-peedie beasties."

"You know," Bowie said carefully, "you don't have to leave right away. You could give it a few days—"

Magnus shook his head. He had no desire to see June again. If he stayed, she'd find a way to corner him. He knew how the lass worked. She wouldn't be able to help herself, even if she wanted to.

"I almost walked away from Katie once," Bowie began. Magnus started to raise his palm for silence since he wasn't in the mood for romantic advice, but then Bowie added, "A honey badger stopped me, though."

Before Magnus could think better, he dropped his hand and turned toward Bowie in disbelief. "A honey badger?"

"Yep," Bowie nodded with a grin. "Katie and I were arguing in the indoor llama shed. In my mind, we were over. I'd just started to storm off when I heard a crash. Fluffy had knocked over an entire dolly of feed, and I couldn't get the stall door open. That gave Katie enough time to get through my anger. I owe that rascal my current happiness. Without him, I wouldn't have worked things out with Katie. Maybe it's why I put up with all the trouble those two honey badgers cause."

But Magnus didn't want to give June a chance to convince him to stay. Not because he didn't think she'd succeed. Nay. It was because he was fairly certain she would. She'd turn those green eyes on him and quirk those bonny pink lips, and he'd cave like an old thatched roof. Aye, the lass held a sway over him that his da had never achieved with all his shouting. And Magnus had no desire to lose his freedom again, even if it was by charm rather than through physical blows.

"I don't want to speak with June," Magnus said.

"Fair enough," Bowie conceded. "So, when are you heading out?"

"As soon as I say goodbye to Sorcha and Savannah," Magnus answered.

"Do you want to feed the camels and llamas too?"

"Aye."

"I guess this is goodbye then. I hope you'll keep in touch, even if it's just so I can keep you up to date on Sorcha." Bowie extended his hand. Magnus took it, and Bowie clasped his upper arm. Then, with a brisk bob of his head, Bowie turned and disappeared into the darkness.

Magnus stood in front of Frida's enclosure a little longer. He could hear the grizzly snoring softly. The old bruin must have fallen back asleep while he and Bowie were talking.

"Farewell, Frida," Magnus said softly as he headed to the main facility. He avoided the nursery and headed to the storeroom instead. He'd leave Sorcha for last. Grabbing treats for all the animals, he threw one into Frida's home before heading to the llama exhibit. Hefting a hay bale, he left it in the middle of the outdoor enclosure before going inside the shed to check on the camels. At the sound of his footsteps, Savannah lifted her long neck. Spotting him, she immediately struggled to her feet, waking her mum in the process. The calf loped over to him and tried to fit her head through the slats of the stall door to reach his pockets. He chuckled softly and lifted the pin to let himself in.

"I'll miss you, lassie," Magnus said as he scratched the peedie camel's woolly head and slipped her an alfalfa pellet. Savannah sucked it up with her huge lips and began to chew noisily, her teeth moving side to side in a grinding motion. Her mother bumped Magnus's shoulder, clearly demanding her own treat. He gave it to her and petted her neck. "You'll both be in my book."

Lulubelle emitted a contented rumbling sound. Magnus gave her another pat before he turned from the pen. It would be morning soon, and he didn't want to linger. If he did, he knew June would find him.

Shoving his hands in his pockets, he took the long route through the zoo. Some of the animals had begun to stir, and when he passed the prairie dogs, a few of their sentries gave warning cries. He could see their short tails flash in the dim, pearly glow as they darted into their holes.

When he entered the nursery, Sorcha raised her head, her black eyes blinking sleepily. Magnus couldn't help but smile. She and the capybara had made a nest out of Sorcha's plush animals. Aye, the little bear loved her toys, especially the snuggly ones. Magnus got down on the floor, and the cub immediately dashed over to him. Even without rubber mats to give her traction, she remained steady. His little Sorcha was growing up.

"I'll miss you the most," he whispered, "but don't tell the others."

Sorcha pounced on him, and he laughed as she began to attack his gloved hand. "Och, lass, I'm not a seal."

The bear, of course, didn't listen. Magnus tussled with the wee beastie until his heart grew too heavy. When he'd left his da's croft, it had been the hardest saying goodbye to Sorcha the cow. He'd never admit it, but a tear or two might have stung the back of his eyes when he'd patted her shaggy head for the last time. Saying his goodbye to her had been the only time he'd succumbed to emotion when leaving his boyhood home.

When Magnus rose, the capybara lumbered to her feet. He rubbed Sylvia's head as she pressed her kidney-shaped body against his leg. "You take good care of Sorcha, you hear?"

The animal lifted her big, brown eyes, bringing back more memories of his old cow. "I'm sorry, lass, but I can't stay. I've got to go, but you'll get along well enough without me."

He swore the animal looked dubious, but he ignored her pleading expression. With one last belly rub for the cub, he left. As always, he didn't look back. Instead, he strode straight to where he'd left his belongings. When he reached the doorframe, he froze, staring in disbelief.

Someone—or rather something—had ripped through his holdall. Clothes lay strewn across the room. Several of his T-shirts appeared ripped.

Baws.

It took his brain only a moment to dredge up the cul-
prit. *Honey*. Only the manky honey badger could have
done something so diabolical.

Magnus walked inside and grabbed his computer. He
didn't even inspect the rest of his belongings. He just
walked away. After all, it wouldn't be the first time he'd
departed with only the clothes on his back. At least now
he had dosh in the bank, but even if he'd been broke, he
wouldn't have lingered to sort through his possessions.

No. He'd had his fill of meddlesome females.

"He's gone," June repeated, her chest aching something fierce as she stood on Katie's front porch. The
dull pain had lingered all morning, and she felt foggy
and out of sorts.

"I'm sorry," Katie said, her expression kind. The
sympathy in her best friend's eyes irked June. She didn't
want to be mollycoddled. Drawing in her breath, she
forced herself to calm. This wasn't like her. This irra-
tional irritation. She was sensible and even-tempered.

"When did he leave?" June asked, each word like a
knife thrust through her heart.

"A couple hours ago. It was barely dawn," Katie said
gently. The understanding in her voice tore at June. She
was tired of being treated with softness. With pity.

It struck June how often she'd extended the same type
of comfort. She'd thought herself the queen of soothing
words. Land sakes, how many times had she uninten-
tionally annoyed the person she'd meant to comfort?

June groaned and dropped her head into her hands.
"I've been such an idiot."

Katie patted her on the back, the swell of her pregnant belly brushing against June. "You're not an idiot. You've just got a big heart, and sometimes you get carried away."

June looked at her best friend. "I've lost him, haven't I?"

Katie didn't respond, but then she didn't need to. Her expression said it all. That, and the surety in June's soul.

"I'm so sorry." Katie's eyes reflected June's pain. Her friend had always possessed a heart for compassion. But June wasn't ready for empathy. Not yet.

June stood abruptly. "I should get back. I left Nan with Josh, and I'm not sure how well he can handle her episodes."

"I can go over and help today," Katie offered. "Maybe you should take some time off. Go into the city. Do some shopping."

June shook her head. "No. I need to keep busy. Taking care of the shop and Nan will keep my mind off things."

"Okay," Katie said. "Do you want me to drive you back? Bowie and I can drop off your car this evening."

"No. It was a breakup, not a death," June snapped and then slapped her hand over her mouth. She did not snap at people, especially when they were trying to show her a kind turn. That wasn't her way.

Katie, however, didn't appear insulted. June almost wished she were. Then she wouldn't have to see her friend's sad expression anymore.

"All right," Katie said with a nod. "But call me if

you need anything. Bowie and I are here for you. If you need help with your nan, there's my mom too."

June bobbed her head. If she tried to speak, she might bite off Katie's head again like an unhinged snapping turtle. At least her friend seemed to understand as she walked June to her vehicle. Katie gave June a quick hug goodbye before she turned and headed back to her house. When June climbed into her SUV, she didn't turn on the engine immediately. She just sat there, letting the pain wash over her. She didn't want to tell Nan that Magnus had left. Part of her almost walked back into Katie's house to take her up on the offer of escaping. But that wouldn't solve anything, and June Winters didn't run.

Not like a certain cowardly Scotsman.

Not that June blamed him. Much. She had given him an awfully big push.

She started her vehicle and drove the short distance to her tea shop. As soon as she headed up the stairs, she heard Josh calling her. He met her in the hallway, his face serious.

"Nan keeps asking for Magnus," Josh told her. "I guess he used to read to her in the mornings? I tried, but she says I sound too much like a Yank. I think I may be insulted."

June managed a weak smile at Josh's attempt at humor. "I'll go talk to her."

She found her grandmother sitting up in bed, her eyes round and cloudy. She swiveled slowly in June's direction and blinked. June's heart skittered at the fear and confusion in Nan's face. The woman needed routine, and June had just blown that to smithereens.

"Where's Magnus?" Nan demanded, her voice high

and a little panicky. "Magnus always reads to me. He didn't come today."

"I'm sorry, Nan," June said as she sank onto the bed. She reached forward and grabbed her grandmother's hand. Her skin felt thin and papery beneath June's. "Magnus is gone."

"Gone!" Nan's thin voice rose even higher. Anxiety swam in her hazel eyes. June swallowed against the well of pain bubbling up from her own chest. She gently squeezed her grandmother's fingers, but she didn't know if she meant to comfort Nan or herself.

"Yes," June said softly. "He went back to London."

"Why?"

Because I was a fool who stuck her nose where it didn't belong.

Instead June said, "It was time, Nan. He didn't belong to us. England is his home."

For a moment, her grandmother's eyes sharpened, and the old Nan returned. "*Pfft.* He's an Orcadian, Junie. England would never be his home."

Despite the hurt in her heart, June smiled. Her grandmother had a point. She patted her nan's hand. "That may be true, but that's where he lives."

The brightness faded from her grandmother. A childish look returned to her face. "But who will read to me?"

"Josh is here for a few weeks."

Nan frowned like a toddler who'd just been told brussels sprouts tasted just like candy. "Bah. He has a horrible accent. It hurts my ears."

June hid a smile. "Well then, I'll read to you."

Her grandmother sank into the cushions, a mulish expression on her face. "It won't be the same."

"No, Nan," June said quietly, "it won't be, but we'll muddle through."

Nan looked dubious, and June didn't blame her. After all, she harbored the same doubts. Somehow, she—the woman who fixed everyone else's problems—had begun to rely on the calm, quiet Scot. He'd become a part of her life, and now he'd vanished.

June hadn't hurt this much since childhood. All the old buried feelings sprang up like zombies, and she felt as helpless as she had as a kid. She couldn't bring Magnus back any more than she could have stopped the Air Force from reassigning her dad. And this time…this time she had no one to blame but herself.

Chapter 16

WHEN MAGNUS RETURNED TO LONDON, HE LOCKED himself in his flat and wrote. And wrote. And wrote. He emerged only to wander to the nearby pub to nurse a whiskey and to type. No one bothered him. Shite, they likely didn't even notice him tucked away with his laptop. He had no one pestering him about working with his stutter or keeping his beard trimmed.

He should have been as jolly as a puffin with a score of sand eels in its beak, but he wasn't. The yawning hole inside him ached, and he couldn't rid himself of the dull pain. He'd never felt emptiness like this before, not even during his recovery from his da's attack. Back then, he'd written to alleviate the pressure inside him. And he did the same now. He wanted to purge Sagebrush Flats as thoroughly as he had Bjaray.

He bled all of his emotions, all of his frustrations onto the page. As he pounded on the keyboard, he didn't mull over his words. He just let them spill over. Although he'd always been a fast writer, the book poured out of him.

Then, he finished it.

He sat at his desk, staring at the screen. It was done. There wasn't any more to write. He felt drained, and he welcomed the sensation.

Scrubbing his hand over his face, he stood up and headed to the toilet. As he washed his hands, he paused at his reflection. He hadn't looked at himself in weeks, and his appearance surprised him. It wasn't because his beard and hair had grown woolly again. No. If anything, the extra hair helped to hide the truth. He looked awful. He'd lost weight. His face was gaunt, his eyes slightly sunken. He pulled at his trousers, and they hung loose. It dawned on him that he'd skipped more than one meal.

Cracking his neck, he headed toward the scullery. When he opened the fridge, he frowned. It was empty. He checked the cupboards and found a tin of beans and a bag of bread. Beans and toast weren't his favorite, but he didn't feel like heading down to the pub. At least the meal was filling, and it only took a minute to heat it on the cooker.

Sitting back down at his laptop with his supper in his hands, Magnus began to skim his manuscript. Generally, he waited at least a day or two before starting his edits. The time gave him more clarity. But he couldn't seem to stop himself. Even though he'd written the damn thing, he felt drawn to it, as if it contained a mystery only he could unravel.

Twenty pages in, he forgot about eating again. Even when his back began to throb from being hunched over the computer, he didn't stop. He sat there reading, unable to pull himself away. Hours ticked by.

When he finally came to the end, he straightened. "Fuck me."

Stunned disbelief ricocheted through him. A part of him wanted to reach forward and delete the whole damn thing, even if it was his best work. Denial whipped

through him, fast and furious, but all too soon, it
slipped away. After all, the truth lay before him,
spelled out in 101,015 words, to be exact. And
he'd written every last one of them.

He'd penned a love letter. To June.

———

"I need your help."

June looked up from her cash register to find
Clay Stevens staring back at her. She didn't know
the man well, but he'd been in her tea shop a few
times. He was a coffee drinker—black. No tea.
No sugar. No milk. She remembered he seemed
offended when she'd asked if he wanted cream.

Clay was an outsider in Sagebrush. It didn't
matter if his maternal granddaddy had roots a mile
deep in this area. Nor did folks give him credit for
the decade he'd spent living on and then successfully running his ancestral ranch just outside town.
He could drink all the black coffee he wanted and
wear all the cowboy hats and boots in the world, but
people would still call him a greenhorn city slicker
and think he guzzled down prissy lattes.

June gave him a smile, even though her heart
still hurt like the dickens. Magnus had been gone
for over a month, and still the pain hadn't eased.
She'd never felt like this after a breakup, but then
again, she'd never loved someone before.

"What can I do for you?" June asked.

Clay glanced around the tea shop. It was mid-
morning and between the breakfast and lunch rushes,
so only Stanley and Buck occupied a table. The

latter was shooting him daggers. After all, the older man blamed Clay's father for giving Buck's son a heart attack.

"Can they hear me?" Clay asked softly as he jerked his head in the direction of June's regulars.

June felt her smile slip. "Not if you talk real low like you're doing, but I won't let you say anything against them. They are just the sweetest fellows, and my best customers."

Clay scowled. He was a handsome man—blond hair, cerulean eyes, even features. Unfortunately for him, he looked like an East Coast blue blood or an Ivy League frat boy, neither of which set well with the folks of Sagebrush. It only cemented his interloper image and reminded them of his swindler father. "Why do people around here always think the worst of me? I just want to ask for a favor, and I don't want them overhearing."

June's grin disappeared altogether as Clay unwittingly caused her a stab of pain and guilt.

"I'm afraid I'm fresh out of favors these days. They tend to get me in trouble."

Clay didn't seem deterred. In fact, he leaned closer, his voice as low as a limbo contestant. "I'm out of options. People around here can't stand me, and I need to change that."

June barely stopped an unkind laugh from escaping her lips. My, my, when had she become so bitter? "I'm not sure how I'm supposed to help you with that."

Clay sighed. "Everyone in this damn town loves you, and we've been here almost the same amount of time. I want to know your secret. How do you get them to like you?"

June had never been one for sarcasm, but it slipped

from her lips as easily as butter over a hot biscuit. "By being nice and smiling."

Clay's frowned deepened. "I do those things."

June quirked her lips and began to wipe down the counter. "From what I've heard, you're more known for yelling during town meetings and stirring up trouble."

Frustration fell over Clay's face, but to his credit, he didn't erupt into anger. "Wanting to protect my livestock isn't stirring up trouble. It shouldn't be so difficult to convince ranchers to see the problem with reintroducing wolves. The difficulty is nobody can say no to Lacey Montgomery. She's Sagebrush's favorite daughter. I can't go up against her. Not with my image. That's why I need your help. If there's anyone who this town adores more than Lacey, it's you."

June leaned across the counter and stared the annoying greenhorn down. "You want me to go up against one of my friends to champion a cause I don't believe in?"

"No." Clay shook his head. "I want you to show me how to be likable."

June's atypical irritation and cynicism fled. She looked at Clay Stevens. Really looked. She saw a flicker of something else in his blue-green eyes. It didn't take her long to recognize it. Loneliness.

This wasn't just about the wolves. June wasn't even sure if Clay realized that. But she did.

The old June would have immediately agreed to his plea. She couldn't have resisted the glimpse of sadness...or the challenge. People in Sagebrush didn't just dislike Clay Stevens. They hated him. A month ago, June would have jumped at the chance to transform him into the town's darling.

But not now.

Instead of fixing others, June needed to concentrate on herself. She'd realized something in the past weeks. She'd never truly wrestled with her own emotions. She wouldn't call herself shallow…just outwardly focused. It had protected her, keeping her heart safe when the Air Force plucked her once again from her home.

But she wasn't a little girl anymore. And she wasn't a military brat either. She had her own store and more responsibilities than she could handle. Although her nan had good days, her mind remained in a permanent fog. The doctors said it likely wouldn't improve much more. June had no business taking on Clay Stevens's issues as well. Meddling in other people's lives could end up hurting them and wouldn't make her own better.

She'd learned that the hard way.

"I'm sorry," June said, and she meant it. "I can't help you."

"Because of what my dad did to this town?" Clay asked. "I wasn't part of his phony investment scheme. Don't you think my life was destroyed too? I was just a teenager when he went to jail."

Sympathy wormed its way into June's heart. She reached forward and patted Clay's hand. "It's got nothing to do with you, Clay, or your daddy. It's not just the favor business that I'm out of. I'm not trying to fix other folks' problems anymore. I'm focusing on my own. And let me tell you, I've got a heap of them."

Clay straightened. June had no trouble detecting the disappointment rolling off him. He'd spoken the truth. He was desperate.

"Just give people a chance," June said. "They'll come around."

Clay snorted. "It's been over ten years. I don't think that's happening."

"I can give you a coffee—black. It's on the house."

Clay gave her a grin, and he looked like he was in an advertisement for an expensive men's fragrance. Yet June felt absolutely nothing. Evidently, a certain surly Scot had ruined her for fair-weather smiles. They seemed so…ordinary now.

"I guess I'll take what I can get," Clay said.

June poured him a cup to go. He raised it to her before heading for the exit. No sooner had the door shut behind him than Buck Montgomery rose to his feet. "Was that upstart bothering you? If he was, I'm not too old to teach him a lesson or two."

June had to hide a smile at the elderly man's protective outrage. She shook her head. "He was just asking me for a favor."

Stanley snorted as he turned in his seat to face June. "Never trust a Stevens. They might act like they're your best friend one minute, and then they knife you in the back the next."

"You can say that again," Buck said as he crossed his arms over his chest.

June shook her head. "Clay Stevens isn't his daddy."

Stanley hmmphed. "He's the spitting image of him."

"Just 'cause they're the same on the outside doesn't mean they're the same on the inside too."

Buck studied her with a worried expression on his leathery face. "You're not going soft for the Stevens boy, are you? I know you're feeling vulnerable since that Scottish…" The old cowboy's voice trailed off, but not before June felt a fresh slice of pain. She tried to hide it, but she saw the regret in Buck's eyes. "My apologies. It wasn't my place, June."

She gave Buck a nod and wished she could think of a witty response that would put them all at ease, but she couldn't. Instead, she felt the prick of tears. Land sakes alive, she hadn't cried this much in years. Maybe ever.

She glanced down at the baby monitor. Her grandmother still slept peacefully, but Buck didn't know that. "I think Nan is stirring. I better go check. I'll be back in two shakes."

As soon as June walked through the double doors to the back of the tea shop, she stopped and pressed her fist against her sternum. Closing her eyes tightly, she willed the pain away. It didn't lessen.

She opened her eyes and said to the silence, "Glory be, how long is this going to last?"

—◆◆◆—

Although Magnus liked fine, smooth whiskey and could appreciate a good beer, he rarely got drunk. With his size, he could hold his alcohol fairly well, and he didn't believe in drinking himself into a stupor.

Until now.

He was completely and utterly blootered.

It probably didn't help that he'd had nothing in his

puggy but half-eaten beans and toast. He stared at his whiskey glass and swirled the liquid, watching it catch the light. He'd broken into the good stuff because he didn't want to leave the flat. A part of him retained enough sense to know he'd regret it, but the rest of him didn't care.

He wanted oblivion.

Instead, he'd become more maudlin. A few moments ago, he'd caught himself singing an ode…to June's eyes. It was a wonder his neighbors hadn't called the bobbies.

Magnus leaned back in his chair, and it almost crashed to the floor. He thought about the time he'd stumbled on the fainting goats and June had rushed to his side, her golden hair hanging over him. There'd been other times when her tresses had fallen like a curtain…more pleasurable times.

He slammed the whiskey glass onto the table. He heard it crack, but he didn't care. He needed to stop thinking about the lass, or he'd go doolally. Pressing his fingers against his forehead, he tried to think. He heard June's voice in his head, telling him he needed to talk about it. And he did, but he had no mates. *Baws*, he'd never even gotten around to buying himself a dog.

Before he could think better—or even think at all—Magnus fished out his mobile. With his coordination absolutely rubbish, it took him a little time to pull up Bowie's number. The other man answered on the third ring.

"Wilson here."

"This is Magnus." He may have hiccupped or

even burped. He wasn't sure. Either way, Bowie was gentleman enough to ignore it.

"How's London?"

"Dddreich," Magnus said, slurring the *d* rather than stuttering.

"We could use some rain here in Sagebrush."

Magnus did not want to talk about the weather. "Would it be all right with you if I FaceTimed with Frida?"

"Come again?"

"I'd like to speak with Frida."

"The bear?"

"Aye. You have another Frida hidden in Sagebrush?"

"Uh, no," Bowie said slowly. "I'm not exactly sure what you're asking. Do you want me to take my phone and position it so you can see Frida?"

"Aye."

"Do you want privacy?"

"Aye," Magnus said, wondering why this was so difficult for the American to understand.

"Uh, I guess I can do that. I'll call you back when I get over to the enclosure."

"Thank you."

"And Magnus?"

"Aye?"

"June's been having a hard time with this breakup too."

Magnus frowned down at his mobile as Bowie hung up. Who said he was having difficulties getting over June? He scratched the back of his head and felt the old scar. His scowl deepened. His mobile beeped, and after several misses, he managed to jab the button to answer it.

He saw Frida and heard Bowie's voice. "Can you see her?"

"Aye."

"Okay," Bowie said. "Uh, I guess I'll leave you two to chat then."

"Thanks."

Magnus waited for a few beats. The picture wasn't the best quality, and he wasn't focusing too well. He doubted the bear even noticed the smartphone with her bad eyesight. It was the best he would get, though.

Frida sat with a block of ice between her hind legs. There appeared to be bits of fruit and vegetables frozen inside it. The bruin scraped her teeth on the edge as her powerful claws gripped the slippery surface.

"I'm glad to see one of us is happy," Magnus said.

Frida just kept on chewing.

"My head's mince right now," Magnus told Frida. The bear appeared unimpressed with this announcement. Most likely, she didn't even hear him although he might have seen her left ear flick.

"I've never been like this over a lass," Magnus confessed.

Frida made a rumbling sound. The old girl's hearing must have been better than her eyesight. She definitely seemed to be picking up his voice. Magnus grinned, inordinately pleased that the grizzly could listen to him.

"I didn't want this," Magnus said, his words slurred even to his ears. "I fancied a quiet life. Alone. There used to be peace in solitude. Now it's just lonely."

Frida moved her large head, clearly looking for him. She emitted a low, almost mournful sound.

Magnus felt his lips slip into a half smile. Aye, the bear made for a good chum. She'd even echoed the dark feelings swirling inside him…along with the contents of a bottle of twenty-five-year old Highland Park whiskey.

"The lass didn't just get into my head," Magnus said. He stopped for a moment trying to think through the fog. His heart took over, and the words flowed. His coworkers from his roughneck days used to joke he transformed into a maudlin poet when blootered. "She got into my soul, and I can't expel her. There's no in-incantation strong enough for her fae magic."

Frida sniffed the air, still trying to locate him. When she couldn't detect his scent, she snorted.

Magnus sighed and wished he could see the old bruin's eyes—even as rheumy as they were. There was something comforting in an animal's gaze. Magnus imagined it was an ancient wisdom that humans had lost in all their philosophizing and blethering. Aye, beasties had an honesty people lacked, including him.

"Och," Magnus said as he hiccuped and then slurred his words. "I suppose you're right. There's no f-f-fairy magic in what June's done to me. I've gone and fallen in love, and that's the truth of it."

Frida stood up on her hind legs in an attempt to see better. She was a magnificent beast, even in her dotage. Old age couldn't completely destroy the raw power nature had bestowed on her kind, just as Magnus couldn't rid himself of his affection for June. It had sunk so deep, it had infected his very cells.

"The problem is," Magnus said, "there's a hollowness inside me, and I'm afraid if I don't repair the hole, it will swallow June and me both."

Clearly giving up on sensing Magnus's presence, Frida sank back to the ground.

"I am not being overly dramatic. I'm a writer. It's how I think."

Frida laid her head on her rock and wiggled her large posterior as she settled into a comfortable position. Magnus wished he could do the same. As drunk as he was, if he tried to sleep, he'd only find himself thinking of *her*.

"June shouldn't have contacted my mum, but I shouldn't have left like I did. I should've given the lass time to explain. She's got a good heart."

Frida grunted as she adjusted her chin. Her eyes drifted closed in pure bliss. Magnus really did envy the bear her peace.

"I've made a bowfin' mess of things, haven't I?" Magnus asked.

Frida popped open one eye. Then she sighed, long and hard. Her entire large body heaved with the effort.

"Aye, I have." Magnus answered his own question.

Frida rolled her head slightly away from him and flung her paw over her face. She shifted a few more times before she stilled.

"Are you trying to tell me I should talk to a human instead of a bear?"

Frida responded with a snore. A very loud one. Magnus chuckled…at himself or at the grumpy grizzly, he really didn't know. But somehow, in his drunken conversation with an old bruin, he'd discovered a way out of his torment.

Because there was someone else in the world

who'd escaped his father's control. Maybe she'd learned to live her life, instead of constantly worrying about losing her freedom if she let another human close. It wouldn't be hard to find her. Not with her unopened letters sitting in the bottom of his cupboard. She'd always included the return address on them, and in all the years she'd been writing, it had only changed once.

Chapter 17

June couldn't remember the last time she'd slept properly. When Magnus left, she'd had Josh to help her with Nan. But he'd needed to get back to San Francisco and his career. June had thought caring for her grandmother and juggling her job would get easier. But it hadn't. It had just become harder... and harder.

The days and nights blended together. She wasn't getting much rest, not with Nan calling her in the middle of the night. The only time she had to herself was when she stepped into the shower in the evenings. She'd broken down and cried in there more than she wanted to admit.

Her parents promised to come for a long weekend in another month, and her brother had two weeks of leave early in the summer. She tried to keep focusing on their upcoming visits. She knew down to the hour when her parents were due to arrive. But she hadn't told them about her struggles. They might insist on sending Nan to a home.

But lately June had begun to wonder if she could avoid that.

She had just started to slip into bed when she heard the baby monitor crackle. "Junie?"

Since Nan couldn't hear her, June exhaled. Long and heavy. Wearily, she got back up and padded into her grandmother's room. Nan was sitting up in bed, her eyes a little hazy. Her gaze latched onto June's immediately.

"I miss the kind young man who used to read to me," Nan said.

This time, June suppressed her sigh. Nan's hearing wasn't terrific, but she could tell when June got irritated. Although June tried to stay even-tempered, she swore at times her grandmother could try the patience of every saint who'd walked through the Pearly Gates.

"I know, Nan." June patted her grandmother's hand as if she hadn't had this same conversation every night since the Scotsman's departure, sometimes more than once. "I miss him too."

Nan's expression turned hopeful, much like a young child angling for candy. "Will you read to me instead, Junie?"

June forced a smile. Reading Magnus's books always ripped open a fresh wound in her heart, but she couldn't say no to her grandmother, especially when his work brought the older woman peace. She'd tried the books on tapes, but it was harder for Nan to concentrate on the words. Plus, she said the recording sounded tinny with her hearing aids.

June found her place in Magnus's second book and began reading.

> The wind howled its baltic breath, and the chill from it sliced through my parka. My first winter in the frigid far North had arrived. Old-timers had plenty of advice, mixed in with a healthy dose of cautionary tales that would make an

auld Orcadian granny proud. Frostbite. Lost
noses. Black toes. Hypothermia. Men lost in
sudden squalls and found frozen during the
spring thaw. I am not sure which ones are
real. Maybe all. Maybe none.

I found it didn't matter. The bitter cold
didn't frighten me. Instead, I found a kinship
with it. When I stood on the edge of the rig
and stared out into the expanse of flawless
snow and ice, I did not flinch at the vastness.
Instead, recognition flickered inside me...
perhaps even a sense of homecoming. In
the emptiness, I found my peace.

June stopped. She'd heard this passage many
times over the years when her grandmother had listened to the audio version. After Magnus's arrival
in Sagebrush, she'd skimmed over the words. Now,
they shot through her, each one hitting her heart
with blazing accuracy.

"He is a lonely man," her grandmother said.
"Lovely, but lonely."

June lifted her head to regard her nan. Propped
up by pillows June had arranged, the older woman
rested her back against the headboard. She had her
eyes closed, but she opened them, and her gaze
appeared clearer.

"Yes, I would say that describes Magnus very
accurately," June agreed, keeping her voice carefully neutral.

Her nan reached forward and patted June's hand.
The action caused bittersweet surprise to ripple

through June. Her grandmother had always been a compassionate woman. For all her British austerity, she'd exuded warmth, especially for her family. But her disease had robbed her of that. She'd turned inward and didn't seem to have the energy or the focus to fuss over others.

"You made him happy."

June felt her mouth twist. She tried to turn it back into a smile and failed miserably. "I chased him away, Nan."

That resulted in another hand pat. "I'm sure that's not correct, dear."

June swallowed hard. Her nan sounded so normal, so much like her former self, that the truth rolled from June's lips before she thought better. "It is, Nana. I tried to fill the barren emptiness inside him and got blasted out instead."

"Junie, I have never seen you give up on something. You go after your surly Scot and make him see reason."

June shook her head. "No, Nan. I've learned my lesson. I'm done being a busybody and sticking my nose where it doesn't belong."

Her grandmother smiled softly, and June's heart gave a pang. Nan seemed to have drifted away again. But then her gaze latched onto June's once more, and she saw wisdom glimmering in those hazel depths.

"Are you certain, Junie, you've learned the proper lesson?"

―⁓―

Magnus was halfway to Orkney by the time he sobered up. He debated about getting off the train at the next village and taking the earliest one back to London. But he didn't because it wouldn't resolve anything. He'd been running since eighteen, and it was time he stopped.

He spent the next couple hours staring at the passing landscape, trying not to think. He'd slept on the train during the night, so he doubted he'd fall asleep even with the remainder of the rail journey and ferry ride ahead of him. Alcohol would have helped, but he needed a clear head. He wasn't showing up blootered on his mum's doorstep. Even if he barely remembered the hen, there were some things a son shouldn't do.

He supposed he should be thinking of what he would say, but he wasn't. If he tried, he would've turned right back around. And that wouldn't do. He was done being a feartie.

—⁓—

Magnus stood at the ferry's rail as the seacraft pulled into Stromness harbor on the Mainland, Orkney. Although Magnus had lived fairly far north of the large isle, he couldn't help but feel a prick of homecoming. To his surprise, he didn't find it wholly unwelcome. In fact, an odd sense of peace crept through him at the sight of the fishing boats in front of the gray-stone buildings dotting the hills beyond. He knew this place, knew these people. Perhaps more of the Isles had seeped inside him than he'd known.

He'd missed Orkney, he realized, and the revelation wasn't as jarring as he would've imagined. Beside him, he heard a couple of auld men havering in the melodious Orcadian accent. He could smell the tang of the sea. Aye, there was beauty here, and part of him still loved it. His da hadn't managed to destroy that after all…but Magnus nearly had.

Instead of catching the bus, he decided to hike first northward to the dramatic cliffs of the Brough of Birsay and then catch a bus to Kirkwall. As a lad, he'd done a lot of walking, and now it helped steady his rioting nerves. This was ancient land. Before it was owned by Britain, the Picts and Norse had made this group of islands their home. As early as the late Stone Age, people had begun building villages and monuments here, and some of those structures still stood. This place was in Magnus's very DNA, and he'd been wrong to try to splice it from his essence.

With the tide out, Magnus walked along an exposed sandy stretch that connected the tidal island to Mainland, Orkney. Although it was off-season, a few tourists and their children stooped to collect smooth rocks and shells. Memories flickered. He remembered scouring the beach on Bjaray for the small cowrie shells that Orcadians called *groatie buckies*. There was a tradition on the isles to keep a collection of them. Magnus had long since thrown his away, but he bent down and gathered a few into his hand and shoved them into his pocket. Perhaps, it was time to start another jar.

Climbing up the steep hill, he stood at the edge of the tall cliffs, breathing in the scent of the blue-green sea and soaking in its power as it crashed on the rocks below. In the dim light, he spotted a few seals bobbing peacefully in the water. As a lad, he'd watch the animals from his da's croft. He'd heard the stories of the selkies — magical creatures who looked like seals in the water but could shed their pelts and become human on land. There were many legends of mortal men and women stealing a selkie's fur, forcing the fae creature to remain ashore with them. The stories always ended with the selkie finding his or her pelt and returning to the sea. Magnus used to imagine his mother as one of those legendary sprites, and he'd dreamed of her coming back, not to stay but to bring him to her ocean home. His mum had returned to Orkney, but it was now Magnus who lived beyond its shores.

Despite Magnus's fantastical musings about creatures of the sea, it turned out Mady Budge lived in an ordinary postwar council home on the outskirts of Kirkwall. Located on a quiet street, it was a nondescript residence with flowers growing in a small, well-tended bed. Magnus heaved a sigh as he made his way up the walk. He paused for only a second before he jabbed the bell. He stood there, resisting the urge to bounce on his feet like a peedie lad.

The door swung open to reveal a tall, stout woman. Even though Magnus hadn't seen Mady Budge in years, he would have recognized his mum on a crowded King's Cross platform. After all, he took after her. Same stocky build. Same dark-brown curls. Same strong features. It shouldn't have come as a surprise to Magnus. The only physical attribute Magnus shared with his rawboned da was the startling blue eyes all Grays possessed.

As he stood looking at an older, feminine version of himself, he felt a roar inside him like a great wind. He swallowed. Gales like this had a tendency to reshape the landscape.

He had no doubt Mady Budge knew him. She

stood there frozen, tears shining in her brown eyes. She raised a shaking hand to her mouth and pressed so hard her lips turned white around her fingertips. She didn't make a sound, though, not even a sob or a gasp. Neither of them did. They remained rooted there—he on the front stoop, she in the foyer, her other hand still resting on the door.

Someone moved on the street. A boy on a bicycle from the sounds of it. Magnus didn't turn, but he did start.

"I d-d-d-drunk-d-d-d-dialed a b-b-b-bear. Thought t-t-t-talking to a human would be b-b-b-better," Magnus said in way of explanation for his presence. Then he winced. Maybe he should have at least considered his first words to his mother. To Mady's credit, she showed no reaction to his bizarre announcement other than stepping back and gesturing for him to enter. He ducked inside and followed her into a comfortable parlor at the front of the house. They stood awkwardly in the small room.

"Tea?" Mady asked. Her voice had a rich timbre to it, and an old memory jangled in the back of Magnus's mind before it flitted away, unformed.

"Aye," Magnus said, grateful for the offer. It would give him something to do with his hands.

Mady bobbed her head before she left the room. She moved like him, quiet despite her large frame. Magnus wondered what else they shared. He heard her in the scullery and considered whether he should offer to help. He thought of June then. She would know what to do in a situation like this. The raw pain started again, and he studied the walls to distract himself and then froze. On a prominent shelf stood every book he'd written. He stepped forward, but then a framed magazine page caught his eye. He stopped and stared. Like all of his publicity photos, he stood with his back to the viewer, his gaze trained on the churning sea. It had been taken early in his career. He'd been practically a lad at the time, but between the camera angle and his bulk, he looked like a full-grown man.

Magnus heard the fall of footsteps behind him. He turned to find his mother watching him, her brown eyes hesitant and guilty. The tea tray clattered, and with shaking hands, she bent to place it carefully on the coffee table. She straightened and nervously wiped her palms on her dress.

"Are you satisfied?" Magnus blurted out, and his mum's entire body stiffened. He realized how aggressive his words sounded and quickly corrected himself. "I didn't m-m-m-m-mean that as an accusation. I just wanted to know if you had—have—a good life."

His mother's eyes held his for a moment before flitting away. She heaved her shoulders and then returned her gaze to his. This was difficult for her. Any nyaff could see that. But she was trying to do it right, and for that, he respected her.

"Aye," she admitted, her voice laced with guilt. "I do."

"Did you remarry?" Magnus asked. He hated asking a personal question, but he needed to know that a body could heal and trust another after a life with his da.

His mother hesitated before nodding. "Aye. To a man named Robert Stewart. We have no children, if you're wondering about that as well."

Magnus hadn't. He should have, he supposed, but he'd never thought about having siblings.

His mother continued speaking as she rubbed her hands nervously. Now that she'd started talking, she didn't seem to know how to stop. "My Robert's at work now. He's a good m-m-m-man—"

"You stutter?" Shock crashed through Magnus, and it felt almost like a physical blow. He nearly stepped back from the force of it.

His mother nodded as she studied him. "You didn't know?"

Magnus shook his head. "No."

"It's a sair fetch for m-m-me to say the letter 'm.'"

Magnus stared at her in disbelief. "Then why did you name m-me M-M-M-Magnus?"

Mady glanced down at her hands. Distantly, he noticed bits of paint on her fingertips before she spoke again. "M-M-Magnus was a Gray family name. Your da wanted it."

"Ah," Magnus said as he immediately understood. His mother raised her chin, and Magnus could see the tears spilling down her cheeks.

"I'm so sorry," she said. "I never should've left you. There's not a d-d-d-day goes b-b-b-by that I don't think of you, my peedie laddie."

To his horror, Magnus felt a burning sensation behind his own eyes. Before he could embarrass himself, he strode over to his mother in two giant steps. When he took her into his arms, her body went as tight as a mooring rope. Then she collapsed against him, her head on his shoulder.

When Magnus spoke, he kept his voice low and gentle. "I never blamed you for leaving."

That startled his mum from her bawling. She pulled back to study him, and he allowed the scrutiny.

"How?" she finally asked, the word as soft as spring moss.

"I lived with him too," Magnus said simply, and his mother's eyes grew wide with something akin to horror. Before Magnus could stop himself, the rest of his words came tumbling out. "But I've never understood why you left me in his care."

His mum stumbled back from him, her face peely walley. "He didn't t-t-t-treat you well?"

Magnus felt his mouth twist bitterly. He couldn't help it. "Oh, he t-t-treated me well enough…if I did exactly as he wanted, which was bloody impossible."

His mum sank into the settee. Magnus found a chair across from her. He sat, folding his hands over his knees as he waited.

"I…" She paused, visibly collecting herself and then continuing. "I thought it was b-b-best to leave you with him."

Magnus couldn't speak. He could only stare. His mother fidgeted nervously as she spoke, "I had no m-m-money. I only went to secondary school to year four. I was afraid I was going to starve on m-m-my own, and I didn't think I could earn enough to put food in your puggy."

Magnus could hear the woman's raw pain. He believed it. Believed her. But he couldn't stop the flow of words spewing from him. "He hit m-m-m-me. For stuttering. For burning the neeps. For not m-m-m-moving fast enough. For b-b-b-blethering to the coos."

His mother squeezed her eyes shut. "I didn't think he'd do that. He had a less violent temper than m-m-my own d-d-d-da who was always guttered at the pub. Your d-d-d-da was always yelling at m-m-me for how I was ruining you. He said it was m-my fault that you stuttered and that you seemed like a sensitive lad. I b-b-believed him back then. I thought you'd be better without m-my influence."

"Aye, he was always one for d-d-d-destroying confidence," Magnus said bitterly.

Her lips formed a trembling line. "I didn't have m-m-much to begin with. I was a 'B-B-B-Blootered B-B-B-B-Budge Lass.'"

Stunned, Magnus sank back. "Fuck me. We're the same."

"I paint," she said suddenly.

He blinked at the non sequitur, but she continued. "Landscapes of B-B-B-Bjaray and T-T-T-Tammay. They sell—not as well as your books—but they bring in a little extra dosh. I started doing it to heal. I put m-myself through university working as a caretaker for a p-p-primary school in Glasgow and got a degree in art therapy. But I never felt whole until I started letting people in. Robert showed me how."

Magnus held himself very still. His mother's expression had softened as she regarded him warmly. A recollection slipped into place. He knew that look. Something unlocked inside him. His throat tightened, threatening to choke him. An anxious feeling chased through him as he debated about standing up and walking over to her. He'd been trained first by his da and then by himself to avoid emotion. But if he wanted to repair things with June, he needed to stop running.

"I know this is not m-m-my place," his mother said

gently. "I've lost all rights to knowing about your p-p-p-private life. But if you were talking to a bear while drunk, I'm assuming you're no longer with the lass who called me."

"No," Magnus said shortly.

His mum opened her mouth, stopped, and then continued, "The lass shouldn't have contacted m-m-m-me without your knowledge."

"Aye," Magnus agreed.

"She wasn't trying to be a wee clipe, though. Her heart was in the right place."

"Aye." Even when he'd been boiling mad, he'd still recognized that. "And I made all go to b-b-b-bruck."

His mom reached forward, her hand hovering near his. They stared down at it, both of them waiting to see what she'd do. She appeared to come to a decision and let her fingers rest on his. "I doubt that, lad. The lass fancies you, and she didn't seem like the type to let a wee b-bit of a temper fleg her off."

"You said Robert is a good man. Are you happy with him?" Magnus asked again, needing further assurance that Mady had managed to find and hold on to joy. "Not just content, but *happy*?"

"Aye," his mum said without hesitation, "I love the man. And we've a good m-m-m-marriage."

"How?" Magnus asked.

His mum sighed and poured herself a cup of tea. Her hands were steady now. Magnus wished he could say the same about himself. She handed him a teacup and saucer, which he managed to keep from rattling as he reached forward to add sugar and milk.

"It wasn't easy in the b-b-b-beginning," his

mother said as she eased back into her seat and took a sip. "Not with my first m-m-marriage, and m-m-my own d-d-da's criticisms in my head. There were times I had trouble catching my breath and times I felt like I had to run again, but Robert understood and he helped me through it. He convinced me it was time to m-m-m-move back here. He told me I shouldn't let my previous husband chase me from the land I loved. He was right. It's b-been healing being back in Orkney."

To save himself from responding just yet, Magnus drank some tea. He didn't know if he could trust June like that. Just the thought of relying on someone made his skin clammy. The china in his hands clinked together. His mum said nothing, but her eyes followed the movement.

"If you want a future with this lass, you need to stop letting your d-d-da win and learn to trust."

Protect. Nurture. Shelter.

New instincts crashed into Honey as she stared down at the tiny hairless creature burrowing against her fur. The sight of something so defenseless should have repulsed Honey. Their kind did not tolerate weakness.

Yet Honey did not want to attack and destroy this new life. She wanted to take care of it, which made no sense. But she could not stop herself.

The kit opened its tiny mouth and squeaked plaintively. It was a pathetic sound, but Honey did not wish to swat the interloper to her den. Instead, she used her nose to guide the blind creature to her belly.

When the little speck began to drink eagerly, Honey

felt content...a new and surprisingly welcome sensation.

———

June sat in her SUV staring at her best friend's house. Katie's mom had volunteered to take care of Nan for the day, and June was supposed to pick up Katie to go shopping in the city. But when she'd pulled up, she couldn't bring herself to ring the doorbell. Because June, the perennial social butterfly, needed a break. From people, of all things.

June pulled out her smartphone and checked the clock. There was still plenty of time before the stores opened, even with the long drive. Pulling out her cell phone, she texted, Mind if I see the animals before we leave?

Katie's response was quick. No prob. Running late anyway. Hubs will let you in.

Bowie met June by the zoo's entrance. Covering a yawn with one hand, he pulled back the gate with the other. Locking it behind them, Bowie said, "Katie told me to tell you not to rush. She had a lot of heartburn and back pain last night, so she's moving slowly this morning."

"Rough night for the mama-to-be?" June asked. "How'd Dad handle it?"

Bowie rubbed the back of his head and smiled. "Well, I'm not the one carrying twins, so you're not going to hear any complaints from me."

June leaned forward and whispered conspiratorially, "She can't hear you out here."

He chuckled and then sobered. "I'm fine. I'm

just glad everything's going well with Katie aside from her stomach issues."

"Doesn't she have the sweetest little waddle already?" June asked.

A huge grin broke over Bowie's face, and she could hear the warm affection in his voice when he spoke. "Yes, but don't tell her I said that."

Fresh pain burst inside June at Bowie's obvious love for his wife. She didn't envy her friends their happiness. They'd had a rough road finding it. But that didn't mean blissful couples didn't remind June of what she'd ruined.

"She's upset enough," Bowie continued. "Honey had her kit last night, and Katie is a tad jealous since she still has months to go."

June straightened. Bowie and Lou had realized a couple weeks ago the little minx was expecting. Since not much was known about honey badger births, they'd set up a webcam in the den Honey had dug. The feed had been getting a lot of traffic from researchers and the interested public.

"My word, that was a short pregnancy."

"Six to eight weeks," Bowie confirmed. "That's why Katie is so irritated."

"I would be too."

"Thanks for going into the city with her today. She could use some time away."

"Happy to be of service," June said, but she knew the truth. She was the one who really needed the escape.

After June said goodbye to Bowie, she walked through the deserted zoo. One prairie dog sentry gave a cry of alarm as she strolled past. Not many of the little guys were awake, but those who were hustled back into their burrows. As she watched them scurry to safety, a bittersweetness filled her. It was here she made her first breakthrough with Magnus when he'd offered to talk to her nan in exchange for help with his vlog.

June sighed as she kept walking. Frida was snoring when she passed by her enclosure. The silly bear was resting her chin on her favorite rock. June had no earthly idea how a stony pillow would be comfortable, but the old girl apparently loved it. She swore the animal even had a slight grin teasing the corners of her mouth.

June pushed open the door to the main facility. Although Sorcha's permanent exhibit beside Frida's was complete, Bowie was still in the process of getting the cub comfortable with her new home, so the little fur ball spent her nights in the nursery.

June smiled when Sorcha lifted her head at June's entrance and immediately scrambled in her direction. She'd grown bigger in the last month, looking more and more like a miniature polar bear rather than a cub. She'd packed on muscle, giving a hint of how powerful she'd become when full grown. Despite her increased brawn, the little girl still retained her playfulness.

Sorcha missed Magnus, though. According to Katie, the cub had moped for two days after his departure. The only time she'd perked up was when she'd played with Frida. Luckily, her natural energy hadn't let her stay glum for long. By the third day, she'd been back tussling with her toys. More than one

stuffed animal had met its untimely demise between her
sharp teeth.

June put on the long, tough gloves that protected
her when the bear pawed and chewed at her arms. She
wasn't as good as Magnus at cub wrestling, but Sorcha
appeared to enjoy it. Her black eyes shone as they
played tug-of-war with a rope. Her hind legs splayed out
behind her as she pulled. June knew that the bear could
easily rip the toy from her hands, but the imp wanted to
prolong the game.

Sorcha had just begun to lose interest when June
heard the door scrape behind her. She turned to see Katie
standing there, her hand on her lower back. Although
her friend claimed she looked like a blimp, she actually
had a very cute baby bump. The hormones had given
her a glow, and with her naturally red hair, she looked
as bright and fresh as a Johnny-jump-up in the spring.

"You look good," June said.

Katie responded with a groan. "I must be hiding the
constant heartburn well."

June frowned. "Do you need some more of my apple-
ginger jam? I was meaning to make a batch, but—"

Katie waved away June's concerns. "Don't worry
about it. I have my trusty bottle of Tums."

"Are you sure you're up to shopping?" June asked.
"We can stay here if you want."

Katie shook her head. "I've been looking forward to
this all week. I'll be fine."

June had a feeling Katie was mostly just saying that.
Her friend didn't mind picking out clothes, but it wasn't
her passion like June's. June started to protest again, but
Katie turned and began to waddle away. June had no

choice but to follow. Once Katie started walking in a direction, she didn't like to stop until she arrived at her destination.

As they climbed into June's SUV, Katie sighed as she settled in. "I'm so glad the seat was already pushed back. I'm getting tired of having to adjust every one."

"I can imagine," June said, forcing her voice to sound bright and casual. The seat had been moved back to accommodate Magnus's massive frame, and she'd never changed it. Evidently, June didn't modulate her voice just right because Katie shot her a confused look that quickly drifted into concern.

"Oh crap," Katie said. "Magnus sat here last."

"Yep," June said in the same overly cheerful tone. She really could not turn it off.

"Do you want to talk about it?" Katie asked softly.

"No."

Katie studied her. "June, you always want to talk."

"Not about this."

Katie gave a long and heavy sigh. "We're all worried about you."

"Well, don't be," June said, and she knew her voice sounded waspish. She couldn't help it. After years of always knowing the right thing to say and do, she felt adrift. It was like a compass inside her had been smashed, leaving her with an uncontrolled arrow spinning in every direction.

"June, you're so used to fixing other people's problems, I don't think you know how to let your friends help *you*."

June pulled over to the curb and turned off the engine to swivel in the direction of her friend. She was not going to drive while emotional, especially with a pregnant passenger. "That's just about the silliest thing I've ever heard."

"Is it?" Katie asked gently. "Who is always giving people advice?"

"I don't do that anymore," June said. "Why, just the other day Clay Stevens asked me to help him improve his reputation, and I turned him down flat. I'm done being an armchair psychologist."

"Clay Stevens came to you…" Katie straightened with interest before she cut herself off with a shake of her head. "No. I'm not going to let you distract me. This is about you."

"Yes. And I would like to change the subject."

"If the roles were reversed, would you let me do that?"

"Yes."

The look Katie gave was as dry as an overbaked, three-day-old biscuit. June crossed her arms. "Well, the new me would."

A single red eyebrow arched. June shifted uncomfortably. She wasn't accustomed to this much scrutiny from Katie. Impending motherhood must have gifted her friend with better interrogation techniques. Maybe June could even learn a trick or two…if she was still in the business of ferreting out personal information.

"Fine," June huffed. "I wouldn't let you distract me."

Katie reached forward and laid her hand on June's shoulder. "And I won't either. You need to unload. You've just had so much to deal with. Your grandmother. Magnus. Your two businesses."

To June's horror, big, fat tears began to roll down her face, and not the type a lady might shed. No. This crying fit was going to be uglier than a hog's backside, and June couldn't stop it.

"Oh, June," Katie said and rubbed her shoulder. "I know it's been hard."

"It's my fault," June blubbered.

"That's not entirely true," Katie said. "You shouldn't have tracked down Magnus's mother, but he shouldn't have left like he did."

"I'm a fraud, Katie," June said. "I go around taking care of other people's problems so I don't have to worry about my own."

"You're not a fraud, June," Katie said earnestly. "You truly do have a big heart, and you want to help people. There's nothing wrong with that."

"I'm pushy."

Katie smiled softly. "Well, maybe there are times you should dial back the helpfulness, but that doesn't mean you should stop altogether."

June sniffed, trying to hold back the torrent of tears. "Are you saying I should reach out to Clay Stevens?"

Katie gave a fond chuckle. "No. I think you have too much going on. This is the time for you to ask for help, not give it."

"I'm handling everything fine," June said. She tried to force a smile, but it turned into a truncated sob. Katie responded with a knowing look.

"Oh, I'm just weepy today."

"Juuune," Katie said, stretching out her name.

June sighed. "All right. I'm a mess."

Katie's expression turned solemn. "June, about your grandmother—"

"I know," June admitted in a small voice. "I'm not managing everything."

Katie patted her arm. "We're all here to help, whatever you decide. You've let my mom watch Nan a couple times, but she would do it more often. Me too. Even Buck and Stanley have volunteered. Lean on us. Let us help. Okay? It's what you've always said you love about small towns."

June nodded with a sniff. "I don't want to be a burden."

Katie's face softened. "Oh, June, you and your grandmother could never be that. You're both institutions in Sagebrush Flats."

Pleased amusement shot through June's misery. "An institution?"

Katie grinned good-naturedly. "Just as much as tumbleweeds, hot summers, and dust devils."

June blinked away her tears. "Even with me being a southern belle and my grandma being an English rose?"

"Absolutely," Katie said without hesitation. "Joking aside, it wouldn't be Sagebrush without the two of you and the tea shop."

June smiled. It was a watery smile, but it was real. "I needed to hear that."

"Good," Katie said emphatically. "Now, are you ready to shop up a storm?"

"Why, yes," June said, wiping the corner of her eyes with her knuckles. "I think I am."

"How about you let me drive?" Katie asked.

"But you're pregnant with twins, darlin'!"

"Hey," Katie protested as she scooted from her seat, "I'm not so big I can't fit behind a wheel."

June gave her friend a head start before she unbuckled her seat belt and climbed into the passenger side. Even with Katie driving, it took June half an hour before her stress began to unfurl. Settling further into the leather upholstery, she laughed at Katie's stories as the scenery passed by.

Katie had been right. June was glad she'd let her take the wheel. She needed the chance just to sit… no obligations, no demands, no juggling multiple tasks. There was something healing about leaning back and watching the wide expanse of land rush by. With a twinge of pain, June thought back to a passage in Magnus's book.

> When I stood on the edge of the rig and stared out into the expanse of flawless snow and ice, I did not flinch at the vastness. Instead, recognition flickered inside me…perhaps even a sense of homecoming. In the emptiness, I found my peace.

June exhaled, trying to relieve the pressure once again building inside her chest. Katie glanced over in concern. "Thinking of Magnus again?"

"Yes," June admitted.

"Over time, it'll get better," Katie said.

June nodded. She'd truly loved Magnus, and losing him was a grief all in its own. But she was strong. She'd get through this. All of this.

Maybe it was time to rely on folks. Stanley and

Buck could entertain Nan in the mornings, and Katie's mother wasn't the only one who'd offered to sit with her grandmother while June ran errands.

Sometimes, June realized, it was okay to let a friend climb into the driver's seat as long as she knew the way home.

Chapter 18

MAGNUS PAUSED AT THE DOOR OF THE PRIMROSE, Magnolia & Thistle. Through the glass, he could spy June. It was closing time, and the tea shop was empty. She had her head bent as she cleaned the counter, and he knew from experience she was humming softly.

He'd imagined her like this, even when he'd tried to shove her from his consciousness. At night when he lay abed, he'd think of her working on her latest jam. She'd be blethering happily as she chopped a piece of fruit or stirred the pot on the hob.

And he'd thought of her as he wrote. Her joy and spirit had bled into the pages, just as they'd bled into him. He could travel back to the Arctic Circle, and he'd still never manage to freeze this woman from his heart. She'd become a part of him, and he'd been an utter bampot to leave her.

He pushed the door open. At the tinkle of the bell, June glanced up. Her green gaze caught his, and her entire body stiffened. The washrag dropped from her fingers, and her bonny, pink lips parted ever so slightly. She'd never looked more braw to him, and he wanted to cross through the tea shop and kiss her.

But he didn't. If things went as he'd hoped, there'd be plenty of time for snogging later. Now, as much as he hated to admit it, was about talking.

He flipped her sign to *Closed* and locked the door. Her eyes widened, but she didn't move otherwise as he strolled forward. He didn't stop until they stood opposite each other with only the counter between them.

During the four plane rides and the long drive to Sagebrush, he'd crafted an entire speech, tweaking it each time he replayed it in his head. Despite the long journey, he hadn't slept much. Over and over, he'd gone through what he planned to say. He wanted to make this right. Make this perfect.

But when he opened his mouth, he said the first damn words that popped into his head, like a newly hatched gull. At least this time he didn't blurt out he'd drunk-dialed a bear...although that might have been a wee bit less dramatic.

Over the past month, June had imagined Magnus walking into her tea shop countless times. Sometimes, he'd stroll right over, sweep her off her feet, and kiss her long and deep. Other times, he'd apologize for leaving. Most often, he said he understood why she'd contacted his mother and that he forgave her. Even she, however, had not possessed sufficient foresight to envision his actual words.

"My da hit me upside the head with a shovel when I told him I was leaving the croft," Magnus announced without a single disfluency, even though he normally stuttered when he mentioned his father.

Ice sluiced through June's veins. "What?"

An angry look crossed Magnus's face, but June knew it wasn't directed at her. "Fuck. That wasn't how I planned to tell you. I'm m-m-making a m-m-manky steer of it."

June stared into Magnus's blue eyes, and she could tell he was hurting something fierce. His beard had grown woolly again, obscuring most of his features. In contrast to his dark hair, his skin looked pale and drawn. Purple pooled under his eyes, making him look like he'd just lost a bar brawl.

June moved around the counter and gently took his arm. It warmed her heart when he didn't pull away. "Let's go upstairs. Nan's resting and won't hear us."

"I'm sorry I left like I did," Magnus said as he followed her. "That's what I was trying to say. I shouldn't go b-b-b-blurting things out like that."

"It's okay," June assured him.

When they reached her bedroom, Magnus took the chair, so June perched on the edge of the bed. He looked so miserable she wanted to reach for him. But she didn't. This time, she would let him go at his own pace. No more pushing for June Winters.

He sighed heavily and shoved back his unruly hair with his hands. "I've never t-t-talked about it."

June nodded. "Don't worry about it, darlin'. Take your time. I'm not going anywhere."

He jerked his head stiffly. When he finally did speak, he kept his voice low, his eyes trained on the throw rug her brother had brought back for her when he was stationed in Jordan. "I was taught not to speak m-m-m-much by him."

June didn't need to ask who the "him" was. She knew instantly he was talking about his father. The man who'd hit him with a shovel.

"He didn't like m-m-m-m-m-my s-s-s-s-s-stuttering," Magnus said, his disfluency worse than normal. June couldn't help it. She leaned forward and rested her hand on his knee. Magnus swallowed. Hard. When he spoke again, he seemed more in control of his voice. "But that wasn't all. He never stopped the insults. I was a pleeping b-bampot, a lazy nyaff, a m-m-manky b-bawbag. I never could do anything right, and I had to live by his schedule. If I didn't rise from bed at exactly the time he wanted, he'd wake me with a b-bucket of water to the face. He did it even if I was late by half a minute."

June involuntarily squeezed Magnus's knee. He glanced at her, and the torment in his eyes nearly slayed her. He'd suffered more than she'd imagined. His beautiful, caring spirit had been nearly pulverized under the hands of a tyrannical bully.

"I had no quarter. He controlled everything, June. What I ate. The order I did my chores. When I went to b-bed. He left every d-day in his trawler, but he'd interrogate me about what I'd done. He terrified m-me as a lad. I'd answer him by nods and shakes because he couldn't stand my s-s-stuttering. When I didn't respond fast enough—or how he wanted—he'd hit me."

"I'm so sorry, Magnus," June whispered as a crushing pain settled on her heart.

"I escaped," he said thickly and then repeated the words in a steadier voice. "I escaped, June, and I swore I'd never let another person tell me what to do."

June felt her mouth twist into a self-effacing smile. "And then I came barreling along with all my poking and prodding."

To her surprise, a fond grin broke over Magnus's

solemn face, momentarily chasing away his gruffness. He reached for her and cupped her face. "Och, lass, you're good for m-me. I need your b-brightness like the Scottish p-p-primrose needs the sun to grow."

June's heart—already malleable from hearing about his childhood—turned into a puddle of goo. She turned her head and kissed his palm. At the contact, his eyes fluttered closed as if savoring her touch. When he opened them, his cobalt gaze had turned electric. June smiled. "That's just about the sweetest thing anyone's ever said to me."

Little flags of color appeared above Magnus's beard. June kissed each spot and then sank back to address him. "But," she continued, "I need to watch that I don't shine too brightly and give you sunburn."

Her statement surprised a bark of laughter from Magnus. Rising from the armchair, he lifted her into his arms and then settled them both on the bed. "Aye, you can be a wee bit intense, lass."

"I'm trying to work on that, cross my heart and hope to die," June said as she settled against his chest. He tucked her head under his chin, and she could feel the sigh of contentment rumbling through him. She snuggled closer and felt her own tension ebb away. My, my, she could get used to this sense of homecoming.

"I missed you, lass," Magnus said, his voice as thick as molasses left in an icebox.

"I missed you too," June said. "I'm sorry about what I did. I shouldn't have tracked down your mama."

"No, you shouldn't have," Magnus agreed, although his voice lacked bite. "But you meant well. I shouldn't have dashed out like a stoat caught trying to kill the chickens. I felt t-t-trapped, lass."

"I'm sorry about that," June said. She started to say more, but Magnus's next words stopped her.

"M-m-my d-d-da nearly killed me when I told him I was leaving. I'd just received n-news I'd snagged the roughneck job. We didn't have a phone out on B-B-B-Bjaray, so I'd come from rowing our dinghy back from T-T-Tammay. D-D-D-Da was still on the trawler when I returned, so I said goodbye to our animals instead. Even after he came back to the croft, I lacked the courage to tell him at first. Then, when we were milking our coos, I told him real fast. I didn't even stutter once. I remember that. His face turned red, but since I'd grown bigger than him, he didn't slap me as much. I didn't want to hear his abuse, so I turned. He p-p-picked up the shovel and hit me across the b-back of my head. Knocked me right out."

June gasped and shifted in Magnus's arms to look at him. He was staring stonily ahead, his face granite. She reached up and stroked his cheek, but he didn't react. He'd gone back to that place of horror, June realized. She wanted to talk, to pull him back, to try to fix his pain with words. But she didn't. Right now, she should just listen. He didn't want advice or a gentle distraction. He only needed her to understand and accept.

"From what he said during the sentencing hearing, he thought he'd killed m-me. He claimed he hadn't meant to. He'd been in a b-b-b-blind rage. I didn't believe him. He'd sooner see me d-d-d-dead than abandoning him like m-m-m-my m-m-m-mum did. I do believe, though, he panicked after I collapsed. T-T-Tammay was small, and even though we lived on B-B-Bjaray, someone would know if I went m-m-missing. I had a few weeks left until graduation, so he couldn't say I'd bunked off to start a new job. And I think the idea of m-m-me leaving shamed him, so he decided to m-m-make it look like we'd been robbed. So, he grabbed the shotgun we had for p-p-protecting our chickens and the feed from vermin and shot me in the back."

June made a sound. She couldn't help it. Magnus's blue eyes softened. He immediately gathered her into his arms. "Hush now, lass. That shot saved m-my life. Some tourists were on B-B-Bjaray looking at one of the Neolithic structures near the croft. They came running at the sound. D-D-D-Da's story didn't hold up long. He was already under arrest when I woke in the hospital. They'd flown me to m-m-mainland Scotland, and I only went back once to t-t-testify."

"Oh, Magnus," June said as she crushed him against her.

"So you see, lass," Magnus said softly, his chin resting on her shoulder as she clung to him, "I wasn't really running from you. I was escaping. M-my whole life has been trying to escape him or anything that could tie me down."

Fresh loss shredded June's hope. She steeled herself for Magnus's confession that he could never commit, could never attach himself to one person. June promised she would understand, that she wouldn't push and try to mold him into something he couldn't become. But it hurt. Oh lordy, did it hurt.

"Nay, June," Magnus said quickly, "it's not what you're thinking. I'm tired of running. I've gotten so used to it, I didn't realize it's been him who's been chasing m-me the whole time. That isn't freedom, lass. The only time I've felt rid of him was when I was with you."

Tears pricked the back of June's eyes. "Really? You truly mean that?"

A soft smile touched Magnus's lips, and June wished his beard didn't obscure half of it. She wanted to see his grin in its full glory, but even part of it was magnificent. Her heart squeezed as sparks of happiness lit inside her as if someone had just released a thousand lightning bugs. She never felt such a mixture of sorrow and joy.

Magnus wiped a stray tear from her cheek. "Aye, I do."

"So, what does this mean?" June asked softly, hesitantly.

"It means I have to get used to small-town *clish-maclaver* again." Magnus gave a wry smile. "I'd wager all my dosh B-B-Buck and Stanley already know I showed up at your shop right before closing and shut and locked the door."

"Okay," June admitted. "You'd probably win that bet."

"There'll be times when I'll be as b-b-blustery as the north wind," Magnus warned. "And you'll have to coax m-me to your parties."

"Uh-uh," June said. "My coaxing days have ended. That and fixing things...*and* sticking my nose where it doesn't belong."

Magnus laughed. The hearty sound reverberated around the room. Despite her echoing happiness, June lightly poked him in the ribs. "I'm being serious. I've learned my lesson. I've been trying real hard to mind my own beeswax."

He sobered instantly. "You weren't wrong about m-my m-mum, June. How you went about it, aye. B-b-b-but that I should speak with her, nay. It was right, and past time for both of us."

"Past time?" June asked.

Magnus bobbed his head. "I had a wee visit with her afore I came back to the States."

"And?" June prompted before she realized she was pushing again. She clamped her fingers over her mouth. Magnus chuckled as he gently disengaged her hand. "You don't need to change completely, lass. A little m-m-moderation would be good, but you care too m-m-much about people to stop. And I don't want you to. If you did, you wouldn't be the woman I fell in love with."

Everything stopped. June's muscles tensed as she processed his words. She felt Magnus's gaze on her…warm and more than a little nervous.

The joy came then, as sweet as honey and as powerful as a swollen river. She let out a squeal of delight, and relief broke over Magnus's face. He kissed her. It was a sloppy, wonderful kiss. With more enthusiasm than finesse, their lips slid hungrily over each other's. She giggled. He laughed. June had never found anything more magical.

"I love you too, Magnus Gray," June told him when they broke apart.

———

Emotion clobbered Magnus. He pulled June close, unable to respond verbally with the maelstrom rushing through him. He'd lived a life devoid of affection. At first, that choice had been thrust upon him. Then, he'd purposely walled himself off.

Until June.

She'd come hurtling into his life, and it had terrified him. Part of him still felt as unsure as a newborn lamb. Yet even that uncertainty was threaded with cautious joy. He wanted this. Craved it.

He remembered as a child watching male hen harriers swoop across the skies performing an elaborate sky dance to attract a mate. He'd gaze up in awe as the bird would pirouette, dive, whirl, and swoop effortlessly through the air. As he'd leaned against the old stone walls, he'd wonder what it would feel like to soar with such freedom, to feel his body dip and sway with nothing restraining him. Sometimes when he'd lay awake in the old cottage, he'd close his eyes and imagine it. In his mind, it felt just like this, exhilarating, yet peaceful. There was a rightness to loving June, and a thrill Magnus knew would never fade.

"I was hoping you would, lass," Magnus whispered, his voice sounding husky even to his own ears.

"And here I thought I was as transparent as glass," June said. "I've never chased after a man the way I did you. I should probably be too ashamed to admit that, but I'm just too tickled pink for discretion."

A wolfish satisfaction filled Magnus. "Is that so?"

"Yep."

"So, I was never just a project?" The idea had stopped plaguing him, but he still wanted assurance.

June's green eyes clouded in confusion. "A project? I don't understand."

"The night afore I left, I was talking to your m-m-mate

Josh." Magnus explained, and June knitted her eyebrows. "He mentioned you had a habit of m-m-making over people. Like him. Like me."

June's lips formed into a perfect O before she spoke. "I swear I am going to wring his scrawny neck."

Magnus shook his head as he brushed back a strand of June's hair. "He meant no harm. He was trying to m-m-make conversation. As you know, I'm not the easiest bloke to talk to."

"That may be true," June conceded, "but he shouldn't have suggested you were just a project to me. He's a real-life genius, and that was a dang-blasted stupid idea."

Amused and a little touched by June's indignation, Magnus kissed the top of her head. She still steamed like a kettle, though.

"Don't be too hard on your mate. The whole world called me a wunderkind, and I'm rubbish at relationships."

June's entire face softened, and she gently patted him on his cheek. "I wouldn't say you're rubbish."

"I'm learning," Magnus said, "because of you. I never would have talked to my m-mum if it hadn't been for you."

"It went well?" June asked.

Magnus nodded. "Aye. It's hard to explain how I felt toward her. I wasn't angry about her leaving. I understood. I think…I think I just cut off my emotions. I cut everything off until you went and turned it all on again."

June snuggled close, tilting her head so they

could still look at each other. "You opened something in me too."

Magnus snorted. June was one of the most unguarded people he'd ever met. At his dismissal, she gave him a mock glare.

"I'm being serious."

"Aye, right."

"I am."

"You're off your head."

June gently pushed on his chest as she leveraged herself to better gaze at him. Her eyes glowed like emeralds. "When I was a girl, we were always moving. I'd just build a new friendship, and my daddy would get orders. So, I focused on making folks happy, and that way I didn't have to worry about myself. If I was working on improving other people's lives, I didn't need to examine my own. And I could be involved without getting too close. Until you. When you left, you caused me to start some long overdue self-exploration, and there isn't another person on earth who could've managed that."

Emotion, thick and heavy, swamped Magnus. He swallowed against the swell in his throat as his heart ached from the force of it. He'd never expected a connection like this. Never sought it. Never thought he could inspire such love. The last of his doubts washed away, and the torrent inside him burst through the walls he'd built to survive his childhood.

He buried his face against June's neck and just held her. He couldn't speak for a moment. He could only feel. June seemed to understand. Her arms wrapped around him, and she held him close. Squeezing his eyes shut, he breathed in her familiar scent. Peace, like he'd never known, flowed through him as his body relaxed against her warmth.

He kissed her, slowly and deeply. Her lips parted under his, and his sense of homecoming felt complete. There was power in this embrace. Not the thrill of new discovery, but something stronger and right and even more electric. This was a joining of souls, not just bodies.

June moaned. The low sound detonated the want inside Magnus. Cupping her head, he slanted his mouth over hers. Her hands laced around the back of his neck, pulling him deeper into the maddening sensations. Desire and need pulsated as he felt her body press against his in clear demand.

His hands moved to undo her blouse as she tugged at his T-shirt. Breaking their kiss, he allowed her to pull the fabric over his head. Her fingers skimmed along his spine, sending lust spiraling through him. He buried his lips against her neck as he continued to work on her buttons. June emitted a sound between a cry and purr as the material fell away. He unhooked the front of her bra with his teeth and buried his face in her breasts. She shouted when he took one into his mouth. He sucked and teased as she writhed. Supporting her with one arm, he used the other hand to stroke the velvety softness of her other nipple. It had already pebbled, and he ran the callused pad of his thumb over the tip. Her fingers pressed into his back. She said his name, a guttural sound drenched in need.

His boabie jerked, and he pulled back and bit his inner lip to stop from coming right then and there. June touched him, wrenching a groan from him. "Lass…" he managed between clenched teeth as she pulled down his trousers. As soon as he bobbed free, June bent and kissed him. Magnus squeezed his eyes shut, his fingers digging into the sheet. "Lass…"

"We have the rest of the day and all night," June whispered, her voice as decadent as honey. Then she took him into her mouth, her long hair brushing the insides of his thighs and the lower part of his belly. He opened his eyes, and the sight of June transfixed him. She looked so sweet and determined as she concentrated on giving him pleasure. The joy in his chest burgeoned as he stared, utterly mesmerized by the fae lass. A tightness inside him unfurled as he gave himself over to her. His release shuddered through his body, shaking through every last restraint. In its wake, he found a peace and a wholeness he'd craved his entire life.

June smiled at Magnus as he lay with a contented look on his face. He opened his brilliant eyes, and the affection in his gaze settled over her like a warm coat fresh from the dryer. Oh, she *did* love this man.

He cupped her chin, stroking her cheekbone with his thumb. "You undo me, lass. I don't know how, but you do. There isn't a wall I could build that you couldn't bring down."

Joy erupted inside June. For once in her life, she couldn't speak. Her happiness was just too great.

Magnus lifted her from her kneeling position, settling her gently on the mattress. His big body bracketed her slender one. "My turn, lass."

He unhooked her pants, his movements slow and deliberate. Fascinated, she watched as he pulled down the zipper. He separated the fabric and kissed the small strip of skin between the placket and her panties. She'd never felt anything so splendid. A cry tore from her, and he smiled wickedly. He removed her khakis, first one leg, then the other. Each time he lingered at her knee, his callused fingers playing at the sensitive skin, before he kissed and licked.

By the time he'd finished, she lay panting, and he hadn't even removed her underwear. He kissed his way back up, pausing when he reached the lacy fabric. She'd thought he'd slip them off. He didn't.

Instead, he traced their outline, his tongue flicking against her skin with wicked little licks. Desire pooled inside her as she squirmed against the onslaught. His big hands cupped her buttocks as he continued his teasing path around her inner thighs. She gripped his shoulders, feeling his hard muscles beneath her fingers. Her cries morphed into staccato gasps as he lathed her. Just when she thought her body could no longer withstand his delicious assault, he inched down her underwear and pressed his mouth against her. Pleasure rushed through her as bright and magical as a fall sunset in all its colorful glory.

When the brilliance finally faded, she could only cling to him. She felt as limp as a rag doll left out in the rain. Magnus's face appeared in her line of vision as he pulled her close.

"I've m-missed you, lass."

"Uh-huh," she managed. She didn't know when she'd think coherently again. She'd never experienced anything like that. Until this moment, she'd never truly let another person take charge before. But it was easy with Magnus.

"You know," he said, reaching down to play with her damp curls. "I m-might be ready for you soon, lass."

She sighed as his hands caressed her already sensitized flesh. He pressed his lips against her belly and began to work his way up. Slowly. It was glorious lying there. Feeling his tongue and lips against her skin. He moved as languidly as she felt. When his mouth finally closed over hers, the hard ridge of him pressed against her center. As if wakened from slumber, her body lifted to rub against him. At the contact, he moaned into her mouth. Galvanized, she wiggled more.

"Och, lass," he whispered against her mouth, "I'm trying to take it slow."

She reached and grabbed his butt. "I don't want finesse. I want you. I want to celebrate. I want it wild."

—∞—

Wild. With the way Magnus's blood was pumping, he could do wild.

"You're sure, lass? We haven't been together—" His words ended in a guttural moan as she reached down and slid her finger along the tip of his boabie. Gently, she guided him to her entrance, and he needed no further encouragement. He sank into her slick warmth, burying himself inside her. She cried in pleasure, her fingertips pressing against his arse. He pulled out and plunged downward. This time, they both shouted.

He'd never experienced this before. This sense of pure abandon. Despite their urgency, they moved as one. Their bodies slid in rhythm as their gasps and moans mingled. He'd never imagined feeling so in tune with another soul.

The intensity of their lovemaking didn't just come from molten-hot passion. This went deeper. He no longer held back any of himself, and neither did she. There was trust, and that faith engendered a freedom that allowed them to soar.

She came first, her muscles clenching around him. Pushed to his own edge, he tumbled over, free-falling into sheer bliss. Pleasure rocketed through him like a thousand shooting stars tumbling to earth. But the landing wasn't hard. It was like sinking into a warm bath after a hard day. Luxurious and relaxing.

He barely stopped himself from collapsing on her. Instead, he managed to roll them both on their sides. They remained joined, and he made no effort to disentangle from her. He craved their closeness and wanted to bask in it a little longer. The connection between them didn't worry him. Not anymore. He'd finally accepted the rightness of it. With a smile, he drifted off to sleep.

Honey quite enjoyed being a mother, even if it meant spending most of her time in a burrow. Recently, she had the urge to move her lair again. Carefully carrying the newborn in her mouth, she dug another cavity in the dirt. Hopefully, this time the humans would not plant odd-looking things inside it.

When her new home was complete, Honey curled up and felt her baby nestle against her. She sighed as her eyes drifted shut. She did not mind this new adventure. She had a feeling it was going to turn out to be an exciting one. Once her kit grew old enough to leave the den, Honey was going to have so much fun showing her heir how to properly stir up mischief.

―∾∾―

June woke to find Magnus watching her. He gently brushed back her hair, his blue eyes glowing with affection. "Good morning, lass."

She smiled and stretched in the circle of his arms. Admiration mixed with the tenderness in Magnus's eyes. Leveraging herself up, she laid a kiss on his lips. She meant to just give him a peck, but it turned into a longer one. She sighed. "Now that is how a girl should wake up."

"Is that an order?" he asked, his voice teasing without any trace of tension. Given what Magnus had confessed about his past, June recognized what it meant for him to say those words so easily.

She laid her palm on the side of his dear, familiar face. "Do you want it to be?"

"Aye," he said, "one I'll willingly t-t-take." He turned his head and kissed her hand before he rose from the bed. The sheet slipped, and June exhaled in appreciation as he walked stark naked over to his duffel bag. When he bent to shuffle for his clothes, lust bolted through her. The man did have one fine-looking heinie. She could spend all day ogling it.

He turned and froze when he caught her looking. His eyes heated, and her body immediately started tingling. Memories from yesterday flooded her, and heat flared.

Mercy, she'd never thought of sex as transformative, but she felt all shaky and new.

"If you keep looking at me like that, hen, we'll never leave the b-b-bed."

June did not stop. "Is that a problem? The tea shop isn't open today."

Leaning forward, he gave her another explosive kiss. Unfortunately, he pulled back. She made a mewling sound in protest. Before she could reach for him, he dropped a fat manila envelope in her lap. Curious, she glanced at him.

"What is this?"

"My latest manuscript. It's due to my editor in a week."

June froze. "I thought you never let anyone read your work until it was published."

Magnus sat down on the bed, his expression solemn. "I don't, lass, but you aren't just anyone."

Joy sparked as she clutched the papers to her chest. Magnus leaned over and tucked a strand of her hair behind her ear. "You're who I wrote this b-b-book for. It'll be dedicated to you and Frida."

June blinked at the last statement. "I share billing with a geriatric *grizzly*?"

Magnus chuckled. "Just read it, June. I'll take care of your nan."

"She missed you," June told him as he started over to his duffel bag again. While Magnus had been sleeping from his long journey, she'd taken care of Nan and gotten her ready for bed. Clearly exhausted, Magnus had slept straight through the night.

"How is she?" Magnus asked as he pulled out a pair of boxers and pants.

June started to give an upbeat response but stopped herself. This was Magnus. She didn't need false cheer. "There've been a lot of bad days. Some good ones too. She's not getting worse, but she's not getting any better. The doctors believe she's plateaued."

Immediately, Magnus stopped putting on his shirt. He came back over and sat on the bed. "How have you been handling it?"

June teared up. She didn't try to hide it. Love meant honesty, even when it came to sharing the uglier emotions. "It's been hard. I've even considered putting her in a nursing home. Katie convinced me to let folks help out. Her mom comes at least one evening a week, and Buck and Stanley watch her during the mornings."

Magnus reached over and pulled her close. "I'm here now, lass. I'll help take care of her."

June rested her head against his shoulder, feeling his heat and strength. "That's a lot to ask."

Magnus shook his head, and she felt his chin scrape against her hair. "Nay, not at all. I've never minded spending time with your nan, and I can write while sitting with her. I'm t-t-tired of living my life alone, June. It will be good for both of us to have a spot of company."

A heaviness lifted from June as she flung her arms around Magnus. He held her tightly and kissed her temple. The simple tenderness in his embrace wrapped around June like her favorite wool scarf. The fear and grief that had clung to her since her nan's hospital visit fell away. Yes, her grandmother might never return to her normal self, but she and

June would muddle through this just as June had promised her gran.

"Junie?" Nan's thin voice came over the baby monitor.

Magnus planted a kiss on June's forehead as he rose. "I'll take care of her, June." He paused and jabbed his thumb at the stack of papers on the bed. "You read."

As Magnus left the room, June picked up his manuscript, but before she could even glance at the title page, the monitor crackled to life.

"Magnus?" her grandmother's voice sounded full of wonder. June felt a stab of relief that Nan recognized him so easily.

"Aye, in the flesh," Magnus said.

"You came back."

"I couldn't stay away from the two b-b-bonniest lasses I've ever m-met," Magnus answered.

"Oh now," Nan protested, but June could hear the pleased smile in her voice. She heard the old wooden chair creak as Magnus sat down.

"I won't leave either of you again," Magnus promised, and those darn tears pricked the back of June's eyes.

"Well, you better not," her grandmother said, sounding every inch a Brit with her clipped tone.

"I promise I'll m-m-make it up to you."

"*Hrmph.*"

"June is reading my latest m-m-manuscript right now, but when she's done, I'll read it to you."

"I would like that," her grandmother said, clearly mollified.

When Magnus spoke, affection suffused his tone. "As would I."

"If you're planning on staying, you might as well call me, 'Nan,'" her grandmother said, sounding so much like her old self that June squeezed her eyes shut.

There was a beat of silence before Magnus said gravely, "Aye, Nan, I'll d-do that."

"Will you read to me now?" Nan asked, her voice childlike again. June smiled softly as she turned off the baby monitor. Glancing down, she started on the first paragraph.

I didn't expect the sharp cold...or her. I've always imagined the American desert to be insufferably hot with a dryness that causes a man's very cells to wither. Yet when I arrived, I discovered a crispness to the air. It is a new chill, not as baltic as the Arctic Circle or as dreich as Orkney. The sun still blazes overhead, a harbinger of the sweltering days to come.

After checking into my lodgings, I popped over to Sagebrush's answer to the pub—the Prairie Dog Café. It is a larger establishment than I'd envisioned and is festooned with antlers and old farm equipment. Like the American West itself, the restaurant is a wide-open space, with no charming nooks and crannies for a man to tuck away in. I attempted to secrete myself in one of the booths the Yanks are so fond of, but I soon received my first lesson on hospitality in the United States.

I heard her voice first...slow and honeyed. It

makes a man think of Spanish moss, magnolia trees, and steamy moonlit nights. I
turned and found myself staring into eyes as
green as newly sprung grass. Dreich, surly
soul that I am, I tried to resist her sunny
warmth, to retreat back into the vinyl bench
currently serving as my cave. But the fae
lass persisted, grabbing my hand, pulling
me into the merriment and light behind her.

June shifted as she read Magnus's description
of their first encounter. It was strange, seeing
herself on the page and knowing this book would
be distributed around the world. Yet, despite the
slight twinge of vulnerability, she didn't worry. She
trusted Magnus, trusted he'd tell their story right.

As she flipped the next page, she forgot her
momentary discomfort. Magnus's beautiful prose
pulled her into the story. Even though she'd lived
it, she found herself riveted. He wrote of his talks
with Frida and his fondness for little Sorcha and
Savannah. Magnus captured details of the zoo
residents' personalities that June had overlooked,
and those observations were what really made the
animals come to life in the reader's mind.

He wrote about his struggles with disfluency
and how he'd finally come to accept it as part of
him. June's eyes grew damp. A tear or two might
have dripped down her cheek when he alluded to
his strict upbringing.

But mostly, her heart soared as she read his
wonderful, wonderful tale. For it was a love story.

Theirs. She appeared everywhere in the manuscript.
Even when she frustrated Magnus, she could still detect
his underlying fondness.

She couldn't stop reading. Magnus checked in on her
a few times and even brought her lunch. He'd reported
that her nan was doing fine, so June kept turning pages.
When she read the last paragraph, her heart galloped
faster than a runaway stallion. The tears in her eyes bubbled over, this time from sheer joy. If she ever doubted
the Scot loved her, this chased the thought away.

> I have returned home from my sojourn in the
> States, but London no longer suits me. The green
> in the pub's stained-glass windows reminds me
> of her bonny eyes, and though the fire chases
> away the dreich of a London spring night, it
> cannot warm my soul. I am a half-awakened man.
> Just as a seed needs the sun's rays to sprout
> through its hull, I need the warmth of her smile
> and the heat of her touch to push through the
> husk of my past. I have been running since I left
> Bjaray; perhaps now it is time I changed direc-
> tions and returned. Not to the dark, windy Isles,
> but to the sun and dust of the American West.

June rose and walked to her grandmother's room. Nan
lay asleep on the bed, while Magnus typed on his laptop.
At her entrance, he immediately glanced up. He took one
look at her face and set his computer aside. Wordlessly,
he arose from his chair and followed her out into the hall.

"Did you like it?" he asked, his tone slightly hushed
even though her nan would never be able to hear them.

"How could I not?" June asked, wrapping her arms around him as she lifted her chin to regard him with all the love she felt. "It was the most magical thing I've ever read. I'm so honored, and touched, and... Well, I don't even know how to describe how glorious I feel, Magnus."

"I didn't realize what I was writing until I was finished," Magnus admitted. "After I read the first draft, I got blootered. I was so blitzed I called Frida."

"The *bear*?"

"Aye, I suppose I owe Bowie a thank-you for not letting on about that," Magnus said. "I was still guttered when I headed to Kirkwall, but I sobered up afore I reached m-my m-mum's. It was good, seeing she'd made a life—a good one—after a childhood of ugliness and m-marriage with m-my da. I'd been going about it wrong, trying to keep myself shut off and thinking it was freedom. I was still under his control, his words in m-my head."

"Oh, Magnus," June breathed.

"But I'm done with listening to him and with worrying that committing m-myself to another will mean losing my autonomy. You've released m-me from so m-m-many of the chains I put on m-myself...and not just those I forged because of m-m-my d-d-d-da. I've accepted who I am June, even the stuttering, because you kept pushing. I meant what I wrote. For the first time in my life, I'm ready to come home."

"Sagebrush is home?"

"Nay, lass, you're home."

The truth of Magnus's words rang through June.

"You know, darlin', my whole childhood I was looking for a place to put down roots, and I did here. But when you left, I felt as empty as a larder after a hard winter."

"What are you saying, lass?" Magnus asked, his voice husky with hope and joy.

"That you're my home too."

He kissed her then. It was sweet and tender…and even a little innocent. It was a kiss of homecoming and belonging.

Epilogue

"So, I am going to ask the lass to marry me on Monday when the zoo is closed to visitors," Magnus told Frida.

The bear looked up from her ice treat. She licked her lips as she regarded Magnus. He'd been back in Sagebrush Flats for a month now. Life had fallen into an easy pattern. To his surprise, he'd become accustomed to having his breakfast at the tea shop with Nan, Buck, and Stanley. The locals didn't even appear to notice his stutter anymore. They just gave him the time he needed to get out whatever he wanted. Although Magnus would never become a gossip, he'd begun to appreciate the rhythm of small-town life.

"And I'm planning to get a dog, a friendly one who won't mind cozying up in a corner of the tea shop."

Frida snorted, the sound indignant. Magnus smiled. "Don't fash yourself, lass. I'll still be volunteering at the zoo and stopping by to see you. I might bring Nan along too." Although the older woman remained on antianxiety medication, she'd slowly improved to the point where she could handle short outings. She had good days and bad days. While June managed her two businesses, Magnus kept Nan company and wrote. Yesterday, he'd finally persuaded June to agree to try having a home healthcare worker watch her grandmother a few times a week. June had protested at the cost, but they could afford the expense, especially after the last call from his agent.

"I have good news," Magnus said to the bear. "You're going to be more famous. There's to be a movie about the Sagebrush Zoo."

Frida appeared more interested in the apple slice she had dislodged from the ice than his revelation of her potential star status. She nosed the frozen fruit before gobbling it down. Magnus smiled. June's response had been a wee bit more enthusiastic. There were benefits to having a human confidant.

"You'll have to wait your turn, though. They're first making two films based on my books about Orkney and the Arctic. The final one will be my favorite. It's a love story, after all."

Magnus's editor had fully endorsed his manuscript. Then the vlog had gone viral, and Magnus's agent was now in the process of negotiating a three-movie deal. She'd called last night to go over the compensation, which would give June and him more than enough to provide for her nan. With the onset of tourist season, June's businesses were also booming. He'd talked her into setting up an appointment with the local bank to see about a loan to expand her jam-making operations.

"Things are settling where they should," Magnus told Frida. "I just need to come up with a proper proposal for June. I'm a practical sort, but June fancies more flash. I want to make it pure magic for her. Bowie said he'd help me execute the details, and Abby's over the moon with excitement. Here's what I've been thinking…"

Although no one could hear him, Magnus leaned over the fence and whispered his plans to the old bruin.

———

June hurried through the zoo carrying two tattie scones, a tea for Magnus, and an iced latte for herself. He'd told her this morning he'd wanted to meet her for a late lunch at the prairie-dog enclosure. The new healthcare worker was watching her grandmother this afternoon. Although June hadn't initially liked the idea of a stranger taking over like that, she'd warmed to Lily almost instantly and, better yet, so had Nan. The woman was both cheerful and competent.

Thoughts of the caretaker and Nan fled when June rounded a corner and spotted Magnus. At the sight of him, she gave a cry of delight. "Honey, I thought you said you would never wear a kilt."

Magnus stood in full formal Scottish attire, the flags of color in his cheeks almost as red as in his tartan. "Aye, lass, but I did it for you. I asked m-m-my m-m-m-mum if we are descended from any of the Highland clans since her folks came to Orkney from mainland Scotland. I have some M-M-MacGregor blood running through me, so I thought I'd wear their plaid."

June ran her eyes over his tall form swathed in the bright-red and green colors. With his broad shoulders, neatly trimmed beard, and strong features, he looked like he belonged on the cover of a romance novel. "Darlin', you do not disappoint."

His flush deepened, a reaction June never failed to find charming. Magnus shifted, and June could sense tension rising from him like steam from a boiler. She frowned at his nervousness. Lately, they'd become as comfortable with each other as two worn shoes. His disfluency had decreased too. Although Magnus still blocked on words, he'd gained more control over his stutter. Since his return to Sagebrush, he'd been diligently working on speech therapy techniques.

Magnus gestured toward the prairie dogs and then the bench across from the exhibit. The little rodents had retreated into their burrows at her approach, but a few had begun to peek out. June caught a glimpse of their adorable little faces as they regarded Magnus and her with curious brown eyes.

"D-D-D-Do you remember the first time you b-b-brought me a tattie scone? I was sitting right there."

June nodded. "You'd just learned your editor wanted you to do a vlog."

"Aye," Magnus nodded. "I thought it was the worst idea, b-b-but it turned out to be the best thing that ever happened to m-m-me. If it hadn't b-b-b-been for his request, I would've kept avoiding you. I'd be b-b-b-back in my London flat now thinking I was free when I was really trapped in the same world of gray I'd spent my life trying to escape."

Magnus swept his hand over the vista surrounding the zoo. Seeing her town through his eyes, June gazed at the familiar red dirt dotted with vibrant green sagebrush. Orange, pink, and white cliffs rose from the ground with hazy mountains looming behind them. "You're like this land to me, lass…full of color and brightness and warmth."

June swallowed at the joy rising up. She felt so alive with happiness it almost hurt. "I love you, Magnus."

"I love you too, and I didn't think I was capable of that emotion."

She stepped forward and brushed her hand against his cheek. "Magnus, you've always had a deep capacity for affection. I brought it to the surface, that's all."

Just then, she heard the crunch of gravel on the path. Bowie appeared with Hank, Lulubelle, and Savannah. The girl camels had wreaths of flowers on their woolly heads and silly grins on their faces. Hank wore an equally absurd smile and a saddle on his back. Wordlessly, Bowie handed Magnus the lead rope. He gave a bob of his head, then turned and disappeared the way he'd come.

June raised an eyebrow as a giddy ball of excitement began to form inside her. "Magnus, what do you have up the sleeve of your Prince Charlie jacket?"

"Would you like to take a ride on Hank and see?" Magnus asked.

"This is beginning to sound like quite an adventure," June said as she let Magnus help her onto the massive camel.

"June, my life has been an adventure since the moment you walked up to me in the Prairie Dog Café."

June paused in settling onto Hank's hump. "What kind of an adventure? That statement can go either way, darlin'."

Magnus chuckled. "The kind that's pure magic."

Satisfied with the response, June made herself as comfortable as she could. It wasn't easy considering the male camel's height, broad body, and swaying gait. Horseback riding was definitely easier, but without the pizazz, and June did love pizazz.

Magnus led their small caravan through the zoo. When they wound past the grizzly's exhibit, he paused. "See, Frida, I told you I'd bring her by."

Frida lumbered over to the edge of the moat and sniffed the air. "I'm here," June called, knowing the elderly bear couldn't spot her from this distance. Frida gave a grunt that sounded almost like approval. Then, without any fanfare, she turned and walked directly over to her favorite rock. With a sigh, she rested her chin on its edge and promptly fell asleep.

Magnus chuckled. "I suppose she thinks her work is complete."

"What work?" June asked.

Magnus responded with a broad grin. "Wooing you, lass."

Before she could respond to *that* interesting statement, Magnus pulled on Hank's lead and brought them past Sorcha's new exhibit. June looked for the little cub, but she didn't spot her among the rocks or in her pool. "Isn't Sorcha out?"

"She's back in the nursery. She has a surprise for you."

"What kind of surprise?"

"You'll see."

"Why, aren't you full of mystery today," June observed as they reached the maintenance facility. Bowie and Abby came out. The tween was trying hard to stay

solemn, but a giggle escaped her lips. She clasped
her hand over her mouth, but she couldn't mask the
joy that had overtaken her pixie-like features. Her
father did a better job of staying stoic as he gave
Magnus an indecipherable signal, but his gray eyes
sparkled just as much as his daughter's. Excitement
zipped through June as Magnus helped her dismount.
Leaving Bowie and Abby outside with the camels,
they headed straight for the nursery. When they
reached the door, Magnus gave her a little nudge.

"You go first."

Curious, her heart beating like a snare drum at
a military tattoo, June pushed on the handle and
peered inside. Sorcha glanced up from the toy she'd
been tussling. The polar bear lay on her back, her
paws in the air as she tossed the stuffed animal. She
paused, her bright eyes focusing on them. When
the cub spotted Magnus behind June, she scrambled
and dashed over. Although she'd put on weight and
muscle, she still remained a baby. Making happy
sounds, she pawed at Magnus's thick boots.

That's when June saw it.

A huge bow hung around Sorcha's neck with a
jewelry box nestled in its center. Although June had
been half expecting it, the sight of the velvet container triggered a rush of joy. Bringing her hands
to her mouth, June watched as Magnus got down
on one knee. Carefully removing the ribbon from
Sorcha, he opened the box.

"Will you m-m-marry me, lass?"

June nodded, tears springing to her eyes. A few
welled over as she dropped to her knees beside him.

Unable to speak, she could only nod. They gathered each other close as Sorcha watched them curiously. Magnus kissed June, long and deep. When he broke away, he framed her face with his hands and stared down at her, his blue eyes bright.

"You are home to me, lass. I'm finally ready to put down roots. Will you show me how?"

She nodded her head, ignoring the tears trickling down her cheeks. Grasping his hand in hers, she squeezed tightly. "We'll make sure to plant them good and deep because you're home to me too, Magnus Gray."

Author's Note

Although Orkney is a real island chain to the north of Scotland, Magnus's home isle of Tammay and the nearby Bjaray are wholly from my imagination. With its treasure trove of Neolithic, Pictish, and Norse monuments, Orkney has long held my fascination. As I researched the isles, I fell more in love with their natural beauty. After I finished my first draft of *Sweet Wild of Mine*, I was fortunate to travel to both Mainland (the main island in the chain) and Papa Westray, one of Orkney's northern most islands. I pictured Tammay and Bjaray as even farther north and to the east, almost between North Ronaldsay (another Orcadian island) and Fair Isle, which is considered part of the Shetland island chain. It is truly a magical place with breathtaking sea cliffs, verdant green hills, ancient stone structures, incredible wildlife, and welcoming locals. Orkney's roots are both Norse and Scottish, making for a culture and language that is uniquely its own.

Fluffy and Honey's relationship was interesting and, at times, challenging to write, especially in the context of a romance novel. Given their acerbic temperaments, honey badgers are unsurprisingly very antisocial. In the wild, the adults rarely interact, except to mate. And, like many couplings in the animal kingdom, it isn't exactly rose petals and mood music, especially for the female. Luckily for the purposes of the tale I was telling, there is evidence of captive honey badgers forming attachments to each other. The original Houdini honey badger (Stoffel of Moholoholo Wildlife Rehabilitation Centre in South Africa) had a girlfriend who aided and abetted in his escapes. Since both Honey and Fluffy have been around silly bipeds their entire lives, I thought it was very likely that they would bond with each other and discover that getting into mischief together was more fun than doing it alone.

There is also conflicting information regarding the gestation period of honey badgers. Some sources say that females are pregnant for six months, while others state six to eight weeks. This is a significant variance. HoneyBadger.com speculates that this difference may depend on whether the honey badgers are living in colder or warmer climes. I chose the shorter time frame as it fit better with the plot.

Acknowledgments

I want to extend a special thank you to my editor, Deb Werksman, who saw the potential hiding in my original draft of the first book in the Where the Wild Hearts Are series. Her insightful recommendations helped guide me to create the vivid world of Sagebrush Zoo and its delightful animal residents.

I also owe a huge thanks to my agent, Sarah Phair, who was the first person in the industry to believe in my writing and who worked hard to make sure this series would become a reality.

The entire Sourcebooks Casablanca team has done such an amazing job in marketing Where the Wild Hearts Are. Each time, the art department perfectly captures the emotional heart of the book with their wonderful covers.

Thank you also to my family, who has always supported me—from answering my endless questions about my latest draft to challenging me with their constructive criticism.

I also want to thank the people of Orkney for not minding all the inquiries made by an eager American tourist.

Don't miss the first book in the
Where the Wild Hearts Are
series by Laurel Kerr.

Meet all of Sagebrush Zoo's
rambunctious characters and fall in love!

Wild on my Mind

THE INCREASINGLY INSISTENT SQUEAKS BROKE
through Katie Underwood's intense concentration.
Cocking her head to the side, she paused in her drawing.
The chirping grew more and more demanding, the sound
bouncing off the sandstone rocks surrounding her. At
first, Katie thought a flock of birds was scolding her for
invading their sanctuary, but she didn't spot any flying
overhead in the waning light.

She started to turn back to her sketchbook, intent on
taking advantage of the last rays before the sun dipped
below the horizon, but something stopped her. The
squeaking had the plaintive quality of an animal calling for help, and Katie had never been able to resist a

wounded critter. Shoving her art supplies in her
backpack, she followed the direction of the sound.
Climbing a few feet above the ledge where she'd
been sketching, she realized the cries originated
from a cave that she remembered from childhood
games with her four brothers.

Dropping to her hands and knees, Katie peered
inside the crevice, wishing she had a flashlight. The
pearly glow of twilight barely reached the back of
the small alcove. She would have crawled inside,
but both cougars and wolves haunted this sandstone promontory. As much as Katie loved wild
creatures, she did not wish to encounter a wounded
predator in a tight space.

Once her eyes finally adjusted to the gloom,
Katie's heart simply melted. Tucked into a corner
lay three squirming cougar cubs. One of the disgruntled fluffs chose that exact moment to howl its
displeasure. A tiny pink mouth, framed by delicate
whiskers, opened wide as the kit mewed in frustration. Katie could just barely make out the black spots
peppering its grayish-brown fur.

She started to crawl forward and then stopped.
Katie didn't know what would happen if she got her
scent on the little guys. Resting on her haunches,
she debated her next step. The mother might return,
but Katie couldn't shake the feeling that the kits
were either orphaned or abandoned. A neighbor-
ing rancher had recently been complaining about
attacks on his livestock by pumas, which is what
he called cougars or mountain lions, and he'd been
known to shoot them in the past.

Katie reached for her cell phone. No signal. She would need to climb down to the old homestead and use the landline. Before she left, Katie stared back into the crevice where the cubs clumsily toddled in search of milk. "Don't worry, babies," she promised. "I'll be back with help."

As Bowie Wilson made the sharp turn onto the old Hallister spread, the suspension of his ancient pickup groaned loudly. He had a hell of a time keeping the vehicle running. The zoo sorely needed a new truck, but funds were tight and getting worse. They'd barely staved off foreclosure this past winter, and attendance hadn't picked up this spring. They were down to just a handful of volunteers and staff—a far cry from the animal park's heyday.

Pulling up to the old homestead, Bowie cut the engine and turned to wake his passenger, the former owner of the zoo. The eighty-year-old had fallen asleep on the twenty-minute drive to the ranch. Bowie had debated whether to bring Lou, since the older man generally headed to bed about now. But, unlike Bowie, Lou was a trained vet, and he could immediately start treatment on the cubs if they were seriously dehydrated or malnourished.

As Bowie waited for Lou to descend from the pickup, the front door to the old ranch house banged open. A woman, backlit by the porch light, waved. Although Bowie couldn't make out her features, he could easily spot the flash of her fiery-red hair. As she stepped out of the brightness and moved closer, the moonlight washed over her and gently illuminated her face. Her brown eyes widened at the sight of him.

Bowie couldn't quite read her emotion. Shock? Dismay? Recognition? Considering the size of their town, the latter was likely, but despite the fact that she seemed vaguely familiar, he couldn't place her. And he was pretty certain he'd remember a woman like her: all curly auburn hair, curves in the right places, and expressive chocolate-brown eyes. She exuded an earthy sexiness that appealed to him, awakening sensations that had lain dormant for far too long. Between his responsibilities as a single dad with an eleven-year-old daughter and his duties at the zoo, Bowie hadn't been with a woman in years.

Unfortunately, he had no time to appreciate this one. At least not now. Not with abandoned cougar cubs to rescue.

The woman focused her attention on Lou. "My parents are inside if you want to wait with them. It's a pretty difficult climb to the cubs."

Lou thanked her and headed to the homestead. The woman waited until he had disappeared into the house before she whirled back to Bowie. She thrust a headlamp in his direction, smacking his chest in the process.

"Here, take this. You'll need it to see," she bit out before she turned and strode gracefully toward the rock promontory silhouetted against the starry sky. Something about her gait reminded him of an Amazon warrior. An irate one. Although he'd spent most of his youth with adults angry at him — some with cause, some without — Bowie wasn't accustomed to facing a hot blast of fury anymore. He lived a quiet life now, and he had no idea what he could've done to upset this particular woman. It would be his crappy luck that the one female who attracted him also instinctually hated his guts.

When the woman reached the base of the rock formation, she bounded up the lower boulders with the sure-footedness of a mountain goat. Even if she had taken an immediate dislike to him, Bowie found his eyes following her lithe shape in the dim light. She moved with a combination of fluidity and unbound energy that made him wonder what she'd be like in bed.

Forcing those unprofessional thoughts from his mind, he concentrated on finding footholds. It wasn't easy keeping pace. His reluctant guide clambered up the cliff almost as quickly as she walked. Bowie figured she must know the land pretty well, since only moonlight illuminated the landscape, and she hadn't turned on her headlamp.

"I guess you've climbed here before," he said.

She nodded, but she still didn't seem too happy. "Yes. My mom's folks, the Hallisters, lived out here, so I grew up playing on these rocks with my brothers. My parents moved out here after my dad's retirement."

That could explain why she looked vaguely familiar, but not her anger toward him. Perhaps he'd seen her around as a kid when she'd visited her relatives. She looked close to Bowie's age, and in his early teens, he'd worked on a ranch nearby. That was until he'd broken his leg and the rancher, who'd been his foster parent, had thrown him right back into the system. Bowie had never known a real home before Lou and his late wife, Gretchen, had taken him in after yet another guardian had kicked him out on his eighteenth birthday when the reimbursement checks stopped.

Deciding to try one more time to befriend the woman, Bowie asked, "So did you come to Sagebrush Flats a lot as a kid?"

She gave a snort of patent disgust. Even though the climb had just become more difficult, the woman picked up speed. Confused as hell, Bowie had no choice but to follow her up the cliff.

If the lives of baby cougars hadn't hung in balance, Katie would have left Bowie Wilson stranded on the rocks until morning. After all, he'd done a lot worse to her back in high school. And despite all his horrible pranks, he'd apparently forgotten that she had ever existed.

That angered Katie more than anything. With all that Bowie had made her endure, she deserved at least a sliver of room in his memory. Even after high school graduation, she would wake up in her dorm, dreaming of her old classmates laughing at her. Because of Bowie.

Oh, she knew Bowie was the mastermind behind all the awful tricks. His high school girlfriend, Sawyer Johnson, might have taunted Katie since elementary school, but it had never amounted to more than snide and not very clever remarks before Sawyer had started dating Bowie. Sure, some of Sawyer's comments had hurt, but they hadn't scarred and certainly hadn't caused the all-consuming humiliation that Bowie's pranks had.

And what horrible thing had Katie done to Bowie to warrant such malicious attention?

She'd had the temerity to form an innocent, school-girl crush on him. That was all.

Katie had never even acted on her feelings. She doubted that Bowie would ever have noticed her if Sawyer hadn't pointed out Katie's secret infatuation. Through the years, Katie had never been able to figure out exactly why Bowie had decided to target her so viciously. Sawyer had never liked Katie, and Bowie might have just enjoyed making other people suffer. Either way, she'd become his favorite mark. And it had all started in the worst way possible.

Bowie had duped Katie into believing that he returned her feelings. For two weeks, Katie had lived in euphoric bliss, oblivious to the fact that Bowie was dating Sawyer. In retrospect, Katie should have realized that the cute bad boy would have had no interest in the nerdy girl. However, teen TV shows told a different story, and she'd stupidly believed the fantasy they peddled.

Which was how Bowie had managed to trick Katie into kissing a pig in the janitor's closet. Even worse, Sawyer had filmed the entire horrifying episode and slipped a clip of Katie puckering up to the hog into the student-run morning announcement program that ran on the televisions anchored at the front of each homeroom. For the rest of her high school career, she'd become known as "Katie the Pig-Kisser." That is, if they weren't calling her the oh-so-creative "Katie Underwear," a name Sawyer had coined in the first grade.

When Katie had left Sagebrush for college twelve years ago, she'd been more than happy to leave high school behind. Unfortunately, her escape hadn't turned out quite as she'd dreamed. She'd planned to become an artist, maybe in New York, LA, or even Tokyo. Instead, she'd traded a small town with tumbleweed for one with trees. Worse, she'd found herself the oddball out again in the male-dominated mulch plant in Minnesota where she'd worked designing packaging and performing the secretarial tasks that her boss assigned to her instead of her more junior male counterpart.

All told, it hadn't been hard to quit her job when her father, a retired police officer, was shot by an ex-con, Eddie Driver. Even if Sagebrush didn't offer many career opportunities, Katie's family had needed her. Her mother had never handled crises well, despite being the wife of a former chief of police, and Katie's four brothers couldn't handle their mother in a crisis.

Unfortunately, Katie hadn't counted on running into Bowie again. As wild as he'd been as a teenager, she'd figured he would have left their dusty hometown long ago. But it appeared that he hadn't. She knew one thing for certain, though. After publicly humiliating her and effectively ending any chance of her dating anyone else in high school, Bowie Wilson had simply and utterly forgotten her.

"Uh, ma'am? Where exactly are we headed?"

Ma'am? Really? Although she supposed it *was* better than Katie Underwear.

"Up."

"I see that, but where did the mother cougar leave her cubs?" The patience in Bowie's tone irritated Katie even more. How dare he act like *he* was the rational one?

She whipped around to glare at him. Even in the harsh light of the LED lantern, Bowie was a handsome man.

"We're headed to a cave," she bit out.

Twelve years ago, Bowie could have doubled for a teenage heartthrob with the shock of jet-black hair that had always dangled over his piercing gray eyes. Now, with that hair neatly trimmed and a five-o'clock stubble dusting his jaw, he looked like a model posing for an outdoor magazine. As an immature youth, he'd possessed a bad boy prettiness that appealed to girls—even self-proclaimed geeks like her. The years had toughened his features, hardening his male beauty into something more alluring and dangerous, even to a woman who should have known better.

Much better. Darn the man if he still didn't have the capacity to make Katie's hormones dance a happy little jig.

She steamed. If time hadn't mattered, she might have taken them on a more difficult path. Even then, she doubted that it would have fazed Bowie. Despite never climbing on this particular rock face before, the man moved like a machine. She could just imagine his muscular forearm extending as he reached for the next hold. His bicep would flex as he hoisted his body…

Katie cursed at herself. Sometimes she found her vivid imagination more of a burden than a gift. It had certainly brought her more difficulties than successes.

Thankfully, they quickly arrived at the small cave. Katie started inside, but a warm hand rested on her shoulder. Even through the fabric of her T-shirt, she could feel Bowie's heat and the strength of his fingers. An unbidden shiver slid through her.

"Let me go first." Bowie's breath caressed the

sensitive skin on the back of Katie's neck, and she had to fight to suppress another shudder. "The mother cougar may have returned."

Bowie dropped to his knees and used the light from his headlamp to scan the cave before crawling inside. With his larger frame, it took him a few seconds to wiggle through the narrow passage. As soon as Bowie moved far enough into the alcove for Katie to enter, she crawled over to the cubs. They moved clumsily about, searching for milk and their mother's warmth. One yawned. Its tiny whiskers flexed as it emitted a long squeak. The others followed suit. Katie's heart squeezed. She resisted the urge to gather the little fluffs against her chest. She still didn't know the protocol on handling kits this small, and she didn't want to harm one inadvertently.

"Their eyes aren't even open yet!" she said.

Bowie nodded. "Nor are their ears at this stage. They must be less than ten days old." The awe in his voice caused Katie to turn sharply in his direction. He appeared just as infatuated with the cubs as she was. Was this the same man who'd once tied granny panties to the undercarriage of her car along with the sign HONK IF YOU SEE MY UNDERWEAR?

Bowie reached for one of the mewling cubs and cradled it against his muscular chest. The little guy burrowed against him, and Katie's hormones went crazy again. Just when she thought the scene couldn't get any sweeter, the kit yawned, showing its miniature pink tongue. Then with one more nuzzle against Bowie's pecs, it heaved a surprisingly large sigh as it fell asleep. Bowie's handsome features softened into a gentle smile as he stroked the baby cougar's spotted fur with one callused finger.

If Katie hadn't suffered years of Bowie's cruel teasing, she would have found herself halfway in love with him. He'd appeared to be the ideal boyfriend once before, but it had all been a veneer, the perfect trap for a geeky girl with silly dreams of romance. And Katie, the woman, would not fall prey to his outward charms again.

"Can I pick up one of the cougars too?" The cuteness of the cub would serve as a nice distraction from her unwanted feelings.

Bowie nodded. "They'll need to be hand-reared, so they're going to end up imprinting on humans anyway. Unfortunately, we won't be able to reintroduce them to the wild, but we can save them."

Katie lifted one of the furry bundles, marveling at the softness of its fur. The little guy emitted a small, contented sound and immediately snuggled against Katie's warmth. She could feel a cold, teeny nose against her skin as the cub rested its head in the crook of her arm. And right then and there, Katie fell in love. With the tiny kit. Definitely not with the man.

Although she hated putting the baby puma down, she knew the little trio needed more than just a warm cuddle. "Did you bring something to carry the cubs back down the mountain with?"

Bowie grimaced and shook his head. "I didn't know the climb would be so steep."

And, Katie realized, she hadn't given him time to grab something from his truck either. To her surprise, Bowie was too polite to point that out.

"Do you want me to run back to the house to get a backpack?" she asked.

Bowie shook his head. "We'll have to improvise. I'm not sure how long the cubs have been without milk, and we need to get them out of this cave as soon as possible."

Katie scanned the dirt floor of the alcove and saw nothing—not even a twig. She turned back to ask Bowie what he planned on using and stopped. He was halfway out of his shirt. Normally, Katie wouldn't blatantly ogle a man, but...those abs. And pecs. His biceps flexed as he ripped his shirt down the middle so it made one thick band. Bowie Wilson might be just as bad for Katie as an entire carton of rocky road ice cream, but he looked just as temptingly scrumptious.

—⁓—

Bowie froze as he lifted his head and found the auburn-haired woman watching him as if she wanted to lick him all over. Something equally hot and elemental whipped through him. He'd never had this much of a visceral response to any woman. If it weren't for the baby mountain lions, he might have been crazy enough to accept her unspoken offer... even if he didn't know whether she'd jump him or push him down the cliff.

The lady—who he'd mentally taken to calling Red—might be showing an attraction to his body, but she didn't appear to like him. At all. She reminded him a bit of the zoo's honey badger, Fluffy—all snarls, bad temper, and teeth. In the

wild, Fluffy's relatives were known to take down king
cobras, and Bowie couldn't shake the feeling that Red
viewed him as one giant snake.

Still, Red had looked soft, sweet even, while cuddling the runt of the litter against her breasts. Sugar
and spice—that was Red. And damn if the combination
didn't intrigue him.

As a single father, Bowie should know better than
to lust after a woman who was all fire one moment and
pure honey the next. If he ever started dating seriously,
he'd need an even-tempered partner who could handle
the ups and downs of parenthood. He'd already dated
one female chimera and learned a lesson about falling
for someone with a dual personality. His high school
girlfriend, Sawyer, had been classy and elegant with an
outward poise that had impressed and intimidated the
hell out of his teenage self. But inside, she had a childish
mean streak that could strike at any time. She had never
wanted anything to do with their daughter, and for that,
Bowie was actually grateful. He loved his baby girl and
wanted to protect her from the Sawyers of the world for
as long as possible.

"Is that going to work?" Red asked, jerking her head
toward his ruined T-shirt. She still snuggled the kit to
her breasts as she peered at him.

"It should," Bowie said, withdrawing his Leatherman
from his pocket. He cut two slices near the bottom of
his shirt and then tore them off to use as bindings. With
the zoo's piss-poor budget, he'd learned to find cre-
ative solutions with the supplies on hand. Within a few
moments, he had jerry-rigged a semblance of a bag. He
tested it with a few rocks first. Satisfied it would hold

three pounds' worth of wiggling cubs, he carefully placed the babies inside, including the one in Red's arms.

"You always were smart."

Bowie glanced up at Red. That hadn't sounded like a compliment, but it wasn't the only thing that confused him. She certainly acted like she knew him, but he still couldn't place her.

"How do we know each other?" he finally asked.

She glared, looking every inch like an irate Fluffy during one of his particularly bad moods. "Think a little harder."

Somewhere, a memory flickered. A fleeting glimpse of red hair. But then the recollection floated away, out of reach. Bowie shook his head. "Sorry, ma'am. You seem familiar, I promise, but I just can't remember from where."

Rather than mollify Red, his words only fanned the flames shooting from her eyes. Still on her haunches, she spun around and then scrambled out of the cave. Sighing, he gathered his bundle of cubs and followed.

Bowie noticed that Red moved slower descending the cliff than she had going up, probably out of consideration for the cougars that he carried. When they reached the bottom of the rock formation, Bowie spotted Lou standing under the porch light next to a lady with the same fiery mane as Red's. Instead of Red's flowing cascade of curls, though, this woman's hair formed a frizzy halo about her cherubic face. Something jangled in the back of Bowie's brain, but before he could zero in on it, the older woman called out to Red, waving her hand cheerfully.

"Sweetheart, I was just telling Lou how you came back home to help out your father and me and that you're looking for work."

Red shot Bowie a sidelong glance and then spoke through gritted teeth. "I do have some paying projects, Mom."

Lou, always the peacemaker, quickly added, "Helen was also telling me that you're designing labels for Clara Winters's granddaughter's new jam business."

So, Red was acquainted with June Winters, Bowie thought, although that clue didn't help him much, since everyone in Sagebrush Flats knew June. The woman had breezed into town a little less than a decade ago and revitalized her family's tea shop. What used to be the domain of little old ladies after Sunday church had become the local hot spot. Even the most taciturn ranchers stopped by for the fussy desserts and fancy drinks. Although June's cooking was the best in town, the food wasn't the only draw. It was the woman herself. June had long blond hair and eyes as green as the grass during the month after which she was named. But unlike her surname, Winters, her personality was as bright as a summer's day. Bowie had stopped by the tea shop himself, but he much preferred Red's earthy sexiness to June's more classic elegance.

In response to Lou's comment, Red's mother bobbed her head like the zoo's cockatoo, Rosie, when the bird was shaking her plume in time to her beloved punk rock. "Yes, and I told Lou how you redid the menus for June's tea shop and that the Prairie Dog Café agreed to use the place mats you're designing—the ones with ad space for local businesses."

"Your mother thought you could help us with the zoo's website and our general marketing strategy," Lou said, looking first at Katie before he turned to address Bowie. "What do you think?"

"Well, it hasn't been updated since before I started," Bowie said carefully. Red looked like the zoo's camel, Lulubelle, right before the animal spit. Clearly, Red didn't appreciate her mother's interference. Keeping his voice neutral, Bowie decided to give her an out. "How high are your fees? Our budget is pretty tight."

Honestly, Bowie wouldn't mind improving the zoo's internet presence if he could do it at a reasonable cost. He and Lou needed something to draw folks through the gates. He'd never really had much of an artistic side, and unlike most of his generation, he sucked with computers. Except for the occasional use at school, he hadn't had much access to them growing up. He certainly didn't know anything about web design. But Bowie didn't want to strong-arm Red into helping him, even if it would benefit the zoo.

"I'm sure my daughter would give you a discount," Red's mom said. "Wouldn't you, sweetheart?"

Red's jaw clenched, and she was back to looking like a mulish honey badger. "Mom, Bowie and Lou haven't even seen my work."

"I'm sure it's wonderful," Lou said quickly. Too quickly. Bowie barely prevented a groan from escaping his lips as he turned from Lou to Red's mom and then back again. This wasn't just about building Red's business or getting low-cost marketing advice. It was a matchmaking scheme, plain and simple. And from the way Red's shoulders stiffened, she recognized it too.

Before Lou and Helen drove Red into finally losing her temper, Bowie turned to her and asked, "Why don't you stop by the zoo tomorrow and bring some samples of your work? We can see if it will be a good fit for both of us."

Before she could answer, her mother beamed. "That sounds like an excellent idea! Doesn't it, sweetheart?"

Red made a sound that Bowie figured was supposed to be noncommittal, but it came out like a honey badger's snarl.

Sensing the need for a diversion, Bowie turned to Lou and gestured to the bundle of squirming mountain lions. "Lou, do you want to check on the cubs?" Bowie asked. "I think they're all right other than they'll need milk as soon as we return to the zoo." After Lou took the bundle from him, Bowie turned to Red and her mom to explain, "These little guys are going to need formula about every four hours."

"Ooo," Red's mom said, "that sounds like a lot of work. Will you be looking for volunteers?" She turned to Red. "What do you think, sweetheart? Would you like to help care for them? You've always loved taking in strays."

"Mom, I'm here to help you with Dad."

Helen waved a hand dismissively. "He's stronger now, and you've been so much help. It's time you took a break and did something for yourself. We'll be fine. You could even work on the zoo's marketing while you watch the cubs."

"Uh, we can talk about that tomorrow as well," Bowie said as he quickly swiveled in Lou's direction. "Are the cubs in good enough shape for the return trip?"

When Lou nodded, Bowie placed his hand on the older man's upper arm and gently steered him to the truck before either he or Helen could attempt more matchmaking. Considering the zoo's skeletal staff, Bowie couldn't afford to turn down volunteers, but if anyone pushed Red further tonight, she would explode. Although he wouldn't mind watching the fireworks from a safe distance, Bowie was a little too close to the danger zone. Plus, he and Lou really did need to get the cubs back to the zoo.

Waiting until Lou got settled in the truck, Bowie helped arrange the bundle of kits on his mentor's lap. As Bowie climbed into the driver's seat, Lou yawned and said, "Nice, sweet girl. Good family."

Bowie grunted. He really wanted to learn Red's name and hear what had brought her back to Sagebrush Flats, but he was afraid that any interest would just encourage Lou and Helen's matchmaking. Maybe if he kept Lou talking, the information would come out naturally. As Bowie considered how to dig innocuously for more details, he heard a snore. A fond smile crossed Bowie's face when he glanced over at Lou and realized the eighty-year-old had fallen asleep again.

Oh well. Regardless of who Red was, Bowie had a feeling that tomorrow's meeting with her was going to be interesting.

About the Author

Two-time Golden Heart Finalist Laurel Kerr spent a few weeks each summer of her childhood on family road trips. That time packed into the back seat of her grandparents' Grand Marquis opened her imagination and exposed her to the wonders of the United States. The lessons she learned then still impact her writing today. She lives near Pittsburgh, Pennsylvania, with her husband, daughter, and loyal Cavalier King Charles spaniel. Laurel always enjoys interacting with readers on her social media accounts: facebook.com/laurelkerrauthor; twitter.com/laurelkerrbooks; and instagram.com/laurelkerrauthor. You can also learn more about Laurel and the Sagebrush Zoo on her website, laurelkerr.com.

Also by Laurel Kerr

WHERE THE WILD HEARTS ARE
Wild on My Mind